The

Scent of

Gardenias

LORRAINE HAAS

The Scent of Gardenias

For permission requests, write to the publisher:
Attention: Permissions Coordinator
Morewellson, Ltd.
P.O. Box 49726
Colorado Springs, Colorado 80949-9726

Library of Congress Cataloging in Publication Data

Name: Haas, Lorraine, author
Title: The Scent of Gardenias / Lorraine Haas
Description: Colorado Springs, Colorado. : Morewellson, Ltd.
Identifiers:
ISBN: 978-1-950452-57-6 (paperback) | 978-1-950452-50-7 (hardcover), 978-1-950452-58-3 (lg print)
Library of Congress Control Number: LCCN 2021921866
Library of Congress US Programs, Law, and Literature Division
Cataloging in Publication Program
101 Independence Avenue, S.E. Washington, DC 20540-4283

The Scent of Gardenias is a work of fiction. Names, characters, places, and incidents either are the product of the author's imagination or are used fictitiously, and any resemblance to actual persons, living or dead, business establishments, events, or locales is entirely coincidental. In order to provide a sense of place for the story, business establishment names have included under the aspect of "nominative fair use" of products or services. Where real people, events, establishments, organizations, or locales appear, they are also used fictitiously. All other elements of the novel are drawn from the author's imagination.

Editing by Red Adept Editing
Formatting by Rik Hall Wild Seas Formatting

FIC044000 FICTION / Women
FIC014050 FICTION / Historical / World War II
FIC008000 FICTION / Sagas

DEDICATION

For Elaine, who understands

July 1941
Milton, Florida

The night air, hot and thick, clung to Margaret Rose as she threw her weight against the hulking behemoth. Her hands had grown slick with sweat against the Packard's trunk. Her fingers slipped, and she stopped to wipe them against the cotton dress she'd borrowed from her sister, Franny. A moan escaped her lips as she followed the line of sweat running past her knees to her best pair of bleached white cotton socks, already covered in red clay dust.

Margaret bit her lip. She dared not break down there, or her brother, Edsol, would tell her to stay home. It was her chance to escape the farm for one night and have an adventure such as she'd only dreamed of during days of endless chores and caring for the younger children. Almost seventeen, she would soon be a woman, and nothing, not even her father, would hold her back then.

Beside her, her brother whispered, "Maggie, put your back into it."

"What?" Nellie called out from her perch in the front seat. With a boost from a wooden milk crate, she sat steering the family car toward the main road.

Edsol peered around the Packard and mouthed, "Quiet." He shook his head and sighed. Margaret knew that he would bear the brunt if they got caught. Bringing Nellie into the plan had been a last-minute decision. While Nellie had crossed her heart and hoped to die not to say anything, the chance of them being found out was still a possibility. After they made it to the main road, Nellie would run home, quietly climb through the girls' bedroom window, and go to bed. But only after the promise of a penny candy reward.

They had to hope Nellie would keep their secret—at least until they'd returned. As long as punishment came after the dance, Margaret could deal with it. By then, she would already have won.

Edsol grunted as his bronzed, muscular arms tensed with another effort. At least she'd been spared helping out in the cotton fields that year. Her arms retained the alabaster glow of her childhood.

Focused again on the task, Margaret Rose pushed, but the hulking Packard fought against any forward momentum. After what seemed like an interminable time of inching the behemoth up the steady incline of the driveway, the car's tires increased their rotations. The crunch of gravel came as a welcome reward for their efforts and was heaven to her ears. They had made it to the main road.

Margaret could barely contain herself as she grinned at Edsol. He winked and returned her smile. Another big push and they would have the vehicle far enough away from the house to start the engine. She let go of the bumper as she swept the dirt from her dress. The cloud of

2

debris floated up before settling back on her and the car. She frowned.

Edsol clenched his jaw. "Come on. You wanted to do this."

Her chin quivered, and she forced back her anger. "I didn't know it was going to be this hard. Look at my dress. My shoes and socks." Tears sprang to her eyes, but she fought against them. This wasn't how she'd imagined showing up to her first adult dance, soaked to the bone with sweat staining her dress and covered in a coating of the all-too-familiar clay.

His mouth pinched, and the gesture reminded her of her father's disapproving glare.

She sighed, not wanting to act like a child or to appear ungrateful. "I'm sorry. I should have put them in the car to change later."

Edsol shot her another derisive look. She clamped her lips together, praying her apology would have the desired effect. At that point, he could take the car and refuse to take her if she continued with her tirade. She'd daydreamed all week of what to expect and what she would wear. The anticipation had been a delicious respite during the unending cooking, cleaning, and childcare.

They were so close. She couldn't give up. Not now. As soon as they cleared the rhododendron hedge, they would be safe.

The sound of a shotgun chambering stopped them in their tracks.

Her eyes met his. In them, she spied the mirror of her own resignation.

And fear.

A knot formed in her chest as her lips trembled, and her face turned ashen. Her stomach clenched. They'd been caught. She grabbed Edsol's arm, but he shook free from her as beads of sweat dotted his upper lip and forehead. He wiped them with his hand while his legs locked, and his back straightened in anticipation of the confrontation.

They moved toward the front of the car, where their father stood. J.T. Locke was not a tall man, but what he lacked in stature, he made up for in bulk. Decades of working in the cotton fields as a youngster had transformed the pale Irish boy into a leathery-brown man who cracked walnuts with his calloused and gnarled hands, spat tobacco through stained teeth, and wielded a power in the community unseen among those not endowed with wealth or privilege.

Nellie, with her button nose and scraped shins, had leaped from the car. She stared wide-eyed at their father. He tilted his chin with a simple "Get." The timid girl of eleven scampered back to the house, her wails trailing behind her on the air. Margaret wondered if it was less of being found out or more that she'd lost out on the candy reward for helping them.

J.T. widened his stance, planting his worn leather boots in the dirt, blocking their path. Worse than the shotgun propped against his chest was his penetrating stare. Margaret Rose dropped her gaze to the ground and clutched her arm behind her back. Her hand twisted her wrist, the discomfort keeping her focused.

Their father spat tobacco juice, and as it landed, a few wet droplets hit Margaret Rose's Mary Janes before sliding off the toecap. Heat rushed into her body, but she clenched her jaw for fear of saying something she would regret. Every fiber sought desperately to fight back, but she couldn't—wouldn't—win against the man. Besides, a foot out of line on her part would affect her brother's punishment. Shame flooded her. After she'd cajoled Edsol to take her to the dance, he, not she, would face the harsher consequences.

The seconds ticked on, the only sound disturbing the night's silence was the choir of crickets and frogs. Sweat dripped against her neck as she kept her gaze on her shoes.

Finally, their father spoke. "Seems like I caught me some car thieves. I wonder if I should call up the po-lice."

Margaret Rose took a step forward, her hands balled into fists, but Edsol pulled her back to his side. "It's my fault, sir. I accept full responsibility."

"Do ya, now?"

"Yes, sir. I do. As the eldest, I shouldn't have been a bad influence on Maggie here. I led her astray to help me."

Margaret Rose wanted to cry out that it wasn't true, but Edsol's grip on her arm tightened. He would take the punishment their father would mete out. Not that she would get off scot-free. Cold sweat made her weaken, and she worried she would faint. She chewed the inside of her mouth nervously.

Her father glanced at her before he motioned to the hedge. Margaret Rose bit her cheek harder so as not to cry. She would never give him that satisfaction.

She stepped over to the bushes and surveyed the branches. Experience had taught her that picking a weak branch meant he would pick his own, much tougher one or that more licks would be in store.

Her legs quivered at the agony to come. She looked further into the hedge and found a medium branch with a thickness she suspected would meet his approval. After snapping it from the bush, she stripped the leaves from the bark, cutting her palm. Her desire to suck at the stinging cuts was strong, but she simply handed the branch to him. Then she faced the back of the car, bracing herself.

But her father spoke, "You two got this up here. You take it back—the same way you got it here."

Margaret bristled at the thought of pushing the car back down to the house, but Edsol only nodded. He went to the driver's door, put the car in neutral, and manned the steering wheel. Margaret gritted her teeth as she struggled to push against the trunk, each turn of the wheels taking her closer to her fate. After a difficult three-point turn, Edsol steered the car back toward the house. Finally, with the help of a downward slope into the yard, they parked the vehicle in its normal spot.

The two of them panted at their efforts. Her arms shook from the hard work as they waited for further instruction.

"You wait for me behind the barn." He motioned at Edsol with his head, and her brother stole her a glance before stalking off into the night.

Margaret's face reddened, and her eyes squeezed shut. She faced the car, hitching up the dress with one hand to expose her calves. She took a deep breath as she waited for the first strike of the branch.

Slap.

Tears slid down her cheeks, but she didn't cry out. She bit her lip so hard, she could taste the blood.

Another one.

But it wasn't the sting of the blows affecting her. It was her desire to scream, "I hate you!" Margaret cursed under her breath.

Finally, he lowered the switch. "I expected better of you." With that, he dropped the branch and turned toward the barn.

Her legs pulsed with the heat of the stings. She still clutched at the dress, but it had already fallen over the wounds, and red marks dotted the dirty fabric. She pushed her shoulders back and limped toward the house with its peeling white paint. A single bulb cast a yellow glow over the door as miller moths circled their doom.

She made it inside without slamming the screen or screaming at the top of her lungs. Poor Edsol would receive the leather strap, and it wouldn't be confined to his legs.

Margaret rushed through the dim living room where a solitary lamp shone. She made her way through the bedroom where the boys slept then from there into the girls' room. She glanced back past the last bed to the closed doorway of their parents' bedroom.

Does Mama know? Or even care? Her expression hardened, and her mouth pinched. She would never be like her mother, who put up with a mean drunk to stay stuck in a five-room hovel with ten children. Margaret Rose would leave as soon as she could and never come back.

Moving past the girls' room, she made her way to the lean-to attached to the kitchen that they used as a bathing area. She tore off the filthy dress and flung it to the ground. Underneath, her mended full slip, pair of white cotton panties, and bra were dark with stains of sweat.

Pumping water into a chipped ceramic bowl, she grabbed a frayed washrag with her free hand and wet it before wringing it out, avoiding the cuts on her hand. Even with a light touch, the broken skin on her legs brought a rush of stinging pain. She bit her lip to suppress the moan but found the cut there swollen too. She swallowed and took in a calming breath, not wanting to wake the sleeping girls. She raised one leg to see the tracks of welts and blood where the switch had torn her flesh.

Gingerly, she applied the cloth to the areas, wincing with each dab. After one leg had been cleaned, she set the washrag back in the bowl, watching the water turn dark pink from the blood and clay. She finished tending to the other leg before her emotions got the best of her, then she slumped to the wooden floor. Deep sobs overtook her. Her stomach clenched as she curled into a ball, rocking with the multitude of emotions pulling at her.

How she hated her father. He never allowed her or Franny to go anywhere for fun or do anything that didn't require her younger brothers and sisters to tag along. Every day was a constant array of chores and more chores. She helped with the young'uns. Washed the dishes. Worked in the garden. Cleaned the laundry. Their father had even forbidden a radio for them to listen to at night. He considered it a foolish waste of money and time that could otherwise be spent on more chores or learning. By learning, he meant understanding how to be wives and mothers. Yet that didn't stop him from heading out to his fraternity meetings. Those were the nights their family cowered in their beds as he stumbled home, belligerent and drunk. Even Edsol had taken to sleeping in the barn on those nights.

She wiped her nose with the dress she'd discarded. Then she wadded it up and threw it against the wall. How she wanted to rip it to shreds, but it was the only decent dress Franny owned, and she'd let Margaret borrow it for tonight. Margaret's dresses consisted of flour sacks her mother had sewn for the girls. Of those, any with a pattern had been reserved for church or going to town for supplies. Margaret begged her mother for a store-bought dress, reasoning that her younger sisters would also wear it. But Ma had refused.

It wasn't fair. Franny had a store-bought dress. But their father had only approved it since she would need one for any fella courting her. As Franny had grown older, her father often commented on her becoming an old maid. At nineteen, Franny was the oldest child still at home. Margaret worried about her sister, who had a childlike nature about her.

She sighed and stared at the dress. But instead of remorse, more anger bubbled up inside. Like their mother, Franny simply accepted a life of children and poverty. Ma's horrible excuses for Pa and his actions, though, were what made Margaret so upset. On the rare occasion that Margaret had questioned her about Pa's behavior, her mother had replied that he hadn't been like that before the war. Margaret didn't care for her constant talk about the Depression and the war. That had been a lifetime ago. Before her time.

She rested her cheeks between her fists. All she knew was that she would never have the life she wanted if she stayed close to home.

She wanted to travel, to be her own woman. *Why is that so hard?* Everyone always telling her to "remember her place." Her attitude had kept many of the mothers in the church steering their sons toward other prospects for marriage.

Margaret used a towel to wipe her eyes. As she pulled herself up from the floor, the slip fell from her shoulder. The fabric stretched against her body. Where Franny's frame was thin and willowy, Margaret Rose's body blossomed toward womanhood, and her shapely figure often caused a head or two to turn when she walked by a group of men.

Perhaps that was where her power lay. In the way she looked. She swiveled in the mirror, pulling the shift tight against her body. At first, she'd felt dismayed by the burgeoning lumps that strained against the buttons of her blouses and caused her brothers to make jokes. Thankfully, her mother had allowed her a new brassiere, which she quickly filled. For the first time, she realized that growing into womanhood would help her find a way out. Her thoughts took on an urgency. She was no longer a child, and she would make her own decisions on how to live her life.

She rubbed her arms and flexed her shoulders, tight from pushing the car back to the house and from the tension she'd held during the punishment. She tried not to feel sorry for herself, but resentment had taken hold like a burr and wouldn't let go.

Margaret Rose brushed her honey-colored hair and braided it behind her. As her fingers flew through knotting the braids, her frustration bounced from her father to her mother to Franny. Franny was so mild-mannered. She felt the need to go along with everything and was always so good-natured. As if she didn't long for a different life like Margaret did. Then there was Edsol. He could easily escape but didn't. *Am I the only one who feels imprisoned?*

She promised herself she wouldn't end up trapped like her mother, with so many mouths to feed and so little to provide. Her days wouldn't be spent wiping noses or bottoms and kowtowing to a brute of a man.

She took the bowl of dirty water to the back door, hitched the screen door open with her hip, and listened. Thankfully, the only sound was of crickets and not the slapping of leather. She dumped the bloody water onto the ground before closing the door behind her. She switched off the light then made her way through the stuffy room to the bed with the aid of moonlight filtering through the lace curtains. Faint snores and a smattering of sniffles from Nellie carried to her ears. Walking past the bed with the younger girls, she made her way to her bed. Nellie sprawled in the middle of the bed, and Franny's back faced the wall.

As the springs squeaked at her weight, Franny stirred. "How was it?"

"Later. Go back to sleep." The iron bedstead creaked as she settled on the lumpy feather mattress. She pulled the light sheet over her and shoved a pillow under her head, tears spilling again.

"Maggie?" A warm hand found her arm.

"Go to sleep, Franny." Margaret Rose's breath caught as she remembered the damage to Franny's only good dress. She hoped she would be able to get the blood out. *Why am I such a horrible sister?* She pounded her pillow as conflicting emotions roared inside her.

Exhausted, spent, and sore, she fell asleep in the dimming moonlight. As she drifted off, resolve coursed through her body, and with it came a new vision of her future. She could be—and would do—better.

She could feel it. Change was coming.

CHAPTER TWO

Light filtered through the window as the sound of buzzing came to her ears. Margaret turned over and buried her head in the pillow, stained with last night's tears. Not only had her punishment been swift, but her father had also forbidden her from going to any dances until the following year.

In the corner, she noticed a spider sitting patiently as a fly made its way around the window. Margaret wondered if the fly was oblivious to the fact that it would soon be the prey. Or maybe it thought it would escape without harm. She gazed at the dance of life and death before flinging back the covers and sliding her legs over the side of the bed. *Wait, today is Sunday. Did I oversleep?*

Her stomach hurt. Oh yes, that was it. The last few days, a stomach bug had hit her, and she'd spent more time than usual in the outhouse in back. Pain clawed her awake, and she clutched at her stomach until it passed. She pulled off her nightdress and shrugged into a shift hanging on a nearby hook. Margaret shuffled into the kitchen, where Franny stood at the sink, cutting up a chicken.

"How did you get out of church this morning?" Margaret pulled out one of the oak kitchen chairs and sat.

Franny turned from the sink. "I told Ma you had a stomachache and I would stay behind to watch over you. I think you're about to get your first monthly. You've been very moody lately, and it's past time you did."

Margaret sighed. Ma and Franny knew about monthlies, but Ma hadn't spoken to her about it. She guessed she would know when it happened. Maybe she could ask Franny. Instead, she put her elbows on the table, resting her chin in her hands as she watched her sister work.

Franny set the chicken in a roasting pan then wiped her wet hands on her tattered apron. "I saved you a biscuit and a piece of fatback."

Franny placed a cloth in front of Margaret, but she pushed it away. She had no appetite.

"Where's everybody? Did they stay at church for a potluck?"

"They've gone over to the Simpsons'. Old man Simpson needed help to split wood. Missus Simpson invited the family."

Margaret rose from the cane-back chair, invigorated. "Ah, now I see why you didn't want to go." Margaret bumped her sister's shoulder with her own.

"Yes, Robbie's been coming around."

Robbie Simpson's wife had died in childbirth the year before. It was no secret that their parents wanted Franny to marry Robbie and Margaret to marry their other son, Bud. She picked at the biscuit. If they were over at the Simpsons', they wouldn't be home until late. She smiled at the prospect of doing nothing all day.

"Franny, we should go to the picture show."

"No. It's Sunday, and I'm saving my money."

Margaret sighed. "You're an ol' stick-in-the-mud. Don't you ever want to have fun?" She perched on a nearby chair, pulling on a pair of mended socks.

"I have fun." Franny used the back of her hand to push the flaxen hair off her face.

"You do? When? Even now, you're doing chores."

"Maggie, sometimes I think you don't understand the world at all. Sometimes you, well—I don't mean to be unkind—but sometimes, you're selfish." Franny pulled down a canister of flour to make a pie.

"I understand it more than you do. And what's wrong with being selfish, anyways? I've seen how Ma always puts others first. Look where it got her."

"It got her a family, a home."

Margaret rolled her eyes. "It got her children hanging onto her skirts, a drunk of a husband—"

"Bite your tongue! How can you speak ill of Pa?"

"Because it's the truth."

Franny glowered at the dough as she pressed it with a rolling pin. "You don't understand what our parents had to go through—the hardships they endured. We have it easy compared to them."

"Easy?" She laughed derisively. "I plan to have it easy and soon. A few more years and I'm leaving. Then I'm going to do what I want when I want."

"And how do you plan to do that? You have no husband, no money."

"Not everything is about getting a husband. But mine won't be one of the Simpson boys. No way am I marrying a farmer."

Margaret slumped back in her chair. She didn't want to fight with Franny. Maybe she could talk her into walking down to the pond. But first, she needed to work on cleaning Franny's dress from last night. She rose from her seat when a commotion at the front door startled them. Edsol rushed in, the chill air following him inside.

"Where's Pa?" His face flushed as his gaze darted toward the chair where his father normally sat. "Where is he?"

Margaret rushed over. "They'll be at the Simpsons'. Why? What is it? What's going on?"

He looked down at her. "The Japanese attacked Pearl Harbor in Hawaii. It was on the radio. We're at war!"

Her hand flew to her cheek. "What? No. This can't be. Are you sure?"

His face was solemn as he stared at his sisters. "It's coming across the wires. Thousands dead."

"What?" Margaret gasped, taking a step back and clutching at her stomach. It was as if the world had gone crazy overnight.

A powerful wailing broke through her thoughts. Margaret swiveled to see her sister, collapsed on the floor. "Franny!"

Margaret took deep breaths as she tried to calm the fragile woman, who rocked back and forth, keening with grief. Of all the children, Franny had the most sensitive nature and felt any tragedy deeply.

Could it be true? Thousands dead. No, it can't be.

"Franny, stop. We don't even know what happened yet. It must be a mistake. It won't affect us."

She jumped as Edsol grabbed her by the shoulders, his eyes rapidly blinking. "This is real, Maggie. We are at war with Japan."

~

Later that day, after Edsol had left, Margaret heard a truck pull up outside. She bit at her nail, a jittery sensation cascading over her body. Once their family had alighted, Bud Simpson backed up the truck before shooting back down the dirt road.

Margaret surged forward to meet them in the driveway. Ma's face was grief-stricken, but she jolted as Margaret rushed toward her.

"Ma, what's going on? Is it true?"

Her mother's mouth opened, but no sound came forth.

"Not now, Maggie." Franny had come up beside her and helped Ma inside.

Margaret followed behind them, fidgeting with her hands as she waited for Ma to settle into the chair. Margaret bent down in front of the woman, while Franny held her mother's hands as tears slid down both their faces.

Even the other children were subdued and remained silent as they entered the house. Pa wasn't with them.

The dark cloud that had settled over them was too much to take. Margaret spun on her heels and fled outside. She paced back and forth in front of the house. What had happened was horrible. The most horrible thing imaginable. *But why does everyone think it would affect them? Hawaii is so far away.* But something deep in her heart nagged at her.

She stopped. Edsol. He would be stupid enough to want to fight. She couldn't let him leave her. He might get hurt. Or worse, killed. For the first time, the reality of what it meant for her and their family hit.

She had to talk with someone. It was already too late by then, but tomorrow, she would go speak to her best friend Alice. Her father was in the Air Force.

She waited up until she saw Edsol walking toward the house. She flew to him. "Edsol, is it true? Are we really at war?"

He nodded, a grim determination on his face. "They'll be opening up the recruitment tomorrow. I'm going to join up."

"No! Please don't go."

He brushed her aside as she attempted to cling to his arm. "Maggie, at some point, you have to grow up. It isn't always about chasing silly dreams. Sometimes, life is putting your wants and desires aside and even sacrificing them."

"No. Don't talk like that. I won't listen to it. You can't go. Please." She latched herself back onto his arm. "I need you—we need you here."

He shook his head and pushed past her, leaving her standing outside alone. The evening's humidity cloaked her body, but she shuddered as a cold shiver crept up her spine.

After what seemed like forever, Pa came home, having spent the day in town with other men. Her dread grew as her father swigged whiskey from a jug, his silence speaking more than simple words. He was planning something, and it never boded well when he drank. She wanted to snatch the jug away from him but fought with the terror building inside her. *I'm useless. There's nothing I can do.*

She escaped to the back porch, her body feeling hollow as she picked at the peeling white paint from the house post. There, Edsol paced like a caged tiger but refused to respond to her questions. Finally, she gave up her probing and went inside. The house was eerily quiet, like it, too, refused to breathe. She undressed by the light of moon in the bedroom she shared with her sisters. She glanced at Nellie, Patsy, and Norma, the youngest of the girls, sprawled on the bed, asleep without a care in the world. She covered them with the blanket before making her way over to her own bed.

She looked over to where Franny slept. Her brows were drawn down and together slightly, anxious even in sleep. Her long, slender fingers clutched at the sheets. She was the only one of the siblings who slept on her back, and her ivory skin almost glowed in the moonlight.

Margaret knew the unsettling quiet wouldn't last. She slid under the covers, her chest thumping, and waited.

The first crash woke her from a tortured sleep, but she didn't move from her spot. The clatter of broken dishes and glasses sounded against the floorboards. When her father had exhausted himself, she heard him stumble to his chair. As heavy snores sounded from the front room, the wisp of a broom against the wooden floorboards made its way to her ears. Once again, Ma was cleaning up the debris of his anger.

Why does she put up with these outbursts? While they had lessened over the years, with a new war on their doorstep, his rages might return with a vengeance.

She turned over and spied her sisters asleep. Oh, to be as innocent as Nellie and as calm as Franny. As for Margaret Rose, her father had called her headstrong. That trait suited her brothers just fine but not her. Her feelings jumbled inside her chest as she tried to make sense of everything but struggled with it. She closed her eyes and sighed.

Her plans might not be going the way she'd hoped, but leaving would solve everything.

CHAPTER THREE

The following morning, Margaret walked into town with Nellie. People crowded the sidewalks like sleepwalkers, their eyes glazed, their mouths set. Young couples clung tighter to each other, their heads bent together. Women spoke in hushed voices tinged with dread, and outbursts from the men revealed outrage and simmering anger. Husbands and sons of fighting age would enlist or be called to arms, leaving the women behind to bear the hardship and fear of them never returning.

In front of one store, men and boys formed a line down the block. The younger boys seemed excited at the prospect of joining to do their duty. The older men, who she guessed had fought in the last war, looked lost to their own battles, their gazes fixed on something she couldn't see.

Margaret moved past as the line went around the block and out of her sight. She gasped as she spied two friends from school, Philip and Oscar. Her eyes fell on even more boys that she recognized from class. They were her classmates, not soldiers. She wanted to rush over and pull them from the lines. So intent was she on her thoughts, she forgot about Nellie at her side.

"Ouch. Let go, Maggie!" Nellie pulled her hand from Margaret's.

"Sorry, Nells. I didn't realize I was squeezing your hand."

As they walked, the crowd thickened around a newspaper stand bearing a Sold Out sign. People stopped on the sidewalk to scour the *Jay Tribune*, while others stared at the newspaper headlines taped to a storefront window.

"I want to go home, Maggie. Everyone looks so sad. I'm scared."

"Yes, let's go home."

~

That night, the family traveled over to the Simpsons' to listen to President Roosevelt on the radio. Crackling noises came across the radio as he spoke of a day "which will live in infamy."

The air of silence was profound as everyone sat glued to the radio. Even the babies were quiet as if a blanket of disbelief had settled on the room. Margaret's heart quickened as the speech went on, her mind racing at the thousands who had died and the thousands more who would die in the coming war. Hatred and revenge bloomed toward an enemy. For the first time in her life, Margaret tasted the vast fear of war, which would inflict untold pain on mothers, fathers, siblings, and lovers.

The grandfather clock chimed and broke the spell of calm that had descended in the room. As they gathered themselves to leave, Margaret watched as her mother and Mrs. Simpson caught each other up in an embrace. Each of them had sons, and they'd experienced the loss of brothers and uncles in the Great War.

Margaret watched them but felt adrift. She didn't know where she fit in the picture unfolding. She was saddened by the multitude who had died at Pearl Harbor. She'd watched as folks in town had cowered in fear anytime a plane's engine was heard or a car backfired. The truth of what had happened sank into her core. Yet she also felt guilt and shame. Because her world was shifting, and in that change, excitement had taken hold. It was as if everyone had awakened from slumber.

Something new had come. Life would never be the same again.

CHAPTER FOUR

Bacon sizzled in the iron skillet as Margaret cracked eggs into a bowl, whipping them with a frenzy. Because she'd stayed home on Sunday, her penance for the following week was to get up at the crack of dawn to help Ma fix breakfast for everyone.

But Ma wasn't in the kitchen. The sound of her mother's pleading voice reached her ears. "No, please, J.T. Think of the children. Please!"

Margaret pulled the pan from the fire and went to the back door, the screen creaking on its hinges as she pushed it open. She leaned on the splintered doorjamb as she watched the scene unfold.

Pa had Bessie by a rope and was pulling her toward a trailer. "Woman, stop your squalling. I've made my decision. You can buy milk from Simpson."

Margaret's chest tightened. They barely had the money to buy anything from the grocer, and there was already talk of rationing coming soon. It made more sense to keep their only cow. Her father's logic made no sense.

Franny bumped her arm as she rushed past Margaret and to their mother. "Ma, I can take on one or two more students. I've heard that the Nelsons want to have their children take piano lessons. I have some money saved up. Here." She pressed a few coins into her mother's hands.

Ma pushed the coins away. "No! You'll be wed soon and off with your husband. I won't be taking your money."

"It's a gift. Please accept. I want to." She covered Ma's hand with her own long fingers. Ma and Franny watched as the trailer left, Bessie letting out a final moo before it made its way around the bushes.

Margaret rushed forward to join Ma and Franny but stopped short. She wanted to scream at Pa, but the consequence would be a backhand for insolence. A huge lump formed in her throat. Down the road, they watched as the Simpson boys helped unload Bessie into the bed of the panel truck.

She felt a pull on her dress and looked down to see Nellie clinging to her side. "Are we going to be okay, Maggie?" Nellie's eyes were full of unshed tears.

"Of course, we are, peach. We can buy milk from Mr. Simpson. That's the way people do now. Only poor people have cows."

Nellie's lip quivered. "But will, I mean…"

Margaret bent down. "What is it?" She wiped Nellie's tears.

"Will Pa send me away too?"

Margaret wrinkled her brow. She gathered Nellie up in an embrace. "No, of course not. Why would you think that?"

"I know some kids that got sent to live with relatives on other farms. Pa says the only thing I'm good for is to make him smile."

"There you go. See, that means you're his favorite. He'd never send you away."

Nellie hugged her neck tightly. "You're the bestest sister in the whole wide world."

"Even better than Franny?" She pursed her lips and made a funny face.

"Um, well, Franny is nice."

"Okay. Franny *is* nice. What about me?"

"You're strong. You're the bestest, strongest sister." Nellie smiled, revealing the gap where an adult tooth was finally pushing through. Her baby teeth had taken longer to fall out, and it gave Nellie a childish quality.

"Good answer. Now you go off and play." She swatted at Nell's bottom, and the girl skipped off. Margaret swiveled to see Franny helping their mother inside. When she followed, she found Ma sitting at the table, peeling apples for a pie as if the recent episode hadn't occurred.

"Where's Edsol?"

"He's gone." Her mother set the peel into a bowl to make vinegar.

"Gone where?"

"You know he volunteered."

"But he hasn't left yet." She felt as if her chest would explode. She rushed out of the house, the screen door slapping against the wood.

"Edsol. Edsol!" She shouted herself hoarse, fearful that she hadn't had the chance to say goodbye. Barefoot, she ran toward the

26

main road, ignoring the chill in the air, her feet and legs protesting in discomfort against the cold. She had to catch him before the bus came that would take him into town. Her heart raced, and her breathing grew labored as she ran.

At last, she made it to the main road. She leaped back as a car sped past, honking at her. *Did Pa take Edsol when he left earlier?* She had been so busy with breakfast, she hadn't seen Edsol leave. She would never catch them if they had gone in the car and not on the bus. She bent over and placed her hands on her thighs, gulping down breaths of air. Then she stood and turned back to the house.

After Franny left to go seek a teaching position with the Nelson children, and the children were off playing, Margaret had a moment to herself. She sat on the porch swing, one leg tucked up under her shift, and used her toes to push it. In her lap, she held a stoneware bowl. She picked up a basket of black-eyed peas and shucked off the shells, glancing toward the road now and then for a hint of her brother or her father. The sound of an engine let her know her Pa had returned. She stopped swinging, setting the bowl down on the seat beside her. Pa pulled up then shut off the ignition, the engine clicking as it began cooling. Her father pulled himself up and out of the car, retrieving a can of chewing tobacco from his pocket. He stuffed some between his cheek and gum before motioning to her.

She knew what he wanted. In the past when he'd had a "fit," as Mama called them, he would arrive with dishes from the local thrift store to replace the ones he'd broken the night before in his drunken rage. She walked over to the car.

"Get your brothers to help with these." He pointed to the back seat.

She bent over and stared through the back window. The boxes inside were from a big department store and looked new.

"You gonna stand there all day, girl? Go get your brothers."

She pointed. "They're playing in the back."

He spat some tobacco juice. "Then go get 'em. And come back. I got something for you too."

Margaret gathered the boys from the backyard, and they took the boxes of plates and bowls inside. Pa reached over and opened the passenger-side door.

Another large box sat there on the front seat, but she could tell from the picture what was inside. She gasped. A radio. "You got me a radio?"

"Don't be daft. That's not it. Next to it."

A bag sat on the floorboard. Inside, it held a clothing box.

"Now you wait until we get inside to open it." He hoisted the radio, and she followed him to open the screen door.

"Mother!" he yelled.

Ma jumped up from the kitchen table and scurried toward him. She unplugged the lamp to make room, and he set the radio down on the table.

A radio! At last. Margaret felt giddy. She couldn't wait to tell her classmates. They would be so jealous.

Pa sat down in his chair next to the table and spat into a rusted Folgers coffee can. "Go on. Open yours."

She'd been so enthralled with the radio that she'd forgotten the other item. She found the bag and removed the box. Opening it with trembling fingers, she stared at the dress inside. It had a Peter Pan collar and white polka dots on a blue background. Her first store dress.

"Pa. Thank you!" She rushed over and hugged him.

"Well, with things going on, you'll need to be getting married soon. You'll need a dress for courting. I know Bud Simpson has good prospects. His pa's going to give the farm to Robbie as the eldest, but Bud's a hard worker. You could do worse."

Margaret knew better than to openly object to the Simpson boys. Not only did she not have any desire to be a farmer's wife, but she refused to live where she would be one more worker for his mother and share a room with the rest of the family.

He turned to Ma, whose gaze was fixed on the radio. He patted it. "Ol' Bessie fetched us a good price, and with the war, we need to know what's happening. Now we can know what's going on with Edsol and the other boys."

Ma's hands flew to her mouth, and she stifled a moan.

"Now, Netha, I know it's hard, but we have to be strong for the boy. Edsol's not quite old enough yet, so they're letting him help with construction. Maybe he'll take an interest in it and work at it after this dad-blasted war is over."

Ma gasped at her father's cursing, looking around to see if any of the younger children had overheard him. Seeing they were outside, Ma's shoulders dropped as she twisted the tattered dishrag in her hands.

Margaret's mind raced. Edsol's age meant a reprieve for the moment, but it wouldn't keep him out of the fray for long. "What can I do? I could do something."

"You are doing something. Helping your mother with the young'uns. It's good preparation for you."

She fought back the urge to reply, "I don't want to be a wife and mother." Instead, she calmly said, "But I could work too. That would give us some money for milk and other goods." She recalled Franny's offer to get more students. He hadn't seemed to have a problem with Franny doing more. Maybe he thought Margaret wasn't sincere about finding work.

He gazed at her, spat more juice, then replied, "We'd have to see if it interferes with your work here. I know that they're going to need some help at the commissary when that opens. Let me talk to some folks I know, and we'll see." He rocked back and forth in his chair.

"Thank you, Pa." She swallowed a laugh that was bubbling up from inside. A job. Away from the house. Her own money. Freedom. A thought flew to her mind. "What about you, Pa? Are you going too?"

He shook his head. "They're wanting the young'uns, not us soon knocking on death's door at fifty. War's a young man's game. When they found out I was a barber, they said that would be needed as they expect lots of men to come here for training. They're setting up more quarters for the men and other housing for workers."

"Where are they coming from, Pa?"

"From all over the country." He spat in the can.

Margaret Rose's pulse raced, and a gleam came into her eye. She had a new store-bought dress. She'd convinced her father that a job would help the family. Men from across the states would be arriving soon. Men seeking wives. Men with prospects. Men who weren't farmers. Or barbers. Or mired in the past.

One of them would be her ticket out of there forever.

CHAPTER FIVE

The following weeks and months saw huge changes to the once-quiet small town of Milton. The roar of large trucks passing, and the smell of diesel fuel mixed with the clash of cigarette smoke assaulted Margaret's senses. With so many men coming to the naval base in Pensacola, construction had also increased in her town. The housing needs for more defense and military personnel multiplied, spilling over into neighboring towns. Strangers were arriving from all around to take advantage of the new economic boom of Pensacola and the surrounding area.

Every day brought with it some new experience or disturbance. Rationing had begun, with blue or red stamps or points for other items. Shop windows that used to display neighborhood items boasted patriotic posters invoking everyone to "Do With Less So They'll Have Enough." Recycling and scrap-metal drives saw many vehicles missing bumpers, while schoolchildren got involved in finding and saving aluminum cans. As the desire for victory gardens increased, Pa had Nellie sit under a poster declaring "Your Victory Garden Counts More Than Ever!" with seeds Ma had saved from their garden. Nellie could easily sell seed packets to anyone walking past the barbershop.

Every day felt like a thrilling adventure as contractors and local lads not old enough to be called into service took on new work where the new recruits left job openings. As often as possible, Margaret would take Nellie and walk downtown to see the people arriving. While Pensacola had most of the activity, her small town was experiencing a large influx of families who followed their husbands and fathers who had joined in the efforts. The once-sleepy little town was bustling. Pa had been right about his work growing too. He'd hired on another barber, and the two chairs were always full of the town's elite and the carpetbaggers who were always found where easy money was to be made.

Besides the constant stream of men coming and going, Margaret also noticed a lot more women in the local stores as well. She couldn't help but stare at their caked-on makeup and full red lips. Their dresses emphasized their figures, and they didn't seem self-conscious about the leers they received when passing groups of men.

Today, she spotted two such women. After hearing catcalls from the men, one woman turned and called out a famous Mae West line, "Why don't you come up and see me sometime?"

The young men, barely out of their teens, cajoled each other forward, but the women ignored their jostling. Instead, the woman fixated on a younger man who hung back. Margaret couldn't look away as one of the gorgeous women made a point of surveying the sailor from head to toe. The other woman made her way around him, and the boy blushed beet red. As one of the women drew closer, she leaned in so he could see her cleavage. His eyes grew big as saucers. As their fragrant perfume wafted in the air, Margaret was as entranced as the men were. It reminded her of the time she'd gone to the zoo and seen exotic animals for the first time. She was spellbound by what was taking place in front of her.

"What do you think, Irma?" The woman picked up his tie then let it slide through her fingers.

Irma ran her lacquered red fingernails across his shoulders. "I think we need to throw this one back. I don't think he's ready yet."

As the boy's face flushed at the attention of the women, the older men guffawed and slapped each other on the back.

"Later, boys." Irma nodded at her friend and flashed her white teeth before taking the woman's arm in hers. "Come on, Bunny."

Margaret let out a breath as the women stalked toward her. The one called Irma dropped her clutch in front of Margaret, who bent over and picked it up.

"Thanks, hun."

Margaret gawked. *Is she talking to me?* She blinked as she realized Nellie wasn't beside her anymore.

Bunny looked her up and down. "Looking for work, honey? I'm sure we could get you top dollar."

A male's voice yelled out, "You don't want the kind of work they're talking about, kid!" Men's laughter and jostling behind her caused her to gasp.

Irma's friend, Bunny, lifted her skirt high enough that the men could see her garter. Whistles ensued, and the woman threw back her

34

head and laughed loudly.

"Just teasing, hun." She winked, and the pair walked past, leaving a stunned Margaret in their wake.

Flustered at the attention, Margaret found Nellie, who'd spied something in a shop window. She grabbed her little sister's hand and rushed down the street, the men's laughter trailing behind her.

Did I just speak to a woman of the night? Her heart raced. Of course, she wasn't naïve, but it was the first time she'd actually seen one. She hazarded a glance back over her shoulder at the women, who were already strolling away. Her eyes went to their ankles. Nylons. They weren't wearing socks. They had on stockings, and they weren't the thick, sagging cotton kind she'd seen on so many older women like her mother.

"Ow! You're hurting my hand!" Nellie pulled back from Margaret.

Margaret bent down. "Sorry, Nellie. I wanted to get us away from—"

"Those women weren't very ladylike, were they?" Nellie searched Margaret's face.

"No. They weren't. Now let's go get the towels from Pa's shop and get the wash going."

When they arrived, men crowded the benches under the revolving red-and-white pole while others stood to the side, smoking and discussing the war efforts. The barbershop had always been the hub for the men, just as Judy's Hair Salon had been the place for women to catch up on the latest gossip. The men looked over her and Nellie, but there would be no catcalls or teasing there. Pa might only be a barber, but he knew most of the town's secrets and wielded power with his knowledge. She wondered often about the meetings he attended, but she never asked and never would.

As they entered the shop, Margaret spied the pillowcase she used for the towels and quickly stuffed them inside. Nellie enjoyed flitting from man to man, playing in a way that only a young child could do so that they would offer her sweets or some other treat. But today, the mood in the shop was somber. Word had gotten out about a convoy of captured Germans who would be helping with construction projects.

Margaret didn't understand what she overheard. *I thought we are at war with Japan. Why are they bringing Germans here?* She wished more than ever to speak to Edsol, but as soon as he turned eighteen, he would leave to start naval air training. He was already away, helping with the building of housing, and except for his few weekends home, she had no way to meet with him.

She added some towels to the second pillowcase so Nellie could help carry them home. "Is that all, Pa?"

"Did you get the ones by the sink?"

"Yes, sir." Margaret grasped the case but walked over to the sink to check again. "Yes, I got them all."

"Okay. That'll do."

The man in Pa's chair swiveled to face her. Even with the layer of soap on his face, Margaret recognized the town's mayor. "Here, you girls. Go get you some gum."

Margaret glanced at Pa, who nodded his approval. One thing her father instilled in all of his children from an early age—in most cases—was not to be on the receiving end. He'd state empathically, "Trust me, power is more important than gifts. When you have control, you can ask for anything you want. And they can't refuse you."

Margaret slipped the dime into the pocket of her dress and took Nellie's hand. "Thank you, sir. That's very kind."

As she made her way to the door, Pa called, "Tell your ma to save me a plate. I'll be late getting home tonight!"

Margaret bristled. She wouldn't tell her mother Pa would be spending the evening drinking and throwing away the money he'd made that day in a poker game. Instead, she replied, "Yes sir."

Back at home, Margaret toted the towels back to the yard and started up the fire. She pumped the water into the pot in which she would boil the soiled towels. After the steam rose from the pot and bubbles popped on the surface, she plunged them into the hot water, pushing them under with an old oar. Margaret's thoughts drifted back to her trip to town. Inside the mercantile, she'd glimpsed women standing in line, patiently waiting to purchase nylons. Margaret had overheard two smartly dressed women concerned about getting pairs—there'd been talk of nylon production converting into manufacturing of parachutes.

She'd rubbed the coin in her pocket as she'd debated how to save up enough for nylons before they were gone. She'd even considered keeping the dime and finding a way to make more. But in the end,

Nellie would've squealed if she hadn't gotten a treat, so Margaret had reluctantly parted with the money for two packs of Wrigley's Doublemint gum.

She stabbed at the towels in the pot, wiped the sweat from her brow, and sighed. With the large oar, she punched at the towels, driving them under the boiling water and the strong lye soap. She needed a way to make money of her own. She needed to ask Pa about that job again.

Her mother's voice called, "Margaret Rose!"

Margaret set the oar down to the side of the boiling pot and trudged to the back screen door. She entered the kitchen. "Yes, Mama?"

Her mother lifted the load of potatoes bundled in her apron then dumped them on the table. Her shoulders were bowed and stooped, her face drawn and wrinkled, and her knobby, rough hands rarely sat idle. During the thirties, when the prospect of feeding so many mouths loomed daily, Ma had taken in laundry, and Margaret recalled the days she'd spent washing and ironing to help her mother. Margaret recalled how each month, the soup had grown thinner than had their old cow, Bessie, who'd kept them supplied in milk and butter. With Bessie gone, it meant one more area they had to find the money for each week.

The haggard woman sat down at the table and pulled a yellowed handkerchief from her pocket. "I need to get some flour and a bit of sugar from the grocer. How much do we have in the account?"

Margaret had always had a knack for numbers. Even when she

was a young child, her mother recognized her gift. Ma spoke to a local retired teacher who tutored Margaret in exchange for laundry. As it turned out, Margaret's gift was a combination of math skills and an extremely good memory—some called it photographic—though the term the tutor used was "eidetic." As Margaret got older, it benefitted her mother, whose lack of schooling left her illiterate. She'd often traveled with Ma to the store, where she would scan the information and report it later. That way, her mother had kept up the appearance of understanding the figures in public.

"We have fifty cents left on the account." Margaret unwrapped a tea towel and pulled a cold biscuit from inside. She tore off a piece of the dry bread and slathered it with a dollop of beautyberry jam.

"Okay, use that to get some salt, sugar, and—" She dug in the pocket of her dress. "Here's a dollar. Get as much beef as you can with our rations."

One dollar. All she would need was twenty-five more cents, and she could buy nylons. Her mind raced. If she could promise Nellie a full stick of chewing gum instead of a quarter or a half, she might be able to get her to work her charm at Pa's shop. She could save it up and no one—

"Girl, did you hear me?"

"Sorry, what Mama?"

"I have to go visit old lady Weathers. Her husband passed, and both her boys have joined up with the war effort. I'm going to take her some of these potatoes and an onion. Lord knows we've been blessed to have enough that we can share our good fortune with others."

Good fortune? Margaret couldn't understand how her mother thought that they were doing well. "Where are Bobby and James?"

"They're down by the pond. I 'spect they'll be back soon, and they can use the rest of the water for bathing. Franny's taken the girls with her to the church to practice piano for service. So I'll just leave you to it."

Ma gathered up a woven basket, which she stuffed with the potatoes and recently dug yellow onion. She wiped her hands on a wet towel and then removed her apron before setting a worn brown felt hat on her head. "Get Nellie to help you peel the rest of them taters for dinner when she gets back."

"Mama, can I ask you a question?"

Her mother raised her eyebrows. "What's on your mind, child?"

"How old were you when you married Papa?"

Ma smoothed her dress. "Fifteen."

Margaret did the math in her head. Her mother would be in her late thirties then. She looked run-down after birthing so many babies and living such a hard life. Margaret knew from Franny that two of their siblings had died young from influenza and another one from a tragic accident. It explained the gap in ages between the older children and the younger ones. Her brows knit together, and she frowned.

Ma patted Margaret's hand. "Don't you worry none. You'll be married soon enough with a family of your own."

Margaret stared at her with wide eyes. She had no intention of ending up like her mother. A husband might be nice, but she wasn't sure about children. Probably two. One boy. One girl. That would be the perfect family.

Ma gathered up the basketful of items. After she left, Margaret sat at the table, forgetting the towels boiling outside. She needed to look into the commissary job. Her mother had said herself that she was good with figures. She needed Pa to allow her to work. She was deep in her daydream of nylons and picture shows with a handsome man when a wail cut into her thoughts.

The shouting grew louder. She lurched from her seat, dishrag in hand, and flew through the back door to where her younger brother, Bobby, came running with the Thompson boys.

"What is it?" Margaret yelled over the cacophony of the boys' voices. "I can't understand you all at once! What's happened?"

Bobby wheezed from his running, putting his hands on his legs as he bent over. "James cut his hand real bad like."

Staggering toward them, James clung to another boy Margaret didn't recognize. Her brother, who wasn't much older than Nellie, moaned and limped to Margaret before collapsing in her arms. The boy helping James sat on the ground, huffing and puffing.

"Let me look at it." She held out her hand.

James clutched his injury to his chest. Once he let go of it, blood oozed from a deep gash in his palm.

She quickly wrapped the dishrag around his hand then helped him inside. Over her shoulder, she yelled, "Bobby, you fetch Doc Rogers. James is needing some stitches. Now get!"

After she settled James in a chair, her little brother clutched his hand to his belly. Even at twelve, he bore the baby face of a younger boy. He sniffled and looked up at her with huge eyes. "Do you think Pa's gonna give me a whupping?"

"No. What were you doing to cause that?"

"We was just playing out in the barn. Jumping off the hay store down onto the hay below. But I missed the last jump and landed on the thresher."

"Oh, my gosh! You could have been killed. You're lucky you only cut your hand."

"Well, I—"

"What? Spit it out?"

"I think I hurt my leg too. It don't feel so good."

"Take off your pants."

His eyes grew wide, and he shook his head violently.

Margaret stifled her frustration. She wanted James to be ready for when Doc came. She took another tactic, lowering her voice to a calm tone. "I have to see if you hurt your leg, and I can't do that with your pants on."

"Maggie, I can't let no girl see my drawers even if you are my sister."

She held back a chuckle. "Fine. Let me look at least to your calves, okay?"

He nodded. She knelt down in front of him and rolled up his pants, but he cried out from the slight movement of his legs. Tears rolled down his face.

One leg showed mottling of cuts and bruises but appeared to be okay. However, as Margaret pulled up the other pant leg, the bruising was darker and more pronounced. That leg was swollen and hot to the touch, and the shin didn't look straight. Chances were it was broken, but his fall must have been cushioned by the hay bales. It was not as bad as it could have been. At least his hand hadn't been sliced through.

She stared at James, whose focus was fixed on the blood-soaked dishrag. She reached up and put her hand to his head. No fever. He didn't feel cold and clammy, either, which was a good sign.

Her gaze moved to the door. *Where are those boys?* It was taking forever for them to return. She took a deep breath and pushed herself up from the table. "I'll be back."

Hurrying outside, she checked on the towels still boiling in the cauldron. Finding a rake, she combed over the trail of blood from James's hand. She had no idea how he'd managed to walk back to the house on his bad leg.

A howl of pain punctured the air. She flew inside, where James clutched at the chair, where he'd tried to stand up.

"I don't feel so good, Maggie." Vomit spewed from his mouth.

Where is the doctor? Maggie called for help as she rushed to the window, but there was no sign of him or the boys.

Trembling, she returned to James. "Sit down." She wet a cloth and wiped his head and mouth before finding a bucket to place by him. She gathered towels and cleaned up the mess, but as she glanced at James, she spied the towel, saturated with his blood. She prayed for the doctor to arrive quickly as she pumped water to clean up the floor then moved the bucket closer to James in case he needed it again.

The door flew open, and the boys raced in, talking over one

another. "He's not there. The doc's not there. He went over to Roeville."

Margaret hung her head. James couldn't wait. She had to do something. With a new determination, she took charge. She pointed at the older boy. "You go get your Pa's horse and bring it here. Tell him James is hurt, and we have to use it to take James to Doc Albert in town. Bobby, go get Ma's sewing kit."

CHAPTER SIX

Margaret pumped water into a pot and struck a match to light the burner on the stove. Glancing back at James, who moaned and whimpered, she struggled with how she would get him to sit still so she could wash and stitch up his hand. Bobby came in with Ma's kit and stole a glance at their brother.

"Bobby, why don't you go see if you can help get the horse ready?"

"Well, um, if you don't need my help—"

"I know you'd be a big help, but there's not much you can do here. So scat!" She winked at him, and he rushed out the backdoor before she could change her mind. The last thing she needed was for him to turn green at the gills or faint on her while she needed steady nerves. She just had to think of stitching James's hand as if she were mending a quilt.

After putting the needles, the scissors, and clean dishcloths in the boiling water, she went to her brother's side. "Listen, James. I have to stitch that hand up. Now, I know you're tough, but if you can sit as still as possible for me and not scream, that will help a lot."

"I dunno, Maggie. I—" Tears spilled down his cheeks. "My hand hurts something awful, and my leg too. I want Mama."

"Look, I wish Ma was here right now too. But she's not. So how about this? I want you to try your hardest to sit still for me, and I'll give you a full piece of chewing gum."

His eyes grew wide. "A full piece? All to myself?" He nodded forcefully.

"Great. Now I'm going to put this here belt around you to hold you to the chair. That's it." She tied a towel with the belt. If he fainted, at least he wouldn't fall out of the chair and injure himself more.

She went over to a cabinet and pulled out Pa's jug of whiskey. She poured a bit of the liquor into a small glass, the alcohol assaulting her nose with its strength. Scouring the table, she finished by washing her hands with lye until they almost hurt from the scrubbing.

"Give me strength." She took a deep breath and made her way to the pot. She winced as she gathered the needles, scissors, and cloths from the scalding water then laid them on a clean cloth on the table. *It's now or never.*

She smiled at the boy. "James, you get to be a real man today."

His eyes narrowed, and a confused look came over his face. His reply was strained. "I do?"

She nodded. "Yes, this is the first day you get to be like Pa. Now, I want you to drink this down in one big swallow. Do you think you can do that for me?"

His eyes grew wide. "But that's the demon's drink."

"Not when you have to use it for medicine. Okay?" She held it to his lips. Once he opened his mouth, she forced it in then pushed his head back before he could spit it out.

He coughed and hacked as the liquid slid down his throat. "It burns!" He tried to move, but the ties held him securely to the chair's back.

"It's just a minute. You'll see. You'll feel much better soon." She stroked his head. Sadly, she couldn't wait for long. She unwrapped the bloodied towel and dabbed at the cut, surveying the best way to work. As she felt James relax, she bit her lip and poured some of the whiskey onto the cut hand without warning. James screamed, but the whiskey was already taking hold.

Margaret worked quickly, and by the time she heard voices in the back, she'd stitched the wound up nicely. She wiped the sweat from her brow as the boys came inside. She stood and stretched. "Were you able to get the horse?"

They nodded, their faces transfixed on James, whose head lolled on his shoulders.

"Is he dead?" Bobby whispered.

"More like dead drunk. Now I'm going to need you to help me get him up on the horse and hold him until I get up there."

Margaret washed her hands of the blood before untying a limp James. She and the boys carried him out to where the horse stood tethered to the back porch. She climbed into the saddle and turned to the boys. "Be careful of his hand and his legs."

With a bit of finagling, they finally managed to get a barely conscious James up in front of her. While Margaret would have liked to move fast, she didn't want to cause any more harm to his leg, so she steered the horse on back paths away from any cars that might spook it.

The trip into town was uneventful except for a few times when she stopped to let James puke over the side of the horse's neck. Soon, they were arriving at Doc Albert's house, where he had his offices on the ground floor.

Margaret called to a young girl of about Nellie's age sweeping the porch. "You, there. I need help. Get the doc!"

The child dropped the straw broom and hurried inside.

A few minutes later, Doctor Albert rushed out, the chain on his pocket watch hitting against his brocade vest. His white shirtsleeves were rolled up, and his gray hair stuck to his head with pomade. "What is it?"

"He cut his hand pretty deep, and I think he's broken his left leg. The other looks to be pretty bruised as well, but I think it's okay."

A black man wearing a pair of overalls appeared from around the side of the house. Together, the men carried the moaning child into the front room of the house. Margaret followed the group before realizing she should have changed her dress. She stank of iron, sweat, whiskey, and vomit.

The doctor unwrapped the cloth from her brother's injured hand. "Who did this?" He pointed at the stitches.

Margaret swallowed, wondering if she'd done something wrong. She bowed her head and choked out, "I-I did, sir."

"Well, I couldn't have done a better job myself. Those stitches are perfect. Did you clean the wound first?"

"Yes. I made sure that there wasn't anything in there, and then I—um... well, I—"

"Out with it, girl. You used whiskey as a disinfectant?"

She replied "yes" then recounted how she had sterilized the needles and put a dressing around the wound.

"Smart. In a pinch, it works, and I gather from this young'un, he got a swig too. Good thinking on the restraints. If he would have pulled back, it could have made it worse. So for now, we'll keep an eye on his hand. I'll give you some gauze and ointment, and then you need to watch for any redness or infection at the site. Now let's look at this leg."

The doctor cut through the pant legs, and she could already hear Pa complaining about having to pay for another pair when those had another season at least in them. She watched as the doctor took his time probing the legs.

"Yep, this one here's broke. But not bad." He motioned to the other man, who stood near the doorway. "Ceril, grab him under his shoulders and hold him."

Ceril came around and cradled James in his arms.

As the doctor repositioned her brother's leg, James cried out. Next, the doctor attached a splint, but he looked up at Margaret as he worked. "How old are you, girl?"

"Sixteen, sir. But I'll be seventeen next month."

"I think you could have a future being a nurse. What with the nurses being sent off to help our boys, lots of us are facing shortages.

My nurse, Ethel, left just last month." He cocked his head at her. "You look familiar. Who's your Pa?"

"John Thomas Locke, sir."

The doctor stopped his work and did a low whistle. "You don't say."

Together, they moved James to a sitting position.

"You bring him back in a week, and we'll check out his hand and his leg. For now, I'll get my man to help put him back on the horse." He turned, wiped his hands on a towel, then pulled out a piece of paper. "Here. Give this to your Pa, and then tell him to come see me. We may be able to work out a deal."

He instructed Ceril to carry her brother out. Before they left, the doctor pointed at Margaret. "Don't forget what I said. Tell your pa to contact me."

"Yes, sir." Margaret stuffed the paper into her dress pocket and followed behind Ceril, who held James like a sack of potatoes. She turned to see Doc Albert close the door behind them. She dreaded telling Pa about the bill. He would be furious. Her stomach knotted as she thought of the ordeal ahead of her. She would get in trouble for not watching the boys. Even worse, Pa would further suspend her attending the dances. She had dreamed about it for months. She sighed. *Well, there is nothing I can do about it now.*

Outside, the old horse happily munched on an apple provided by the girl Margaret had seen earlier. She stroked the horse's muzzle. Seeing them, she jumped down from the railing and scooted back around the house like a timid mouse.

Margaret mounted the mare before Ceril positioned James in front of her. She pulled James in toward her, wiping his hair, then slick with sweat, away from his brow. At least his normal color was returning to his face.

"Is that your daughter?" she asked Ceril. "I don't think I've seen you here before."

"Yes, ma'am. We came down from Mobile. Doc needed a hand with painting his house."

"I noticed his new shingle outside. Did you do that?"

He smiled. "Yes, and Cassia helped me a bit with it." He pulled off his fedora, wiped his brow with a frayed red bandana, then pushed it back into his overalls. "Do you need me to lead the horse home for you?"

"No. Thank you."

She accepted an apple he offered her from a nearby basket. "For your trip." He tipped his hat then moved swiftly around to the back of the house.

She thanked him again and clicked her tongue to get the mare to start home.

Margaret wondered if she should stop in at the barbershop to speak with Pa but decided it would be best to take James home first. She needed to get out of that filthy dress. Plus, she didn't want Mama to come home and see all the mess she'd left in the kitchen. She should have enough time to clean up the house, get James settled, and wash up. As she made the edge of town and the path that would lead her home, she took a bite of the apple. It crunched in her mouth, and her stomach rumbled. She couldn't remember when she'd last eaten. She looked down to see if James wanted any, but his face was crushed against her breast, his soft snores coming in puffs of air. As she chewed, she thought back to the doctor's words.

A nurse. She hadn't thought of being one, but she had heard about the nursing training. It had been for older girls, but maybe she could think of a way to help. She bit into the crunchy, sweet apple, and after she munched on the last bite, she gave the core to the horse.

Her thoughts drifted, and she smiled at the praise she'd received from the doctor. "Couldn't have done it better myself." That's what he'd said. He'd also praised her for not panicking and keeping a clear head. She sat up a little taller in the saddle and went to move the reins to the other hand, but her fingers were sticky from the apple. As she wiped her hands on her dress, the paper in her pocket rustled. She pulled it out, looked at it, and gasped.

Eighteen dollars! Pa was not going to be happy. She had no idea how they were going to pay. At least James wouldn't receive any other punishment except for maybe some more chores. She shoved the paper back into her pocket. Stroking her younger brother's hair, she knew James would have a hard time living this incident down. She would miss having her share of the gum, but it was worth it for what he'd undergone.

Tiredness set in as she approached the last leg before home. As she made her way down the road, she was surprised to see a car in front of the house. Franny stood on the porch with their guest and let out a laugh that lit up her face. She possessed an ethereal beauty and seemed to glow from within. Margaret supposed that all the goodness in Franny needed some way to escape, and it showed up on the outside.

Margaret squinted but couldn't make out who the man was. He wore a tan suit, the shoulders broad with the jacket cutting into a narrow waist. In contrast to the suit, he wore black brogans. Franny waved to her, and the man turned too. He strode over then took hold of the horse's bridle.

Franny peppered Margaret with questions, worry dotting her face. "Is James okay? Did you make it to the doctor? The boys told me what happened."

The man held the horse while Margaret shifted on the horse's back. "He's okay. But he's going to be hurting for quite a while." Fatigue had set in over the ride home, and Margaret sighed deeply.

The man motioned to James. "Need some help?"

"Yes, if you can take him and put him in his bed, I can take care of the horse." Margaret moved her arm away, and the man lifted James so that he rested on his shoulder.

Franny patted James's head, cooing over him with tender words. As they reached the porch, she motioned to the man as she held the screen door open. They disappeared inside.

Margaret dismounted, her muscles taut with exhaustion. She found a bucket and began pumping water. As the water filled it, she scooped up a handful and took a deep drink. She set the bucket in front of the horse, who dipped her snout in gratefully. Margaret returned to the spigot and splashed water on her face. She arched her back, still tight from the journey and the tension she'd been holding.

Franny appeared at the door with the man, who took her hand before he strode over to the car. With a wave, he drove away.

"Who's that?"

"Paul."

"And?"

"And what? You know, sometimes you don't need to know everything." Franny shrugged and went back inside with Margaret following behind.

Margaret raised her eyebrows at Franny's uncharacteristic rebuff. "You better watch out. I think you may have a case of the gumptions."

Franny laughed and took Margaret's arm. Inside, the kitchen had been cleaned and everything returned to its place.

"Did you do that?" Margaret asked.

"Yes. I knew that you'd worry about it. The boys told me everything. They're around back, and they'll take the horse home now." She stuck her head out back and called for them.

As the boys flew inside, they assaulted Margaret with more questions, but she refused to say anything until they took the horse home. Defeated, they stole a quick glance into the bedroom, where James was sound asleep.

"See, I told you they wouldn't have to do no ampu-station." Petey hit Bobby on the arm with his fist.

"Did not."

"Did too."

"Boys, horse. Home." Franny pointed toward the door, and they tussled with each other on their way out.

"Hold on." Margaret held up her hand for them to wait. "For all your help today." Their eyes lit up and their mouths gaped open as she pulled out a piece of Doublemint gum from her pocket. She split the piece in half and offered it to them.

"Thanks, Maggie!" They hugged her neck before pulling the horse behind them, their lively voices discussing eating the treat then or saving it for later.

Back inside, Margaret slouched on the edge of the kitchen chair, the energy draining from her.

"Come on. I'll pour you a bath. Go get out of those things." Franny set the pot on the stove as Margaret made her way into the girls' bedroom. On the way, she stopped and kissed James on his forehead.

His eyes fluttered open, and he murmured, "Can I stop being a man now, Maggie?"

"Yes. Though you did a very fine job of it." She ran her fingers through his hair. "Now you go to sleep."

"You're the best sister ever." He shut his eyes.

She smiled, hoping he would think that later when he would most likely wake up with a horrible headache. Shucking off the clothes, she enjoyed the pampering Franny provided. She soaked in the tub until the water turned cold. After slipping on a clean shift, she rummaged through the dirty dress until she found the note from Doc Albert. She debated on what to do with it. *I could give it to Ma first. But that might make Pa angrier.*

Franny took the decision away from her by asking what she was holding. Margaret gave it over, then Franny let out a gasp.

"I know. Pa's going to be angry."

Franny stuffed it into her apron pocket. "I'll take care of it. I'll think of something." She gathered Margaret up in a warm embrace. "I'm so proud of you, Maggie."

Tears stung as she allowed the words to wash over her. Maybe she did have a purpose. For the first time, she wasn't worthless. Even more exciting, maybe she was meant to be a nurse. The possibilities blossomed in her mind. She smiled at Franny.

The front door hinge squeaked. "Where is everyone?" Ma was home.

CHAPTER SEVEN

Ma took off her hat, sticking the pin back through it before looking at the pair of them. "What's happened?" Even when they were children, it had always felt like Ma could read their minds and look into their souls.

Margaret pushed forward, but Franny held her back. "Ma, James got hurt, but he's okay now. Margaret Rose showed real bravery and got him the help he needed."

Brave? She'd only done what needed to be done. A rush of emotion crashed down on her. In the next moment, she flew into Ma's arms, weeping at the ordeal she'd been through with James. "It was so awful, Mama."

Ma gathered her in a soothing embrace, stroking Margaret's hair and cooing. "It's okay. Mama's here."

Margaret buried her face in Ma's jacket, inhaling the comforting smell of VEL soap on her skin.

Ma took Margaret's face in her hands. "Let's sit down and have Franny make us some hot tea. Then you can tell your mama all about it. Okay?" She smiled as Margaret sniffed and nodded.

After Margaret had shared what had happened, their mother went in to check on James. They listened to the boy wail from the other room. "Mama, it feels so bad!"

His cries were followed by more soft words from their mother, her voice a haven of calm in a sea of fear.

When Ma finally returned to the kitchen, she sat on the chair, taking the cup of black tea offered by Franny. "Margaret Rose, I'm proud of you. You kept your head and did what needed doing." She patted her hand.

"But Mama, here's the issue." Franny pulled the doctor's invoice from her pocket, unfolded it, then slid it across the table to their mother.

Margaret rubbed her arms as she watched Ma's brow crease. She pursed her lips before setting the paper on the table. Folding her hands, Ma closed her eyes and prayed. Margaret licked her lips and waited. *What are we going to do?*

Finally, Ma glanced up at both of them. "Tell me again what Doc Albert said about you helping him in exchange for payment."

Margaret shared about Doc's nurse leaving and help being scarce because of so many nurses serving in the war effort.

Ma tapped her finger on the table. "Yes, I think this is a good idea. You can work for Doc after school and on Saturdays. I can speak to your teacher so you can leave at lunchtime." She placed her hands on the table before pushing herself up to stand. "Right, then. We have work to do. Tonight, we'll have fried pork chops, mashed taters, and gravy, along with apples and cabbage—to celebrate that James wasn't more seriously hurt and for your quick thinking, Margaret Rose. You go pull some taters and a cabbage from the cold cellar. Franny, I think vinegar pie for dessert."

"Yes, Mama. I'll work on it now." Franny walked to the cupboard, opening up the flour sack. "This will use up most of our flour if we make two pies."

"One pie will be enough."

Margaret caught her mother's eye. "Ma, what about—"

She stroked her hand down Margaret's cheek. "Don't you fret none. Leave it to me."

Ma was true to her word, and after dinner, when Pa was satiated with one of the best meals the family had enjoyed for a while, she shooed all the children from the room. Unable to bear it, Margaret crept into the boys' room, her ear close to the door. She heard the moment Ma handed him the paper. A string of expletives grated on her ears. His rocking chair creaked then slammed into the wall as he got up. For several minutes, all she could make out was his shoes stomping as he paced, muttering to himself. No word was heard from Ma.

Finally, after Pa had spent his energy and Margaret heard him resettle into his chair, Ma spoke about the doctor's offer for the first time. In that moment, Margaret understood her mother to be smarter and wiser than she'd ever realized. She listened as Ma led Pa directly to where she wanted him to go with his decision. Margaret crept closer to the door, pressing her ear tightly against the frame. She wanted to hear what Pa would say about her.

"Margaret Rose."

She jumped when she heard him call her name. Taking a deep breath, she tiptoed back toward the girls' room and waited until his voice rose.

"Margaret!"

She ran to the living room. "Yes, Pa?"

"I'm thinking that your brother got himself into trouble 'cause you weren't watching out right for him."

"Yes, sir." She bowed her head.

"Am I correct that Doc Albert offered you a job to help pay off your debt?"

"Yes, sir." She noted his use of the word "your."

"What about your schooling and the chores? You still have things to do. Can you handle this job too?"

She pinched her hand so as not to scream out "yes" too quickly. Ma's brows were raised, and Margaret calmed herself before replying, "I do. I can get up earlier and finish my chores in the morning, and if Ma can speak with my teacher, I think I should be able to help Doctor Albert."

Ma stood. "Nellie can help with the younger girls, and as James won't be going off anywhere for a while, I can have Bobby stay close and keep him company while he heals."

Pa stood. "Okay, it's settled, then. I want you to tell Doc Albert you'll work for him to pay off this debt. It'll teach you some responsibility and help you settle down a bit."

Margaret forgot herself and sprinted over to Pa. "Thank you, Pa."

She kissed him on the cheek. "I won't let you down."

"I know you won't, girl." In an unusual display of affection, he pressed his lips to her forehead.

"Ma, I'm going to the lodge." He walked out the door without another word.

CHAPTER EIGHT

As Doc Albert gave her the tour of his office, Margaret took in the surroundings with new senses.

The room reeked of antiseptic, and one of her jobs would be to use the heavy rubber gloves to wipe down the table, chairs, and other surfaces. A wood stove sat in the corner with a large pot on it to sterilize various instruments.

On a table in the corner sat a wooden instrument with a rubber ball attached to a larger piece of material that she learned took blood pressure readings. On a hook nearby, a stethoscope hung. Along the other wall, a glass-faced cabinet held bottles of various liquids and powders. On the bottom, two drawers opened to reveal gauze, plasters, and elastic rubber bandages for sprains. Margaret was also shown a metal tray displaying various scissors and other tools. Those were to be cleaned and boiled daily before she left then covered with a clean cloth for use the next morning.

Her mind whirled at all she would need to do and learn to be a competent helper. But she realized that the doctor needed her as much as she wanted to learn. Because of her lack of skills, he'd only agree to twelve cents an hour. That meant that Margaret would have to spend more time clearing off the eighteen-dollar debt, but it would also give her more time to learn.

As soon as she'd started work, Margaret soon realized Doc hadn't hired her simply out of charity, either, or because he needed some aid. His nurse must have done most of the stitching. She would often watch him squint while doing a procedure even though he wore spectacles, and the tremor in his hands increased the more the day wore on. It made more sense, then, why Doc Rogers spent his time attending to people who couldn't come into town to see the doctor. Those patients would require a good eye and a steady hand of a younger man like Rogers.

While Margaret was excited about learning and getting away from the house, she'd been dismayed to find she wouldn't get to wear a nurse's cap or uniform. However, she'd convinced Ma that she needed a white dress and shoes, so her mother had sewed her a jacket with large pockets and matching skirt in the seersucker fabric she'd seen on many nurses.

Her best friend, Alice, had been elated for Margaret and wished she could find something to occupy her time. Her father had been shipped off to Europe, and that worried Alice. They hadn't heard from him in months. As Alice shared her fears, Margaret could only think of when Edsol would be leaving. So far, he'd been able to stay in Pensacola, training and working on projects. But as the war continued to ramp up and men were sent to fight against Germany, she knew it wouldn't be long before he would be gone too. Her heart beat faster, and her stomach ached with worry when she thought about it. The thought of Edsol leaving was unbearable, and she fought constantly against her feeling of powerlessness against the unseen enemy. Thankfully, being able to work for Doc Albert helped to keep her mind on daily tasks, and for that, she was grateful.

With her hair pulled back into a bun, Margaret surveyed herself with pride. In the few months she'd worked for Doc, she'd honed her skills and had taken in as much learning as she could. So much so that Doc gave her books to read when she wasn't needed to assist with a patient or complete other tasks for the day. She was diligent about showing up early to school to get more work done before she left for the day.

Margaret wore her nursing outfit proudly to school, even though her sister, Franny, had admonished her about arrogance. But she *was* making a difference with Doc Albert by helping people. Though she had to admit, it felt good when some of the girls who lived in the nicer homes looked at her uniform with awe. Of course, she would never let on that she was paying off her family's debt or that she hadn't yet earned the title of assistant, but none had stopped and questioned her.

While Doc was training her, he wouldn't pay her. Margaret felt that wasn't right, but there was not much she could do about it. She'd done the math. Working for him a couple of hours a day meant she would have half the debt paid off in a few months. During the summer, she hoped to work more, and he seemed agreeable because kids tended to get hurt more over the summer. She reasoned if she could work four hours a day, that would be two dollars and forty cents a week. She could pay off the debt by her birthday in May. But as she worked, she enjoyed learning. Even while the money went to the debt, to know that she'd earned money for the week put a skip in her step. Even though she was still too young to join the nurses, she could look into any training she could take.

On Friday afternoon, Margaret shucked off the rubber gloves, put them in a nearby sink, then ran hot water over them. While she was tired after the day's efforts, it felt good to know she'd been able to stitch up Mary Young's toddler, Mabel, who'd fallen and hit her head on the coffee table. With Margaret's sewing skills, she had made it to where the scar wouldn't be too visible. She'd also told Mrs. Young about putting arnica salve on it. That was the first time she'd been chastised by Doc Albert, who instructed her not to recommend anything but store-bought products that he sold. Then, as quickly as he'd gotten angry with her, his demeanor changed, and he asked her to come into his office.

Oh, no. If he fired her, they would still owe the money. Margaret clutched at her jacket top, worry rearing its head as she shuffled into his office.

He sat behind his desk. "Close the door, please."

She did as she was told before he motioned for her to take a seat.

"You've been doing good work here. You're eager to learn, and you've grown in your skill." He sat back in the leather chair burnished with the oil from his head—he often stole naps during the day, his snores echoing across the long hallway. "I was going over the figures, and I'd like you to stay on after the debt is paid. What do you think about that?"

"I'd like that, but I'm not sure what Pa will say about it." It was the truth. Pa still believed a woman's place was in the home. She hoped there would be a way to convince him.

He nodded then slid his fingers across his bushy mustache. "I thought as much." He opened a drawer and pulled out a quarter, sliding it across the scarred wooden desk. "However, I want to give you some incentive to make that happen. You always come in early and sometimes stay later, so I'll pay you for two hours directly. I'm sure a pretty girl like you would like a bit of mad money."

Margaret nodded, unsure how to respond. "Yes, sir."

"Good. Now we'll keep this arrangement between ourselves for now. You can leave."

She picked up the quarter and backed out of the room. Running the coin over her palms, she could barely contain her excitement. *My own money!* With the quarter burning a hole in her pocket, she rushed over to the drugstore, where she chose a *Calling All Girls* magazine and a bag of penny candy. After handing over the quarter, she pocketed the ten cents in change. She would stop home to change then head over to Alice's. She couldn't wait to tell Alice that she'd bought the candy and magazine with her own money.

Margaret was becoming a woman of the world.

CHAPTER NINE

Margaret spent a lot of time making herself scarce whenever Bud Simpson showed up at the house. The last thing she wanted was to give him an incentive to pursue her. She fretted when Franny asked her to be nicer so as not to hurt his feelings or make her Pa upset at her rebuff of Bud's advances. In the end, she'd decided the best way was to hide or leave when he came around. His brother had been able to avoid enlistment because of having his younger children and no wife. If the war continued to build, it wouldn't be long before Bud would be called up next.

The sun beat down on her as Margaret walked to Doc's. When she arrived, he had an errand for her. She gathered up the list of items to pick up from the shop and made her way over to the drugstore. As she went, her mind was lost in a daydream instead of focusing on restocking the surgical kits.

She strolled along the boardwalk, feeling smug and cheerful as she touched the coin purse in her pocket. After a recent incident involving a young girl from a wealthy family in town, the mother had taken her aside and given Margaret a whole dollar. The girl had cut her leg, and Margaret calmed the child enough for Doc to check her wound. Margaret had handled the stitching. Along with the quarters Doc had given her, she felt rich indeed.

She fingered the coins again. She'd been saving for weeks but didn't know what to spend it on. She was imagining all the things she could get when catcalls stopped her in her tracks. She'd been so deep in thought that she hadn't noticed the gaggle of sailors she'd just passed.

She turned around. "What did you say?"

"Hi, peaches. You rationed?"

Margaret froze, and a blush rose on her chest and cheeks. It was no one's business if she had a beau or was going steady. She struggled to come up with a strong retort but only squeaked instead.

The sailors, barely out of their teens themselves, laughed and slapped each other on the back. She wanted to run away, but her feet refused to move.

A deep male voice spoke. "Leave the girl alone."

Margaret swiveled to see a man in uniform. He towered over her five-foot-four frame, and she had to crane her neck to view his entire face. His hair was shorn close to his head, but it still revealed a hint of red.

The man spoke again, invoking his friendship with their superior, then the sailors scattered like rats. The man glanced down at her with a smile that revealed his straight teeth, but her gaze had become fixed on the dimple on his chin. She longed to reach out and touch it.

Shaking her head, she came back to her senses. "Thank you."

"It's my pleasure. I have a baby sister at home, and I hope some other guy would do the same for her in this situation." He looked at her dress. "You in the nurse's corps?"

"No, I work for Doc Albert." She turned and pointed down the street to where the doctor's shingle hung from the large Victorian home office.

"Okay, well, I can walk you back there just to make sure those goons don't bother you again."

"Thanks, but I'm on my way to the drugstore to get some items."

He rubbed his head. "Be okay if I walk with you over there? I hope you don't think I'm being too forward, but this would be a good time for a soda float."

"Okay. I guess that would be all right." She walked toward the store, glancing up at him every now and again. She knew he had to be older than Edsol, but she couldn't tell by how much.

"Where are you from?" She gazed up at him, taking in his handsome face and how self-assured he appeared.

"Texas, ma'am. Have you ever been there?"

She shook her head. "Is it all cactus and sand?"

He roared with laughter. "No, though that's what lots of people think. We have trees, though not with as much moss and lichen as y'all have on your trees."

"Do you wear a cowboy hat and boots?"

"No, not usually. Only my six-shooter."

"Really?"

He grinned.

She laughed. "Ah, you're pulling my leg!"

"Yes, I am. I don't suppose you could take a little longer on your errand. I'm enjoying our chat so much."

She smiled, trying her best to appear calm when, inside, her heart was doing somersaults. "I suppose I could take a little more time. We could cross the street and then circle back here."

"Killer-diller." He stuck out his arm, and she wrapped hers in his, a flush of warmth flooding her.

She stole glances at him as he talked about his family back home and how he'd joined the merchant mariners once the war had started. So far, he'd spent much of the time since he'd arrived in Florida stocking inventory and supplying the next convoy. After the next group, he anticipated that his fleet would be next.

"It won't be long before we'll be shipping out. But that's going to be even harder now that I've met you."

Margaret blushed. "You're just saying that."

"No, I'm not." He stopped. "I feel like we—I don't know what it is. Ah, geez." He fumbled with his words. "I've only met you, but I feel like I've known you forever."

She wanted to tell him she felt the same. Instead, she tilted her head, beaming up at him.

"I don't suppose, well, you'd consider—" He stopped as they reached the store and held the door open for her.

Inside, the ceiling fans whirled, the swishing sound echoing on the clapboard walls and wooden floors as the owner fought to keep the trapped interior heat moving. A few scowling women, some holding babes or with small children clutching their skirts, stood in line with their woven baskets and ration cards, waiting their turn for the paltry provisions they were allotted for that week. The shelves that had once been lined with other goods looked bare in spots. In their place, plain white boxes or canned meats held center stage.

Yet Mr. Mason, the shopkeeper, had seized an opportunity with so many young people in town. He had converted part of the storefront to a soda fountain with a counter and barstools that swiveled. She'd yet to get to sit on one, but as she watched the younger girls spinning around, flirting with dashing men in uniform, a touch of envy rose in her throat.

"What d'ya say? Up for a float?" He cocked his head toward the counter.

"I can't. I have to get these things for Doc and get back."

He stuck out his lip in mock sadness. "Come on. What's the harm? My treat."

She licked her lips and tucked a strand of hair behind her ear. Just as she had made up her mind to say yes, the door opened, and in walked Edsol.

"Edsol!" She flew over to him, and he wrapped her up in his arms, twirling her around. "When did you get here?"

"I got my orders to ship out soon. They let us have leave, so I wanted to come home and see everyone before I head out. I don't know how long we'll be gone or when we'll come back."

Margaret's chest clenched. *Or if they'll come back.* She wanted to wrap her arms around him and force him to stay. She wished it was as simple as kidnapping him until the war was over. Yet she was also proud of his honor and desire to serve his country.

"Ma is going to be beside herself if she doesn't expect you. You know how she likes to make a good meal for her boys."

"It's all good. Whatever she makes, I'll eat." He held her back at arm's length, looking at her outfit. "Well, look at you. Ma told me you was doing some nursing training with old Doc Albert."

The man who'd accompanied her interrupted their chatter with a clearing of his throat.

To her surprise, Edsol grasped his hand in his hand. "Eugene! Good to see you again. Are you down here too?"

The men slapped each other on the back. "Yes, for a bit. Until I get shipped out. Say, is this your sister? As ugly as your mug is, I'm surprised to find you have such a pretty sister."

Edsol took the ribbing in stride. "Funny. Yes, this is Margaret Rose."

Eugene turned. "Nice to make your acquaintance, Margaret Rose." His brow furrowed for a moment. "Wait, I thought your eldest sister was named Franny."

"No, you're right. Franny, me, then Maggie."

"But that means you're only—"

"I'll be seventeen soon." She avoided Edsol's look and puffed out her chest, but the widening of Eugene's eyes had Margaret wishing she could sink into the ground.

"Well, it's a good thing I came along when I did. There were some boys acting ungentlemanly toward your sister, here." He cocked his finger at Margaret.

"Thanks. I'm sure Maggie appreciates your chivalry. Don't you, Mags?"

She nodded, dejected at missing out on the ice cream soda.

Edsol turned back to Eugene. "I've got to catch the bus back to base. Headed that way? We can spend the time catching up." He bent and kissed Margaret on the cheek. "I've got leave starting tomorrow, so tell Ma to expect me for supper then."

Eugene followed Edsol but turned before exiting the door. "Nice meeting you, kid."

Margaret's fists balled, and she bit her lip to keep from crying. She wasn't a child.

The jangle of the coins in her pocket brought her back to the present. She would buy her own soda float and sit on one of those barstools. She didn't need a man to do it for her. Pleased with her decision, she noticed the bus pull up outside. As Edsol and Eugene waited for the people to exit the bus, a group of ladies rushed off it and bustled toward the store.

The cacophony created by the ladies entering made heads turn. Dressed in professional suits or dresses, the women were young to middle-aged. Margaret backed up against a table of stacked goods as the women moved as one, not unlike a gaggle of geese, honking at anyone who might get in their path. It appeared the women were on a mission, but she hadn't the slightest idea what kind.

CHAPTER TEN

The women's laughter and voices carried across the shop as they made their way toward the back of the store to the women's section. There, the fabrics and other ladies' items were kept more discreet from the general public. Soon, they jostled one another to move to the front by the counter.

Margaret grabbed a young clerk as she started toward the women. "What's going on?"

The girl stopped. "It's the nylons. The factories are now going to make parachutes instead. From the size of the group, they must have heard we got a shipment in, so they're going to grab some nylons while they're still available."

She gestured toward the women, whose voices were growing ever louder. "I gots to get on, or Mr. Mason will—"

"Susan, quit dawdling!" Mr. Mason's voice reverberated as she scampered off to the line of women.

One woman's voice rose above the rest. "I want to buy three pairs!"

"That's not right. If she can buy three pairs, I want two pairs!"

"I'll pay more!"

"I'll pay double!" a woman in a smartly belted suit called out. She unclasped her black handbag before pulling out a wad of dollar bills.

The surrounding women gasped at the display of wealth. A woman close by shoved her, loudly proclaiming, "Who do you think you are, trouncing in here, all hoity-toity like?"

"Stop it!" The woman pushed back. It looked like a catfight was on the verge of happening.

"Tsk, tsk." Margaret swiveled to see some older women in line at the butcher counter, shaking their heads.

Mr. Mason joined the shop girl. "Ladies, ladies. Please!" He held his hands up. "You know full well that you are only allowed one pair. Now, you must give Susan your money and wait in an orderly—and quiet—manner for your turn. To be fair, you will also give her your name so that she can write it down in the book to ensure everyone receives one pair only."

He handed it over to Susan, who waited on the first customer as women in the back of the line fumed.

Margaret's mind raced. *What if I never get to wear nylons?* Today might be her only chance. She could get an ice cream soda another day.

Margaret rushed over and took her place in line, imagining all the envious looks she would receive when she showed up to the dance in nylons. It would be held in a few weeks, and Pa had given her his consent to attend—as long as she went with the Simpson clan. The idea of having to dance with one of those farmer boys repulsed her, but missing out was not an option. The line moved forward, and she was startled from her reverie when Susan asked her what she wanted.

"Oh, sorry. I'll have a pair of nylons, please."

Susan's eyes grew into saucers. "Really? They're a buck and a quarter."

"I know. I have my own money." She pulled out the dollar bill given to her plus the five nickels—all her money. She fingered the bill then, with a "hurry up" from other women behind her, slapped it down on the counter. Susan handed her the package, and Margaret fought down an urge to squeal. Instead, she lifted her chin and walked away from the counter as if it wasn't the most exciting thing she'd done in ages.

So intent was she on being able to open her prize that she was almost out the door before she realized she needed to retrieve the items for Doc Albert. She stuffed the package of nylons into her top and made her way back to Mr. Mason's line to wait her turn.

She was gathering up her supplies when the door swung open. Irma and Bunny sashayed into the store. Irma wore an emerald-green dress with a fox stole across her shoulders. On her head, a hat was perched at a jaunty angle, with a lace veil that covered part of her hair and forehead. Her lips were painted a vibrant red, and her gloved hands were linked with Bunny's, who wore a simpler cornflower-blue A-line dress. Irma carried a tapestry purse, Bunny a floral-basket purse. Each wore a set of party-time pumps, with Irma's Kerrybrookes featuring an ankle strap. As they walked past her, Margaret also noted that Irma's hosiery had a black seam up the back.

Glamourous.

The word jumped into Margaret's mind. They looked like something she'd seen in the magazines, *Silver Screen* or *Movie Life*. Whenever she spent time with Alice, they devoured the gossip magazines Alice's mother bought, entranced by the clothing and fashion of the movie stars. It was as if those pages had come to life right in front of her.

Irma and Bunny strode toward the back, their heavy heels announcing their presence as their spicy perfume filled the stale air. They kept their gazes focused forward, either oblivious or ignoring the gaping mouths and nasty whispers of the women and the leers of the sailors at the lunch counter. Some of the mothers turned their children's faces away. Despite the unwelcome reception, Margaret supposed Irma and Bunny had to shop somewhere too.

She bristled when she overheard a lady from her church make a cutting comment about the pair. She faced the woman and hissed, "Judge not."

"Well, I never." The woman gathered her packages tied with string then fled the store.

Shocked at her own brazenness, Margaret prayed the woman didn't know her mother. She turned back, and as Irma and her friend made their way to the counter, another lady was already yelling at Susan. "What do you mean, you're out? They arrived today!"

"I'm sorry, ma'am, but we sold out." Susan whimpered and huddled like a rabbit at the woman's assault.

Irma squeezed by the woman, who said, "Well, I never."

"Probably true," Irma replied.

The woman clamped her mouth shut, her face ruddy with humiliation.

Irma turned back to Susan. "Child, what's your name?"

"Susan, ah, ma'am." She glanced around for someone to come to her aid.

"Honey, I ain't no one's ma'am except maybe some young boys." She chuckled heartily along with Bunny, whose laughter echoed through the store. She focused on Susan. "But I appreciate your saying it and your respect and all. A few people could learn from you." She turned around with narrowed eyes, and her gaze targeted the other rude women in the shop with surprising accuracy. Those hecklers quickly turned away, their faces red at being called out in public.

Irma patted Susan's hand with her gloved one. "Now, when will the next shipment be coming in? We'd be happy to pay in advance."

Susan tittered at the touch. "I don't know."

Mr. Mason joined her at the counter and cleared his throat. "Miss, um, Horace—"

Susan fought back a giggle, and he shooed her away before beginning again. "Susan is telling the truth. We don't know when they'll send more or even if we'll get another shipment at all, so we can't take any payments."

Irma twisted her head to the side and looked up at Mr. Mason. Sweat collected on his forehead as he tugged at the bowtie around his neck. Irma bent toward him, and Margaret knew that she was most likely showing off things she shouldn't in decent company. "Now,

Ron, you wouldn't be lying to me now, would you? I'd hate to think that we weren't... friends."

He shook his head. "No. I'm telling you the truth. As soon as the current batch sells out, that's it. I've ordered more, but they've already said this is probably the last we'll get in here. Most shipments are going to larger establishments in cities."

Irma sighed. "Well, that's a fine kettle. Come on, Bunny. Let's take a powder." She trounced past the women, still holding their breath, but as she reached the door, she turned back around. "Give my regards to your wife, Mr. Mason." She flipped the fox fur over her shoulder, and out the door she went, Bunny behind her. "Ta-ta." She waved.

A collective sigh went through the store as the women went back to placing their orders or gathered in hushed conversations. Margaret looked toward the vacant door. *Something happened here, and I don't know what it was.*

She gathered up the items for Doc and spent the rest of the day folding bandages and restocking the shelves of Mercurochrome and plasters. Every once in a while, she would adjust the belt on her dress and pull the package of nylons out, still secured between her bra and slip. She longed to touch the fabric, but she knew she needed to be careful with them. She also needed to figure out a place she could stash them. The more she thought about it, the more she was worried they would be discovered by one of her sisters. She couldn't have that.

Doc popped in to say he was leaving, so to lock the door on her way out. As she listened to his footsteps receding, she went over to the sink and washed her hands. While she had always kept her nails short, she rubbed them to make sure that there were no nicks that would catch or snag the hosiery. Finally, she applied a generous dollop of lotion, letting it soak into her hands. When it had dried and she had checked her nails once more, she pulled the nylons from her dress. Gingerly, she opened the package then, with reverence, picked up the stockings. They were cool against her skin and slid across her hands like a butterfly's wings. She held her face to them, wanting to take in an imaginary scent of culture or something she couldn't even name. After allowing herself to caress them and run them over her hands, she carefully laid them back inside the package, deciding that she would try them on later.

She couldn't let them be discovered at home. One of her little sisters might ruin them by poking around inside with their grubby little hands. No, she needed to protect them until the dance. She rolled back on the stool and glanced around the room, her eyes fixing on a sturdy chest of drawers used for linens. She wiped her hands on her dress, tore off a piece of butcher paper, then wrapped the package of nylons. Then she went over to the cabinet and slipped the package behind it. It would be easy enough to retrieve before the dance.

Walking home later that day, she hummed to herself. The next time that Eugene saw her, she wouldn't look like a kid. She would show him.

CHAPTER ELEVEN

The air was fragrant with the smell of orange blossoms as spring took hold. The dogwood trees blossomed, covered with white flowers. But as much as the natural beauty surrounded the inhabitants of the small town, for Margaret, their showy display held little allure. Her mind was fixed on her upcoming birthday and the dance.

For her seventeenth birthday, Franny would travel with her to Pensacola. Margaret had asked for a store-bought dress, and with Ma insisting that she had money saved for such an extravagance, Pa had finally given his permission. Giddy with excitement, the sisters prepared to take the bus to the city. Each dressed in the best they could manage, fixing frayed hems and polishing their shoes. Franny borrowed Ma's best gloves and hat, while Margaret wore a crocheted pair.

Once they'd exited the bus, the pair entered the large department store. Unlike the smaller stores they normally spent time at, the hustle and bustle inside added to Margaret's thrill.

Passing the cosmetics counter, they made their way to the staircase, which took them up to the second floor. Racks of clothing unlike anything she'd seen before dotted the space.

A shop lady arrived. "May I help you?"

"I'm looking for a dress for a dance."

"An evening gown?"

Franny cleared her throat. "Something like a nice church dress."

The woman nodded. "I understand perfectly. Follow me." She glided ahead, and Franny shot Margaret one of her mother's looks to behave.

So much for trying on evening gowns.

"Here we are. I think this should suit you." The woman gestured to a rack of dresses. They thanked the woman, who said to call on her if they needed any further help.

Margaret's eyes fell on a rack of long evening dresses along the back wall. She folded her hands in prayer and whispered to her sister, "Please?"

Franny shook her head no, but a large grin crossed her face.

Margaret rushed over and held one up to her body as she looked at herself in the nearby mirror. She set it back and picked up another one. The blue offset her blond hair. "I think I'll try this one on."

"Don't be silly." Franny frowned.

"Franny, don't you ever do anything just for fun?"

"It's wasteful."

"Why do you say that? It's not wasteful trying on beautiful clothing. I'm doing it, and you should do it too. Um… this one." Margaret pulled a winter-white dress with epaulets at the shoulders and a silver waist. "Take it. This would look lovely on you."

Franny shook her head.

"I didn't realize you were scared." Margaret tipped her chin toward her older sister.

"I'm not."

"Then I dare you to try on this dress. Come on."

"Fine." Franny rolled her eyes.

They entered the dressing room to help each other with the zippers. Finally, they stood in front of a three-paneled mirror.

"I'm... I'm beautiful." Tears welled up in her sister's eyes.

"Of course, you are. You look like Ann in *Topper Returns*."

Franny twirled in place. "You really think so?"

Margaret nodded. "I do. I want to have a negligee like Joan Blondell wore. One day, I'm going to wear beautiful clothes like that and have a fancy bedroom."

"Oh, Maggie. You and your daydreams." She turned around and lifted her hair. "Now, let's get to the real reason we're here. Unzip me."

After shucking out of the evening dresses, Franny helped pull dresses for Margaret to try on. As Margaret exited the dressing room, Franny clapped her hands. "That's it. That's the one. Too bad it's red."

"What's wrong with red? I'm sick and tired of all the navy and black clothing. I want something with color."

"But Maggie, we need to consider the war—"

"Why does the war mean we have to go around in funeral colors? If anything, we need to wear brighter colors to keep our spirits up."

"I don't know. But it does look very nice on you."

"I love it, but look at this." Margaret showed her a small rip at the waist. "I think I could fix it, but it would be better with a pretty belt just to be safe."

Margaret twisted her lips, deep in thought. She didn't have the money for both. She glanced down at the price tag and quickly calculated how much she would need the dress discounted in order to purchase a belt. As she put her own outfit back on, she got an idea.

Bypassing Franny, Margaret walked out from the dressing room to one of the approaching shop ladies. "I saw you in that dress. It's perfect for your coloring and figure."

Margaret sighed. "Sadly, it has a rip. See here? It would cost money to have it repaired and would probably still need a belt to cover the flaw. Oh, well." She handed the dress to the woman. "Come on, Franny. Maybe we can find something at our next stop."

Franny rose from the chair where she'd sat waiting on Margaret, and they linked arms. But Margaret made no real move to leave, wondering if her ploy would work.

"Um, miss? Maybe I could talk to the manager about a discount."

Margaret tapped her chin, pretending to think. "I don't know. I'd still need the belt."

"Why don't you both have a seat, and I can speak to the manager? What belt were you thinking?"

Margaret walked over to a rack of belts. Even though she quickly spotted the best one for the outfit, she surveyed the group before landing on her first choice. The belt was a white woven number, which would emphasize her waist nicely. She stole a glance at the price tag.

They would have to discount the dress at least a few dollars for her to afford both. She went back over and sat down next to Franny, who'd remained quiet the entire time.

In a few minutes, the woman returned, a smile on her face. "I've got good news for you. Mr. Andrews says that we can discount the dress and belt to twelve dollars."

Margaret couldn't believe that she'd actually been able to get a discount. While it came in under her budget, she wanted to test how far she could take it.

She sighed deeply and looked over the dress and the belt. "Well, hm. I'm not sure." She scrutinized the dress. If she changed out the plain buttons for pearls, it would make the dress look much better. "Is that the best you can do? I'm not sure."

The woman gawked. For a moment, she almost regretted her question and wondered if she'd taken it too far. Then the store lady collected herself and replied, "What were you thinking?"

Margaret calculated the price of the buttons in her head. "One dollar?"

"I'll go ask, but I don't think we can discount that much." The woman swept from the changing room, and Margaret paced the floor.

In what seemed like a long time, the woman returned. "Seventy-five cents off in addition. That's as far as we can go."

"Yes. I'll take it." Margaret bit the inside of her cheek to stop herself from jumping for joy. With her new pretty dress and stockings, no one would dare call her a kid.

Franny rose from her place and squeezed Margaret's hand. She bent next to her ear and whispered, "I need to take lessons from you on dickering over prices."

Margaret grinned at her older sister's praise. She met the attendant, who was wrapping up the dress in tissue paper while Franny paid the salesclerk with the money Pa had given them.

Leaving the store, Franny turned to Margaret. "Okay, where next? I know you must have plans for the money you saved."

"You're right. I'm going to change out these buttons, so let's head to the notions store."

At the next store, Margaret marveled at all the colors and styles of buttons. Finally, she selected a discounted package that had one button missing. They spent more time in the five-and-dime section, looking at the various items in slotted areas on the counters or hanging on racks. Unlike the shops in Milton, they could admire the things for sale and even pick them up for closer inspection.

Franny moved over to the ribbon rack. "Look at this color grosgrain ribbon. This would look so pretty in your hair, and it pulls some of the color out of the dress."

Margaret did quick math. "I don't have enough after I get these buttons."

Franny reached over, pulled the ribbon from the rack, then handed it to the woman behind the counter. "We'll take a yard, please."

"But—"

Franny raised her hand. "I want to get this for you. I'm getting extra because I bet you can do something with it. If not, I'll save it for

Nellie's birthday."

Margaret gathered her sister up in a hug. "Thank you."

The woman handed over the ribbon, which was held together with a folded piece of paper and a staple. Franny thanked her then said, "Now, let's go to Woolworth's and grab some lunch. I'm starved."

"I couldn't. It's so expensive."

"I've been saving up my money from piano lessons. If I can't spend some of it on the day my sister gets her first dress to go to her first dance, then I don't know a better time." She smiled.

"Okay, but let's share something."

"Sounds good. That will leave us some room for ice cream."

The two made their way to the counter, where they ordered Hires Root Beer and shared a tuna sandwich and chips. For dessert, they each picked a scoop of ice cream, with Franny settling on orange sorbet and Margaret choosing chocolate.

Gathering their packages, they stood in the shade of an oak, waiting for the next bus. The air was hot and thick with moisture, signaling the daily rain shower was imminent, but Margaret was cheerful. When the bus finally pulled up, she was glad for the bit of breeze through the open windows as they traveled.

She smiled as she hugged her packages. She looked over to Franny, who had closed her eyes once they'd settled in their seats. A lump formed in Margaret's throat, and tears gathered as the love for her sister overwhelmed her. Even if they didn't agree on everything, Franny always had her back and wanted the very best for her. Margaret leaned her head on her sister's shoulder. It was enough to wake the dozing Franny, who clasped Margaret's hand in her own. As she stared at their hands, Margaret felt the bond between them. She prayed it would never be broken.

CHAPTER TWELVE

They arrived home to find the house busy with activity for supper. Nellie sat plucking a chicken with more hindrance than help from the younger two girls, Patsy and Norma, who picked at another one. James limped in from the back door, waving his hand, which had healed nicely. He made his way to the long bench seat next to the table then pulled an ear of corn from a wooden bucket. As James and Bobby shucked the leaves, Ma gathered the corn silk into a bowl for medicinal teas. On the stove, a pot of water boiled for scalding the chickens before plucking them.

Nellie jumped up at their arrival, the half-plucked chicken swinging from her hand. "How was your trip? What did you see?"

Franny laughed. "Let us get changed, and we'll tell you all about it."

Margaret wanted to get to work on the dress right away, but she changed out of her town clothes and put on a simple shift to help with preparing the food. She wished Pa would let them wear overalls, but he wouldn't abide a woman wearing pants in his house.

A few hours later, the family gathered around the table while Pa said grace before they dug into the meal. Along with the corn and roasted chicken, the evening's meal comprised black-eyed peas, collard greens, and cornbread.

Margaret had been told to divvy up the buttermilk, with the youngest getting a quarter cup, the middles a half cup, and the eldest three-quarters of a cup. She finished with pouring a full cup for her father and a half cup for her mother. The jug contained just enough for everyone.

As she looked at them, she saw Franny take her cup and add some of her milk to her mother's cup. Shame washed over Margaret. Franny was always so conscientious of others. Even today with the ribbon for Margaret's hair and treating her at the lunch counter.

Today, she'd had more food than she'd had in quite a while, and on the bus ride home, her full stomach and the motion of the bus's wheels had lulled her to sleep. With Edsol gone, that left more chicken, and it was easier to divide up the plates with a combination of white and dark meat. She set a chicken breast and thigh on her father's plate and the same on her mother's plate. Most likely, her mother would end up giving much of it to the younger boys or saving it to make a casserole, but she put the full pieces on her plate anyway.

The younger kids were all ears as they listened to Margaret and Franny share about their adventure to the city. Most were excited about them eating out at the lunch counter and the idea of root beer. Ma was concerned about its name and questioned if it was sinful.

After washing up after dinner, they settled in to listen to a radio program. Pa dialed into *The World News Report* while the younger kids went off to play. Margaret hoped he would leave for the lodge soon so they could be thrilled by the stories of *Nick Carter: Master Detective*. Sometimes, Ma preferred listening to *The Judy Canova Show*. They would all laugh or sing in unison during those. Nellie, especially, would act out the singing to the delight of the younger kids while Mama smiled as she watched from her rocker, darning someone's socks from a basket that never seemed to empty of its load.

That evening, Pa stayed home. Once his droning news program was over, the youngest went off to bed, and Pa went outside. Ma continued rocking, her gaze intent on her darning.

Franny pulled Margaret over and whispered, "Show Ma your dress, belt, and ribbon, along with the buttons."

"Why?"

"Sometimes I wonder about you, Maggie. Because mothers want to take part in their children's lives. Soon, you'll be off and married. Let her enjoy this day with you."

"If you think so."

"I know so." She motioned toward their mother.

"Ma, would you like to see the dress I bought today?"

Ma's face lit up. "Yes. Don't mind if I do." She set down the pair of pants she'd been mending and, using the arms of the rocker, rose from her seat. The three of them headed into the girls' bedroom.

Margaret grabbed a match and lit the kerosene lamp. She stooped over and pulled the box holding the dress, belt, and buttons from underneath the bed. Her mother sat on the edge of the bed, the springs creaking under her weight as Margaret withdrew the dress and held it up in front of her.

Her mother clapped her hands. "Oh, my. That is smart. I think that's the prettiest thing I've seen in a while."

Franny had told her to ask her mother's opinion, so she replied, "Ma, I got these buttons. I think they'll look better on the dress. Um, what do you think?"

Her mother stood from the bed and held the buttons next to the dress. "Yes, sure as spots on a baby deer." She glanced down at the box with the red ribbon.

"Oh, Franny got that for me to wear in my hair."

"What are you planning to do with the other?"

Margaret shrugged. "I don't know."

"You know, if you made a bow, you could attach it right here on the collar." She motioned for Margaret to lay the dress on the bed. "See here?" She made a small bow and placed it on the dress.

Margaret leaned forward, her head nodding slightly as a huge smile played on her lips. "Ma, that makes the dress. I love that. Can you show me how to make one?"

"I can, but how's about you let me fix the dress for you? You have chores and your work. I can easily change out the buttons, fix the rip, and add the bow."

"Oh, Ma. Thank you!" She grabbed her mother up in a tight embrace.

Her mother laughed. "It pleases me to take part in your first dance." She gathered up the dress then folded it back into the box with the ribbon and buttons. She patted Margaret on the arm. "Leave it to me."

Margaret watched her mother's back, realizing with a sinking heart that she'd been praised for doing something she'd only done because Franny had told her to do it. She fought the urge to rush after her mother and tell her she would try harder, do better, but she simply stared at the empty doorway.

The days seemed to drag, and Margaret could barely contain her excitement about going to the dance. She would often hum as she worked at Doc Albert's, but try as she might, she never saw Eugene again. Perhaps he'd already shipped out. She fought back her worry but couldn't help but wonder if he was still around. If he was, she hoped she would see him at the dance. If he asked her to dance, she would act like she didn't know him. But as a flutter filled her chest at the thought of him, she knew she was only kidding herself. He was so worldly and handsome. She would be a fool not to dance with him. Plus, since the last time they'd met, she'd changed. She had her monthlies then, which she'd hated at first, with the belt and all the washing involved, but she soon realized it sometimes kept her out of doing the hard chores. But only when Pa was around. Ma would simply laugh at her carrying-on and tell her to get to work.

But it was the day her friend, Alice, came into the clinic that Margaret forgot everything that had been on her mind. Because everything had changed.

CHAPTER THIRTEEN

The door to Doc's house flew open and Alice ran in, her eyes wild, searching. Alice doubled over, her voice loud with weeping. "Maggie!"

"Alice, are you hurt? What's happened?" Margaret rushed to her friend.

Doc Albert charged in from the back of the house, where he'd been taking lunch. "What is it? Are you hurt?"

The girl shook her head, the sobs causing her to lose her breath. "It's Pa. They brought the telegram. My ma—I never seen her like that. She was in such a state. I-I couldn't stay there no more."

Margaret gathered her up in an embrace, smoothing down Alice's hair and cooing as she did with her younger brothers and sisters when they were afraid. "It's okay. Everything will be okay."

Alice moaned. "No, no, it won't. She's talking about sending us to live with an aunt. I don't want to go away. If she makes us go, then I want to live with my sister."

The old man pushed his glasses up on his head. "Young lady, I'm sorry about your father."

She'd heard those words or similar ones countless times. Every day brought more news of death or missing brothers, husbands, or fathers. Others came home, shells of the men they used to be.

"Margaret, why don't you go on and take her home?" Doc offered.

Margaret gathered up her things, and the pair walked in silence for a while. Finally, Alice spoke. "I wish I were like you, Maggie. You have a job, your own money. You can do what you want. I can't do anything on my own. I can't even get the money to go to my sister's."

She hadn't let Alice know that she had been paying off a family debt when she'd first started, and the money she received from the doctor wasn't much. But it felt good to earn her own money. She fought back against her wish for her friend to stay. She had to think about Alice's future, not what she wanted. If only she hadn't spent the last of her money on the nylons, she could've helped Alice out.

"I'm sure your ma's just talking crazy right now. You know how adults are. They're always carrying on about something or 'nuther."

Alice stole a glance at Margaret Rose. "I-I never told you, but she's not my real ma. My real ma died when I was young. We were already struggling with Pa gone.

"Alice, why didn't you say something? I could have helped you."

Alice shook her head. "I was too proud. I didn't want anyone— least of all you, Maggie—knowing how hard it was."

"That's what friends are for. You should have said something."

"It doesn't matter now. I'd heard her on the phone before saying that if she could get rid of me, it would give her more money." She wiped her nose. "I only have my sister now."

"Oh." Margaret was shocked Alice had kept such a huge secret from her. "How do you know your sister will let you stay there?"

Alice sniffled. "I called her. She said there's more than enough room, and it would work out well for her, too, as she helps her husband at the store. But she can't come get me right now, and Ma's determined to send me to her aunt in Mobile. I don't want to leave. My sister said she could send me the money for bus fare, but not for another few weeks. But Ma is already clearing out of the house we're staying in now. With me gone, she figures she can take care of my younger brothers. What am I going to do, Maggie?"

"Leave it to me. I have an idea where I can get some money."

~

After bidding goodbye to Alice, she hugged her friend and assured her that all would be well. Margaret rushed back to the doctor's house and crept in through the dark front hallway lined with heavy wooden chairs for waiting patients. She stole a glance into what had once been the parlor and was now Doc Albert's office. Thankfully, he wasn't inside. She released her breath. She would hate to lie to him on why she had returned. She needed to make it into the surgery room and out without him finding her. When she found that room empty, too, she rushed over to check behind the cabinet.

For a moment, her fingers hit dead air, and a tightness formed in her throat. Tears pricked at her eyes as she leaned closer to the wall. She stretched her arm toward the back and finally brushed the package. But try as she might, she still couldn't grab it.

"Whatcha doing?" a child's voice asked.

Margaret swiveled to see Ceril's daughter, Cassia, her head cocked to the side in curiosity.

"I—a package I need dropped behind this bureau. I can't get it. Do you think you can reach it for me?"

The young girl knelt down next to Margaret and stuck her thin, brown arm behind the cabinet, easily latching onto the hosiery package. She pulled it out then held it up to Margaret, a big gap-toothed grin on her face. "I did it!"

"So you did. Now listen up, this is a present. It's a surprise, so no telling, okay?"

The girl nodded and twisted a pretend key with her fingers in front of her lips.

Margaret rose, and as she did, she remembered she still had a stick of gum in her pocket she'd been saving for a while. She bent down and ran her hand along the child's cheek, resting on her chin. "You know what? I never could have done this without you." She reached into her pocket. "Here, this is for you. Don't swallow it, now. You have to spit it out. Okay?"

Cassia nodded, her gaze fixed squarely on the sugary treat.

Margaret tore the piece in half and then again. "Here's what you do. You eat this piece here now, and that gives you enough for three more days."

The little girl reached out her hand, but Margaret closed her hand over the treat. "Remember, this is our secret. I don't want to spoil the surprise by someone finding out."

"Yes, ma'am. I won't tell nobody. Cross my heart and hope to die, stick a needle in my eye."

"Fine, then." Margaret handed over the gum, then Cassia scampered out of the room. "Don't swallow it!"

Margaret pushed the hosiery between her bra and slip then adjusted her belt on her dress to hold it in place while she walked. A knot formed in her stomach, but she pushed back her apprehension and made her way outside. Avoiding everyone's eyes as if they knew her plan, she walked to the end of the boardwalk then crossed the street. There it stood. The house of ill repute. Right there, in front of God and everybody. Margaret bowed her head and said a prayer for protection for whatever evil awaited her inside. She took a big breath in and walked up to the large stained-glass front door.

She knocked.

No one answered.

She knocked harder.

A young girl answered the door, her dark hair tied up in a handkerchief. She looked surprised to find Margaret standing there.

"Is Miz Horace—"

"Who is it, Dot?" a voice called from somewhere inside. "Tell them we're not open yet. We've barely had our coffee." It was Irma's voice.

"No ma'am. It's a—"

"It's me, Miz Horace. I'm Margaret Rose Locke." She tried to steady the trembling in her voice.

The woman swept toward her, a silk robe flowing around her. Her hair was wrapped in a turban, and Margaret could see a few pin curls at the front. "Child, what are you doing here?" She looked to see if anyone was watching before pulling Margaret inside. "You foolish girl. Did anyone see you come here?"

Irma crossed her arms, waiting for Margaret to speak. But Margaret's gaze was transfixed by the interior. It looked like many other large homes she'd visited with Doc Albert when he'd gone on house calls. The parlor had a big piano beside the front bay window, and horsehair sofas and chairs dotted the room. A rug had been rolled up, most likely for dancing, and set to the side.

"Well?"

Irma's words brought her back to the moment. Margaret cleared her throat. "I have an offer for you."

"You do, do you?" She glanced at Margaret. "Come on. My coffee's getting cold. Dot, go get Miss Locke a cup of coffee and bring it into the dining room."

The girl nodded and fled through the back hall, which must have led to the kitchen. Irma pulled open the wooden doors, and the interior revealed a long mahogany dining table with fourteen chairs. On the windows, heavy velour draperies were tied back with golden tassels, and over the fireplace, a large, gilded mirror held center stage. But it was the oil portrait of Irma in a red velvet dress with a low-cut bodice that captured Margaret's gaze.

"It's beautiful. I mean, you're beautiful."

Irma had joined her in pondering the painting. She took a pull of a sweet-smelling cigarette in an ebony holder. "In my prime then." She swiveled and took Margaret in with her eyes, telling her to twirl around in front of her. Margaret obeyed.

"I don't normally take in local girls—"

"Oh, no!" Margaret yelled, shocked at such a thought.

Irma threw back her head and laughed. "Honey, I was teasing you. Though you have a decent figure under that sack of an outfit you're wearing."

Dot came into the room from a side door, pushing a cart. Irma motioned to a chair as she took the high-backed gold one at the head of the table.

As Dot approached the table, Margaret started, "So, I—"

Irma held up her hand. "First rule. You never discuss business until after the staff leaves and you've had your first drink."

"Oh, sorry." Margaret folded her hands in her lap and waited until Dot set a cup of coffee in front of her, along with a side of toast cut into strips. She finished by placing a curious thing in front of her—an egg sitting in a porcelain cup with roses decorating the sides. Margaret had never seen such a thing. *Why put a boiled egg in a stand?* Not that it mattered. They normally ate eggs scrambled with additional milk powder and water to stretch them. An entire boiled egg would be a treat.

Dot poured coffee and set a small bottle of a brown liquor and a pitcher of cream next to Irma. Last, she added a plate of oranges, cheeses, and grapes to the table. "Will that be all, ma'am?"

"Yes, thank you, Dot."

Margaret watched as the servant went through the door, closing it quietly behind her. She turned back to face Irma, who was scrutinizing her. Irma poured cream into her coffee then handed the pitcher to Margaret, who followed suit.

Real cream! It had been so long since she'd had some. She resisted licking the spoon thick with it.

While Margaret fixed her coffee, Irma used a smaller spoon and cracked the top of her egg, exposing the yellow inside. She dipped a toast strip into the gooey mixture then stuck it in her mouth. "Ever had a soft-boiled egg before? I had a... friend who was from England, and he showed me this method of doing eggs. I love them this way." She picked up another strip of toast and waved it at Margaret. "Try it."

Margaret picked up the tiny spoon and tapped lightly against the eggshell. Inside, the egg was golden yellow liquid. Her stomach rumbled. The first taste was pure bliss. The gooey delight was certainly better than the cold potato she'd eaten earlier in the day. She forgot where she was and licked the crumbs off her fingers.

Irma held up the plate of fruit and cheeses to Margaret. As she reached to take an orange, Irma shook her head. "No, you take the platter, and then use that small fork to put items you desire onto your plate."

"Sorry." Margaret took the extended plate and placed a few items on her own plate before setting it on the table.

Irma rang a small brass bell, and Dot popped back through the door. "Dot, bring Miss Locke another egg and some more toast, please. Also, more coffee."

"Oh, I couldn't. This is already—"

Irma waved her protests away. "Honey, I thought you were making love to that food, the way you were moaning."

Margaret's face turned beet red. She wiped her mouth with the linen napkin, more to hide her embarrassment than to get rid of any food on her lips.

Irma laughed. "Child, there's nothing wrong with enjoying the flesh. At some point, you'll discover that."

Dot returned with the coffee, but that time, Irma picked up the small brown bottle and tipped a bit into Margaret's coffee as well. "For Dutch courage. It's brandy. Think of it like the Victorians used it, as medicinal." She winked. "Now, you've made me curious as to your offer. What could you possibly offer me?"

"Well—"

"Wait."

Dot had reappeared. She removed the old egg stand before replacing it with a new one and a new set of what Irma called toast fingers.

Irma nodded to the delicacy. "You eat that first while it's still warm."

Margaret didn't need more coaxing. She dug into the egg and toast while Irma smoked, appraising her like a cat might study a mouse intent on a piece of cheese.

Finally satiated, Margaret took a sip of the coffee, forgetting the brandy. She coughed into her napkin as Irma stubbed out her cigarette in a crystal ashtray.

"Okay. Now down to business. What's your offer, Miss Margaret Rose Locke?"

Margaret took another sip of the coffee, that time allowing the warmth to coat her throat. "I have some nylons for sale." She rushed on. "I saw you in the store the other day, and there's no telling when they'll get any more. Maybe never. You pay me a dollar and fifteen cents, and you can have them."

Irma squinted her eyes at her. "How do I know you even have the stockings?"

Margaret pulled them out from her dress. "I've never worn them. I was going to wear them to the dance in a few weeks, but I have a friend... um, never mind."

"So, you're selling these to give the money to a friend?"

Margaret nodded, her words spilling forth in a rush. "Her pa died in the war, and her ma—well, she's really not her ma—is sending her to live with an aunt. It's another state away, and she hates, I mean, she doesn't want to go with the aunt. She'd only be a housekeeper to the old lady. She wants to go to her sister's, but she needs money for bus fare."

"What's her name?" Irma took a sip of coffee.

"Alice."

"Well, I'm glad to hear you want to help your friend. But I can get those nylons elsewhere for less."

Margaret's chin dropped. She hadn't thought of that. She blurted out. "How?"

"I have my ways. I'd need to feel I'm getting a good deal."

Margaret hesitated. She needed to help Alice. "I'll let you have them for one dollar, ten cents. These are brand new too. Never been worn. You may get some elsewhere, but that's a steal." She pointed at the hosiery.

Irma sat back in the chair. "One dollar, five cents. That's my last offer. What do you say?"

Margaret's mind raced. She hated losing the money she'd spent, but she could help Alice. "Fine. But you have to fix my hair for an upcoming dance." She crossed her arms, but her legs were shaking.

Irma grinned. "Okay. We have a deal." She rang the bell, and Dot came back into the dining room. "Fetch me my purse and also a roll of gauze."

When Dot returned, Irma counted out four quarters and a nickel. She laid them on the table in front of Margaret before holding out her hand for the nylons. Margaret sighed as she passed the nylons over to Irma, who set them down on the table's edge.

"You're a good friend, Miss Margaret Rose. Alice is lucky to have you." She rose from the table.

"Dot, Miss Locke is going to bandage your left hand. You're right-handed, correct?"

She nodded. "Yes, ma'am."

"Okay, good. She's going to bandage your hand. Oh, best to get some lard and add that on first and then the gauze. Wait!" She rushed from the room and returned with lipstick. Using it, she made a red streak down the center of Dot's hand. "Now, go get the lard and bring it back in here."

The woman disappeared as Margaret sat in confused silence. Dot hadn't looked injured. The servant returned, her hand glistening with a reddish hue. Margaret glanced over to where Irma was smiling.

"Perfect. Now Margaret, you bandage her hand, but make sure some of that red shows through it. Dot, as soon as she's done, you'll gather up a basket, and I'll make you a list of shops to stop at. You'll tell them you burned your hand, and I sent for Miss Locke to come have a look-see."

She put out her hand to Margaret. "Nice doing business with you, Miss Locke. Now, bandage Dot's hand, but never darken our front door again. When you come to get your hair done, you come to the back door through the alley, and Dot will let you in that way. Wear your uniform, and bring your dress here. Then you can claim your work clothes the next day. I'll have Bunny put all your things in a case by the back shed." She strode over to the door and took hold of the brass inserts in the door.

"Just so you know, I would have paid you the dollar and twenty-five cents *and* done your hair. Let this be a lesson to you. Always stand your ground on what you deserve, Margaret." She smiled and pulled the heavy wooden doors together to shut them.

When Margaret had finished wrapping Dot's hand, she was escorted out to the front door. There, Dot made a spectacle of the entire proceedings, pretending her hand was hurt and thanking Margaret for helping her. Though Margaret saw no one, she knew that just the sight of her close to Irma's house could set tongues to wagging. Even coming close to such a place, it would quickly find

Pa's ears, and a licking would be waiting for her. She would need to retell Irma's excuse to Ma straight away when she got home. But first, she needed to see Alice.

She felt the coins in her pocket. She might have let Irma beat her at bargaining, but she had enough to help Alice. She hated that her friend would be leaving, but she wanted her to be happy. That was more important than any nylons or any money. She relived the time spent inside Irma's house, committing everything to memory as she walked to Alice's. She couldn't wait to tell her the good news and to help her make plans to join her sister.

CHAPTER FOURTEEN

"So I bandaged her hand and left." How she longed to tell the whole story, but she kept to the premise of her helping Dot.

Ma wrung a towel in her hands. "Oh, my stars. I can't believe you even stepped foot on that porch, much less darkened their doors. What will the neighbors think?"

Margaret wanted to say that it didn't matter what the neighbors or townsfolk thought, but she knew in her heart it wasn't true. Later that night as they lay in bed, Franny and Nellie begged Margaret for details on what the inside of the house was like. They were disappointed to hear it was like any big home owned by the finest families in the area but continued to ask her to repeat the meal she'd had while there. Nellie especially would groan and moan about her desire for toast fingers dipped in thick egg yolk.

The next morning, Nellie couldn't contain herself. "Ma, please. Can we have soft eggs with toast?"

"Don't be silly, child. Be content with what the good Lord gave us."

Nellie frowned, crossing her arms over her chest. "One day, I'm getting me some of those eggs."

"Well, today, you can go get some eggs from the coop for making some tater salad. Now get." Ma popped her dishtowel toward Nellie, who yelped then scrambled off to gather eggs.

Once she and Franny were alone, her sister looked at her. "You're holding something back. I can feel it."

"Best you don't know. You'll just have to trust me that I didn't get into trouble. In fact, I was doing something good for someone."

"I don't know. These things can come back—"

"Not this." She hugged Franny. "I love you."

"Love you too. But please be careful."

"I will."

A few days later, Margaret and Alice cried and hugged each other with a fierceness before Alice boarded the local bus. Margaret waved at her friend until the bus was out of sight, wishing she was on a bus to somewhere too. She turned away as she caught two women staring at her. *The town's grapevine must already be at work.*

Over the next week, people might drop their voices or stare at Margaret curiously, but her reputation remained unsullied. Dot had done her part in spreading the story invented by Irma about the burn.

Finally, after what seemed like forever, the day of the dance arrived.

After finishing her work with Doc Albert, Margaret gathered up her dress and shoes. She took her time walking down the alley toward Irma's house. She envisioned how the evening would go, knowing that her mother had tailored the dress so that it fit Margaret perfectly.

In addition, Ma had affixed the bow to the collar, piped the sleeves with the extra ribbon, and made her a handkerchief for her purse. Margaret would wear her polished Oxfords and Franny's best socks. She just hoped that the dress wouldn't be too wrinkled.

Arriving at the back of Irma's, she looked up and down the alley but could see no one. She raced to the shed in the back.

Bunny was waiting for her. "Wait until I make sure the coast is clear before you go up to the door."

Soon, Margaret was hustled into the back screened porch. Bunny took her through the kitchen to a small room off the back. There, a vanity with a large mirror sat against one wall, and a smattering of older sofas and chairs dotted the rest of the room. A table and chairs sat in the corner. *This must be where the other women were the other day when I visited.*

"Okay." Irma sat her in front of the vanity. "Bunny is the queen with hair. What did you have in mind?"

Margaret dug in her purse and pulled out a magazine. She pointed to a picture of Betty Grable.

"Oh, no, honey. That's not right for you." Bunny tsk-tsked, and Irma pinched her lips and shook her head.

Irma, dressed in a shirtdress, walked over to a magazine lying on the table. She flipped through it. "Yes, this one." She came over and showed the photo to Margaret. It was Rita Hayworth, her locks pulled back from her face and soft curls cascading down past her shoulders.

Margaret nodded.

The women got to work prepping Margaret's hair, and she

enjoyed the pampering and listening to their laughing and joking with one another. Finally, they told her to get dressed and pointed to a screen in the corner.

"Just for you." Irma winked.

Margaret pulled her dress down from the hook, and the women asked, "Where are your shoes?"

Margaret pointed at the flats she wore.

"No. That will never do. Dot!" Irma yelled.

Dot appeared, and Irma turned to Margaret. "Give me your shoe." She handed the shoe over, and Irma spoke to Dot, who nodded and disappeared. Bunny worked on Margaret's hair in the meantime.

"Now, here's something from the girls here for your first dance." Irma held out a package. Inside were garters.

"I don't know what to say."

"Well, we don't have new ones, but we got these mended, and since you don't have to worry about them being seen—"

Bunny giggled, and Irma shot her a look, so she stifled her mouth with her fist.

Inside the paper was a pair of nylon hose. The upper thigh portion had been mended and one part had been patched, but the lower legs were still in good shape.

Irma looked at Margaret. "Do you even know how to put on hosiery?"

Margaret shook her lowered head.

"Okay, watch and learn." Irma instructed Margaret to lotion up her legs first, starting at the toe and working her way up. Last, she would add the garter to hold them in place. After a few false starts, Margaret was able to get the nylons on and the dress on. Bunny draped her in an old sheet then continued on her hair, pulling the curlers they had put in earlier.

"These curls won't stay as well as if you had them in for a while, but they should work for a few hours. What do you think?"

Margaret stood up and faced the mirror. In place of the girl who had entered the room stood a poised, beautiful young woman. Tears sprang to her eyes. "I-I don't know what to say. Thank you." She rushed to Bunny, who tsk-tsked but wiped her own eyes.

"I can't thank you enough. Truly," Margaret said to Irma.

"Ah, it's nothing. Though I couldn't be prouder if you were my own daughter. Now, don't forget to bring Lucy's shoes back, or she'll be coming after you. Now, get so you have time to arrive."

Margaret hugged Irma before Bunny hustled her into the Cadillac. They'd decided it would be the easiest way for her to make it on time and join the group riding on the bus back into town. Margaret ducked in the back seat until Bunny found a safe spot to let her out where she wouldn't be seen. Bunny waved goodbye, and Margaret ducked behind a tree just in case. It wouldn't be too long before the bus arrived that would take her to the hall where the dance was being held.

After a few more minutes passed, the bus pulled up. Margaret handed over her fare and spied Franny waving at her from the back. She held her head high as she walked down the narrow row between the vinyl seats.

"Wow, you look—" But Margaret barely heard Franny's words. She was more enamored by the reaction from the Simpson boys. She didn't know whether to tell them to stop gawking or to enjoy the admiration.

When they arrived at the hall, the music was already spilling out into the night air. She stood for a moment outside, telling the others she would catch up in a minute. She wanted to make sure that she could remember every minute of that night.

Lost in her thoughts, she almost missed the deep whisper that tickled her ear.

"Hello again."

CHAPTER FIFTEEN

Margaret swiveled to see Eugene. He cut a fine figure in his short-sleeved khaki shirt and pants, with black shoes polished to a high shine. On his head, he wore a garrison cap, but Margaret's eyes were drawn to the gold eagle on his chest and bars of various colors, along with what appeared to be gold leaf insignias on his lapels. Even though he wasn't in full dress, his casual military attire still proved to be impressive.

However, she had to stay focused and stick to her goal to appear above noticing how handsome he looked. She thrust her chin high in the air and moved her shoulders back. "I'm sorry, do I know you?"

His laughter boomed. "Oh, so that's the way we're going to play this."

"I don't know what you mean."

"Oh, yes, you do." His eyes crinkled as he gave her a leisurely smile.

Flustered, Margaret flounced inside, where the band was playing and couples were joining the dance floor. Eugene followed and shook his finger at her as he passed by. Margaret could smell the alcohol on his breath as he leaned in closer.

Is he going to ask me to dance?

But in the next moment, he spun around and grabbed another girl's hand. He swung her onto the dance floor with the Lindy Hop, leaving Margaret flushed and flustered at his easy dismissal.

Margaret's eyebrow twitched. This was not at all how she'd imagined this night. In her mind, he would have been conciliatory, and she would deem him worthy of forgiveness. Instead, there he was, dancing with that horrible Martha from school. Margaret fumed.

Deciding to simply ignore him, she joined her friends and the Simpsons, laughing loudly and expressing herself with huge gestures. She leaned closer to Bud Simpson, hoping Eugene caught her actions.

She whispered in Bud's ear, "It's so hot in here. I wonder if a drink would help." She touched his arm, giving him a coquettish smile.

The boy, delighted to have been chosen from the others nearby, scampered off to fetch her a drink.

Margaret glanced over to see that Eugene had spotted the event. But her smug smile faded when he caught her looking and his face broke into a huge grin.

Oh, that man. He's so frustrating.

Margaret turned from the dance floor after Eugene winked at her. No matter what she did, it wasn't working. Some girls could wrap men around their little fingers just like that. She'd seen guys falling all over themselves to do things for particular girls at school. She must have missed the lesson on seduction but needed to figure it out and soon.

Margaret laughed gaily. The boys stole glances with one another, wondering what was so funny. Finally giving up the charade, she waited until Bud arrived with a glass cup of cherry punch. She sipped at it politely, wondering how she could turn back toward the dance floor without being obvious. She looked down, and her cup was almost empty just as another song began.

Oh, no. Bud Simpson was going to ask her to dance, and it was a slow song. The thought of his arms around her sent a shiver down her spine.

Bud twisted his hands. "Um, Margaret Rose, um, I, would you like—"

"Sorry, pal," a deep voice boomed. "This here young lady already promised me this dance. Hadn't you, Miss Locke?"

It was the moment of truth. She would take her defeat gracefully. "Yes, I had. Sorry, Bud. Next time."

Eugene glided her onto the dance floor, and when his hands when around her waist, it felt like she had always belonged there. They moved in sync, neither speaking until they had made it to the far side of the dance floor.

"Okay, I give. At least tell me why you're mad at me."

She lowered her head, not daring to look up at him. "You called me a kid."

He chuckled. "Is that all?"

He must have felt her stiffen, as he removed his hand and lifted her chin to look at him. "I know you're no kid."

She felt the blush from her toes all the way to the top of her head.

Her body radiated heat as a tingling sensation she'd never experienced before coursed through it. While they were in the middle of a crowd, her senses had narrowed to the man in front of her—the starch in his shirt, the feel of the muscle beneath it, the smell of his aftershave, and the pressure of his hand against her back. All her life, she had been asleep and had finally awakened. Their eyes met, and as she gazed into them, she felt her breathing increase. Gone was the playful smile from his face. In its place, his eyes were firmly fixed on her face as if to memorize it. His lips parted with an unasked question.

The dam broke. As much as Margaret had wanted to remain coy and have him pursue her, she had fallen hard for Eugene. She broke eye contact if only to regain some composure, but as their eyes met again, she longed for him to kiss her. As they moved with the music, it felt like they were the only two people in the world. Ignoring decorum, she rested her head on his chest, listening to his heartbeat. She never wanted the song to end.

As the music slowed, they stopped for a short moment, their eyes only on each other. They stared, neither willing to break the spell.

As couples moved from the dance floor, Margaret finally said, "Well, um, thank you for the dance."

He reached for her hand, warmth radiating up her arm. "You don't want any of those boys. You want a man. Don't go."

"Okay."

The music started up with a fast number, and she laughed as he spun her around the dance floor. As she was being twirled, Margaret caught a few envious looks from her schoolmates. Other males tried to cut in for a dance with her but were quickly informed that she was off-limits.

As they danced, the hall grew hot with sweat and cigarette smoke, choking the room's edges. She wiped her forehead. "I'm exhausted. I need to take a break."

"Let's go outside." Eugene captured her hand in his large one and led the way. Outside, the cool night air felt nice against her skin. He left her for a moment, returning with punch they gulped down.

"Short walk?" He offered his arm.

The music followed them as they strolled down a side street dotted with houses lined with picket fences. Normally, Margaret would have been preoccupied with one day living in a house like the ones they were passing. In that moment, her mind only had room for Eugene.

Neither spoke, but she accepted it when he took her hand in his strong, masculine one.

She sighed. *Is this the way love feels?* Because she felt absolutely giddy.

"Margaret Rose." His voice was quiet on the air. "No, that's not right." He shook his head.

She stopped and gazed up at him, admiring his strong jawline and dimple.

"I mean, you're not a rose. No, you're not like that at all." He glanced around, and his eyes settled on a gardenia bush on a lawn of the house they'd passed. "Wait here."

He sprinted over and, with a snap of the branch, released one flower from the rest. "Here."

"I can't believe you did that. What if they saw you?"

"What if they did? I'd just plead guilty to falling in love."

Falling in love? He'd just said it. It wasn't just her feeling that way.

She smelled the fragrance, and her arms tingled as he brushed against her to place the flower in her hair.

"There. Every time I think of you, I'll remember this scent."

"Don't be silly. You don't have to remember me. I'm right here." She moved away from him and over to a mature oak known as the Old Man. She leaned against its dense trunk, glancing up at the thick branches that bent low and, in some spots, almost touched the ground, forming a secret cocoon away from the eyes of the world.

Will he kiss me? She wanted that desperately yet was reminded of her mother's warning about kissing before marriage. She waited, but instead of moving toward her, he pulled a flask from a pocket and took a swig.

The hairs on her arms stood up. *No, not like Pa.* Her mind raced. She waited, hesitant yet expectant, when it occurred to her they were hidden and away from everyone. She made to move from the tree, but he placed his hands on either side of her. She laughed and bolted under his arm. But that time, he was more insistent.

"No more games."

"I don't know what you mean."

He came closer, and she found she was back up against the trunk. His breath stank, and she realized he was slurring his words. Thrill turned to terror. She had to get away.

"How's about a kiss?" He leaned over, and she turned her head. But instead of falling back, he buried his face in her hair. "Mmm, you smell so good."

His left hand had moved down, and before she knew it, she felt his hot hand on her thigh, inching upward.

"Stop it!" She gathered her strength and pushed against him enough to run away from the tree. "You ever touch me like that again and you'll pull back a nub." Her eyes burned with tears.

"I'm sorry. I don't know what I was thinking. I forgot myself. I thought—"

"Well, you thought wrong!" Her eyes darted around, seeking escape.

"Margaret, please. Let me take you back to the dance." He stepped forward, but she moved away.

"No. I'd appreciate it if you don't escort me back."

"Margaret—"

But she turned and ran like a chased animal fearing capture. Tears streamed down her face. She was foolish to think that he truly loved her. He must have thought she was one of those easy girls. *Did I give him that impression?*

She roughly wiped her eyes, anger building at feeling betrayed by an older man. She finally slowed her jog once she realized Eugene wasn't pursuing her. Outside by the privy, she took time to compose herself, berating herself once again for being so blind and allowing her feelings to take her down a wrong path. She had straightened her dress when she heard noises from the bushes.

Margaret peered into the darkness. She drew back, her fist against her mouth in shock. It was Franny with that man she'd seen at the house. They were kissing.

Oh, my gosh! Franny was going to become pregnant. Mama had warned them of the dangers of kissing. She wondered if she should go in and stop them. Instead, she watched from the dark, wondering what it would be like to experience her first real kiss. *If only Eugene hadn't been a drunk.* Tears spilled onto her cheeks.

She pulled the delicate white flower from her hair, threw it to the ground, then stamped on it, twisting the petals into the dirt. As she did, its fragrance rose. She stifled a cry, knowing the scent would always remind her of her heart breaking into a thousand pieces.

~

The following day, Margaret Rose waited until everyone had settled, with Pa enjoying his Sunday nap. She grabbed a burlap bag and put in the newly cleaned shoes she'd borrowed. The walk into town calmed her spirit, and when she reached Irma's house, she cut through the back alley to where her items were stowed by the shed. But instead of dropping the shoes and leaving, she picked up her items and walked over to the back door. Dot opened it, a look of shock on her face.

"Can I help ya, ma'am?"

She held up the burlap bag. "I've come to return these to Lucy, and to say thank you." She glanced over Dot's shoulder to where women were seated around a table, drinking coffee and eating a meal. "Is it okay if I come in?"

Dot's protests got her nowhere as Margaret slunk under her arm. "I've brought your shoes back."

"Here, have a sit." The girl, who didn't seem much older than Margaret, gestured.

Another older woman pulled a Chesterfield cigarette from a pack and tapped it on the table before lighting it. "So, give us the whirl. How was the dance?"

"It was a blast." She sat in the chair.

Dot set a cup of coffee in front of her. "Egg and toast, miss?"

Margaret had picked at the lunch meal of white beans and cornbread. *How can I eat when my life is over before it even started?* Franny had been in a good enough mood. Margaret's sad attempts at responding to questions about the dance finally proved to be enough for the family to seek out other conversation.

Though she still wasn't all that hungry, she wouldn't turn down a chance to have that delicious treat again. She gave a crisp nod. "Thanks ever, Dot."

As Dot went over to the stove, Margaret regaled them with tales of the band, the new dances, and what the other girls had been wearing.

"Well, I know you were the belle of that ball. I doubt any other girl had no heels and hosiery."

"That's true. I noticed a few envious glances from some of the Parktown girls."

"And this fella you danced with? He sounds like a handsome guy."

"He is." She faltered.

Lucy reached over and touched her arm. "He didn't—he wasn't forward, was he?"

Margaret choked up. Luckily, Dot saved her with the egg and toast. Margaret had dipped into it while the other women sipped at their coffee or smoked. Finally, she finished her snack and recounted what had happened under the tree.

Lucy stubbed out her cigarette. "Honey, all men want the same thing."

"You mean a kiss? Don't worry. My ma told me about kissing and getting pregnant."

"What?" Lucy covered her mouth to stifle the laughter while the other women just glanced at one another and giggled.

Irma's voice was sharp. "What's going on here?" She waltzed into the room and pointed at Margaret. "What are you doing here?"

Margaret swallowed the toast and wiped her mouth. "I came to give Lucy back her shoes." She pointed at the bag on the chest by the door.

"Okay, you've done that. Now you need to get." She pointed toward the door.

"But I—"

Irma brooked no further conversation. She went over to a chest, put the shoes inside, and held out the empty bag to Margaret.

Margaret set her napkin on the table, thanked Dot for the meal, and took the bag from her. Irma folded her arms across her breast and waited. "Our business is done. Don't darken this door again." She pointed toward the door.

Margaret trudged down the stairs, the sound of the door's lock clicking shut behind her. Feeling shunned and humiliated, she gathered up her things from the shed and made her way home.

She found Nellie jumping up and down on the porch, waving at her. "Maggie, Maggie! A man came and wanted to talk with you. Pa told him to leave, but look!" She ran over to the side of the house and came with cupped hands, holding a wilted gardenia. "He told me to say that he would be by that Old Man tree on Friday at four if you wanted to meet him."

Maybe he'd come to his senses. She took the flower and shoved it into her dress pocket.

Inside, Pa was in his rocker and Ma was sitting opposite, working on her sewing. He spat tobacco into the rusted can next to his chair. "Who was that fella that came by today?"

"He's a friend of Edsol's."

Pa sat forward, elbows on his knees. "He's not for you."

"I like him, Pa."

"No." He leaned back and started rocking to show the conversation was over.

Margaret stiffened. "I'm walking out with him on Friday."

"Are you, now? I said no." He pointed over to where Franny sat, reading a book. "Why can't you be like your sister? She's got a good head on her shoulders."

Margaret wondered if he would keep heaping praise on Franny if he knew that she'd been out kissing a man last night. "Pa, I—"

He cocked his head, and his hands gripped the arms of the rocker. "Are you questioning me, girl?"

She bent her head low, shaking it. "No."

"What did you say?"

"No, sir."

Nellie rushed into the front room, holding the hosiery. "Maggie, where did you get *these*?"

The room started spinning. Her mouth felt full of cotton. There was nothing she could do or say to prevent what was coming.

Then a soft voice came to her ears. "Nellie, those are mine. Pa, one of the students' family couldn't pay this last month, so she offered me this hosiery. I let Margaret Rose borrow them for the dance last night. Isn't that right, Maggie?"

Stunned, Margaret could only nod. If her father found out about Franny's lie, the consequences would come swiftly.

"Bring those here." He held up his hand. Nellie rushed over to her father's chair. He held up one leg of the nylons. "I won't have my girls behaving like trollops."

Margaret moved to speak, but Franny squeezed her wrist. She glanced over to see a subtle reassurance in Franny's eyes, but Margaret feared for what her older sister would say next.

"Pa, I was saving those for my wedding."

"Wedding? To who?"

"Paul Rogers." Her shy smile couldn't hide the glow on her face.

"He's coming by tomorrow to see you."

"Isn't he that car salesman over in Pensacola?"

"He's the manager, and one day, he'll have his own business."

"Robbie Simpson has already asked for your hand. I've given him my blessing."

Franny's hand dropped from Margaret's arm. "Papa, I love Paul."

"Robbie needs a wife. He's got two young'uns to care for after his wife, Rebecca, died. He needs help on the farm."

"No. I don't want to marry Robbie. I don't love him."

"You'll do what I say!" He spat tobacco.

"I won't!"

A hush descended on the room. No one ever spoke back to their father, and to see Franny do so was tantamount to an earthquake.

He stared at her. The quiet grew heavy as he chewed on the tobacco in his cheek.

He spat into the tin can. "Is that so?" He glared at Franny as his voice lowered. "Old man Tate had a rebellious daughter. He had her sent to the sanitarium. She's better now."

A shiver went through Margaret. They didn't know what had happened to Julia in that place, but after, she sat all day on their front porch, eyes unseeing, spittle forming in her mouth.

"No, Papa. Please!" Franny cowered behind Ma's chair.

"We won't speak of this again. I've given my blessing to Robbie for your hand."

He got up, and they watched as he crossed through the kitchen then out the back door. Margaret rushed to the door with Franny. The boys were burning the trash out back, and Pa threw the stockings onto the fire, sparks flying into the air, the only memory of what had been.

CHAPTER SIXTEEN

A month later, Margaret watched as Franny married Robbie Simpson. She wore the same antique lace gown Mama had worn for her wedding. Margaret had to hold back her tears when Franny approached.

"It'll be fine," Franny said quietly. "You'll see."

Margaret wondered if her words were to calm Margaret or for her own ears. They stood outside Saint Gennie's Episcopal Church on Oak Street, waiting for Robbie to bring the truck around.

Franny tucked a piece of hair behind Margaret's ear. "I want you to have this." Margaret looked down to see that her sister had tucked some dollar bills in her hand.

"No! I can't take this. You'll need it."

"I want you to have it. I know that you're going places, Maggie. I never was." She shook her head. "I got a bit uppity there for a while. But my place is here."

"I won't use it, but I'll keep it safe for you. If you need it, you let me know."

They hugged, then Franny went over and climbed into Robbie's truck. Her new husband sat a toddler on her lap, walked around to the other side, then hustled a young boy in between them before he got in. The door slammed shut, and Margaret watched as they drove off with two of Robbie's brothers in the back, next to Franny's upright piano.

As the truck moved out of sight, anger burst from Margaret. James tried to grab at her, but she shook off his hand. She marched over to her mother. "Why did you do this? Why did you allow this to happen to her?"

The other kids grew quiet, and her mother remained silent.

"You should be—" Margaret froze when her father strode out from around the back where the men had been talking.

"What in tarnation is going on?" He spied Margaret, breathless from anger with clenched fists. "Are you sassing your ma?" He took a step forward.

Margaret couldn't bear to be there another minute. She ran off down the road and continued until her legs burned and sweat dripped from her brow. She slowed but kept walking, taking in huge gulps of air. Her stomach churned when she thought about Franny. She raised her hands, noticing they were shaking. Her breathing had grown fast and shallow, causing her mouth to become dry.

She couldn't go back. She wouldn't. Not if her choice would be between a loveless marriage to Bud Simpson or a life spent as a vegetable like Julia. She shoved her hands into her hair, a guttural sound escaping from her lips. *I have no control over my life!*

Margaret continued walking toward town, the realization of what she'd done, what she'd said, haunting her. Lost in her thoughts, she didn't notice that she'd headed toward the courthouse and the Blackwater River.

Her mind raced as she reached the water's edge. She stopped and stared into the water. She would never be forced to marry someone she didn't love.

She fought the urge to throw herself into its murky water and let it take her away. She licked her dry lips as her thirst became more insistent.

A man walked by, breaking her reverie. She turned away from the water and headed toward Main Street for something to drink. She didn't care if it was frivolous to spend money on a pop. She dug into her purse and found enough coins for a cold 7-Up from the grocer. Outside, she made her way to the Old Man and flopped down in its shade, not caring that her dress would be grass stained. She took a long swig then rested her head on her bent knees, daring herself not to cry or to sink any further into despair.

A noise startled her. She looked up, surprised to see Eugene. He crouched next to her. "You didn't come."

"No."

"Listen, I was a cad that night. You had—have—every right to be angry at me. I didn't respect you, and I'm sorry. Please forgive me."

He pointed at a spot next to her, and she nodded. He sat across from her.

She laid her head back against the tree. "Today was my sister's wedding."

"You don't seem happy, or am I missing something?"

Margaret ran her hands through her hair, pulling it together then letting the strands loose again. "She didn't have a choice."

"Oh, you mean…?"

"No! She wasn't in the family way. My *pa* didn't give her a choice. She wanted to marry someone else, and he said no."

"What do you think he'd say to me if I asked for your hand?"

Margaret bolted at his words. "What?"

"I mean it. Since the dance, well—truth is, I haven't been able to get you off my mind. Back then, I thought that we could have some fun, and then that would be it. But this is more. It's something I've never felt in my life. You push me. You say what you mean. You're different from other women."

She crossed her arms, frowning.

"No, I don't mean it in a bad way. I've never met anyone like you. When we're together, it feels right." He ran his hand across his jawline. "Ah, I'm not doing this very well.

"Look, here's the thing. I've been given my orders. In a month, we'll be shipping out soon, and from what I'm hearing, between the Jerries and their subs, us getting through with supplies is going to be like a duck in one of them shooting ponds at the fair. We have to take a long way around to divert suspicion of where we're really going."

He paused. "This may be my last chance. I want to be married before I ship out." He rose on one knee. "Margaret Rose, I love you. Will you marry me?"

Her heart swelled. Like Eugene, she couldn't go through the day without thinking about what he was doing or if he was thinking of her. It didn't matter that they didn't know each other well. She didn't hesitate. "Yes!"

He stood and pulled her up from the ground. She rose to her tiptoes to put her arms around his neck.

Eugene leaned toward her. "Now may I have that kiss?"

She nodded, and as his lips met hers, a tingle traveled through her. She let herself be caught up in it and his embrace, his kiss supplying an excitement like she'd never experienced. She would be married, and after the stupid war was over, she would leave that place once and for all. She would move with Eugene to Texas, far away from her father and his control.

She gazed up at Eugene as he set her back down on the grass. "You'll have to talk to Papa."

"Okay, when?"

"Come for lunch on Sunday. I'll tell Ma to set another place." She kissed him on the lips again, butterflies exploding in her chest.

After their lips parted, Eugene escorted her back down the street. "Should I walk you home?"

"No, it's better if you don't."

He took her hands in his and kissed them tenderly. "I love you, Margaret."

"I love you too." She smiled and reluctantly pulled her hands away from his. "Until Sunday."

"Sunday."

She flew home, lighter and happier than she'd been in months.

She was going to be wed.

But when Sunday came, it was clear that all wasn't going to plan. Her father was not happy to see Eugene at the table.

"Let's talk outside." After lunch concluded, he cocked his head toward the door, and Margaret scrambled over to the window to hear what they were saying.

"Sir, I want to ask for your blessing for me and Margaret Rose to be wed."

"No."

Stunned, Margaret's grasp tightened on the chair back.

"But sir, I have a good job. I can take care of your daughter if that's what concerns you."

"How old are ya?"

"Sir?"

"You heard me." Even though Eugene towered over him, Pa's presence commanded a response.

"Twenty-nine."

"Why ain't you been married before?" He spat more tobacco into the weeds nearby.

"I was in the navy and spent most of my time out on ships, so it was hard to find a nice girl."

"I bet you could find some not-nice girls though. Am I right?" He winked at Eugene.

Margaret had never even considered that he'd been with any other woman. She knew that he was older, but she hadn't realized by how much. Lots of couples had an age difference though. Even Ma was ten years younger than Pa, so she couldn't understand why that was an issue.

"Sir, respectfully, I know what you're saying, and I would remain faithful to your daughter while I'm away."

"Away?"

"Yes, sir. I ship out in a little over a month. So, with your permission, Mr. Locke, Margaret would stay here until I return, and we can set up a house when I get back."

"Here?"

"If Margaret would want that, but most likely, we'd move back to where I'm from in Texas."

"Mm-hmm." The older man kicked at the dirt, stirring up dust that floated in the air.

"I bet you like a bit of drink now and again."

Eugene cleared his throat. "I sometimes take a drink. Yes, that's true."

"And when you 'take a bit of drink,' you get into fights with the younger guys."

"We're just blowing off steam. I think everyone's a bit on edge. You know how it is. I believe Edsol said you were in the first war."

"Yes, 'the war to end all wars.' We thought." His countenance grew dark. "I know what it's like to look death in the face every second of every day. To see your friends alive one minute and torn to shreds the next. I also know what men get up to in war, and it ain't nice. My Margaret Rose doesn't need the likes of you now, after, or ever."

"But sir—"

"You heard me." He walked away and left Eugene standing outside.

Margaret dashed out to Eugene, and he gathered her in his arms. She lifted her face to his. "I told you. He's horrible. He doesn't want me to be happy."

Eugene kissed her forehead. "Let me think on this. I have to get back now, but I'll stop by Doc's office this week. We'll figure this out." He strode off, and Margaret hurried inside then flung herself on her bed.

"Sissie, what's wrong?" Nellie stood wide-eyed by the bed.

"Go away! You're just a child. You wouldn't understand." Margaret buried her head in the pillow as Nellie ran wailing from the room.

Will I ever find happiness? Margaret wept until she fell asleep.

~

The following week, Eugene showed up at Doc's office. Pulling her outside, he took her in his arms and kissed her. "Elope with me, Margaret Rose."

"What? How? When?"

"You turn eighteen in a week, right? You may still need permission here, but we could drive over to Mobile and get married. Say yes, Maggie." He took her hands in his and kissed her knuckles.

"Yes."

They plotted their elopement for the following week on the day

Margaret was to turn eighteen. Eugene had been granted leave, and they would escape to Mobile then return a few days later, man and wife.

That morning, Margaret packed the dress she'd worn to the dance, along with her nightgown, into a small travel bag. Leaving a note for her mother to find later, she slipped out before anyone could see her packed. The morning dragged by, and as the clock chimed ten, she could hardly contain herself. A familiar car drove up, and she spied Eugene behind the wheel. He was wearing a smart dark-blue uniform with brass buttons and an insignia of gold stripes on the arms. His white hat with a gold crest sat on his head. He came around and opened the door for Margaret before putting her case in the back.

Looking around, Margaret said, "This looks like Bunny's car."

He swiveled to face her, a strange look on his face. "How do you know Bunny?"

"Long story." She took his hat before sliding in next to him on the bench seat.

"Hm, well, I think I better hear that long story at some point. But for now, she knows... a friend of mine. But this is Irma's car. When she found out that we were eloping, she wanted us to use her car instead of taking the bus."

"That's so thoughtful." Maybe Irma wasn't mad at her anymore, yet she wondered how the woman had learned of their impending nuptials.

The drive was uneventful, and before she knew it, she stood before a judge, stating her vows. "For richer, for poorer, in sickness and in health..."

She smiled up at Eugene as the presiding judge pronounced them man and wife. They shook hands with the couple who had witnessed the proceedings then signed the register.

Margaret Rose Miller. She grinned as she wrote it in the book.

"Come on, Mrs. Miller. Let's grab something to eat before we go to the motel." He twirled her around in his arms, her laughter spilling over with joy.

They found a diner, and while they both ordered meals, they picked at the food. Finally, Eugene paid the bill, then they headed to the motel. Margaret had learned that kissing wouldn't make her pregnant after she'd asked Franny, but she didn't know what to expect beyond that.

While she fidgeted in the car, Eugene went inside and got the keys to their room. He drove around back to an area where a dozen green doors beckoned.

"Hold on a minute." He got out and unlocked the room before coming back to open the passenger door for her. She alighted from the car, and he swung her up into his arms.

She hesitated and pointed to the back seat. "I need my case."

"For what?"

"It's got my nightgown in it."

"Darling, you ain't going to need that." He whooped and gathered her up in his arms, carrying her over the threshold. "This isn't our real home, but when we get one, I'll do this again."

When they made it inside, he kissed her and kicked the door shut.

Then Margaret Rose found out what all men wanted.

And what women did too.

CHAPTER SEVENTEEN

Margaret stretched her body like a cat. She pushed up on her elbow to study the man sleeping next to her. Then she moved her hand out from under the crumpled sheets and held it up to gaze at the gold band that adorned her left hand. She let her thumb rub against the ring before reaching over and running her hand down his arm.

His eyes fluttered open. "Good morning, wife." He let his fingers slip through the silk of her hair.

"Good morning, husband."

He moved toward her, the urgency and intensity of last night's passion satiated, shifting toward a slower tenderness that made her heart swell. She had heard about "two becoming one" in church and at weddings, and finally, its meaning became clear. They were joined in love so powerful and rich, there was no wonder it was referred to as ecstasy.

Later, they roused themselves to go out to eat, their appetites having grown with all their efforts. As they ate, they shared glimpses of their lives and funny stories with one another before returning to their room.

As their days together dwindled, the tension built. Even with the aid of mouthwash, Eugene had come to her the evening before, smelling of alcohol. Their lovemaking had gone from passionate to tender to demanding.

Will this be the last time we'll be together? Each clung to the other with a renewed sense of not wanting to let go, of never leaving that moment.

Exhausted, Margaret couldn't suppress the tears at the thought of Eugene leaving. "I can't stand the idea of you being away from me."

"I know." He cupped her chin and gently kissed her lips. "I feel the same way. Like a piece of me is being torn away." He gathered her close, where she nuzzled into his chest. Neither spoke, afraid of the words that would make their fears real.

Finally, they slept, but Margaret tossed and turned with the knowledge that the first battle would be tomorrow when Eugene took her back to her parents' house. Because he was leaving so quickly, getting housing for her would be too tricky, and it made more sense for her to remain close to family. That last day, they didn't leave the room except to get food from the diner next door.

On the drive home, they stopped at roadside parks, taking pictures of one another so they would have them while he was away. As they made their way to Florida, Margaret sat shoulder to shoulder with Eugene. When they neared Milton, she shifted in her seat, clasping her hands tightly in her lap.

They pulled up back at the house, then Eugene faced her. "I hate to leave you, Margaret. This stupid war. Make sure you write to me every day. I promise I'll try to come back as soon as I can."

"Just come back to me, Gene." She stroked the dimple on his chin and kissed him.

He got out, and when she slid over to exit on his side, the entire Locke clan was standing on the front porch.

Margaret ran up and hugged her mother. When they drew apart, she flashed the gold band on her finger. "I'm married, Mama."

Pa stood in front of the family on the porch.

The two men locked eyes, and Eugene came forward and extended his hand. Pa looked at it but said nothing.

Margaret rushed over to Eugene, linking her arm in his.

He took her face in his hands. "I have to go. I'm due back, and I have to get the car back first. I love you. Write to me."

"I love you too." Margaret bit at her lip, realizing that she didn't know when she would see him again. She walked him to the car, its door still open. She wondered if he would kiss her in front of everyone.

Sure enough, he removed his cap, bent down, then kissed her tenderly on the lips. "I'll think of you every day."

"Me too."

He sat the cap back on his head and turned to her parents. "Mr. and Mrs. Locke, I love your daughter, and I aim to be a good husband to her. Please watch over her until I return." He tipped his hat toward her parents.

Then, after hugging Margaret one more time, he moved in behind the steering wheel. Shutting the door, Margaret leaned over and kissed him once more as he squeezed her hand.

"Keep me in your prayers, Maggie."

"I will." She swiped at her tears.

As the car churned up dust, she waved until she could no longer see him. Then Margaret faced her father, feeling triumphant. "I'm married. There's nothing you can do now."

He spat tobacco off the porch. "We'll see about that."

CHAPTER EIGHTEEN

When the next day began like any other, Margaret wondered if the elopement had only been a beautiful dream. Though her family knew of their marriage, Eugene hadn't told anyone, as he'd volunteered as a single man. For the moment, it was a closely held secret between them and her family.

But the gold band on her finger kept her doubts at bay. During the day, she would wear it on a chain around her neck, fingering its cool band and thinking about him, praying he was well and safe. She spent her evenings writing him letters but was disappointed when she received none from him.

Eugene had told her it would be harder for him to get mail to her since he would be at sea, but he would try. He was supposed to write her every day. She would rush over whenever she saw the mail carrier, asking if there was a letter for her. But days passed with no word from her husband.

At night, he'd told her to look for the North Star and he would do the same. So every evening, as the night air teased her, she would gaze up at it, kissing two of her fingers and raising them to the sky.

But even with her nightly outing, praying, and writing of letters, she struggled. Days became weeks until those glorious and precious moments they'd shared seemed a sweet, distant memory.

At night, she would think back to their time together and enjoy dreaming of their new home in Texas with its picket fence and arbor of roses. To prepare herself for when Eugene returned, she focused on growing her skills as a nurse so she could save more for decorating their first home. She couldn't wait for their lives to start together, far away, just the two of them.

~

Adjusting the cap on her head, Margaret opened a bobby pin with her teeth then secured it to her hair. She hummed a tune, thankful that Doc Albert had recommended her to a nurses' training program.

Margaret's training took her to the hospital in the morning, and she would spend a few hours with Doc in the afternoons if he needed help. But she started noticing that she struggled in the afternoons as fatigue set in. *I must not be sleeping well.* But that was odd since she and Nellie were the only ones sharing the double bed. She figured it was due to her fretting over not hearing from Eugene.

Margaret yawned as she made her way into the patients' ward. She'd been sent to prepare the beds for incoming patients when she heard her name being called.

"Miss Locke, you're needed in Ward One as soon as you're finished making that bed." The nurse reviewed the paper on her clipboard before marching away to find the next trainee. Even though she was married, she'd signed up for the training under her maiden name. Often, they wanted single women for the training, and it kept things easier for her.

Margaret gathered up the dirty linen and put it in a bin before taking a quick bathroom break. As she sat, she yawned again, her eyes fluttering closed for a moment. Making herself presentable, she washed her hands, patted some of the cold water on her face, then dabbed it dry with a rough brown paper towel.

She walked to the ward and met the nurse, who nodded a welcome to her. Margaret rolled a tray over with gauze as the other nurse exposed the young man's leg. He'd been one of the charmed ones to make it home from the war, but his feet and legs had suffered from standing too long in wet, cold trenches.

The sight of the damage made Margaret's stomach jump, and bile rose in her throat. She turned away and took deep breaths, knowing the charge nurse was not happy with her response.

"Mr. Talbert, I want to confirm with you that the doctor came by to tell you he will be operating later."

The patient, who wasn't much older than Margaret, nodded, the fear evident in his eyes. If he was lucky, he might get to keep some of his foot. Margaret busied herself with preparing the new gauze. The blackened and open wounds still needed tending. As she turned back to face the patient, she became so queasy, she had to flee the room.

Her face burned as she bent over the toilet. Margaret wiped her mouth just as the nurse in charge came in. "That was very unprofessional."

"I know, ma'am. I don't know what happened. I can go apologize."

"No. That won't be necessary." The older woman glared at her. "Are you well?"

"Yes, ma'am. I'm sorry. I guess it—well, maybe the smell affected me."

"Is that all?" The nurse crossed her arms across her white uniform.

"What do you mean?" Margaret wobbled and caught herself on a chair next to the sink. She lowered her head between her legs, pursing her lips and taking slow breaths.

"We can't have trainees that aren't able to perform their duties. It upsets the patients. Is that clear?"

She rose to look at the nurse and nodded. "I'll do better, ma'am. I'm sorry for my actions."

The woman strode out, and the day nurse of the ward came in to check on Margaret. "How are you feeling?"

"Fine. I think I'm just not eating enough before I come to work in the mornings."

"Not eating?" She washed her hands in the sink with lye soap.

"It doesn't taste good and upsets my stomach. I think I may have had a bad apple or ate something that didn't agree with me."

The woman chuckled. "It's no bad apple, sweetie. What you've got is a case of a bun in the oven."

"What?"

The nurse wiped her hands on a towel then threw it in a metal bucket. "You better not let Nurse Mathers find out. Sorry, but your days here are numbered. No pregnant nurses, and certainly none with children."

Margaret broke down crying. "But I can't be."

"I'm pretty sure you are. Now wipe your nose, wash your hands, and put on some lipstick. Bedpans are calling your name."

The nurse left Margaret alone with her thoughts.

Pregnant? She wanted to be happy, but with Eugene so far away, she didn't know how to feel. She loved her work as a nurse and had seen it as a potential career. Minus her morning outburst, she'd been praised by the nurses and doctors for her work. But if it was true that she was pregnant, her dreams of becoming a nurse were swirling down the drain like water from the tap. She gazed at herself in the mirror, biting at her lip to stop the sobs building up in her throat.

Tonight, she would write to him. *He'll be happy, won't he?* Lots of women were waiting on husbands to return, and she would be no different. But her heart mourned the loss of her dream of her and Eugene starting out together in their first home. Things would change forever.

She didn't know how to be a mother when she hadn't even truly been a wife.

CHAPTER NINETEEN

Margaret walked to the bus after her shift was over, her mind a jumble at the possibility of being with child. She found her seat, her hand resting protectively on her stomach as the bus lurched away from the curb.

Visions of Eugene playing ball with their son while she made dinner went through her mind. Or maybe a girl. Margaret would make sure her daughter had the opportunities she'd never had. She would read their children books and watch them sprint past the fence to the ice cream truck. She smiled at her daydreams. They would be a family just as she'd always imagined.

The bus pulled up to the stop, then Margaret exited with the other riders. As she walked home, her thoughts swirled with possibilities. She wanted to think of a wonderful way to break the news to Gene. Maybe she should wait a bit just to be sure it was true. But by then, she felt it in her bones. The tiredness, the upset tummy—it all came together. As a nurse, she should have realized sooner.

As she made her way up the road past the hedge, she caught the sound of angry voices rising. Margaret's eyebrows knit together as she rounded the corner. Pa and Franny were across from one another, their faces flushed. As the confrontation went on, she saw Franny almost crumble. They turned as Margaret rushed across the patchy grass to Franny.

"What's happening? Franny, are you well?"

Pa faced Franny again. "Remember what I said."

Franny flew to Margaret, tears running down her cheeks. "I'm sorry, Maggie. I'm so sorry."

She kissed Margaret on the cheek, and with a glance at their father, climbed into the truck waiting for her. Robbie tipped his hat at Pa before grinding the gears and going off down the road.

"What's the matter with Franny? Is she okay?"

"Mama!" Pa called out, and Ma came out on the front stoop, wiping her hands on her apron, her face a mask of hurt.

"What is it? You're worrying me. Is it Nellie? James? One of the others?" Margaret sought assurance from her mother, whose hands twisted at the worn fabric.

Pa spat tobacco before addressing Margaret. "I got word. The telegram came today."

"Word? What do you mean?" She looked back and forth between her parents, worry building in her chest. "What is it?"

"Mother, come help your daughter." Pa took a step back, and Margaret's stomach clenched in fear.

Mama rushed to Margaret and tried to pull her into an embrace, but Margaret brushed off the advance.

Word? Telegram?

Then it registered why they would be receiving a telegram, and her eyes grew wide. But if it was Edsol, then Pa wouldn't have called on Mama to come to her. It could only mean one thing.

No. It's not true. Her breathing became shallow, and she moved back from them.

"Baby, I'm sorry." Her mother reached for her again.

"No, you're wrong." She shook her head violently. "You're wrong. It's—it's a mistake."

Her father replied, "His ship went down. He's gone." He strode away.

An anguished howl came from Margaret as she crumpled to the ground. Her mother tried to soothe her as she rocked back and forth, mourning the life she would never have.

Mourning the life that was gone and the one that would never be seen.

CHAPTER TWENTY

The following days crawled on in a haze. Everything and everyone remained a blur. Grief's talons clung to her, and the pain would strike from out of nowhere, doubling her over in pain and sorrow.

She'd taken leave from the training, as she couldn't concentrate. She fluttered between accepting the loss to believing it wasn't true. If only Eugene had told her the name of his ship. At the time, she hadn't even thought to ask. Maybe it had been a different ship. Maybe he was still alive.

She wrote to him, her father looking at the letters and shaking his head. "You have to give this up, Margaret Rose." But she couldn't give up. He might be alive or hurt somewhere. Finally, Pa had agreed to talk with someone on her behalf in order to settle it once and for all. So Margaret waited for news. In the meantime, she tried to get on with her life, but that proved difficult.

Her morning sickness grew stronger, worsened by grief and her not eating well. In order to gain some motivation, she helped Ma by running errands, Nellie accompanying her. As they walked along the familiar streets in town, she moved in slow motion, her heart heavy.

How can you people walk around like nothing happened? She wanted to scream at them. But no one approached her. No one cared. It was as if Margaret was encased in a bubble of grief, and no one could enter it.

Pa had been furious to discover her pregnancy. He stomped around the house, spent nights at the lodge, and drank heavily. He came home one night and yanked the radio's plug from the wall before leaving the house with it. When he'd returned, he brought a much smaller radio and set it on the table. No one questioned why he'd taken the first radio or even what he'd done. No one dared.

But Margaret felt that something had occurred, and she didn't know what. Weeks passed, and she could no longer hide her swelling abdomen. While she'd stopped her nurse's training, she hadn't expected to lose her job with the doctor too. When Doc Albert had learned she was pregnant, he reluctantly said there was no way he could keep a woman in her condition working for him.

Losing all the income she had, Margaret felt adrift. All she knew was that there was no way she was going to end up like Franny. When she'd talked about looking into any pension or monies due, Papa said he would take care of it, but the merchant mariners didn't receive anything. Plus, Eugene had joined with the knowledge that they only accepted single men. She wouldn't be receiving any help that way.

Some days, she still refused to believe it had happened. Even after Pa had been adamant that it was fact. It *couldn't* happen. Not to her. Not to Eugene. If only Papa hadn't burned the telegram. He'd said it was to protect her, but it only prevented her from verifying Eugene's death.

She wept until she felt hollow inside. As she encountered old school chums enjoying their lives, she knew this child had ended any romantic notions of dances or stepping out with a fella to go to the picture show.

The days dragged on as morning crept into night. They grew longer and wearier as the life inside her grew, and she grew heavy with its fruit. A fruit its maker would never see.

~

"Come on, Maggie."

Margaret struggled with the weight, her hands clasped behind her back as she waddled down the boardwalk to where Nellie jumped up and down, a sparkle in her eyes.

"Look! Look!" A cinema rose above Nellie, and they were opening with a movie that had premiered last year, *Casablanca*. "We *have* to go. I'll die if I don't get to see a moving picture show."

"You won't die. Stop being so childish." Margaret turned away from the building, and they crossed the street to retrieve the canning lids Ma had ordered.

Margaret Rose had gotten used to the stares and whispers. Her fingers had swelled up so much, she could not wear her wedding band, so she wore it around her neck. Those days, she would often touch it or pull it from her top so that everyone could see it as she walked by them. Yet she knew that some were even calling her a "convenience" widow, where girls who'd gotten in the family way said they'd been married and widowed. She wanted to spit the truth at them, and some days, she daydreamed ways to enact her revenge, but it only tempered her frustration.

"Let's go." Margaret held onto Nellie's hand as they exited the shop. She turned to her right, and she couldn't believe her eyes.

"Gene!" she screamed. "Eugene."

The uniformed man was too far to hear her. She rushed forward, pulling Nellie's hand as she fought past couples on the sidewalk, her heart pounding.

Nellie cried out, "Stop! You're hurting my hand."

"Come on. Didn't you see? It's Gene." She pulled again, but Nellie fought back, wrenching her hand away.

Frustrated, Margaret pointed at a nearby bench. "You sit here. I'll be back soon." She scurried off to where the man had disappeared around the corner. She panted at the effort she made as she turned the corner. In her current state, she couldn't go any faster.

Finally, she spied the man farther down the street, stopping for a woman and children to pass in front of him.

Gene. She ran the last bit and pulled at his arm. "Gene!"

The man turned and faced her, but it wasn't Eugene. Her emotions fought between disappointment and embarrassment. "I-I'm sorry. I thought you were someone else."

His expression as he looked at her said that it wasn't the first time a desperate lover, mother, or wife had accosted him. "It's okay, ma'am. Can I help you?"

"No. Thank you." She managed to get out before she walked

away, sobs tearing from her throat.

She made it around the corner before she allowed herself to rest against the building's brick front. She took deep breaths until she had calmed herself. Then she remembered Nellie. But when she reached the bench, Nellie was gone.

Margaret sat on the bench and allowed herself to cry. She didn't care who saw her. She was so tired. The grief might never release its hooks from her soul.

A shadow passed in front of her. Margaret sniffed and looked up to see a black woman with three children behind her. The woman was also pregnant, and as their eyes met, the warmth of her brown eyes resonated with Margaret. "Here, honey." She held out a blued handkerchief.

"I couldn't."

"It's fine. I know those hard days. Don't you worry your pretty head none. It'll get better. You have to trust me on that." The woman started walking away as Margaret struggled up from her seat.

"Thank you." She handed the damp handkerchief to the woman, who shook her head.

"Just doing what the Good Lord says about doing unto others." She herded the children off down the street just as Nellie raced up to Margaret.

"Where have you been? Don't scare me like that!" Margaret pulled her little sister into a tight hug.

"Maggie, you're squishing me."

"I'll squish you some more if you ever do that again."

"Well, did you find him?" Nellie's gaze met Margaret's.

"No. I didn't find him."

~

At home that evening, Nellie danced around the room, excitement in her voice. "It's a new cinema. Papa, please. I want to see a picture show." She batted her eyes at the man, who laughed at her antics and swatted her away.

"I ain't spending no money on some silly picture show."

"But my birthday is coming up. Can't I go this once? Please, Papa?"

Maggie had an idea. "What if we can get our own money, Papa?"

He set down the paper he was reading. "And how do you plan to do that? You're as big as a whale. No one's going to hire you like that."

"I'll figure something out. If I do, will you give us permission to go?"

He shrugged. "Suppose. Now fetch me my tobaccy."

Margaret lay in bed that night, a renewed sense of purpose in her mind. She would get the money if only to show Papa she could do it. Plus, what a great birthday present for Nellie it would be. Much better than the embroidered handkerchiefs she'd received when she'd turned thirteen.

A week went by with no hope of extra monies when her mother came in, followed by two of the younger Simpson kids. They were carrying wooden buckets full of pears. But it was the sight of Franny that made Margaret squeal with delight.

"Franny! I've missed you." They met and laughed as they touched bellies, each pregnant.

"I've missed you too." Franny lowered her head and coughed.

"Are you okay?" Margaret helped Franny to a chair, the hacking cough continuing. "Nellie, get Franny a glass of water."

"Just something I caught. I'll be fine." She took a few inhales before she smiled at Margaret. "See? All better now."

Margaret wiped Franny's hair from her face. She couldn't help but notice that it felt thinner beneath her fingers. "Are you sure you're okay? Are you eating enough?"

"I'm fine. Truly. Now stop fussing." She pointed toward the pears. "Robbie got these on his last trip, and there's so many that I thought you all could use some for canning."

"That's mighty kind of you." Mama brushed the top of Franny's head with a kiss.

Margaret pointed at Franny's belly. "How is it that I'm so much porkier than you? I can barely tie my shoes now."

Franny lowered her head as Mama said, "Don't go nosing in where it ain't none of your business."

Margaret furrowed her brow. "What are you talking about?"

Franny addressed the children, "You go on outside and play now." After they left, Franny looked at Margaret. "I lost our first child."

"What?" She swiveled to her mother. "Why didn't anyone tell me?"

Franny shook her head. "You were grieving Eugene. The last thing I wanted to do was add to your burden."

"But you're my sister. You should have told me."

"I'm sorry." She reached out with her hand.

"No. *I'm* sorry. I shouldn't have said that. Oh, Franny, I'm so sorry. But don't you think you should have waited a bit to get pregnant again?"

"Robbie wants a big family. It'll be fine." Franny smiled, but it didn't reach her eyes.

"Come back home. I'll take care of you." Margaret reached for her sister.

"Don't be silly. You'll be having your own baby soon. You'll have your hands full. Trust me on that." She used the table to stand. "We need to get back. I'll come visit again when you have the baby." She kissed Margaret and Mama on the cheeks before leaving.

"Mama, what's going on with Franny?"

Ma shook her head. "Margaret Rose, as you grow older, you learn that we each have our own struggles to bear. The best we can do is be there for others when they're going through theirs."

The memory of the woman gifting her the handkerchief came to Margaret's mind. The images of people stopping in their tracks as the pair talked, harsh disapproval on their faces. The woman had hurried off so quickly. *Was it because of them?* Maybe those people were why Pa hadn't allowed her to play with some of the migrant workers' children.

"Well, it looks like we'll have plenty of pears for this winter."

Her mother's voice interrupted her thoughts.

"This is a ton. What are we going to do with—?" An idea shot into her head. "Mama, will you let me use some to make preserves?"

"Why?"

She turned to Nellie. "Because we have a picture show waiting for us."

After Ma agreed to their plan, they canned the preserves, then Margaret took a few jars into town with them. She went to Mr. Mason's and to other places along the boardwalk that sold preserves. She even had leftovers and placed a few jars on the back porch of Irma's house. But the door remained firmly shut.

By the time they were done, Margaret had not only made enough money for her and Nellie to go to the show but had convinced Mama to go with them.

Nellie bustled about the front room with excitement the day of the picture show. After paying for the tickets, they settled into the seats, each holding a small paper bag of popcorn in hand. Scenes flashed across the screen of news from the front, and as Mama tensed, Margaret took her hand. They hadn't heard from Edsol in a while, and each day, they fought hard not to think of receiving another telegram of bad news.

Finally, the movie began, and Margaret was swept along in the love story of Ilsa and Rick. But his parting words to Ilsa caused Margaret to suck in a breath as tears spilled down her cheeks. The dam broke, and she wept for so much that had been lost—her first love, her dream of a family and a home, and her desire to escape their small town and all it meant.

After they exited the movie theater, the three of them sat down on a bench outside to wait for Pa to pick them up in his car. They sat silently, each lost in their own thoughts, Nellie with a big smile at having attended her first picture show.

Realization hit Margaret like a punch to the gut. She'd been holding on to the idea that maybe, just maybe, there had been a mix-up. But the truth was, Eugene was never coming back to her. Her dreams of a little home with a white picket fence were not to be. That night, she went home, and as she stared at herself in the mirror, she unclasped the necklace that held her ring. After kissing it, she wrapped the ring in paper and put it in a jewelry box Franny had given her on her birthday.

Then she shut the box and locked it with a key.

CHAPTER TWENTY-ONE

Margaret cried out and grabbed the counter. A sharp convulsion racked her. She waited until the agony had subsided before she turned from the counter, water splashing between her legs to the floor. Another swift wave of pain shot through her.

"Mama!" Margaret screamed as her legs shook. Her mother came in from outside, where she'd been hanging up the sheets on the line.

"Oh, child. It's time. Let's get you into bed."

Nellie ran in to see what all the commotion was about, and Ma said, "Go get Mabel Steel. Tell her Maggie's babe is coming fast."

Nellie raced out the door to collect the midwife, the screen door slapping loudly behind her.

Once in bed, the pains stopped for a bit, and Margaret felt well enough to talk. "Mama, it hurts bad." Her eyes welled up with tears. "I think I'm dying. I don't want to die." Deep, wrenching sobs caught in her throat, causing shallow breaths to escape. "I'm dying." She moaned.

"Don't you fret. You need to take some deep breaths. That's it. Now you know Mother Steel delivered you, and her daughter is training up after her. It'll all be over before you know it."

Ma bustled about the room, bringing in old towels and basins of water, then helped Margaret into her nightgown. The midwives arrived, and Margaret swung between flashes of pain and exhausted sleep as the contractions waned. Then another wave overtook her, and through her daze, she heard Mrs. Steel say, "Push!"

A wail cut through the air. Margaret wiped the sweat from her eyes and face to catch a glimpse of her child before she fell back on the pillow, exhausted from the quick and strong labor. She allowed her mother to sponge her with a cool cloth as she rested.

"You have a beautiful daughter." Mabel's daughter, Selma, laid the child on Margaret's chest. The baby was soft and pink with a light dusting of red on her head, and she blinked in the light.

Margaret broke into laughter and cried tears of joy. "Hello, baby girl. I'm your mama."

As if understanding, the child wrapped her hand around Margaret's finger.

As Mabel moved around the bed and began palpations on Margaret's stomach, Selma cleaned up the detritus of birth by removing the towels.

Placing clean towels under Margaret, Selma looked up to the new mother and her child. "You have a name picked out?"

"May," Margaret replied. "May Eugenia."

CHAPTER TWENTY-TWO

Margaret had a spring in her step. She was finally fitting into her regular clothes, though her breasts were still heavy with milk. Five months had passed, and Gennie had begun to change and grow. It wouldn't be long before she started scooting and crawling, which meant more work for Margaret.

Frustrated at not being allowed to get her job back from Doc Albert, she'd given up and looked elsewhere. Finally, she'd admitted defeat and asked Pa to get her a position at the commissary. She could work in the mornings, which wasn't much, but it gave her a bit of money. Then, when she arrived home, she could nurse Gennie, and the pair could nap for a bit before helping with other chores. Every day, Margaret's mind went to how to get out from under her father's roof.

She spent her mornings at the register, checking out young mothers and calling out the prices as she compiled the items in her head. She didn't even have to record the figures before announcing the total. Her line started getting longer. Customers clamored to be in her line since she never made a mistake, which kept them from losing hard-earned dollars and cents, so precious with ever-growing families.

But it was the days when the recruits would come in from the base that Margaret liked best. It served as a bit of fun in an otherwise fairly boring life. At home after work, her primary desire was to pull off her shoes, collapse on a chair, and prop her feet up. However, being a mother to a child whose demands never seemed to end was taking its toll. Even more frustrating, Gennie seemed to be fussy all the time. Margaret would often pace the floor, barely awake. When Gennie finally settled, Margaret would climb into bed, the baby next to her in a crib made by James, and fall asleep in seconds, so profound was her tiredness.

A male voice pierced her thoughts. "Miss, I'm sorry. Did you hear me?"

Margaret jolted upright. She looked up to see a young man with jet-black hair slicked back on his head. He looked at her with piercing dark-brown eyes, and she noticed one of his eyebrows bore a scar that traveled up into his hairline. But as she focused on the handsome man, she realized he wasn't the one speaking to her.

"I'm sorry, sir. What did you say?" She turned toward the man standing next to him. Unlike the other man, his hair was a muddy brown but had been trimmed neatly compared to his eyebrows, which were bushy and full. He had a lazy smile, which contrasted with his square jaw. They were both dressed in Air Force uniforms.

"Cigarettes. Looking for Camels, and I don't see any here." He pointed to the display.

"Let me look." Margaret went to the rack and found a pack. She came back, handing them to the brown-haired man.

He put up his hands. "Not me. Wouldn't touch the things. Bad habit. This guy was asking about them." He stuck his thumb out at the other man, who pulled out a dollar bill.

"Oh, sorry. I must not have heard you." Margaret made change, and the pair left with a "see ya 'round" chorus.

Her coworker Mildred came over and tapped Margaret on the shoulder. "Oh, my gosh! So dreamy. Do you think he'll ask you out?"

"I don't know. He didn't say much to me."

Mildred's brow wrinkled. "What do you mean? He was talking to you."

"Oh, him."

"You don't mean—you like the other guy? Too dark and brooding."

Margaret shrugged. Maybe she liked dark and brooding, but it was Mr. Warm-and-Willing who came back a week later, asking her out to the movies.

In the theater's dark, she stole glances, realizing she was comparing him to Eugene. Where her husband had been tall and stout, Leland was the opposite. He had a lanky frame, a straight nose, and narrow lips. His teeth weren't stained from tobacco like so many others, nor did he stink of its smoke. Yet the spark she'd felt with Eugene evaded her. However, as long as Leland would keep wining and dining her, she enjoyed the attention, and it kept her away from home. As of late, her father had grown increasingly obvious with his push to see her married to Bud Simpson. That idea filled her with dread, but she didn't know what to do with May Eugenia to take care of.

The following week, she went to pick up the towels from Pa's barbershop and was surprised to see Leland in Pa's chair. The pair were laughing and looked to be at ease with one another. She hadn't told Pa about Leland, so she didn't know what to do. If she went inside, she knew Leland would speak to her. If she didn't, Pa would be upset she hadn't taken care of the laundry. In the end, the decision was made for her.

"What you doing, girl?" Pa yelled. "Get in here."

She stepped into the shop, and Leland turned to see her. He leaped from the chair, the cloth wrap twisting around him. "Maggie!"

Pa looked between them. "Do you know each other?"

Instead of answering, Leland faced Pa. "Are you her father? Well, this is a fine how do you do." He reached out his hand, and Pa plied it with a vigorous handshake.

"Maggie?" Pa left the word hanging.

"Pa, Leland is a friend." She emphasized the last word, not daring to say more. If only Leland had remained quiet.

But to her surprise, Pa's face actually took on a look of approval. "Come on, son. Sit back down in the chair. So, you know my daughter?"

"Yes, sir. We met at the commissary, and she's been nice enough to show me around town while I'm here."

Margaret let out a breath she'd been holding. Leland must have taken the hint.

"Maggie, this here boy is looking to stay around these parts after his tour is up. He's got a good head on his shoulders." He picked up his comb and shears again without another word, but Pa's message was clear. Leland had been deemed acceptable. With that nod of acceptance, a spark of hope and an idea took shape in Margaret's mind.

She started gathering the towels into the pillowcase but overheard her father. "My Maggie will make someone a good wife one day. All she needs is the right fella."

"Yes, sir," Leland replied, glancing over toward her.

She left the shop, a sense of purpose in her step. She'd never thought she would witness her father make the case for an outsider marrying her. It was certainly better than marrying Bud when he came home from the war or someone else in town.

She walked down the street when a woman dressed in a fine tweed suit passed her by. But it was her fragrance that almost caused Margaret to drop to her knees. Gardenias.

She would never love another man like she'd loved Eugene. But she would have to marry or live with her father. Neither choice was a good one.

~

On Saturday, Margaret went with Ma to see Franny and to bring some things for the new babes. Franny had given birth to not one baby but twins. Margaret couldn't imagine dealing with twins. They'd had to bring in a wet nurse, as Franny had struggled on her own.

They arrived at the house that sat back from the larger Simpson house with its two stories and gambrel roof. Franny and Rob's place reminded Margaret of the old homestead, white-washed clapboard siding, two long windows barren of shutters, and a door with a torn and oft-mended screen that kept dogs out but didn't prevent the access of flies and mosquitoes.

Carrying May Eugenia, Margaret pushed past the screen, and her heart dropped.

Poor Franny.

The entire house comprised one big room, with beds on one wall and a table and chairs toward the back, where a kitchen area had been set up. Franny suckled one child as she rocked the other one with her toe on the cradle. Every bit of her energy had gone into carrying the two children, and her frame almost appeared skeletal after birthing them. Franny started to rise when Ma waved her down.

"No need to get up. Let me put on the pot for some coffee." Mama scurried over to her daughter then placed a kiss on top of her fair hair.

"We're, um, out of coffee right now." Franny's eyes met Margaret's, and Margaret noticed a yellowing around her irises. She fought the urge to grab Franny and pull her away from all the chaos.

"That's okay. I didn't want any coffee anyway. Too hot. Right, Margaret?"

"Yes, that's right." Margaret swatted at a buzzing fly before sitting in the nearest chair. Margaret laid Gennie down on the floor on a blanket, the child's hands and legs pumping in the air.

They waited until Franny finished nursing and handed the baby to Mama, who cooed over her as she walked around the room, burping the child on her shoulder.

Ma faced Franny. "Franny, how are you feeling, honey?"

A coughing fit was Franny's reply. She took in a struggling breath. "Hold on." She walked over to a cabinet, pulled back on a package, then lit up a cigarette. "The doctor says this will help open up my lungs. Have a bit of congestion in them, he says." She took a long drag before another long coughing attack.

"That doesn't seem like it's helping to me," Margaret replied.

"You leave her be, Margaret Rose. You're not a doctor."

Franny sat back against the chair, her collarbones visible against her chest. "Bud tells me he's been writing to you, but you haven't answered. He has a question for you."

There it was. The dreaded question. If he had talked to Pa, she could only imagine the life she would live, stuck in a one-room hovel like Franny, constantly pregnant and barefoot. She had to do something and quickly. She couldn't avoid Bud forever. That night, she constructed her plan.

After donning her nicest dress, she managed to make her way to Main Street with May Eugenia in her stroller. She was conscious of her surroundings, hoping that she'd planned correctly, and Leland would be in town. She hadn't seen him in a few weeks since the encounter at Pa's barbershop. A group of men in Air Force uniforms was approaching. She spied Leland in the bunch, but she needed him alone. She flipped the buggy around and headed in the other direction.

"Margaret?" Leland had spotted her.

"Oh, hello. I didn't see you there." She feigned ignorance, stopped, and faced him. The others moved on past the couple, Margaret thankful for their continued progress.

"Who's this?"

"This is my daughter, Gennie."

"Your daughter? You never told me you had a daughter."

She'd thought of how to approach his question. She only hoped her plan would work. "Well, I figured we were just having fun, right? I mean, you'll be leaving soon, and I—" She pulled out a handkerchief and pressed it against her eyes.

"Maggie, what is it?"

"I guess it doesn't matter now. I think a local boy is going to ask for my hand in marriage. He's serving now, so I guess I'll have to write him my answer soon." She watched him carefully, relieved when obvious disappointment sank his features.

"Marriage? But—"

She brushed against him, kissing his cheek. "I guess, well, this is goodbye, then."

"Goodbye? But I thought—"

She sniffed. "You thought what?"

"I thought we had something."

"What are you saying, Leland?"

He paused, walking back and forth. It was the moment of truth. He pushed his shoulders back and took her hands in his.

"I'm saying why don't you marry me?"

"Marry you?"

He ran his fingers through his cropped hair and sighed. "Yes, why not? I love you. Will you marry me, Margaret Rose?"

"But I'm a widow. I have a daughter. Won't that bother you?"

He hesitated, and she wondered if she'd pushed too hard. "No. I love kids. I'd like to have some of my own. What do you say?"

"I say yes." She threw her arms around his neck and kissed him long and hard. "Let's do it as soon as we can."

"Swell. I love you, Maggie." His lips were soft against her own. "You love me, too, right?"

"Of course."

He kissed her again, laughing.

"You'd need to speak to my father and ask for his blessing."

"Not a problem."

"When will you go?" She didn't want to give him time to think too much about having a ready-made family. She needed him to move soon. "I was walking that way. Should we go together?"

"All right. Sure, let's do it."

He laid his hand on her back as she pushed Gennie's stroller to the barbershop. She waited outside and heard hollering and the slapping on Leland's back as congratulations were passed around. She had done it. She had escaped Bud Simpson or anyone else like him.

~

After Leland was given time off, they decided to marry in a small ceremony at the courthouse with the intention of doing a larger wedding in the church later.

Margaret wore a nice blue skirt suit, and Leland wore his dress uniform. She couldn't help comparing that moment to when she'd seen Eugene, so tall and handsome in his uniform. But she refused to dwell on the past. Leland would be a good husband and father. That was all she could ask for at that point.

No permission for a longer leave meant the honeymoon would have to wait, but they snuck away and consummated the marriage in a grove of pine trees by the river. Base housing wasn't available to families of recruits, so Margaret and Gennie moved in with Leland's sister, Ida, and her husband.

But moving out from under her father's thumb was not as freeing as she'd thought. With no time away from the house, Maggie spent her days reading movie magazines and caring for her daughter. Tension grew between her and Ida, and Leland confronted her.

"Maggie, you can't sit around all day and expect Ida to wait on you hand and foot."

"Is that what she's been saying? I have to take care of Gennie. She's into everything now. I hardly have a moment's peace, and when she's down for her nap, that's when I have a chance to take a break and read a magazine. You can't allow me that?"

"Of course. I'm just saying that you need to do more housework."

"I do. But I need my own house."

Leland ran his hand over his short hair. "We've already been over this. I can't afford a house."

"Then an apartment. There's a block of apartments outside of the base. We could be together. We'd have some privacy. How do you expect me to be a proper wife when I'm not allowed in the kitchen or to cook meals or have any space of my own? We need our own home."

After much cajoling on her part, he finally relented. Margaret was thrilled when he came to her with the news that he'd found an apartment where other base guys lived with their wives and children. The one-bedroom apartment in Niceville was on the second floor, but she wouldn't complain about having to carry May Eugenia down the stairs to where the stroller sat in the entry hallway. Ma helped her to crochet some doilies, and she found some knickknacks at the local thrift store that helped make the apartment look less spartan.

But the newness quickly wore off. Leland, who was training pilots, was gone for days or weeks on field exercises while she was left at home, staring at four ugly, patched beige walls. If only she could work or do something with her days besides cooking and cleaning. Margaret threw the knitting into a nearby bag. The idea of staying inside all day again with nothing to do was disheartening. She couldn't face it.

Since the days had grown warmer, Margaret decided to take Gennie to the playground. She changed into a nice dress and heels before setting a cap on her head. After settling her daughter in the stroller, she pushed it over the lip of the doorway and down the couple of steps to the pavement below. The air was warm on her skin, and she waved to another mother in the building who was pinning laundry to the apartment's clothesline.

She daydreamed as she walked, so she missed seeing the break in the sidewalk ahead. She lurched as her high heel got caught in a crack.

"Here, let me help you." She recognized him as the dark-haired man Leland had been with in the store.

She pulled her foot out of the shoe, and he easily retrieved it. "May I?" Margaret lowered her stockinged foot, and he took her ankle before placing it back on her foot. A shiver went up Margaret's back.

Gennie reached out her arms and babbled. He picked her up, swinging her around to her squeals of laughter.

"And who is this young lady?"

"Gennie." Margaret smoothed her dress and wished she'd remembered to put on lipstick.

"She's a beauty." He turned to her. "Just like her sister."

Margaret didn't correct him, though he was most likely teasing her. She swallowed. "Well, we need to get going, um—"

"Joseph. Joseph Martin."

There was something different about how he said his name. "You're not from around here, are you, Joseph?"

"New York. Ever been there?"

She didn't want him to know the farthest she'd been from home was Mobile. "No."

"You should come visit sometime. I could take you out on the town."

She blushed. He could clearly see the ring on her finger, and he had to know she was married to Leland. Yet he didn't seem to care that he was breaking the bounds of propriety.

"Maybe the next time Leland gets leave."

"Yes, of course. With Leland." He gave her a lazy smile that caught her off-guard.

In that moment, she felt vulnerable, that her emotions were on display, and she had no control over them. She also knew that he was feeling the same attraction as she was.

"Well, I'll be off now. Bye, Gennie. Margaret. Maybe we'll see each other again sometime." He tipped his cap and jogged off toward a waiting car honking its horn.

Margaret followed after him with her eyes, wondering if he was just visiting someone nearby in the apartments.

Margaret took Gennie to the park, where she pushed the girl on the swings and spun her on the merry-go-round, lost in thought.

That night, when Leland came home and they were in bed together, it was Joseph's face she envisioned when she closed her eyes.

CHAPTER TWENTY-THREE

Margaret recognized the signs right away that time. The swollen breasts, fatigue, and morning nausea left no doubt that another child was on the way. Whereas before, she hadn't understood what changes would come to her body and her life, after May Eugenia, she was fully aware of what awaited her. Often, she would break down crying at the thought of caring for another baby. She had no idea how she would manage a newborn with a near toddler on the verge of getting into everything.

Plus, marriage hadn't been the perfect life she'd dreamed of either. Leland was constantly moody and barked at her over meals he didn't like, the apartment not being clean enough, or her spending money on anything for herself. If she couldn't buy magazines, she didn't know what else she was going to do all day. At least back in Milton, she could go into town and walk around. In Niceville, which was closer to Eglin Air Force Base, it wasn't as easy for her to get around while pushing a stroller.

So it was with a bit of trepidation that Margaret planned to surprise him with the pregnancy announcement that night at dinner.

But when he stalked through the door, she could tell he was upset.

"Honey, what's wrong?"

"What's wrong? Everything's wrong!" He spun to face her. "It should have been me. It should have been me." He loosened his tie before whipping it to the floor.

"What are you talking about?" She clenched her hands to her chest.

"We lost good men today. I was supposed to be on one of the planes. But I'd been—I missed the call."

"Why? Where were you?"

"Stop with the third degree, all right?" He fell into his armchair, his head in his hands.

Margaret knelt at his feet and spoke in a soft voice. "Please, Leland. Tell me what happened."

He looked up at her and took in a deep breath. "It was a training exercise. One of my pals was in the plane. I guess he covered for me and took my spot. They were to do a series of flight tests—they crashed. No survivors."

"Oh, Leland. I'm so sorry."

He rose from the chair. "I'm going to take a shower."

Naturally, Margaret was saddened by the tragic loss of life. But at the same time, it had been the first time they'd talked in a very long while, and that gave her a glimmer of hope. That all went away the moment Leland emerged for dinner. He'd retreated into his shell, deepening the chasm between them. He was struggling with something, and she could no longer reach him. The outbursts were hard, but it was his silences cut the deepest. His moving away from her emotionally. She felt it in her marrow.

Margaret decided to wait for better timing, but she wouldn't be able to wait long.

Margaret awoke to the same routine of feeding Gennie oatmeal, making the bed, and sweeping the linoleum floors. The rest of the time was spent moving Gennie back onto a blanket on the floor or changing diapers. The growing girl could finally play by herself for a bit, so Margaret could get things done. But that would be before the new baby arrived.

She'd finally convinced Leland that if she could acquire a portable baby cage, she would be able to get more housework done. With her neighbor watching Gennie, she set off to a local thrift store to see what she could find.

Margaret marveled at all the treasures people had tossed as she strolled through the store. As she rounded the corner, her breath caught. Bookcases full of titles captured her, and she rushed over to them. Gothic romance, mystery—so many things caught her eye. By the time she was done, she had narrowed it down to three books. Two for her and one for Gennie.

The shop owner said that she would keep an eye out for a baby pen, and Margaret left her the apartment's main phone number. As Margaret exited the building, she spied a woman on a bike rush past her. *Oh, a bike would be nice.* At the moment, she didn't have the money for it, but she dreamed of getting one with a baby seat to go on the back. That way, she could take Gennie out on rides. With a spring in her step, she made her way back to the apartment, climbing the steps to drop off the books before going to get Gennie. That afternoon, Margaret got lost in a world of manor houses, ball gowns, and brooding lovers. Looking up, she spied the clock, and her stomach sank. Leland would be home soon.

She was pulling the bread from the toaster when Leland walked into the apartment. She ladled the hamburger and gravy over the toast then set it down in his place.

"Not SOS again!" He slumped in the chair.

Margaret bucked up. "Well, you can eat it or do without. I'm tired of everything I do isn't good enough for you!"

"Everything you do. What *do* you do all day? This is a one-bedroom apartment. It's still always a mess with toys on the floor when I get home."

"Gennie has to have someplace to play. Once I get the baby pen, the toys can stay in there."

His brow furrowed. "You didn't get it, then?"

"The thrift store didn't have one. She's going to call me when one comes in."

"So that's why the laundry is still in the basket on the couch?"

Margaret had gotten so caught up in her novel that she hadn't finished folding it. She struggled to come up with an answer, instead deflecting her anger back on him. "You're never here. You come home in a bad mood, and we don't ever go out and do anything."

He glared at her. "Well, maybe if you tried a little harder—"

"What are you saying? Like the nurses and other women you're around? They're not caring for a baby with another one on the way!"

"What?"

"I'm pregnant. I hope you're happy!" She rushed from the room and threw herself on the bed, crying.

He came to the door and sighed. "I am happy. I've always wanted a child of my own."

She rolled over and glanced up at him. "Are you? Really?"

He hesitated. "Yes, of course. This is good news." He came over to her and kissed her hands. "I can do this."

She squinted. "You mean, *we* can do this."

"Of course. That's what I meant." He rose. Now let's go eat at the diner to celebrate."

"Really?" Margaret smiled.

He nodded. "Grab Gennie, and let's paint the town red. And by that, I mean, let's splurge on a meal out."

Margaret hurried to put the hamburger away in the fridge. They enjoyed the dinner while discussing names for a boy or a girl. That night as they lay in bed, they were joined together by the new life growing inside her. Instead of happiness, though, dread reared its ugly head as she feared another door closing on her life. As Leland slept beside her, she stifled the sobs she couldn't control.

As the weeks passed, and she grew with child, their arguments had mellowed, but the silences between them stretched. Leland started spending more time away from home, coming home later and later. She felt trapped in the marriage, but she had a baby on the way. She certainly didn't want to go home again. She'd hated the commissary job.

Luckily, she'd become friends with a new neighbor, Jan, who had a child around the same age as Gennie. Jan's husband was also stationed at the base, so she understood the long days and nights alone while they went out for training exercises. They had to be thankful that their husbands' health and education had allowed them to serve as trainers and not participants in missions, where many lost their lives or were captured by the enemy.

Over time, they would take turns watching the children so that the other mom could get out without having to drag a baby along. On the day that Jan kept Gennie, Margaret decided to enjoy a stroll, as the weather was nice. She sat on a bench, leaning her head back to allow the sun to warm her face, a light breeze from off the pond teasing her curls. If not for her tight maternity girdle, she could have stretched out for a nap. Hearing footsteps approaching, she lowered her head and put her hand at her brow to see two women about her own age standing in front of her.

"Sorry if we're disturbing you. Is it okay if we share a seat with you?"

"Sure." Margaret waved them over and noticed their outfits. "Are you nurses?"

"In training. We're going to be moving up to New York for more training, but it will be a while yet."

"Training? Why aren't you doing it closer?"

"Adventure!" they both echoed.

The more petite one squealed with delight. "I want to see the country—the world, really. I've never been up north, so that's why I want to go."

"Me too." The other, sturdier woman with sparkling eyes and raven hair checked her nails. "I'm ready to get away from here."

"Can anyone join up? I used to work as a doctor's assistant and had been thinking of doing more training."

The smaller one pointed to Margaret's hand and the gold band on her finger. "No married women, especially not with children."

"Oh." Margaret bowed her head in defeat. It wasn't like she could up and tell Leland she was heading to New York. And certainly not with two children.

"You said you worked for a doctor before?"

Margaret nodded and shared about her time with Doc Albert and also her training at the local hospital. Before long, they were sharing funny stories about the nurses in charge and the patients.

"You definitely understand nursing. I'm sure that your skills would be much appreciated. In fact, I'd venture to say that if this war drags on much longer, they'll open it up to more women."

That certainly wouldn't work for Margaret because she'd have two children by then. It was hard enough with one, and there was no way Leland would want her working outside of the home. Yet the idea of only being a mother didn't sit well with Margaret. Even as a wife and mother, she still had her own interests. If she had a job, she would be contributing to something that mattered, plus she would have her own money.

With Leland holding the purse strings, it was reminiscent of when she'd lived at home and had to do without or beg for anything she wanted. She hated it. She wanted to be able to buy a book from a real bookstore or take Gennie out for an ice cream without pinching pennies.

The petite trainee stood, and Margaret snapped out of her thoughts. "Well, we best be getting back. Nice to meet you, um—"

"Margaret." She held out her hand, and the taller one took it in a firm handshake.

"Nice to meet you, Margaret. Thanks for letting us share your bench."

The second one chimed in. "It's too bad you're married, Margaret. We're looking for one to two more girls for roommates. The apartments are expensive up there in the city."

They were walking away when the taller one turned back. "Hey, a few of us trainees are getting together for lunch next week. I think you'd fit right in. Plus, I'd like to hear more about that style of stitching you told me about. Wanna come?"

Margaret's heart leaped, and a huge grin broke out on her face. "Yes, I would love to."

"Great, now we're cooking with gas. See you then."

Margaret stood. "Where should I meet you?"

"Oh, sorry. Katie's apartment. Got a pen? I'll write it down for you."

Margaret rummaged in her handbag, pulling out a nub of pencil and a scrap of paper. "Sorry, this is all I have."

"That works. Turn around, Sarge." The taller woman put her back to the petite woman, who used it to write the address. She handed the paper and pencil to Margaret. "Say twelve on Thursday?"

Margaret nodded. "Sarge?"

The taller woman laughed. "I'm the oldest, and when we first met, I was, shall we say, a bit bossy with the newbies. They started calling me Sarge, and it stuck."

"Oh, okay. See you next week." She waved at the pair, who linked arms then laughed as they practically skipped down the street.

Margaret spent the rest of the day twirling the scrap of paper in her fingers. As soon as she arrived back at the apartment block, she confirmed with her neighbor for next Thursday. The idea of meeting with other women her own age who didn't constantly talk about their fears and frustrations with deployments, children, or how the commissary was out of something would be a needed change of pace. It would also be nice to have something to look forward to instead of staring at the four apartment walls.

The upcoming outing put Margaret in a good mood. After putting Gennie down for a nap, she worked on prepping dinner for the evening of a roast chicken, potatoes, diced carrots, and green peas. She sang along to the songs on the radio as she prepared biscuits to pop in the oven and set the table with candles. Everything ready, she changed back into her nice dress, brushed her hair, and put on lipstick. If this effort didn't please Leland, she wouldn't know what would.

The clock ticked by. Margaret sat at the table, tapping her fingers on the red-and-white-buffalo-checked tablecloth. Dinner came and went with no sign of Leland. Margaret finally blew out the candles and, kicking off her kitten heels, then picked up Gennie for her bath. Her mind swirled with images of where Leland was or what he was doing, only increasing the anger building inside.

She'd put Gennie to bed and was back in her housedress and apron when she heard the key in the apartment door. Leland came in the door. He looked at the table and the food she was packaging up for tomorrow.

"I'm sorry, baby. I didn't—" He came up behind her, his arms around her waist, the fumes of liquor wafting over her.

Shucking free, she faced him. "Don't say sorry to me. You're never home. Why do I even try?"

He held out his hands. "I said I was sorry."

"Sure, you're sorry!" She picked up a dish and smashed it against the wall. "Well, I'm sorry too."

"Stop it." His jaw clenched.

"No, you stop it!" She threw another plate.

He grabbed her wrist. "Enough."

She yanked free from him and fell into the plastic chair seat, her arms resting on the cool Formica table. Sobs overtook her. "I hate this place. You're never here. It's like a prison."

He crouched down on his flanks next to her, his hand rubbing her back. "Maggie, honey. I meant it when I said I was sorry. I should be more thoughtful while you're in this condition."

"This *condition*?" She sniffled, glancing over at him.

"You know, with the baby. Your emotions are all over the place."

"My emotions are just fine. I need my husband. I need to do

something besides the same thing every day."

He rose and stretched his back. "I got an overseas assignment today. I leave in a few weeks."

She swiveled to face him. "Assignment? Where? For how long? I thought you were only doing training."

"Things are heating up. Eisenhower is setting up a strategic command for Allied forces in Britain. I'll be one of the field commanders."

"But you can't go. What about the baby?"

He shook his head. "Margaret, don't you understand what happens if we don't stop Hitler? It's my duty. This is my chance to prove myself."

"Why do you need to prove yourself to anyone?"

He shook his head. "You don't understand. I've been sitting on the sidelines, sending men off to their deaths. I have to go." He rubbed his hands over his face. "Write to me and let me know about the baby."

She grasped the edge of the table. "Let you know?"

"I won't be here. It's at least a year. Maybe more."

That night, as Leland snored next to her, Margaret stared as the light from the outside streetlamp shifted across the ceiling. The thought of staying in that plain apartment with its patched walls, all alone for over a year, was daunting. She had to find a way out, but she didn't know how.

CHAPTER TWENTY-FOUR

Leland promised to be home every night until he left, but even with Margaret working hard to make an effort for him, their conversations were forced. She could tell that he wasn't giving her all the information about where he was going and what was planned, which was frustrating. Yes, he might not be flying the planes, but England was still deadly, with nightly bombings and reports of German sympathizers also causing havoc. Margaret's fear for her husband, her marriage, and herself grew daily until it was all she could think about.

What if he never comes back? The news of Eugene's death had wrecked her. She couldn't deal with that again. A black cloud settled over her, and Gennie had taken to crying due to teething, causing Margaret to be more upset. Leland had his own worries and rarely spoke of anything he felt. She dreaded the day that she would be alone. The only thing that kept her sane was the upcoming lunch with the women she'd met.

The day of the luncheon arrived, and Margaret sported a new skirt she'd bought. It meant that other things needed would have to wait, but she wanted to make a good impression with the other ladies.

Because she could buy a size up, with the help of her girdle, it would hide a lot of her protruding tummy. By wearing it higher on her waist and adding a larger belt, it also drew the eye upward. Thankfully, she was barely showing and felt confident. Plus later, after the baby came, she could cut the skirt down and probably have enough fabric to make a playsuit for Gennie. Leland had been angry with her spending the money on something so frivolous but later apologized, giving her some extra money for groceries.

Margaret added a hat and gloves and strolled along the street toward the apartment where the girls lived. As she checked herself in the glass of the storefront windows, she smiled. She had done a good job with the new skirt. She bent down to look at a display of glassware, and as she rose, she swiveled to see Joseph.

"Oh, hello. I haven't seen you in a while." She held her purse in front of her tummy, just in case.

"I was away—you know, doing my bit for the country—but I'm back for a short while. Now it looks like I'm headed home."

"Home?"

"Yes, back to New York."

"But I thought—"

"Well, truth is, I got a little banged up. My plane was shot down, and I spent quite a bit of time at a field hospital." He tapped his legs with a cane she hadn't noticed until then. "Finally able to get up and about, but it's desk work for me now."

"Oh, I'm sorry." She tried to focus on his face and not on what may have happened to his legs beneath his crisp, pleated gray slacks.

"Naw. One of the lucky ones. Other chaps, not so lucky. I can deal with a couple of bum legs for now, but it means they're stationing me closer to home."

"Other chaps?"

He laughed, and it was a deep, melodious song that caused her to react with laughter too. "That's what the Brits say. That and blokes. I guess I picked it up." He stopped laughing, and his gaze grew intense.

"Well, I, uh, have an appointment to get too." She held out her gloved hand, and he took it in his own hand. "I'll be sorry to see you go."

"Will you?"

Flustered, she pulled her hand from his, spouting the first thing that came to her mind. "I've been thinking of going to New York."

"You have? What about Leland?"

"He's going off on assignment, so I've been considering going up there with some friends for nurse's training."

"Well, if you come, you should look me up. My pop owns a store up there. Once my tour is over, I'll be working with him." He tipped his hat then limped away, leaning heavily on his cane.

Joseph made her feel so different than Leland. Maybe it was because he listened to her, or maybe it was because something was missing with Leland. She hated the thought, but it kept rearing its ugly head. Did she even love Leland, or had it been simply a marriage of convenience? Joseph stirred things in her that Leland never had. Her face grew hot with shame and regret.

She took a deep breath. None of that mattered. For better or worse, she had taken those vows, and she would abide by them. Once Leland came back, maybe they could find a house. There, she could start up a little garden outside. Or she could ask him to buy her a Singer sewing machine to start making clothes for Gennie and the baby. Either way, she would make the best of it and be the best wife that she could be. She straightened her shoulders and made her way forward.

Katie greeted her at the door with a quick hello before she rushed back toward the kitchen. A group of ladies already sat around the table, their chatter and laughter filling Margaret with joy.

"Hey, Ladies. This here is Margaret. She worked as a nurse trainee for a while, and she shared a stitching technique that holds the stitches tighter so there's less scarring."

Introductions were made around the group, and Margaret took a seat while Katie brought over tomato soup and grilled cheese sandwiches. After they ate, she reveled in the knowledge the women possessed, and it made her appetite to learn more grow. At the end of the day, Sarge even allowed Margaret to borrow a book on medical procedures. She spent the day devouring the information, wishing that she was sitting in the classes with the women as they shared what they'd learned.

That night, Leland came home with a smile on his face. "I bought you something."

Margaret's spirits soared. "What?"

He reached out into the hallway and pulled in a wooden baby pack. "Look, it even has yellow, red, and blue spindles." He spun them with his fingers. His brow furrowed when he spied the look on her face. "What? I thought you wanted this."

"I do. I just thought when you said you got something for me, that it was—"

"It was what?"

"I don't know. Flowers, jewelry, a new book I've talked about."

He harrumphed. "You're never happy, are you? You said you wanted this, and I got it for you. But now that's not good enough."

"I'm not saying that, Lee. I just thought you meant something else, that's all."

"I give up. Nothing satisfies you."

Tears pricked her eyes. "That's not true. Why do you have to be so mean? I just told you what I thought you meant. I'm still happy to get this. It will help me so much with Gennie."

"Fine." He pushed it over toward the sofa. Then he turned, stared at Margaret for a moment, then walked out the door.

Another day. Another failure. *Couldn't I have acted thankful?* She had to do better because Leland's date for leaving was fast approaching.

~

On a whim, Margaret asked Leland to drive her to see her family so she could spend the day with them. Mama was waiting for them on the porch and waved at Leland with a dishtowel. He waved goodbye, promising to pick Margaret and Gennie up that evening.

Gennie's chubby arms waved, and her legs wobbled as she

reached toward her grandmother, who caught her in an embrace.

"Hello, sweet pea. I'm so happy to see you." She gathered the child up, settling her on her hip as she had so many other children in her lifetime. Gennie clasped her arms tightly around Ma's neck, greeting her with a sloppy kiss.

"Mama." Margaret placed her hand on her back and walked over to the pair. "How are you?" She kissed her on the cheek.

"Doing good. Come in."

"It's well, Mama."

"What?"

"You're doing well, not good." Irma had taught her that.

"Oh, you and your fancy ways. Good. Well. It's all the same. Now come inside. I've just fried up some taters, and I can scramble some eggs for lunch."

"I'm not sure I can eat."

"You're eating for two, Margaret Rose. You need to keep your strength up." She adjusted Gennie on her hip and walked over to hold the door open for Margaret.

Inside, the room was darker and cooler, but Margaret could make out a person sitting at the table. "Edsol! When did you get home?"

She rushed over to the brawny man, and they embraced in a big hug. "Ma told me you'd been hurt. What happened?"

He pulled out the chair next to him for her, then Mama lowered Gennie onto Margaret's lap so as to finish the cooking. "A few toes missing and can't hear out of this ear anymore." He shrugged. "Luckier than many."

Margaret stared at the man her brother had become. As she gazed at him, she noticed a patchwork of scars along one side of his face. Her sympathy must have shown, as he quickly changed the subject.

"Been busy. I transferred over to construction work. I've been tapped to head up to D.C. to work on the Pentagon."

"The what?"

"It's a five-sided building. It's almost done, but they work in three shifts, so me and my buddies can still get work there. Plus, there are a lot of temporary buildings going up there, too, to help with the war effort." He clasped his hands on the table. They were rough and bore the cuts and tears from working construction, while the other hand had a large scar from someone stitching it up swiftly.

"Edsol, what are you not telling me? Surely that wouldn't have stopped them from sending you back?"

His eyes met hers. "You've always been as sharp as a tack. Turns out, they found a heart issue that somehow got missed before. I started having a few chest pains. That's when they moved me into construction full-time."

"Why didn't you say anything? Are you okay?"

"I was embarrassed. All my buddies going off to fight for our country, and here I am stuck at home with a messed-up ticker. I didn't want anyone to know."

"But it's nothing to be ashamed of, Edsol. You served in Europe. And now you're still doing your bit for the war effort."

"Thanks, Maggie." He patted her hand. "How about you?"

Margaret knew better than to make up some story about her life being great. Edsol could read her as easily as she could him. Instead, she shared about Leland leaving for somewhere in Europe and her not looking forward to being alone with the two children. That much was true.

Mama set a plate of fluffy eggs, taters, and tomato slices in front of Edsol. "Thanks, Ma." He addressed Margaret. "Why don't you rent our place? It'll be available."

"What do you mean?"

He reached over and pulled a biscuit from the pan. "It's a trailer right around the corner. Easy way over here. Then Ma would be close for you when your time comes."

Margaret had never considered moving back, but the idea had promise. With Ma helping out with the kids, maybe she could go back to work with Doc Albert. "When are you leaving?"

"In a few days. I could put in a word with our landlord, Mrs. Childs. I'm sure she'd be happy to know that a family is living there instead of four guys."

"Yes, please do." She looked at the plate Ma had set in front of her and realized how hungry she was. "Here, Gennie. Let's put you over here for now." She moved Gennie to the side bench, handing the child a piece of biscuit, but her thoughts were on the trailer. She would have her own place and be close to family. Coming home to visit might have been the best thing she could have done today.

That night, when Leland picked her up, she brought up the subject of the trailer, focusing on the fact that she would want her mother when the baby came. Even though he thought she would probably be better off close to the base hospital for the birth, in the end, she convinced him that living closer to family would be better for their child.

They gave notice to the apartment landlord. The apartment had come furnished, so that only meant packing up boxes to take to the trailer. James and his buddies would help, and Franny promised Robbie would bring his truck over too.

The one thing Margaret would miss would be the lunches with her new friends. They were so different from any women she'd met before. They were more self-assured, forceful in their convictions, and more promiscuous. Some stories that Sarge shared had her blushing, which caused the others to laugh at her naivete even after being a married woman. Yet Margaret had never let on that she was a mother or expecting, intending to keep that part of her life separate. The move was good timing, too, as she wouldn't be able to hide her pregnancy forever or claim that she'd been putting on weight.

Whether they realized the truth, they never let on. Margaret felt sure that she'd kept it secret, though some days after being with them, she would struggle out of her girdle, large red marks covering her sides and belly. She hated that her newfound friendship with Katie and Sarge was coming to an end. With them, she could pretend to have lived an entirely different life.

But they would be leaving soon too. Their last meeting was a mixture of laughter and tears as they said their goodbyes.

With her friends headed for New York and Leland leaving, she wondered about the way she would fill the days ahead until the baby came.

As she waved goodbye to Leland, a knot of guilt and remorse filled her. Any love they'd shared seemed lost, and she couldn't guess what it would be like when he returned. They would be strangers. She laid her hands on her belly as the baby kicked. Another life. Another responsibility. She prayed she was up to the task.

CHAPTER TWENTY-FIVE

Margaret happily settled into the two-bedroom trailer. The smell of fresh paint on the cabinets mingled with the furniture and floor polish. She reveled in her newfound freedom of deciding when to have dinner or what was on the menu for the week. With Gennie happily ensconced in her "playpen," Margaret was able to spend a bit of time reading a mystery by a British author by the name of Agatha Christie. When she wasn't busy with housework, she often had her nose in the pages of a book.

The months seemed to pass quickly, and as it had been with Gennie, her pangs left little time to make it to the hospital. Ma and the midwives came to the trailer, where she gave birth in her own bed. While Leland had hoped for a son, they were blessed with another daughter.

Margaret named her June after the month she was born. She wrote to Leland, enclosing a picture of her with the two girls. After some weeks, she received a letter back, but while he noted he was happy about June, much of the letter's tone was stiff and perfunctory at best.

Even though the rent was paid by Leland, there was little extra left for utilities, supplies for the girls, or food, which meant Margaret often found herself at Ma's at lunchtime. That helped stretch her food budget but also allowed her to avoid Pa, who left earlier to head to the barbershop for the day.

While Nellie rocked June, an idea came to Margaret.

"Nellie, how would you like to watch the girls so I can see about getting my job back at the commissary?" She'd tried to get her job back with Doc, but that hadn't panned out.

"I don't know." Nellie stuck her pinky finger in June's mouth when she started crying.

"See, you're a natural." Margaret thought fast to come up with something Nellie wanted. "I would pay you, of course, and if you wanted, I could move June in with me, and you could share with Gennie. You'd have your own bed."

Nellie's eyes lit up. After Franny and Margaret had left, one of the younger girls slept with Nellie, and Margaret had often seen Nellie's bruised legs from her sister kicking while asleep.

"Yes, your own bed. And you would be close to Ma, so you could come over. What do you think, Mama?"

"We enjoy loving on them babies. I think that's a fine idea."

"What about Pa? Will he be okay with it?"

"You leave him to me." She patted Margaret's hand.

With that settled, Margaret contacted the manager and was offered her position back. The pay wasn't much, especially since they'd started taking out what was called "withholding," but it helped her to pay the few bills she had, plus some for groceries.

She was working the day shift when a woman's voice called out, "Maggie, is that you?"

Margaret swiveled and saw the group of nurses. "Sarge!" She rushed over, and the pair hugged. She surveyed the uniform Sarge wore. "Look at you. This doesn't look like the nurses' uniforms I've seen. I thought you were in New York."

"I was. They really need lots of nurses in the service, and I fit the bill, so I joined up. I wanted to go help our boys. It's getting rough, and they need us to be there for them."

"What about the others?" Margaret asked.

Sarge shook her head. "Too young, and you remember Squirt— they said she was too tiny. You have to be a certain height. No worries with me on that score. Plus, Katie's working on civilian training."

Margaret glanced back to her register, glad for a lull in customers. Sarge pulled out a Vantage and lit it. She glanced down and noted Margaret's ring finger bare. "What's the story?"

She didn't know what came over her, but the lie was out quicker than she realized. "He died."

"That's rough. Sorry." Sarge took a puff of the cigarette.

The only reason she didn't wear her ring as she found her hands sometimes swelled after being on her feet all day. She wasn't used to it. But Margaret kept digging a deeper and deeper set of lies with her friends. They would hate her if they knew the truth. Deep in her heart, she knew the reason she pretended with her friends—it allowed her to be Margaret, not a wife, not a mother. Her own person.

Sarge spoke. "You know, with me and another gal leaving, they'll be needing some roommates. You should write and see if they still have a bed." Sarge pulled out a tiny notepad and wrote an address on it. "Here you go if you're interested. Now got to go. Toodles."

"Be safe." Margaret hugged Sarge.

"You know me. Adventure calls. And men." She threw back her head and laughed loudly, causing surprised looks from onlookers.

Margaret could barely finish her shift after what Sarge had said. There was no way she could go to New York. Sadly, that ship had sailed along with all of her other dreams of doing something worthwhile with her life. Yet she desperately wanted to get that training. Unfortunately, the decision was out of her hands. A customer called to her, and she returned to her post, her ears ringing as she punched the keys with renewed fervor.

Arriving at the trailer after her shift, Margaret flopped down in the chair in the living room, rubbing her aching feet and legs. Even with the stockings she wore, each day, she noticed spidery blue veins creating a series of feathery blue lines snaking up her legs. She sighed. Leland would be upset if she kept getting these on her legs.

She'd dozed off in the chair when she heard a car door slam outside. She rustled herself up from the chair, wiping the sleep from her eyes. It was already getting dark, and Nellie had gone home. Maybe it wasn't anyone for her. She pulled back the sheer from the curtain and looked outside.

It was Leland.

After throwing open the door, she clambered down the steps and into his arms, kissing him wildly. "Lee! Why didn't you tell me you were coming home? What a surprise!"

"Stop, stop." He grabbed her arms and set her back.

"What is it? The neighbors won't say anything. They know I'm married." She attempted to draw him closer.

"No." He dropped his arms. "I came to see June."

She cocked her head. "Well, of course you did. And me too."

"Yes, you too." He looked at her, and his gaze made Margaret take a step back. His eyes were blank, soulless, as if the person she had known was gone, replaced by someone she'd never met.

"What's going on, Leland? You're scaring me." She hugged her arms to her chest. "Is something wrong? Are you bringing bad news?"

"Let's go inside." He took her arm, but she wrestled it away.

"No."

"Yes, we don't want to make a scene for the neighbors."

Her voice rose. "A scene. What are you saying?"

She swiveled to see the curtains drop in front of the window next door as Leland pushed past her up the steps. Gennie had stayed over at Mama's for the night, and she had brought June home, who was already tucked in her crib. Leland made his way to the sleeping baby and reached down to pick her up. He held her for a moment, as if memorizing her, then kissed her forehead before setting her back down. Brushing past Margaret, he made his way to the front room, where he stood with his back to her.

"What's going on, Leland?"

He turned and faced her. "I want a divorce."

"What?" She caught herself on the nearest chair.

He rubbed his hands over his face and through his hair. "You know as well as I do that we've never fit. It all just happened so fast."

"What did? What are you saying?" A buzzing sound was growing louder in her brain.

"I-I've met someone. We're in love."

The swiftness of the slap against his cheek surprised Margaret. "How could you!"

He slumped into a chair. "I didn't mean for it to happen. War does strange things to you. You never know if today or tomorrow is going to be your last day on this earth. I want to spend my days with Catherine."

Catherine.

A chill went through Margaret. It was as if by not knowing the woman's name, she didn't exist. The name made her real.

"I refuse! I'm not going to give you a divorce."

"She's going to have my child."

Margaret's stomach clenched. "*We* have a child!"

"I'm sorry. I'll take the blame. I've already told her that I'll have to be the one to bear the adultery charge. She's willing to stand by me."

Margaret's anger boiled over into huge, breaking sobs. She could barely catch her breath as she took in everything he'd said.

"You're hyperventilating. Sit down."

"Don't tell me what to do. You have no right!" She screamed at him before rushing forward and pummeling his chest with her fists. "You have no right." She finally lost her strength, and he set her on the couch, all of her fight gone out of her as the sensation of numbness crept in.

He reached into his pocket and pulled out an envelope. "Here's some money. The housing payment will stop, but this should help until you get on your feet."

She watched as he sat the envelope on the table. "How will I be able to make it with two children and no help? I'm already working and just making ends meet."

"I've discussed it with Catherine, and we would take June."

She shot up from her chair. "Get out. Get out, and never come back. I hate you. I hate you!" She pushed at him, and he hurried out the door. Margaret watched as he backed up the car and drove away, her body shaking with anger.

She went down the narrow hallway that led to the back bedrooms. She walked over to the crib and looked at June, who slept the innocent sleep of babies. Then she went into the kitchen, pulled a scrap of paper from her handbag, and composed a letter.

CHAPTER TWENTY-SIX

Margaret could barely take in everything as her awe of the noise, the smells, the height of the buildings enveloped her. Everywhere she looked, people were rushing past, going somewhere. She'd experienced nothing like it in her life. Maybe she should have stayed inside the train station, but that was where Katie had told her she'd meet her. She set the beat-up satchel at her feet and pulled her embroidered lace handkerchief from her purse to dab her brow.

It had been months since she'd learned her marriage was over and she would have to make a way for herself and her children. It still felt surreal. After seeing if the apartment still had room, Katie had helped her navigate the paperwork for getting into nurse's training.

Arriving after the new year, there was no better way to start off 1945 but with a fresh start. While Margaret hesitated over the boxes that asked her to confirm that she was unmarried and had no children, in the end, she chose to continue the lie. The job at the commissary wouldn't sustain her and the girls. If she could get into training, chances were that she could go back home and find a position in Pensacola.

She'd looked into other work but was met with heads shaking when they asked if she had children. While she hated being away from them when they were still so young, getting a job would affect their future as well. The thought of them growing up in poverty challenged her to move forward and forced her to concentrate. Though she knew that she probably could have done the same thing somewhere closer, she had to take the last chance to do something she wanted before returning to a life of motherhood. Surprisingly, Ma had been able to placate Pa about having the girls stay with them while she went for training. Whatever Ma had said, it'd worked. Plus, with the girls being so young, Margaret doubted they would even notice she was gone.

"Margaret!" Katie hustled down the street toward her, holding onto her hat with one gloved hand while waving with the other. They hugged, and Margaret made to pick up her satchel when a young man grabbed it.

"Stop! That's mine." She reached for it, thinking she was being robbed.

"That's just Tom. Didn't I tell you about him? Oh, we have so much to catch up on now that you're here." She weaved her arm with Margaret's.

He tipped his hat, and when he spoke, his voice held a distinct accent. "Nice to meet you."

"Come on, you two. Stop lollygagging." For such a tiny woman, Katie was a dynamo that cajoled Margaret to follow her. Before she knew it, Katie was pulling her down a set of stairs onto a train platform.

Margaret marveled as trains emerged from the dark tunnel. People would rush off then more on the platform would crowd inside before it shot off again. "What *is* this?"

"The subway." Katie pulled her to a seat inside, and they rode to the sound of the clacking on the tracks, sometimes in darkened tunnels and sometimes on tracks above the streets. At each stop, passengers came and went in a frenzied fashion unlike anything Margaret was accustomed to seeing. The pace in New York was much different than small-town Milton or even Pensacola. Her head swiveled, trying to take it all in.

Finally, Katie patted her hand. "This is our stop."

They exited up the subway steps and stood in a section of town housing and high-rise apartment blocks.

"Hey, Sam." Katie smiled at the doorman, who opened it for her as she swept by, followed by Margaret and Tom. They took the elevator, another new experience for Margaret. Alighting on their floor, Katie thanked the operator, who tipped his cap.

"Come on. I'm beat and could use a drink." Katie fished in her purse for her keys and then let Margaret into a miniscule apartment compared to the exterior of the building. "It's not much, but it's affordable. Of course, if you live on the upper floors, that's where the hoity toity live." Katie pulled out a bottle of gin and motioned to Margaret with it, who declined with a shake of her head.

Margaret went over to the window to watch the people scurrying below. Despite the closed window, the sounds of car horns and other unfamiliar noises filled the apartment. The assault on her senses left her queasy.

That night, as Margaret reflected on the day, she listened to the soft purr of Katie's snores in the bunk above her. The rooms were so tiny that only bunk beds would fit. The other room mirrored theirs and belonged to two other girls who she hadn't met yet.

Margaret thought back over the last few months. After Leland's announcement, things had only gotten worse for her. The money he'd given her didn't last long, and even with her pay from the commissary, she wasn't able to keep up with the trailer rent. Margaret had begged the landlord to give her time to pay, but she was quickly out of money and back home with her parents. She hated every moment of being under the same roof with her father again. He didn't say it outright, but she could tell he blamed her for Leland straying and the divorce. His tone and his support for Leland whenever she would spout off about him told her as much.

While she'd written to Katie on a whim, she'd never expected that she even had a chance in hell of going to New York. Yet every day, she would rush to see if Katie had answered, sure that reading her "no" in print would finally put Margaret out of her misery.

Katie's actual reply was a total surprise. Another girl had dropped out to get married, and she'd been in contact with the head nurse about Margaret. After the suggestion to apply, Margaret had succeeded in gaining Doc Albert's recommendation. The news that she'd been accepted gave her a rush of pleasure. But it was one thing to apply for the training and something else to actually go there.

With Ma taking care of the girls with Nellie's help, she would get the training she needed then find a position in a doctor's office or the hospital when she completed the course. That would give her a stable income. First a widow then a divorcee, her plan had to work. She'd asked Franny about it, and while her sister hadn't been keen on Margaret leaving her children, she, too, saw it as a good opportunity. She'd also hinted that Bud was still a possibility. He was off somewhere in the South Pacific, and Margaret had no desire to wed over a telephone line like so many of her schoolmates had done. No, she had to learn to stand on her own two feet.

Horns honked outside, causing Margaret to jump. She punched her pillow, trying but failing to fall asleep, the cacophony of the city keeping her awake.

~

Training began shortly after she arrived, and it was rigorous. Sarge wrote to them, though much of her letters had black through them or were otherwise nondescript. But it was one letter that came in May that most troubled her. The letter was stained with water marks— most likely tears, and her anguish was clear in the note.

I've been at work for days and nights, tending to the men who survived. The loss. I thought we were safe here. I can't even—the rest was blacked out. Only the last words remained: *Will this horrible war ever end?*

Margaret felt totally helpless. She couldn't do anything for Sarge, and she knew that if the nurses found out she had children, she would be kicked out of the program. So she kept her head down, revealed little of her past except that her husband had been killed in the war, and put her nose to the grindstone, learning as much as she could. Every day, she prayed it wouldn't be her last in the program. But her natural aptitude with memory and math led her to working alongside the pharmacy doctor, and she gained a wealth of information on various drugs and protocols.

She lay in bed on Saturday, exhausted from the week, when Katie threw a pillow at her. "Come on. Let's go to Central Park."

Margaret groaned and pulled the pillow over her head. She ached from standing on her feet and rushing through wards, but the thought of an outing even in the chill weather gave her a burst of energy. She dressed quickly and grabbed an apple to eat. She was already an old hand at riding the subway, and soon, they were at the park, sitting on the grass, shoes and socks set to the side, enjoying the brief winter sunshine.

But overhead, Margaret spied a dark cloud on the horizon. It mimicked how she felt inside, where dread had been forming over the last weeks, rearing its ugly head. Even though she'd been careful with the extra money Franny had told her to use and what she'd saved from the commissary, it was dwindling. Prices in the city were much higher than at home. It wouldn't be long before she would need to pay rent again, plus cover food for the month. She was also missing her girls. Some nights, her pillow was damp with tears as their faces came to mind. She couldn't have fathomed how much she would miss them.

Maybe coming to New York had been a terrible mistake. She shut her eyes and let the sun hit her face before a shadow passed over her.

She opened her eyes as a couple of men strode by. One had dark hair, and it reminded her of Joseph. She'd been so busy with training that she'd forgotten Joseph would most likely be back in New York as well.

She hopped up and found Katie. "Hey, I want to find a grocery store. Can you help me?"

"A grocery store? Whatever for?"

"Well, I want to see if a friend's there."

Katie tilted her head to the side. "By any chance, is this friend a member of the male sex?"

Margaret blushed.

"So he is!" Katie laughed, hooking her arm with Margaret's. "Let's go. I can't wait to meet this mystery man."

They went back to the apartment so Margaret could rummage through her things to find the name and address of his father's store. In the end, the day got away from them, so they made plans to go the following weekend.

Margaret wasn't sure why she was even going to see Joseph, but she couldn't deny she had thought him attractive. Of course, he probably had a girlfriend or even a wife. But it would be an outing.

Tom joined the pair, then they took the train across town, finding themselves in a grocery store with people buzzing about. Tom and Katie wandered off to find some cookies. Margaret was at a loss what to do next. She could ask the owner if he had a son. She glanced down at a stack of fruit, picking up an orange and basking in the sweet smell, which reminded her of home.

"Well, this is a surprise," a male voice interrupted her memory.

Margaret turned, and there he was. "Joseph!"

"In the flesh."

"You look so different."

"No more uniform. Only suits now. Turns out, my running and jumping days are over now with these pins in my legs. Even desk work had its issues. Not made for that type of job. They discharged me, so I'm back helping Pop."

Margaret couldn't help but notice how smart he looked in his navy suit with a tie and polished black shoes.

"You here by yourself?"

"No. Katie is with me, though I don't know where she went. You told me to look you up if I came to New York, so here I am."

"Understandable. It's a good day for an outing with this nice weather."

She felt suddenly shy in front of him. "Yes."

"What are you and Leland doing Friday night?"

"Friday night?"

"Yes, you know, like the last day before the weekend." He smirked.

"Well..." She held up her left hand, sans ring.

"Oh, sorry. My condolences. Leland was a good guy."

Margaret had a different idea on that after he'd treated her like dirt, but she simply nodded. Once she started lying, it was so much easier to continue down that path.

"Um, well, would it be wrong to still ask if you're available on

Friday? We could all go out for dinner or something. You can tell me how long you'll be in town and what you're doing here."

"Nurse training."

"Is that a polite brush-off? I can take a hint."

"No, that's not what I meant. I was simply saying what I'm doing up here. You told me to stop by." She felt foolish for ever coming there.

He smiled at her. "I'm glad you did. Now what do you say about Friday? Any plans?"

"Nothing." She kicked herself for not acting like she needed to check her calendar.

"Great. How's about—"

Katie sidled up to them, carrying a few cans of potted meat in her arms.

"Hi, I'm Joe." He held out his hand to her, and Margaret ignored the googly eyes Katie made when he turned away. After introductions were made, Joseph said, "I was asking Margaret if she wanted to go to the club this Friday. Yous guys could come too."

"Oh, Margie. That sounds fun. Let's do it!" Katie pulled at her arm.

"Okay, I suppose."

"Margie, huh? You look like a Margie. Okay if I call you that too?" He reached for her hand and put his lips to it.

She shrugged. "If I can call you Joe."

"It's a deal. Till Friday, then." He tipped his hat and walked away.

"Wowzer. He's a hunk." Katie nudged her.

"Hey, I'm standing right here!" Tom gestured.

Katie stood on her tiptoes and kissed him on the cheek. "And you're my hunk. Now come on, you two. I think it's going to rain, and I don't want my shoes to get wet." They'd just made it to the subway entrance when the downpour started.

"Whew. Looks like we made it just in time." Katie spoke before taking Tom's arm toward the trains.

Did I? Margaret wondered. Maybe the clouds were a warning to her. Ma had always been superstitious about weather events. Then she shook her head and chuckled to herself. The last thing she needed was to be illogical. It was only rain.

CHAPTER TWENTY-SEVEN

Margaret took her time dressing even though she would be going out with a bunch of people rather than on an official date. She chose the only smart suit she had, the one she'd worn when she'd married Leland. Tom arrived and was waiting on Katie to put on her hat when Margaret realized she'd left her gloves downstairs when she'd picked up the mail.

Skipping the elevator, she scurried down the stairs. As she rounded the corner, she spotted them on the floor, smudged with dirt and grime. She would have to go without gloves unless Katie had another pair. As she turned around, a little boy rushed by, his hand in his mother's, and Margaret stepped back to prevent a collision.

Unfortunately, that put her in contact with a radiator. Before she knew it, she moved forward and felt the pull on her stocking.

No. Not today, of all days.

Then came the familiar sensation of the stockings laddering on her calf.

No, no, no.

She pulled her skirt up to see the damage. There would be no way to mend them or stop the destruction. Her lip quivered with a mix of anger and upset. Other than the white stockings she wore with her nurse uniform, she had no more nylons. She didn't want to show up in socks either. Maybe she could borrow a pair from the other girls.

Margaret rushed over to the elevator and climbed inside. The doors opened, and as another couple moved out, she shot past the elevator operator, who bore a confused look on his face. He held up his finger, but Margaret shot him a look that stopped him. He punched a button, the elevator doors shutting behind her. She didn't have time to listen to whatever he had to say.

She rushed down the hall to clasp at the doorknob. The door wouldn't budge. She hurried to grab her keys, wondering if her friends had already left without her.

The key wouldn't fit the lock. Her brows knit together. She jammed the key harder, but it wouldn't go in. She tried again. *Something must be wrong with my key.*

Finally, in frustration, she banged on the door. "Katie, let me in. The key's not working."

As she waited, Margaret agonized over the destroyed stocking on her leg, most likely beyond repair and only good for holding onions or potatoes or donating it to the war effort.

The door cracked open.

"Will you look at this?" She gestured to the rip. "Of all the times—" She looked up, and her mouth dropped open.

A familiar woman with wavy chestnut hair stood in front of her in a floral silk dressing gown.

"What is it, honey? Cat got your tongue?"

"I thought—I, um, my apartment." She pointed down to the floor. "I—" She lost control, and tears slid down her face. She'd made a fool of herself, and no one would believe her when she told them who had witnessed it.

The woman appraised her with large, saucerlike eyes. "Honey, we all have those days. Come in. Don't stand in the hall. Close the door after you." The woman's voice had a depth to it yet was also lyrical in tone.

Margaret watched as the woman lit a new cigarette off the one in her hand. She inhaled deeply then blew out a heavy cloud of smoke before she gracefully sat on a Chesterfield sofa, her arm along its back. This apartment's living room was bigger than all the rooms in their apartment combined. Glass tables with bouquets of flowers and crystal ashtrays sat next to a magnificent fireplace flanked by two upholstered chairs.

"Out with it. What's got you all hot and bothered?" The woman commanded with her hand.

Margaret swallowed. She searched her head for a lump and wondered if she was dreaming.

Finally, she turned and lifted her skirt to show the laddered stockings. Finding her voice, she said, "I have a date tonight. I'm supposed to leave soon. I must have missed getting off on our floor. I'm sorry to have bothered—"

The woman's deep voice bellowed, "Ethel!"

A maid, complete with a black dress with a white apron and cap, appeared. "Yes, ma'am?"

"Miss—what's your name, dear?" She waved at Margaret with the hand holding the cigarette.

"Margaret."

"That's a mouthful for a little nothing like you." She took another puff of her cigarette then picked some filter lint off her tongue.

"Some people call me Margie."

"Margie. I like it." She rose from the sofa and went over to the drink cart, where she poured two glasses of brown liquid. "Ethel, this young lady needs a pair of nylons. Get her some, won't you?"

The woman nodded. "Yes, ma'am. Right away." The woman scurried from the room.

Margaret pinched her hand. *Ouch.* Yes, she really was in the presence of a famous actress somehow. She swallowed again, trying to keep from gawking at the woman.

"Here." She handed Margaret a drink. "Cheers." She clinked her glass with Margaret's and took a swig.

Margaret followed but choked and coughed at the liquid, which didn't taste as sweet as the one she'd received from Irma so many years ago.

The woman coughed too then laughed. "Sorry, dear. Forgot to ask if you take soda with your scotch. Another?"

Margaret cleared her throat. "No, thank you." Still stunned to be in the presence of a real life movie star, she was flummoxed on what to say. Wait until she told Katie.

Ethel reappeared with a pair of stockings. "Will these do,

madam?"

She waved with her hand, cigarette ash perilously close to falling off onto the floor. She simply tapped it against an overflowing ashtray before lighting another cigarette from the stub of the one in her hand. After taking another deep inhale, she looked at Margaret. "Smoke?"

"No, thank you."

"They keep you thin, you know. Plus, they helped me get this voice." She came and walked around Margaret, surveying her.

"Not bad, but you know what that Windsor woman says—you can never be too thin or too rich." She threw back her head and laughed as Margaret gawked.

Perching herself on the edge of the sofa, she surveyed Margaret. "Where are you going?"

"I think it's some club with a number."

"Twenty-one?" Her eyebrow arched.

Margaret shrugged. "I guess."

"What are you wearing?"

When Margaret didn't respond right away, she said, "Not this!" She waved her hand up and down." No, that will never do. Take off that jacket."

Margaret did, revealing a simple white blouse with a tie at the throat. "Well, that'll have to do. For God's sake, take down those pins in your hair. Men want to imagine running their fingers through your curls."

Margaret did as she had been told, pulling the pins that had held her hair out of her face during her work. Her soft auburn curls fell forward, framing her heart-shaped face.

"Yes, that's better. Now go in there and change into those stockings, and we'll find you a jacket."

When Margaret returned, Ethel was holding a jacket with a large fur collar. She also noted a pair of heels with an ankle strap next to the shoes she'd been wearing.

Margaret slid into the heels and felt tissue in the toe boxes.

"See what you think." The woman waved her over to the full-length mirror by the door.

Ethel set a small hat with a veil on her head just past her victory roll, securing it with a pin.

The movie star had joined her by the mirror. "Now the last thing every woman needs..." She revealed a gold lipstick case, and a swipe of red was drawn on her lips. Next, Ethel handed her a tissue paper. "Pat."

The actress handed over the lipstick to Margaret before she swept away, the robe flowing out behind her. "Now you're ready for the hunt. Right, Ethel?"

The maid nodded.

The woman laughed with that deep-seated tone again. "Men always think they're the ones on the hunt for prey. But it's us women who draw them slowly into the snare." She poured another scotch before turning back to Margaret. "Have fun."

"Thank you, Mrs.—"

"Just call me Bette."

CHAPTER TWENTY-EIGHT

"Where've you been? We waited forever!" Katie shouted over the noise of the club. "The girls said you'd left, so we thought you went ahead without us. I'm a bit miffed. You could have let us know."

"I'm sorry. I meant to go with you. But I got a run in my stocking and then—I'll tell you later."

Katie considered the smart jacket with fur-trimmed collar Margaret wore. "Where did you get that jacket and hat and—"

"You wouldn't believe me if I told you. There's Joe." She waved, and he walked over to her.

"Well, well. You're looking mighty fine tonight, Margie." He offered his arm, and she noticed him glancing at her locks.

Who knew that flowing locks did a number on men? Margaret had never really paid attention to "reeling in prey," as the movie star had put it. Though she might have done it a bit with Leland if she was truthful. But at that moment, all she knew was she felt sophisticated and beautiful for the first time in her life. It was as if she had been a child before and, in a moment, had become a woman. She was going to enjoy that evening with every ounce of her being.

Margaret marveled at how well-known her date was as men shook his hand with a fervent, "Joey, good to see you." Others held glasses up to him from tables in the corners, thick with cigarette smoke clouds gathered over their heads. Women would stop by their table, draping themselves over his back, whispering into his ear, their disregard for her presence next to him blatant. And though he poured on the charm, Joey's gaze kept returning to her.

"Sorry I can't dance the faster dances with you. But when a slower one comes on, hows about we give it a go?"

"Yes, that sounds nice." She smiled sweetly. It would be good to move around, as Bette's jacket had grown hot and tight. She unbuttoned the top button, enjoying a bit of cooling. When Joe pulled a pack of Lucky Strikes from his pocket, tamped them on the table, then offered her one, she accepted it as if it were her standard practice. He handed it to her before cracking open his gold lighter with his initials on it. Trying her best to impersonate Bette, she took in a deep inhale, which immediately caused a coughing fit. It had to be the most horrible thing she'd ever tasted. Joe snapped his fingers, and a waiter hurried over with a drink.

She took a swig, thinking it was water, but sputtered even more when the juniper brew slid down her throat. "I think I—"

Katie and Tom had returned to the table, and she immediately gauged Margaret's distress. "Gentlemen, us gals need to go powder our noses."

The men rose from their seats while Katie led Margaret to the ladies' room. Inside the lounge, she pulled off Margaret's jacket and sat her on the lounge's sofa. "You look green around the gills. I'll be back in a minute." She returned with wet towels, which she applied to Margaret's forehead and neck. "Better, or do you think you're still going to be sick?"

"Better. Thanks, Katie." She leaned back and closed her eyes, taking in deep breaths. Finally, she said, "That stuff is disgusting."

"Which one? The cigarettes or the gin?"

"Both!"

They giggled, and Katie stroked the fur on the jacket. "This is stunning. Seriously, you look so glamourous. Joseph and half the men in here are goners. Where did you get it?"

Two women walked by, and Margaret could've sworn they'd flashed her a look of contempt. *What did I do to deserve that?* She focused on Katie and lowered her voice. "You're never going to believe it." She lowered her voice as she shared the woman's name.

"What?" Katie's eyes grew wide. She punched at Margaret playfully. "Oh, you're pulling my leg." She giggled.

"It's the truth. I missed our floor because I was so upset because I'd laddered my stockings. She offered me a drink and helped me out. She said my jacket wasn't right for here, so she let me borrow this one, plus the hat and the shoes. I had to pinch myself to see if it was real and not a dream." Margaret pointed to the red spot on her hand as proof. "Aren't these shoes divine?" She twisted her foot back and forth so Katie could admire them.

"Can I try them on?"

Margaret slipped them off and Katie put them on, though they were too big for her. "I can't wait to tell everyone—"

"No. You can't do that. This was a favor to me. You can't tell anyone."

Katie flopped on the couch. "Margie. What good is it if we can't tell anyone? This is such a big deal—"

"No. Cross your heart."

She slumped back against the seat and stuck out her bottom lip. "You're no fun."

"Sorry, but it's only right. Anyway, no one would believe you."

Katie sighed. "That's probably true. Okay, fine. Now let's powder our noses for real and get back. I want to dance all night."

When they returned refreshed, Margaret ordered a scotch and soda with a glass of water. When Tom asked if she would like to dance, she turned to Joseph. "Okay with you?"

He hesitated. "Sure." As Margaret stood, she noticed a pulsing tic by the corner of his eye. He caught her hand as she moved toward Tom. "Just this once."

After the dance with Tom, another man came over and cut in, so she danced with him too. Finally, she made her way back to the table, laughing.

Joseph stood as she took her seat next to him. She smiled at him, but he bent toward her, nostrils flaring. "Are you trying to make a fool of me?"

"No. What do you mean?"

"Trying to make me jealous? Are you like all the rest?"

"Joe, I don't know what you mean, but you're ruining a perfectly nice evening. I'm not trying to make you anything, so don't insinuate I am."

He looked at her with sharp, deep-set eyes that were almost black, but then his jaw relaxed. He smoothed down his slicked black hair. "Of course. Margie, let's get out of here."

"Okay." Happy to escape the enclosed confines of the space, Margaret kissed Katie on the cheek but avoided doing the same with Tom.

As Joseph said goodbye to some of the men, Tom approached her, whispering, "You don't want to get involved with him, Margie. I've heard things."

Before she had time to question him further, Joe returned. "Cabbie's waiting outside."

They drove for a while and came to a large store. "We'll just be a minute. Wait for us."

The driver nodded. Joseph exited the yellow cab, and he held out his hand to her. She met him on the sidewalk, happy for the jacket, as there was a nip in the air.

"This is my pop's building. One day, it'll be mine. I have influence in this town, and I'm going places."

She didn't know what he wanted her to say. "It's very nice."

His nostrils flared again, but he kept his voice in check. "It's more than nice." He went over to the cab and opened the door.

Margaret slid across the seat, wondering at Joe's reactions. Once inside, he instructed the cab driver to take them home. Finally, they pulled up in front of her apartment. He paid the driver and stood, waiting.

"Well, thank you for a wonderful evening." She put out her hand.

"Aren't you going to invite me up for a drink?" He reached over and rubbed her arm.

"Sorry, but my roommates are sleeping, and we only have a kitchenette. It's really small, plus we don't have any booze in the apartment."

"I'm sure we could think of something. Maybe your room, perhaps?"

The cheek of him. "I share a room with Katie, and she'll be home soon. I think we better say goodnight." She stuck out her hand again.

"Not even a kiss?"

"We don't even know each other that well." She stepped back before changing her mind and planting a kiss on his cheek. Then she turned and scurried into the apartment building like a mouse in front of a cat.

Inside, she flew up the stairs to the next floor then headed over to the window. Joseph lingered on the pavement below, lighting a cigarette before glancing up toward the building. Thankfully, she could hide behind a large curtain on the landing's window. He pitched the spent match to the sidewalk then set off down the street.

Emotions roiled in her chest. Yes, he was charming, funny, and handsome, but there was something else. A hint of danger. Whether that made him more attractive to her, she didn't know.

~

The following day, Margaret spent time following a nurse around the floor, making beds, and changing dressings. The monotonous work gave her time to think back over the events of last night at the club. Joe's changing moods and Tom's mysterious warning bothered her.

After her shift, she headed home, where she cleaned and polished the shoes, brushed the jacket, and wiped down the hat, placing it in tissue paper. She'd washed the nylons the night before, and they had dried while she was at work. Even though she barely had enough money until her next paycheck, she bought some flowers on her way home.

Gathering everything into her arms, she made her way to the elevator and into the hallway leading to the star's apartment. That time, she noticed the buzzer, and Ethel answered the door. "Hello, miss."

"Hello, Ethel. I wanted to bring these things back and give these—"

"Bring them back?"

"Yes, the things I borrowed."

Ethel shook her head. "No, you keep them now."

"I couldn't!"

The recognizable voice carried to them. "Who is it, Ethel?"

"Come in." Ethel ushered Margaret in the door, closing it behind her. Following Ethel, Margaret made her way to the large living room.

"Margie. To what—" She took a drag of her cigarette then blew out more smoke. "—do I owe this pleasure?" She waved a glass at

Margaret. With her other hand, she threw some papers down on the couch next to her. "Do I look like a Mildred to you, Margie? No, I don't think so."

Margaret blinked, but it seemed that the actress wasn't speaking to her.

"You have to make tough decisions in life sometimes," she went on. "No, I need a role I can really sink my teeth into. Margo, yes. You have to wait for the best." She paused long enough to acknowledge Margaret's presence again. "Don't forget it. There are times you have to turn down the good to get the best." Her gaze centered on the flowers in Margaret's hands.

"I wanted to return these to you and bring you these flowers as a thank you." Looking at the large bouquets situated around the room, Margaret felt foolish at her small offering.

"Wonderful." She took the flowers like they were the most beautiful blooms she'd ever seen, pressed her nose to them as she closed her eyes, then handed them to Ethel. "Please put these in a vase on my dressing table."

The woman took them and left.

"Follow me. I have a bit of time before I leave. Do you enjoy the theater?"

Margaret walked behind Bette, still holding the jacket and other items. Margaret simply shrugged. "I've never been." There was no way she could afford tickets to an off-Broadway production, much less a Broadway play.

"If you're in New York, you simply must go to the theater. I'll leave you some tickets for you and your friends. You just tell me the day, and I'll take care of it." The woman sat in front of a vanity with a large mirror.

She could barely contain herself. "Oh, thank you! I don't know what to say."

"I think you just did. Now tell me about your date last night."

"It was nice but a bit of a bumpy ride."

"Hmmm." She took a swig of the drink. "You don't say."

Margaret quickly shared the highlights of the evening, then thanked her again for the items she'd borrowed.

"Listen, I know men. Do you want this fella to pursue you?"

"Honestly, I don't know." Margaret hadn't thought that far ahead. *Am I even ready for another relationship?*

"If you don't, then cut that fish loose, honey."

"I do like him. I—this is going to sound horrible—I just thought we might have some fun. I'm sorry, I can't even believe I'm talking to you about this."

"Honey, women don't need to apologize for wanting to have a good time. Men certainly don't!" She turned back to stare at her visage in the mirror. "Here's what's going to happen. He's going to ask you out on another date. But you're too busy. Maybe another time." She picked up a mascara cake box and brush from the vanity as Margaret waited.

"Then I say yes for another time?"

"No. You make him come back and ask again." She held the small brush in her hand, swiping it across the black cake.

"How do I know when to say yes?"

"When he asks what you want." She stubbed out her Vantage cigarette. "Now, I have to get ready. William will be here soon. And take those things with you. I don't want them." Without a goodbye or any form of dismissal, Bette left the room.

Ethel appeared and guided Margaret to the door, which clicked softly behind her. Margaret stared at the door. So many doors had opened then closed in her life, each containing a new experience or version of herself. It was the shutting of those doors that always broke her heart.

Margaret took the stairs down to her apartment, where she carefully put the gifts away in her closet. If she was living in a dream, she was afraid of what would happen once she finally woke up. After heating some chicken noodle soup on the stove, a knock came on the door.

"Phone call for you!" a neighbor yelled through the door.

Margaret turned off the stove and made her way down the hall to where the phone sat next to a chair. She picked up the black receiver. "Hello?"

"Margie, it's Joseph. Joe."

Her heart jumped, but she remained calm with her voice. "Yes?"

"We had fun last night, didn't we?"

"Yes." She added, "I suppose."

Silence. That second part had thrown him.

He cleared his throat. "I was thinking we could go out to dinner. This Friday."

"This Friday? Oh, sorry, I'm busy that day."

"You are?"

"Yes, sorry." She twisted her fingers in her hair.

"What about Saturday night?"

"I can't." She recalled what Bette had said as she left about no explanations, controlling the narrative. "Why don't you call me either Sunday or next week, and we can figure out another date."

"Well, I—"

"Okay, talk then. Goodbye." She set the receiver down on the cradle, hoping she hadn't made a terrible mistake. He probably would have taken her out somewhere nice for dinner. She stood up and smoothed her dress. *Too late now.*

The next day, when she returned home from work, Katie squealed as she grabbed her by the hands. "Margie, look what came for you a while ago!"

On the kitchen table stood a long box. She unwrapped the red ribbon and lifted the lid to reveal a dozen red roses. She stared at the beautiful flowers. She'd never received store-bought flowers from a gentleman in her life.

"Aren't you going to look at the card?"

Margaret slid the white linen card from inside the tiny envelope. *Until Sunday. Joe.*

She picked up the roses, and as she gathered them, some stray thorns caught her skin. She quickly pulled her hand away as drops of blood formed at the cuts. Shaking off the pain, she used a paring knife and clipped the thorns the florist must've missed. "That's better." She poured water into a jug and set the flowers inside it.

She stepped back, admiring the roses as her soup grew cold, her finger throbbing from the unseen thorns.

CHAPTER TWENTY-NINE

Despite his grand gesture and note assuring her that he would call, Sunday came and went with no word from Joseph. Maybe he'd seen through her little ruse and was playing with her as well.

He finally phoned, but it was only to let Margaret know he would be gone until late summer. As she hung up, Margaret realized that it was probably good—it would give her time to think about her future and that of her girls. So many things would be changing with Germany being defeated. A growing sense of hope was spreading, and Margaret felt it too.

Joe called her weekly, and they would spend as much time as possible talking until the operator would come on, ending their calls. Every time she hung up the phone, her happiness was short-lived as she thought of any future with Joe. Yet she couldn't help but acknowledge the butterflies she felt every time they talked. In some ways, his being gone for business had helped them move away from the physical attraction to learn more about each other as individuals. He made her laugh, and she ended the calls with a big grin on her face.

Weeks passed, and the oppressive August heat caused the air

inside the apartment to be stifling. Margaret decided to head out for a walk on her day off. She found herself once again at the oasis in the middle of the city. Women in light cotton dresses pushed strollers while fathers tickled toddlers, who scurried away on tiny, fat legs.

Her chest ached as she recalled the simple night-time rituals of baths and reading of stories with Gennie or rocking June as she slept. Maybe she only treasured that time with her children because it had been taken away. But it hadn't been *taken* by anyone. She'd been too stubborn, too set on living life on her terms, to consider the emotional toll it would take on her and her girls. *Do they miss me too?* She needed to be able to be with them again. She hoped her determination to succeed hadn't come at a terrible cost to her children.

After a long walk, she arrived home to a quiet apartment, where she ate leftover potato soup along with bread and mayo while she thumbed through a *McCall's* women's magazine—Katie would pick up old issues from the waiting room that would otherwise be thrown away. The free entertainment helped ease the night's boredom.

Margaret opened the window next to her bed, allowing a soft breeze to come in from the fire escape. Soon, her mind went back to the children and the families she'd watched in the park. A knot rose in her chest, climbing into her throat. Even the letters Nellie wrote about the girls' antics only brought her pain instead of comfort.

The pain of regret, of being homesick, and of missing her children overtook her, and sobs wrenched from her. It wouldn't be too much longer before she could receive her nursing certificate, but even if she got it, she couldn't imagine anyone hiring a single mother with two children. She had failed as a wife, a mother, even as a daughter. Margaret curled up into a tight ball, grief overtaking her.

She barely had enough money for the rent that month. She would have to scrape by on food, using the chicken she'd bought to make broth. With the noodles and a can of mixed peas and corn, she could stretch out her meals with soup for a while. She sighed. *What am I doing in New York, so far from everyone and everything I know?*

She had thought too highly of herself, of her capabilities, of what she could do or become. And then there was Joe. *Who am I kidding? He won't want a ready-made family.* Her tears soaked her pillow until she fell into a deep sleep.

When Margaret woke, dusk was falling. The buildings usually blocked out the sun long before it disappeared, so she'd gotten used to the early darkness. The sounds of taxis honking, people's animated voices, and dogs barking came to her ears. She cranked down the window and pulled the cord to lower the bent venetian blinds. Katie was traveling to Boston to visit Tom's parents. Margaret figured they would soon be wed, and she was happy for them. They were a good fit, unlike what she and Leland had been. The other roommates stuck pretty much to themselves, so it was rare they even had conversations beyond basic pleasantries. They'd gone out for the evening, leaving Margaret even more alone and despondent.

A ruckus outside her door caught her attention. She opened it to find her neighbors in the hallway, dancing and laughing.

"What's going on?" she asked the lady who lived next door.

"Didn't you hear? Japan's surrendered! The war's over. My boy's coming home!" The older woman took out a hankie and wiped her eyes.

All at once, she was pulled into their revelry. A man picked Margaret up and twirled her around. A little girl came up and took her hand. "Isn't this the best day ever?"

"Yes. Yes it is." She scooped the child into a hug, drinking in her smell of baby powder and milk.

Then a familiar voice gave her pause. "Hello." It was Joe, his hat in his hands, looking dapper in his suit.

"When did you get back?"

"Earlier today. I was going to call, but the phones were tied up. Then I heard the news. I decided to come on over."

"We won. I can't believe it's finally over." She smiled up at him, tears in her eyes.

He leaned down and kissed her, and she allowed the emotions of the day to melt away into that one kiss. He put his cheek next to hers, took her hair in his hand, then looked into her eyes.

"Margaret." He gathered her in his arms. "What do you want, Margaret?" He bent her head back, kissing her again. "It's yours."

She breathed in his cologne as she rested her head on his chest. *What do I want?* She wanted a husband, a home, and her family, all together. But she also wanted freedom, independence, and autonomy. Each pulled her in different directions, leaving her torn with how to move forward. But for that moment, the war was over. Life could go back to normal.

"I want this moment to never end."

~

After the excitement had died down and people mellowed from all the liquor and wine of the celebration, Margaret sat alone in her room. Joe had left hours earlier, asking if she would go with him to dinner with his family. She'd agreed before heading back up to her apartment.

A mix of giddiness and fear had combined to give her a horrible headache. She couldn't marry Joe. Not with two children. She would have to tell him and soon. She knew he thought Leland had died. And when he'd seen Gennie back in Florida, Joe probably believed she'd actually been Margaret's little sister. A divorced woman with two children wouldn't be on any man's list of desires.

She couldn't go further with her deception. Her attraction to him reminded her of her feelings for Eugene, but they went beyond that. Despite her strong feelings, she wasn't sure she wanted another marriage when the last one had ended so horribly. They would have one more day together, and then she would tell him about her girls. After their dinner. She knew it would mean the end of their romance, but she had no choice.

~

"Come in, come in." Mrs. Martin, a plump, short woman, motioned to Margaret, who was escorted in by a protective Joseph, his arm around her waist. Smells of garlic and onions filled the air, causing Margaret's stomach to rumble.

"Sit. Sit." The woman waved to the living room.

Margaret sat on a sofa covered in plastic as more people poured into the room, welcoming her with kisses on both cheeks. She laughed at the familiarity, not knowing what to do or say.

When Joe's mother bustled into the room, Margaret stood. "Something smells delicious, Mrs. Martin. May I help do anything?"

"No, you sit." She returned to the kitchen, leaving Margaret with other family members, who smiled at her now and again but were busy trading stories with Joe.

Later, they gathered over a spread of heaping bowls of spaghetti, meatballs, and a large plate of olives, salami, and peppers that she'd never seen before. They poured a red wine called Chianti into her glass.

Mr. Martin had come in and welcomed Margaret with the same cheek kissing. A large pan of lasagna was placed on the table, its savory smell lingering in the air.

Mr. Martin regaled the table with stories of customers. "So, I says, 'That'll be sixty-nine cents for them.' My clerk says, 'But you charged Mrs. Cruthers forty-nine cents for the same amount.' And I says, 'But she said she wanted toe-mah-toes, and Mrs. Cruthers wanted toe-may-toes.'" He sliced the air with his knife, and the table laughed.

Later, after everyone had eaten the hearty food and the table had been cleared, Joe Senior turned to Margaret. "Why you no marry my boy yet? He needs a good wife. I like you."

Margaret blushed. "I haven't known your son that long."

He shook his head. "No. He told me about meeting this beautiful girl down in Florida, and he couldn't get you out of his mind. And here you are. So when you going to marry the bum?"

"Pops, enough already." Joe pulled out a cigarette and lit it, puffing smoke up into the air.

"I can vouch for my boy. He's my firstborn. He gets everything when I—" He ran a finger across his throat.

"Franco Joseph, don't." Mrs. Martin crossed herself and kissed her fingers. "Don't tempt fate."

"You'll want for nothing. I'll make sure of it." Joe's father took her hand and kissed it while gazing at her, a strange look in his eyes that suddenly made Margaret uncomfortable. She smiled and pulled her hands into her lap.

"Joe doesn't know everything about me." She clasped her hands.

"What's to know? He can take care of you. In return, you can give him sturdy sons."

If the two daughters she already had were any sign of her ability to produce a son, that might not happen, but she instead focused her attention on drinking from her wine goblet, the warmth relaxing her.

At the end of their visit, Margaret and Joe bid their goodbyes to his family. He drove her home but pulled up by the alley instead of in front of the apartment block. A set of large trees sheltered them. He reached over and took her in his arms, and she yielded to his kisses. To be his wife, she could release her constant worries, but she knew she had to tell him about the girls. His hands moved over her body, and though she wanted to give in to her desire, she stopped him, yanking open her car door. "I can't."

"Let's get married." His voice was husky with lust.

"No. I can't." She rushed off, tears streaming down her face.

Glad that he hadn't followed her, Margaret took the stairs, avoiding the elevator and the inquisitive look from its operator, who held the door for her. Inside the apartment, she dodged her roommates and went directly into her room. Thankfully, Katie was still out, so she had the space to herself.

Pacing the tiny room, she went through the various scenarios in her head, but they all came back to one fact. She couldn't marry Joe no matter how much she wanted to. She needed to go home and be with her children. She shouldn't get involved with anyone, no matter how he made her feel inside. She had to finish her training and get back to her girls. Maybe it was time to admit defeat when it came to men.

She plopped down on her bed and laid back on it, staring at nothing. Later, she was woken by Katie, who was shaking her arm. "Margie, are you ill?"

Margaret blinked and gazed up at her. "No, I'm fine."

"Well, you don't look fine. Why are you still in your dress and shoes?"

"I must have fallen asleep after I got back." She swept her legs over the side and buried her head in her hands. Looking up at Katie, she said, "I need to tell you something."

Katie sat next to her on the bed and took Margaret's hand. "You know you can tell me anything. I'm your friend."

"You may not want to be my friend after what I tell you. I've lied to you."

Katie sat back against the wall. "Spill. It can't be as bad as all that."

Margaret poured her heart out. About Eugene, about her children, about Leland. "I've been living a lie. You must hate me."

Katie gathered her up in a warm embrace, smoothing her hair. "I don't hate you. I couldn't hate anyone. Certainly not you. Fact is, I have my own secret to share."

Margaret cocked her head and waited.

"Tom and I got married."

"What?" Margaret squealed before Katie motioned for her to lower her voice.

"A few days ago. It was spur of the moment. Tom had a fare that took a shine to him, and he's going to be his driver. There's an apartment over the garage where we'll live, and I found a job at a local school, where I will be their nurse. They are okay with married women as they struggle to find help in more rural areas."

"Tom doesn't care that you'll be working outside of the home?"

"No, he says that as long as I'm happy, then that's what he wants. But who knows what will happen when the children come along? His job gives him lots of time to read while he's waiting on Mr.—um, I better not say that." She made a face.

"Don't worry. I understand. Go on."

"Anyway, he's learning everything he can about the automotive business. He wants to have his own company. He thinks that in the years to come, every household is going to have a car, maybe even two."

Margaret didn't want to burst Katie's bubble on families all having automobiles, so she said nothing.

"You're moving out?"

"Yes, plus I'm almost finished with classes. Once Tom serves his notice, we can move into the apartment. Oh, Margie, I'm so excited and scared all at the same time!"

"You sneaky…" She laughed as she hit Katie's shoulder, and they both fell back onto the bed, hitting their heads on the wall.

In unison, they cried out, "Ouch!" Chuckling, they lay down, facing each other on the tiny single bed.

"I have to say, I won't miss this small bunk. I can't tell you how many times I've hit my head on the wall or ceiling climbing up there." She pushed up and looked at Margaret. "What are you going to do now?"

"I don't know." She crossed her arms.

"I feel you at least owe Joe an explanation. Don't leave him hanging."

"I guess you're right. But we need to celebrate. And I have just the thing. When's Tom's next day off? Because we're going to a Broadway play."

"Really?" Katie clapped her hands together. "But how?"

"I know someone." She winked.

After securing the performance tickets, she called Joe, unsure of what reception she'd receive after their last meeting. She looked at her nails. She'd almost bitten them down to the quick, leaving the cuticles raw and red.

Finally, she'd gotten hold of him and told him about Katie and Tom, asking if he would go with her as her date to the show. He didn't seem keen on the invitation at first, so she promised to give him a proper explanation on why she couldn't marry him.

The evening of the play, the group enjoyed an early dinner before the show, compliments of Joe as a wedding gift. As the champagne flowed, the tension finally broke between her and Joe, leaving them laughing and enjoying the evening.

Arriving at the theater, they made their way to their seats. The musical was enjoyable, but Margaret grew anxious as the evening waned, knowing she would have to tell Joe the truth and lose him forever. Her life in New York was not to be. After the refusal of a nightcap, Tom and Katie said their goodbyes.

"Should we get a cab?" Joe asked.

"No. Let's walk for a while if that's okay with you." She took his outstretched arm and linked her hands through it. They strolled in silence, and by the time they reached Central Park, her feet were aching. "Can we find a bench and sit down for a bit? These heels aren't great for walking this far."

He led her over to a bench, and she took in a deep breath. "Joe, I'm sorry for everything. I should have told you sooner. But, well, the fact is, I have two children." She waited for his outrage or some emotional outburst.

"Children? You mean with Leland?"

"Yes. Remember when you met me, and I was pushing the little girl in the stroller? She wasn't my sister. She was my child. June's about a year younger."

"So, you're a war widow of two young children. You think that would stop me from marrying you?"

"But I—"

"Listen, I've got prospects. Pops has influence, and he thinks I could run for mayor of Long Island at some point. Rescuing a war widow with two kids and marrying her, that would be—"

Margaret's stomach roiled. What he was saying nagged at her subconscious. He would be rescuing her. It didn't feel good even though it held a grain of truth. She battled with her conscience. It wasn't her fault she was divorced. As far as she was concerned, Leland's betrayal had made him dead in her eyes.

Joe's voice interrupted her ordeal. "Plus, they're only girls."

Only?

Her brow furrowed. She couldn't see why raising another man's daughters was okay but not sons. Her shoulders tensed, and she sought for words that didn't come. *Something isn't right.*

She made to get up from the bench when he grasped her hand. She faced him, wanting to flee but still feeling a strong pull toward him. Her conflicting emotions froze her in place.

Joseph pulled a box from his pocket. Getting down on one knee in front of her, he cracked open the box. Inside sat a diamond ring. Margaret stared at the precious gem. She'd never owned a diamond in her life.

"Margaret Rose, I know that we haven't known each other long.

But I feel it's right. I think we would make a good team. Will you marry me?"

She should have asked for time to think about it. To get to know each other better. Maybe even turned him down for her dishonesty. Instead, she whispered, "Yes."

Every doubt and hesitation dissolved as she flung her arms around his neck and kissed him. The past could no longer haunt her. Gone were her worries of being kicked out of the training program and living a life of pretend. She wouldn't need to carry on with her training. She was already good enough for Joe and wouldn't have to return home, broke and in need, struggling to get anyone to accept her as a nurse. Marrying Joe, she and the girls would no longer need to live hand-to-mouth. She would get her daughters back, and everything she'd ever dreamed of awaited.

Even with doubts niggling in her mind and murmurs of "fraud," she brushed them away like they were cobwebs. "Yes."

Third time's a charm, right?

CHAPTER THIRTY

Her third wedding differed greatly from her other two. No judge and a simple dress or suit that time. She would marry her love in the church Joe's mother attended. When she'd sent word home of her nuptials, her father had refused to come, as he wouldn't step foot in a Catholic church. Even though Margaret had said that they would pay for the train fare, she was met with rejection. And while he hadn't said as much, she gathered he was against her marrying an Italian, since they'd sided with Hitler during the war. Yet Margaret wondered if it was more than that. Maybe she had become a failure in his eyes, and his absence was more about him thinking her third marriage was another mistake in a long line of them. *Who cares what he thinks?* She could—and would—make her own decisions.

Only one family member begged to come and visit: Nellie, who, like Margaret, had always longed for adventure. She would be Margaret's maid of honor, and Gennie would be the flower girl.

Margaret wore a beautiful antique ivory-satin-and-lace gown. Knowing that divorce wasn't allowed in the Catholic faith, she hoped God wouldn't strike her dead on the spot. After she'd said yes, the wheels had turned so quickly that they buried her secret deeper and deeper into the ground. She was trapped then but constantly reminded herself that marrying Joe would give the girls the wonderful life she'd never had.

The ceremony was solemn, and Margaret caught herself shaking a few times. She didn't know whether to blame it on her deception or something else. But before she knew it, they were marched out the door to be showered with rice and laughter.

Joe Senior had rented out a lovely venue for the reception, and Margaret and Joe were whisked over to the dinner in a black Daimler. Other than the dress and flowers, the wedding, dinner, and dance were all coordinated by the Martin family. With no one from her side attending except for Nellie and her friends, it was easier to let them manage it. Plus, the cost would be another factor. There was no way that her family could have afforded such extravagance.

Nellie looked beautiful in a pale-peach gown, her hair elegantly done up in a chignon like Margaret's. After toasts from Joe's best man, Pete, and a short and sweet message from a visibly nervous Nellie, the dinner began. The Martins had pulled out all the stops. Margaret looked at the stand in front of her plate that held the printed menu.

As waiters in white dinner jackets set the plate in front of her, she inhaled the savory smells. The first course was an assortment of arancini, which, she discovered, were rice balls filled with meat, white sauce, mushrooms, or mozzarella. Each bite was a warm delight. They were accompanied by a cup of wedding soup—baby meatballs and pasta in a flavorful chicken broth.

The next course served was a combination of seared scallops and Saltimbocca. The combination of chicken, salty prosciutto, and herbs melted in her mouth. It was set on a bed of freshly made pasta that Joe's mother and her friends had prepared as Margaret watched with June in her lap.

Just as Margaret thought it would be time for dessert, another plate was set before her. The filet mignon was topped with prosciutto, mozzarella, and a mushroom brandy sauce.

Champagne and wine flowed, all paid for by Joe's father. Having a father-in-law in the grocery business must've helped with bypassing a lot of the rationing and other food shortages that Margaret had seen and experienced in the last few years. Even with the war over, the shortages hadn't stopped.

After cutting a multilayered white cake with an apricot filling, the couple took to the dance floor. As she twirled in her beautiful ivory tea-length gown, she spied Joe's mother and her friends cooing over her daughters. Margaret's heart swelled with happiness.

That time, she'd chosen well. Whereas she'd had feelings for Leland, her love for Joseph was undeniable. Gene would always be her first love, but Joe would be her last. She kissed him.

He grinned broadly. "Mrs. Martin, whatever are you doing?"

"Showing the world that I love this man."

The party went on into the wee hours of the morning, and as guests left, they were given homemade Italian torrone, a type of nougat candy.

Those celebrations of the last few days and on her wedding day gave Margaret the taste for a life she'd dreamed of for so long. She snuggled in next to Joe as they drove the roads that would take them to Niagara Falls for their honeymoon.

Each day was more glorious than the last as they got to know one another, laughed over dinner, and made love. Margaret marveled at the falls, the perfect spot for honeymooners, as they signified love, passion, and forward movement. Margaret took Joe's hand, and with one look, they were rushing back to their room again, the desire to merge mind, heart, and body all-encompassing.

The days flew by, and soon, they were making their way home. *Home.* Not a trailer or an apartment. An actual house. Margaret was giddy when Joe told her he had bought them a home.

At his parents' house, Gennie rushed into Margaret's arms. "Mommy! I missed you."

"I missed you too, sweetie. Now we can have such fun together. Look, we brought you a present." She handed Gennie a set of Little Golden Books. "We can read these new books at night before bed. We also got you this."

Joe pulled a teddy bear from behind his back. "Here you go, Gennie."

"Thank you." Gennie hugged the bear.

"You're welcome." He ruffled her hair.

Her mother-in-law rushed into the room, spouting a stream of Italian. She kissed Joe then Margaret on both cheeks. "Come in. Come in. You must be hungry."

Margaret felt Gennie pull on her hand as they went to the dining room. The table was stuffed with food.

"Mrs. Martin, you're going to make me fat."

"Good. You could use a little meat on your bones."

They ate and passed around postcards of Niagara Falls.

"I wanted to take pictures. It's magnificent," Margaret said.

Joe Senior wiped his mouth. "Get Joe to buy you a camera for your first son."

Margaret bristled. Her only role in his eyes seemed to be bearing sons. He reminded her of Pa with his hold on the family. The sooner they were in their own place and out from under his thumb, the better.

Joe Senior scooted his chair back and stood. Unlike her father, who was strong and sturdy, his belly crept over his belt and pants.

"Now the important thing." He walked over to the mantel, where he pulled down a set of keys then handed them to Joe. Keys to their new home. Margaret could barely contain her excitement. "We got everything ready, as you requested, Figlio."

Margaret helped clear the table and dry the dishes as the men smoked outside. Unlike the unease she felt with her father-in-law, she welcomed Joe's exuberant, friendly mother, who was always seeking ways to help others. While Margaret's mother was meeker and milder, Joe's mother could simply give a look or speak a word, letting others know that they had crossed an imaginary line.

As they left, Joe's mother handed her a loaf of bread, a container of salt, and a bottle of wine along with a picnic basket. Joe's parents would bring the girls up to the new house in a few days after they'd gotten to know the place. Margaret hugged Gennie, and after spending some time rocking June, she brushed her lips against June's forehead and laid the sleeping child in the crib. Joe opened the door for Margaret before climbing into the navy Buick Roadmaster.

After such a substantial lunch, Margaret rested her head on Joe's shoulder as he drove. They were headed toward Long Island and the area known as the Hamptons. It sounded nice, and Margaret's excitement grew as she woke and stretched.

Beautiful homes lined the road, and finally, Joe slowed, allowing her a glimpse. They stopped in front of a house that sat higher than the rest, a white picket fence across the front of the yard and climbing roses around the gate. Her eyes followed the walkway that led to the two-story house.

The car rolled to a stop. "This is it."

Is he pulling my leg? She thought they were only passing through.

"What do you think?"

"What do I think? Is this for real? This can't be our house. Don't dash my hopes, Joe."

He took her chin in his hands and kissed her on the lips. "I wouldn't do that, Margie."

She squealed with delight, wrapping her arms around his neck then kissing him all over the face. "Oh, no." She laughed as he pulled out his handkerchief, wiping the red lipstick from his cheeks and neck.

Margaret swiveled toward the house as Joe came around to open her door. She had never seen a more beautiful home. Even in Florida, the huge Perry and other houses paled in comparison to its buttercream-yellow façade with white trimming. Branches of a large sugar maple framed the rock-walled enclosure, and what looked like a balcony extended off one room upstairs, most likely the master bedroom. She could barely make out the neighboring houses through a row of hedges, allowing for a modicum of privacy.

Joe faced her, propping his arm across her shoulders. "So will this do, Mrs. Martin?"

"I'm speechless. It's beautiful."

"The best things for my girl." He leaned over and kissed her before pulling her behind him.

She grabbed at her hat with her gloved hand, then her heels clicked up the flagstone pathway. They raced to the front entrance, where the door was opened by an older woman in a gray dress with a white apron.

"Hello. We've been expecting you. I'll have John gather the luggage, Mr. Martin."

Margaret's eyes grew wide as saucers. They had help too.

Before she could respond, Joe gathered her up in his arms and carried her over the threshold, setting her down in an entrance hall that was bigger than the apartment she'd shared with the girls in New York. A polished mahogany staircase curved along the side of the wall with an elegant wood banister. Directly in front of them, she spied a hallway that led back toward what appeared to be the kitchen area. A large dining room and living room completed the lower level.

Joe grabbed her hand, and they raced up the stairs, him flinging open doors as they went. "Here's June's room. Here's Gennie's!" He opened another room and winked. "The nursery." They moved past the children's rooms and toward another wing, which opened up into a lovely master bedroom.

Margaret marveled at the size of the room then spotted another large door. "Does this have an—?"

"Yes, an en suite, right through here." He threw open the door, and Margaret's eyes grew wide at the large clawfoot tub, perfect for soaking in. He opened a second door, and it connected to a smaller room with a twin bed.

"What's this?"

"For when I come home late. So as not to disturb you."

"But wouldn't we be going out together?"

"Of course. But this is for when I go to the club with the guys. Play cards."

A memory came back to her of her father and his nights out with the guys. Joe interrupted her thoughts as he picked her up and carried her back into the master bedroom. "Now, Mrs. Martin, let's get to making some sons."

~

When they had first spoken of where they would live after the wedding, it became apparent that the neighborhood was part of Joe Senior's political ambitions for his son. Though she tried not to eavesdrop, Margaret overheard them on numerous occasions. She couldn't help herself. What happened with Joe would affect her and the girls. Over some weeks, she'd learned that political office was the primary goal of Joe Senior for his son.

In order to do so, they'd started with changing the family name from Martino to Martin, as people's prejudice against Italians had taken hold in some areas. They also knew that they would need capital, meaning money and clout. They'd selected an area known for wealthy donors, and its inhabitants spent weekends in the Hamptons. Many of their new neighbors already commuted to Joe Senior's store, so Joseph had been advised to set up another shop there. Joe Senior would send down a truck with the goods, then Joe and a crew would deliver the groceries. At deliveries, Joe would schmooze the homeowners, getting into their good graces with items that were hard to come by. Those favors would be useful later.

Margaret didn't understand much of it, but some of the things that happened left more questions than answers. First of all, there was the expensive house. But she didn't pry, as she thought it would be good to be farther away from Joseph's parents.

After they had settled in, his parents brought the girls to the house, and Margaret cooked a pot roast, potatoes, and carrots. She wished Nellie had stayed a while longer. It was hard unpacking the wedding presents while looking after the girls, but even though Joe's parents had said she could stay with them, Nellie had wanted to head home.

In the evening, Joe would come home, pulling at his tie while pouring a glass of whiskey from the drinks cabinet. She quickly learned that while he was okay with the girls, he didn't want to see them in the evenings, when he preferred to eat dinner with her and relax. Luckily, the girls were still young. She could feed them an early dinner, give them baths, and tuck them into bed before he came home.

That evening when he arrived from work, he greeted her with a kiss on the cheek as she helped him out of his coat.

He surveyed her. "Is that what you've been wearing all day? Why haven't you changed for dinner?"

"I guess time got away from me. We went to the park and had a picnic. I met some ladies from—"

He shook his head. "No. You'll make friends with the guys' wives soon enough. We're like a close-knit family. We stick with our own."

"But—"

He turned, and she saw the now-familiar tic by his eye, signifying his displeasure.

She looked away before replying. "Of course."

He went to the drinks cabinet and poured himself a scotch. "We need to have a housewarming party. Everyone's been asking what's taking so long."

"That sounds wonderful. I can start planning it tomorrow. Maybe in a few weeks on Saturday. "

"Tomorrow we've been invited to a party over at the Rossis'. Seven. Have Mrs. Bohannon get her niece to watch the girls." He pulled off his tie, whipping it from his neck, and a waft of something she couldn't place reached her nose. "I'm tired. I'll be in my study. Just bring me a sandwich."

"But the table's all set, and I made a roast and—"

"Okay, bring me a roast sandwich." He strode off down the

corridor toward his study, which was off-limits to her or the girls.

Later that night, he came to her reeking of booze, cigarettes, and some other strange scent. After he'd finished, he got up from their bed and left the room, leaving Margaret feeling used and unloved. She wept into her pillow.

Everything had been so perfect. She knew they couldn't always be like they had been on their honeymoon, but it felt like their marriage was devolving into lives lived more separately. He refused to talk to her about his work, and she felt adrift after she'd unwrapped all the wedding gifts and sent the thank-you notes. Meeting with the ladies in the park had been nice. She'd been able to get the girls outside and playing with other children. She punched the pillow and flipped over on the bed, staring at the empty space next to her. *Failure.* The word echoed in her mind. *Why am I not enough? I can't make any man happy.* She had everything she'd dreamed of, and the façade was cracking, letting in the truth.

She wondered if she would ever be happy or if happiness was just an illusion.

CHAPTER THIRTY-ONE

Mrs. Bohannon said she could watch the girls the following evening, so Margaret took the free time to enjoy a nice long soak in a bubble bath before fixing her makeup and putting on a freshly pressed dress.

She heard Joe's voice through the intercom in the bathroom. "Margie! I'm here."

She swiped red across her lips and hurried over to the panel on the wall, where she pushed the button. "Coming!"

Margaret slid into her shoes, careful not to snag her heel on her nylons. She walked out to the landing and glanced at the bottom of the steps, where Joe was waiting.

He squinted up at her. "What's that?"

"What do you mean? What's what?"

"You can't go to the party in that old rag."

"But I don't have—"

He bristled. "Didn't I tell you to go buy some new clothes?"

"Yes, but I've been so busy with getting the house set up and with the girls."

He slapped his hat against the banister then put it back on his head. "I'll tell them you were ill." With that, he walked out the door.

Margaret stood clutching her hands as she heard the motor of his car start up and the sound of tires against gravel as he sped away. She walked over to the nursery, where Mrs. Bohannan was reading the girls a story. "I-I'm not feeling well, Mrs. Bohannon, so you don't need to stay. I can bathe and put the girls to bed."

"Not on you. You put yourself to bed. I'll handle the lasses." Her occasional lapse of vocabulary from her Irish ancestry snuck into her statement.

"Thank you." Margaret went to her room then flung herself on the bed. She wanted Joe to be proud of her—she should have made time to go buy new dresses. Margaret slammed her pillow down then threw all of them across the room. If only she'd listened to him. Things were so different here than where she was from. She had ruined the evening with her poor upbringing. She picked up the pillows and clutched one to her chest. Tomorrow, she would get new clothes. She'd try harder for Joe. She would be a good wife. She had to.

Even though Joe didn't come to bed that night after the party, Margaret awoke with a new sense of purpose. His late arrivals and staying out with the guys had increased, causing Margaret to question if he had fallen out of love with her. She had never seen Leland's love fade. Even his betrayal had come as a shock. Her stomach ached all the time as worry over Joe leaving her intensified.

She had to work harder. That was all there was to it. She would try to cook some of his favorite dishes, have a drink ready when he got home, and make sure she had new makeup and a clean dress on when he walked in the door. Joe would be proud she was his wife. But clothing had never been her strong suit. She picked up the alarm clock from her bedside table. Seven in the morning. She glanced over to where Joe's side was still made up from last night.

After swiping the covers back, she strode through the bathroom toward the door to his room, but when she turned the handle, it wouldn't open. She tried again. Locked. Throwing on her robe from the bottom of the bed, she made her way to the hall to the other door. It was unlocked, but inside, she spied ruffled bedclothes but no Joe.

She flew down the stairs to the kitchen, where Mrs. Bohannon sat with the girls, feeding June oatmeal while Gennie ate cereal.

"Good morning, Mrs. Martin. May I help you?"

"I'm sorry to bother you, Mrs. Bohannon. I was looking for Mr. Martin. Has he already left for work?"

"Yes, ma'am. He asked me to give you this when you woke." She handed Margaret a sealed envelope. "I'll be bringing your coffee up to your room, or are you ready for breakfast now?"

"No, no breakfast. Just coffee, please."

In her room, she set the envelope on the dressing table and opened a drawer. She took out a menthol cigarette and lit it, the burning in her throat becoming more manageable. He'd teased her on gaining weight recently. Maybe that was why he was so aloof lately. He no longer found her attractive.

She took a puff of the cigarette, determined that she would cut out the full breakfast from then on. With a housekeeper, she spent more of her time sitting around. She needed to be careful that she wasn't getting fat. Sitting on the vanity bench, she tore open the envelope.

Mitzi's going to help you with clothes. She knows the best stores. She'll call later today.

Love, Joe.

She stared at the note. Maybe she'd been overreacting to his rejection last night. Of course she had. He'd said it right there—Love, Joe. She held the note to her chest. A grin broke out over her face. Not only would she be getting some new clothes, but she would finally get to meet one of the other ladies. She had become so bored lately, and it would be good to have some girl time.

She hadn't realized how much she missed Katie and the friendship they'd shared. Margaret needed a new friend—someone who could help her be a good wife to Joe.

Mitzi called on the telephone, and they set a time for ten next Wednesday. Margaret was waiting in the living room, reading a book to Gennie, when the doorbell chimed.

Mrs. Bohannon ushered in a voluptuous woman. Margaret guessed that she was at least ten years older, if not more, but her makeup made it difficult to determine her exact age. Her white blouse hugged her curves, and the pencil skirt slimmed her hips. She sashayed into the room, perfectly arched brows rising at the sight of Margaret.

"Margaret, we finally meet." The woman seemed to enunciate every syllable of her name. She came over and pressed her cheek to

Margaret's before repeating the gesture on the other side. "We are going to be such friends. Now... clothing."

Margaret was soon sitting in Mitzi's convertible, speeding down the road, the wind whipping at the silk scarf Mitzi had given to her to secure her hair.

After leaving the car with the valet, they entered their first stop for the day, Bergdorf Goodman. After that store, they went to Bloomingdales then Saks. Margaret balked at the cost of the clothing, but Mitzi assured her that Joe had given her carte blanche. Finally, while Margaret struggled with a zipper, Mitzi entered the dressing room at Lord and Taylor.

"Is this your lingerie? Oh, no. We can't have that." Their next stop was all about new panties, bras, slips, and a new girdle.

"That too." Mitzi pointed to a peignoir set. It was a light-peach color with a waist trimmed in sheer lace. The designers had cut the decolletage of the gown sharply in the front. It was beautiful but also the most daring thing Margaret had ever seen. The robe had sheer long sleeves with three pearl buttons to close the front. Mitzi also found a pair of slipper kitten heels with feathers to complete the look.

"Oh, that's a gorgeous set. But I don't think so." Margaret's cheeks burned. "I'm not sure I could wear something like that."

Mitzi smiled. "I know so. Trust me. When you wear it, tell Joey I helped you pick it out."

Margaret tensed. That was an odd thing to share with your husband. But she simply nodded.

Mitzi continued, "I'm famished. Let's go to the Bird Cage."

Margaret noticed that Mitzi often referred to Joseph as Joey, and a grain of jealousy planted itself in her mind. Guys called him Joey, but she wasn't sure about that woman using it. Even Margaret used Joe or Joseph.

They took their seats in the restaurant. As Mitzi picked up the complimentary cigarette and matches on her tray, Margaret followed suit.

Mitzi exhaled a cloud of smoke. "Thank God for these things, or I'd be as big as a house."

The wagon lady came by, and Margaret ordered bread and butter with pickle, Mitzi the liverwurst on rye. They both drank orange pekoe tea.

Mitzi smoked for a bit before stubbing it out on the little ashtray. "You got yourself a good one with Joey. I hope you know how lucky you are."

Taken aback at the frankness of Mitzi's words, she stiffened. "I am very lucky. He's lucky to have me too." In her heart, she doubted that. *What do I really have to offer Joe?*

Mitzi cracked open her handbag and pulled out her cigarette case. She tapped a cigarette on it and lit the end before waving the flame away. "Sons. You have to give them sons."

Margaret laughed, but it sounded hollow. "Well, that's not everything."

Mitzi raised an eyebrow. "I can tell you're still young. You have a lot to learn. What have you been doing with yourself during the day?"

Margaret shared about getting the house in order and planning for the housewarming. Mitzi nodded. "And at night?"

Flustered, Margaret replied, "I'm not sure I know what you mean."

"Don't you?"

"No, I don't. What are you trying to say?"

"When Joey's away. Any 'friends' come over?"

"I can't believe you're asking me that. Are you asking if I'm cheating on my husband? I'd never be unfaithful to Joe."

Mitzi raised her hands in surrender. "Sorry. No harm, no foul. I meant nothing by it. Forget I said anything." She picked up her purse while pushing her cigarette into the half-eaten sandwich. "Let's go."

They drove home in silence, but the entire time, something kept nagging at Margaret. Joe was away that night with the guys, playing cards. As she bathed the children, she realized what had been bothering her—Mitzi knew Joe wasn't at home in the evenings.

CHAPTER THIRTY-TWO

The party was a colossal success. Margaret had also invited the neighbors, and she was happy to see that one of the women she'd met in the park had come with her husband. Ruth waved at her. The woman was surrounded by most of their neighbors in a tight cluster.

Margaret made her way over. "Hello, I'm Margaret Rose. Or some call me Margie."

Ruth introduced her husband. She could tell he was tense from his posture as he said hello in return. "Charles Stone."

"Nice to meet you. I'd love to chat further, but it seems we need to refill some plates. Please, help yourselves to another drink." She smiled and walked past the pair, who stayed fixed in their spot.

Conversely, most of Joe's friends kept to their own group as well. Margaret wondered how to increase their mingling, but she had other things on her mind at the moment. The canapes were running low, and she needed to ensure there was enough food. She didn't want to fail her first time hosting.

As she made her way to the kitchen, she couldn't help overhearing whispered voices—"not one of us," "Maria Corti," and something about a "good Italian Catholic." The voices continued, and Margaret stepped back in shock. Something told her they were talking about her. They must've thought Joe should have married someone else.

She jumped when an arm went around her waist. She turned to see Joe. "Oh, honey, I'm sorry. You scared me."

"You've done well. I'm happy with how everything turned out."

She basked in his praise. "Well, Mrs. Bohannon and your father—"

"I'm not sure about inviting the neighbors again. This time's okay, but don't do it again." He patted her cheek and walked away, leaving her staring after him, wondering if she'd been praised or chastised. She glanced around to see if anyone had heard the exchange, her cheeks burning.

Finally, the evening wound down, and Ruth came over to say goodnight. "Charles and I are leaving, but I wanted to thank you for your invitation and a wonderful evening."

"Are you going to the park this week with your children?"

Ruth nodded. "Will you be bringing the girls?"

"Yes, I was thinking of having a picnic. We could meet up and chat while they play or nap. What do you think?"

She smiled. "That sounds lovely. You know, you look more like a Maggie."

"That's funny. It's what all my brothers and sisters call me. Do I hear a bit of accent?"

"Yes, Alabama, born and raised. Can't help it. That accent won't go away. Up here, it tends to stick out like a sore thumb."

"Who cares if it does? Us Southern gals need to stick together. I'm from Milton, close to Pensacola."

"No wonder. I think we'll make fast friends. I could use a friend, as Charles is away quite a bit as the business is being built up." She gave Margaret a hug. "Thursday?"

"Sounds great." Margaret waved them off as Joe joined her.

"What were you talking about?"

"She was saying how much they enjoyed the evening and thanking us for inviting them."

He stared after the couple then turned to her. "I don't like them. Don't spend time with her." With that, he returned to the last guests, who were gathering up coats and hats.

Margaret's eyebrows knit together. Joe was being so negative. She smoothed down her dress, giving her time to compose herself. He could "not like" Ruth all he wanted, but she felt a kinship with the woman and wouldn't stop seeing her just because of Joe. Plus, she refused to let him spoil tonight's party.

After helping to clear away the dishes, she found Joe in the living room, smoking as he stood next to the mantel. She went over to him and clasped her arms around him. "Happy?"

"Yes." He faced her. "You look beautiful tonight. Those new dresses suit you."

"I have a surprise for you."

"Do you, now?" He gathered her in his arms.

"Wait ten minutes and then come up."

Margaret dressed in the peignoir set, releasing the hair that she had pulled back with combs. She spritzed a bit of perfume on her wrists and walked out to see Joe standing in the doorway.

"I said ten minutes. It hasn't been that long."

"I couldn't wait. Where did you get that?"

"At the store. Mitzi convinced me to buy it. She said you would like it. Was she wrong?"

"No, she's not wrong." He kicked the door shut with his foot.

~

Days turned into weeks, and within a couple of months, and after missing her monthly, she felt the first impending signs of pregnancy. She made Joe's favorite meal of veal piccata and surprised him with a pair of white baby booties under a cake stand.

Joe was over the moon with the news she was pregnant. He grew more attentive, spending more time with her and making sure she had everything she needed. As a present for getting pregnant, she requested a camera before the birth so that she could take pictures of the girls and their family as they grew.

He'd been happy to oblige and found someone who gave her lessons. As the girls played, she would take different shots of them as well as others that intrigued her. She found she had a knack for it and went to see a photographer to have the film developed frequently. After Joe learned she had to continually visit the male photographer, he set up a room for her in the basement to do her own film processing. Margaret felt pride in her efforts for the first time in her life. Happier than ever with her new hobby, she continued to hone her craft of photography, decorating their walls with some of her work.

Margaret arrived for the weekly Thursday afternoon playdate with Ruth, the children falling over one another on their way to the nearby trees. After Joe's statement of not liking Ruth, Margaret had kept those outings as her little secret.

Margaret pulled out a red flannel blanket, laying it on the ground for them to sit while Ruth opened a basket, pulling out baloney and iceberg lettuce. Margaret laid out the slices of white bread, buttering them before Ruth added the bologna.

"I'm not sure I really like baloney, but it's easy and inexpensive."

Margaret nodded. "Agree. Plus, the girls like it. If I couldn't get them to eat it, they'd live on butter-and-sugar sandwiches."

"My bunch too." Ruth chuckled. "How are you feeling?"

"Better. I had pretty bad morning sickness with June, so I'm happy it's hasn't hit me this time."

"Small blessings." Ruth bit into her sandwich. "Mikey, put that rock down!"

They chatted about movies and the latest fashion before the children came over with their cries of "I'm hungry!"

After the children had eaten sandwiches, they enjoyed some sugar cookies for dessert before packing the items away.

"Well, best get them home for naptime." They gathered up the flannel blanket, dusting the grass from it before folding it up. Margaret hugged Ruth then set Gennie in the stroller. It was often easier to leave June at home on some outings so she could spend some time visiting instead of chasing after the toddler or stopping her from putting a bug in her mouth.

She waved goodbye, content with her life. Joe appeared happy, she continually sought ways to make his life easier, and she had her photography. Being friends with Ruth was another blessing. She treasured their visits. Ruth could relate to much of Margaret's upbringing and early life. Over time, they'd learned to trust one another with their fears, hopes, and dreams—even some of their secrets.

That was why Margaret couldn't understand how she had the sense Ruth was holding something back from her. On those days, Ruth would embrace her in a tight hug as if it might be the last time they would meet.

Margaret and Joe's home became *the* place to be for parties. It was a lot of work for her, but if it made Joe happy, then she'd do it. It also appeared that the goal of getting high-profile individuals into their sphere of influence was working. On other days, they would host what Joe called "family parties." Joe made it clear that those were the days that no outsiders were to receive an invitation.

She didn't care for those parties as much because it often turned into the women sequestered with the children in one area and the men off in another. On numerous occasions, it appeared to be Joe Senior holding court in whispered conversations. Once, she'd strayed over to see if they needed anything and was met with total silence. Joe had grabbed her arm and ushered her away. "Never interrupt business."

"But this is a party. It's not the time to talk business." *Why are they talking about groceries, anyway?* Margaret had wondered.

In fact, she wondered about a lot of things. Somehow, the grocery business was profitable enough to allow them to live in the manner they did. All she knew was, Joe took care of the bills and gave her a weekly household allowance that provided a sufficient amount for everything that was needed or wanted. She had never experienced living with such extravagance, and it was rare Joe ever said no to any of her wishes. Especially when he felt it made him look better in others' eyes.

Mitzi had also become a regular visitor, but Margaret couldn't be herself with her like she did with Ruth. She always felt on edge when Mitzi was around, probing about private matters. But that shouldn't matter. Margaret had a loving husband, a beautiful home, a housekeeper, and a gardener. It was far above the life she'd ever even dreamed. The girls were happy and healthy, and she practically glowed with this pregnancy, her mother-in-law stopping by on weekends to bring food and to fuss over her. She wrote to Franny and Nellie, talking about her life in New York but not including too much that would sound prideful. She always ended her letters with "Missing you. Love, your Maggie."

They'd planned for Nellie to come up after the baby was born to help out and spend some time with her, so she was looking forward to the visit from her sister. If only Franny could get away for a while.

News had come that Franny was not doing well after her last pregnancy, but Mama was over at her house, helping with the five children while Franny recovered her strength.

The days drew closer to Margaret's due date, and the pain of childbirth returned with a vengeance. She'd forgotten its intensity, and while she'd given birth at home with her first two children, Joe wouldn't hear of any child of his not being born in a proper hospital. She was quickly rushed away into an operating theater, where a nurse hovered nearby. A woman's screams echoed throughout the room.

Margaret grabbed the nurse's hand. "Please, help that poor woman!"

The doctor replied, "Mrs. Martin, you're the only woman in here."

Margaret screamed again. Something was wrong. Then she heard the words she dreaded, "Breech birth, Doctor."

"Okay, Nurse. I think it's time for twilight sleep."

Margaret felt her arms being tied down and fought against the restraints. "No, stop. I don't want that. Help! Someone help me." But as they lowered a mask over her mouth and nose, it muffled her cries, and she fell into a dreamless sleep.

When she awoke, she was in a hospital bed in a ward with other women. Margaret felt down to her empty womb yet still held its bulk. She moaned.

A nurse looked over from where she stood, holding linens. After setting them down on a nearby counter, the nurse picked up the chart from the end of the metal bed. "Hello, Mrs. Martin. I'm here to massage your stomach."

Margaret licked her lips. A wave of sickness passed through her. "I feel like I'm going to throw up."

The nurse grabbed a bedpan and set it next to Margaret, who dry-heaved into the pan.

She fell back on the pillows, exhausted. "Where's my baby?"

"She's in the nursery. We can bring her in here later for you to see her."

"Her?"

"Yes. It says on your chart that you had a little girl."

Margaret closed her eyes, tears gathering. Joe had wanted a boy so badly. She had failed him as a wife again. Later, when he came and brought roses, she could see that he was trying to make the best of it.

"Joe, we'll have a boy next time."

He smiled. "Yes, next time." Kissing her on the head, he advised her to rest, but it was difficult. Since Annabelle had been born breech, the doctor had used forceps, and Margaret had to deal with stitches from a cut made to prevent more trauma. Where she was normally up and about after her other two children, she struggled with this one.

Margaret was released from the hospital after five days, then Joe drove her and their baby home. But he left soon after, stating that she needed her rest, and he would only be in the way. Nellie, who preferred being called Nell after she'd turned sixteen, had arrived to help. Leaving the children in Nell's care allowed Margaret more time to recuperate, and for that she was grateful. With two young children and a baby, Margaret spent much of her time feeding Annabelle and napping. Joe came in a few times, but mostly, she stayed in bed, waiting for her strength to return.

CHAPTER THIRTY-THREE

After a week had gone by, a tentative knock sounded on the bedroom door. "Who is it?"

"It's me, Ruth. May I come in?"

"Yes, please come in." Margaret adjusted herself on her pillows, pulling the pink quilted bed jacket closed.

Ruth entered, wearing a smart chestnut suit and a cream cap with a short veil that rested behind her ears. A brooch adorned her lapel. In her gloved hands, she carried a bouquet.

Margaret smiled. "Well, look at you. Don't you look swell?"

"Thank you. We're going out to celebrate Charles's promotion. Sadly, it means we'll be moving soon."

"Oh, no. Where?"

"California." She pulled up a chair and sat next to the bed.

"California? Oh, that's so far. I'm going to miss you so much." Margaret reached out her hand, and the woman took it in her two hands. "When are you leaving?" She fought against the tears pricking her eyes.

"Soon. They want Charles out there right away. As soon as I can get the house taken care of, I'll go out with the children. Everything's so rushed. I feel like I haven't had time to even catch my breath." She sat in the chair next to Margaret's bed, clutching her handbag with both hands.

"You always said you wanted an adventure. Think of it as a wonderful escapade, Ruth. I know when I first moved here, I felt like a fish out of water. Like I'd moved to a different country. But that's what makes it fun."

Ruth nodded and took in a deep breath. "Maggie, you've been such a good friend to me. I hate the thought of losing our friendship. And even worse, for our last time together for you to hate me."

"Hate you? Why would you say such a thing?"

Ruth hesitated. "I wanted to come by to say goodbye but also to get rid of something I've had on my chest for a long time. I don't know how to say this without just coming out with it."

"What do you mean?"

She let go of Margaret's hand and paced the room.

"Ruth, you're scaring me." Margaret leaned forward.

Ruth rushed back to Margaret's bedside. "I've struggled with this so much. Normally, I keep my thoughts to myself. I don't interfere in other people's lives. But I feel like you're one of my sisters. I can't sweep this under the rug, and if I don't tell you now, I never will."

"It can't be all that bad—"

"I'm so sorry, Maggie. I don't even know if I'm making things better or worse by coming here."

"What is it? Tell me." A chill went down Margaret's spine.

"It's—well, it's Joe. He's been…" She pursed her lips and bowed her head.

But she didn't need to say it. Margaret already knew the truth in her heart. "Who, Ruth?"

"I don't know for sure. It's just, Charles has seen them on more than one occasion, and—"

"Mitzi." She clutched at the sheets, knotting them in her hands. All that time, the nights out, the times Mitzi had probed about her seeing anyone, and the smell. That's when it hit her. The smell on him had been her perfume. She'd tried to block it out. Think it was all in her mind. What a fool she'd been.

"In some ways, it's good you had a daughter," Ruth continued. "He wants a son. If you have a son, he'll never let you leave. Or he'll try to take the boy away from you."

Margaret moaned. She'd tried to avoid his adultery because she knew what it meant if she faced it. She would have to admit that she'd failed yet again.

She steeled herself before looking at Ruth. With others, she'd had to hide her true feelings, but not with Ruth. "I don't want to live like this. I know other women do. It's often expected or accepted. But I can't. I'm not one of them. I'm trapped." She hung her head, defeat filling her. "What am I going to do?" She held her face in her hands, forcing herself not to break down.

"Well, he'll leave you alone while you're healing, and you can figure out what to do." She wrung her hands. "Charles told me not to say anything. But I'm just not made that way. I tried, but now that I'm leaving, I feel I don't have a choice."

"It's okay. I've always been one to speak my mind too. I think you and I were made for a different time, Ruth." Margaret laughed.

Ruth took in a deep breath, avoiding Margaret's gaze. "The principal thing is you don't want to get pregnant again. He may want to try for a boy again soon. I keep seeing ads in the women's magazines for the mouthwash helping with, um, you know. As soon as you start feeling better, use it if he wants to try again."

"I can't stop a pregnancy. That's my duty as a wife."

Ruth nodded. "Of course. I'm sorry. You're right." She opened her purse and pulled out a card. "Here's where we'll be staying until we move into our house. Please keep in touch, Maggie." She leaned over and kissed her hair. "I'll miss you, my friend."

"I'll miss you too. Write me when you get settled."

Ruth left the room, and Margaret pondered their conversation. She'd known from dealing with men in the past that they strayed— and that it was often accepted and ignored. But she had vowed that she would never be anyone's fool. For the time being, she had to care for herself and her children.

Once she recovered, she would figure out her next steps. Her eyes fell on her desk, which held a bouquet from Joe and her prized camera. An idea formed in her mind as a soft smile played on her lips. She knew exactly what she needed to do to set a trap for the rat.

CHAPTER THIRTY-FOUR

Margaret spent the next weeks resting, but in her mind, she plotted her escape. And her revenge. She began by befriending the women of Joe's business partners, inviting them over for coffee and cake, along with playdates. As they grew more comfortable with her, she would garner who would dish the gossip and who remained tight-lipped. One thing the women had in common was their dislike for Mitzi. Margaret knew that could play to her advantage.

She also knew that the last thing she needed was to get pregnant. If she had a son, her chances of leaving or taking the baby with her would drop dramatically. She made sure not to dress up while Joe was around, instead appearing frumpy or unkempt. On nights when he would go out with the guys, she followed his lead and locked the connecting door to their rooms. But she knew that would only be a temporary fix, and she could only have so many headaches. She needed to find a way forward, and she knew just the person who could help her.

Mitzi sat across from Margaret on the sofa, her legs crossed, sipping at the coffee Mrs. Bohannon had poured before leaving the room. "It's so good to see you, Margie. I know you had a hard time with Annabelle."

Margaret nodded. "I'm just now feeling like myself again. Though I'm still concerned about well, down there." She took a sip, pretending to gather her courage and not to come across as false. "I admire you, Mitzi. You stay so trim, and you've given Pete two strapping sons. Any more on the way soon?"

Mitzi set down her cup and pulled out a cigarette, tapping it hard against the silver case with her initials.

"Oh, that's a pretty case. May I see it?"

Mitzi reluctantly handed it over to Margaret. "Pete got that for me after my last boy."

"Nice."

When Margaret handed the case back to her, Mitzi tucked it in her purse, closing the clasp with a clack. She smoked in silence while Margaret sipped at her coffee.

Finally, Margaret set her cup down then paced the room, clasping and unclasping her hands. "I want to be a good wife to Joe. This last pregnancy did a number on my body. I'm not sure getting pregnant again so soon will be good for us. I only wish I could, I don't know, wait a bit more before I get pregnant again."

Mitzi stamped out her cigarette but said nothing in reply. Margaret had to come up with something to get the woman talking.

"I already have to depend on Joe so much with the other girls and now with Annabelle. Adding another child, I don't know how long it would be before I recovered. Poor Joe would have to miss some of his nights out and business trips. It's really not fair to him." Margaret cringed at her own words. They sounded so phony to her. She turned toward the mantel in case Mitzi could read the lies on her face. She heard the strike of another match.

"That would be awful. You certainly wouldn't want to do that to Joe."

Margaret's face lit up, and she turned with a smile. "Oh, Mitzi, I knew you, of all people, would understand. You're such a good wife to Pete." She went over and joined the woman on the sofa.

"You just have to know how to handle men."

Margaret played the innocent. "What do you mean?"

"Their egos. They want their wives to be like their cars. Attractive. And they want other men to envy what they have, yet they're the only ones with the ability to take it out for a spin. But that's where you have to be careful." She pointed her cigarette at Margaret. "Too much spin and you become the old family car. It's predictable."

"I think I'm following you, but how do you keep them from driving the car?" Margaret hated all the talk around, but if that was the only way that Mitzi would give up advice, she would go along with it.

"Honey, you just need to rev the engine once in a while."

Margaret shook her head. That time, she didn't understand what Mitzi meant. But when the woman explained, Margaret sat back in her chair, a bit stunned. All that time, she'd thought of herself as a woman of the world, but she had been clueless when it came to sex.

"Did I embarrass you?" Mitzi flipped ashes into the ashtray.

"No, I've just never, um, well—"

"Trust me. Men come home, they're tired. You simply release their stress."

"And that satisfies them? The, um, revving the engine?"

Mitzi nodded. "They're happy. You're happy because you're now in control of when and where."

Margaret rose from her chair and went over to the mahogany piecrust table with a lamp beside the front window. She flipped through the woman's magazine and landed on an advertisement for mouthwash about hygiene. "I was thinking of this."

Mitzi shook her head. "That doesn't work. I know of two women right now with bambinos who tried that. You need real protection." She shared about a contraption you could use to prevent pregnancy. "That's a big no-no for most of the women, which is why they look like used-up old—" Mitzi stopped for a moment, but then proceeded, deciding that Margaret posed no harm. "Maria just had her fourteenth child this year. I don't think I've seen her without being pregnant or nursing a child. Sometimes, at the same time." She pulled another cigarette from the silver case. "She had to be institutionalized. I think she's at the nunnery now, where she's recuperating."

"Who's taking care of all her children while she's healing?"

"Well, her older children help with the younger ones, and they have lots of nonnas that help too." She took a puff of her cigarette. "Just imagine. She hasn't even hit forty-five yet."

Margaret didn't need to imagine it. She knew many others around her mother's age who'd had that many.

"And you have and use one of these, um…?" Margaret needed to get Mitzi back to the original subject.

Mitzi's eyes narrowed, and she sat back on the sofa, blowing out smoke.

Margaret had to be careful. She'd cracked into Mitzi's shell, but it could easily close up again. She had to ensure the woman felt comfortable and safe with her. "You know, I think Lorena said that..." And off she went with distasteful gossip. She hated to tell on those women, but they had resented her from the beginning. She would do whatever it took to ensure that she and her children would be safe.

By the time Mitzi left, Margaret felt she'd had a sex education class. She'd learned of times of the month when a woman was most fertile and so much more. She'd even had Mitzi agree to help her purchase the same contraption she used.

She had the first round of ammunition in her arsenal and would use it when the time was right. It was time to start on the next piece of her plan.

~

Margaret pulled through her dresses, viewing each and discarding those that weren't what she wanted. While she had returned to her slim frame with her first two, with Annabelle, her hips had widened, and her breasts were full and heavy.

With the dresses Mitzi helped her buy, she'd added modesty panels to the tops. She set to work, tearing them out and cinching the waists with darts and using belts to highlight her figure. That night, she cooked Joe's favorite dinner. She had put the children to bed early and dressed up. Instead of wearing her hair down, she put it up in a bun on her head.

"Well, what have we here?" Joe had come in the front door.

"Darling. I'm so glad you're home. Let me take your hat and coat." As he shucked out of his coat and she placed his hat on the hall tree, she noticed his eyes on her full cleavage then skimming over her hips. Updating the dresses with a few tweaks had created the desired effect.

"You're looking lovely this evening."

She twirled around. "I'm finally feeling better now. I wanted to thank you for bearing with me. I've been so moody lately. I'm sorry. To make it up to you, I've made steak, baked potatoes, green beans, and for dessert, your favorite coconut cake."

"Sounds delicious."

"How about a drink first? Whiskey?"

He loosened his tie and sat down in the club chair as Margaret went over to the drinks cabinet. She bent over in front of him, playing the harlot, and handed him the glass before going behind him. "Let's take off that jacket. It's just the two of us here." He stood, and she removed his suit jacket, running his hands across his shoulders. As he sat back down, she pulled off his shoes then rubbed his feet.

"Oh, that feels good. You're spoiling me, Margie."

"Isn't that what a good wife's supposed to do? You spoil me and the girls so much. I only want to show you how much I appreciate all you do for us."

He smiled. "It's nice to see a woman appreciate how hard men work."

Margaret couldn't help but catch the word, "woman" versus "wife." She kneaded his foot, causing him to moan a bit. "I could get used to this."

Margaret bit back a retort that if he spent more time at home, he'd receive more attention. Instead, she smiled and went to work on his other foot.

Joe laid his head back on the doily protecting the chair. Soon, he was snoring, and she used the time to get dinner ready. Tonight was one of the nights he "went out with the guys" but was most likely meeting up with Mitzi. She had to see if she had the power to prevent him from leaving. Over dinner, she kept piling the food on his plate.

"No more. I'm already stuffed."

"Don't forget the cake."

As he ate cake, she broached the actual subject of the evening. "Joe, I took your recommendation and have invited the ladies over, but now that I'm feeling better, I was wondering about possibly having another party. What do you think? Would you like that?"

"A party? Um, yeah, we could do a barbecue. Hamburgers and hotdogs. The girls would like that."

"That sounds wonderful. I'll see if I can find something the girls can wear. They're growing so quickly."

"Just go into the city and buy some clothes." He winked. "Get you some things too."

"Thank you. Now why don't you go have another drink, and then I'll clean the kitchen. I know you'll be leaving for your time with the guys, so I'll say goodnight now and go up and have a hot bubble bath."

She exaggerated her hips swaying as she made her way upstairs and made sure she cracked the door to his sleeping area open. As the tub filled with bubbles, she listened for sounds from his room. When she heard him rustling around, she kept her back to him and dropped her robe before pulling the last pin from her hair, sending the curls cascading down her back.

He opened the door.

CHAPTER THIRTY-FIVE

Later, as he slept, Margaret crept from the bed and pulled the concoction she'd made up earlier from its hiding place. Mabel Steel may have been a midwife for her mother, but her daughter had taught Margaret some things too. This was the first time she'd used that marital knowledge to prevent a pregnancy. But most importantly, Margaret felt vindicated that Mitzi had spent the evening waiting for Joe. She could begin setting the next part of her plan in motion.

After returning to the bedroom, she watched Joe sleep. She should feel dirty and ashamed of what she'd done. Never before had she tried to deceive or lie like that, but the anger at his betrayal and adultery and his dismissal of her when she didn't supply him with a son still caused her heart to clench in pain.

Margaret had had enough of living a lie, of men being in control of her life. She was taking hold of the reins, and if this was the only way she could do it, she would. To protect herself and her children.

The next morning, she rang up Mrs. Bohannon's niece to watch the girls. Instead of heading into the city, she went over to another town and found a thrift shop. With money from the household allowance, she bought a few dresses, a pair of comfortable flats, and some items for the girls, but the most important thing was a battered brown suitcase. Thankfully, the money being gone wouldn't raise an eyebrow. She gathered a few things up for the girls they could wear so that he would think she'd gone to the major stores.

The following week was the party. Margaret wore a halter top and tight capris with kitten heels. She leaned over and made jokes with the men, knowing that Joe's pride at having her as his wife would outweigh his jealousy. Pete finally arrived with the boys but no Mitzi. When she'd asked after her, he said that she didn't feel well and had stayed home.

Margaret's stomach clenched. Far too often she'd heard that excuse, and she had learned it usually meant a man taking his anger out on his wife. But not Mitzi. Pete wouldn't dare touch her knowing that she was Joe's. Maybe Pete didn't even know about their affair. She considered telling him, but in her heart, she knew there was some unspoken code between all the men. Maybe they didn't care if their wives slept around because they were doing it too. It made Margaret's head spin with all the underlying drama.

After ensuring that Joe and the guys were well taken care of and the kids were playing, she returned to the group of women, the gossip in full swing. She overheard them sharing about something that had happened in the business and that Pete's business partner was missing. Words floated to her ears as she cleared glasses, pretending not to hear what the women were saying. Compromised. Found out. Cheating. *Is Mitzi cheating on Pete with someone else besides Joe?* Or perhaps this had to do with the family business. More and more, she felt she didn't know half of what was going on outside her home, but rumors of illegal activity made her more aware of her need to ensure her children's safety.

Her mind was spinning. Maybe Mitzi and Joe weren't having an affair. Maybe he was only going out and playing cards with guys on those nights. Doubt swirled in her mind.

She knew one thing. She had to find out the truth.

The next day, Margaret went to Mitzi's, showing up unannounced. Mitzi opened the door before realizing who it was. She hadn't drawn the drapes yet so didn't expect it to be a neighbor or someone she knew.

Mitzi peeked around the doorframe. "Margie, what are you doing here?"

"I heard you were ill. I brought you some chicken noodle soup." She held up the container.

"I'm not presentable for company right now."

"Well, at least take this soup after I've come all this way. If you're ill, let me make you some tea and dry toast. I'm here to help." Margaret stepped closer.

"I'm not dressed. Leave it on the stoop, and I'll get it in a little bit."

"We've both seen each other while dress shopping. Come on, open the door."

Mitzi sighed. "What the hell." She opened the door, and Margaret gasped.

The right side of Mitzi's face bore a horrible combination of yellow, green, and purple mottling. Her eye was half shut, and her bottom lip bore a large cut.

"Mitzi. Sit down. What happened?" She set the container down on the hall table and led Mitzi over to a chair covered in chintz.

Mitzi didn't answer. She reached forward, clutching her ribs with her hand.

Margaret picked up the cigarettes and lit one for Mitzi and one for herself. "I'm going to go put on some tea. You sit there, and I'll be back shortly." The kitchen was a mess, and she realized Mitzi must have told the housekeeper not to come in. As she set the pot on the stove, she worked to clean up the dishes and wipe down the counters. "I'll be just a few more minutes."

Jogging up the back stairs, a knot in her throat, she made her way to Mitzi and Pete's bedroom. She searched until she found what she was looking for. She wadded it up and stuffed it under her shirt. Making her way back to the kitchen, she found a paper bag and put the garment in it before setting it outside on the back stoop. She closed the door softly before finding a tray. She buttered some toast, poured some orange juice, then put the tea bags in the cups, along with the hot water jug. When she returned to the living area, Mitzi was weeping softly.

"Oh, Mitzi. I'm so sorry. What can I do?"

A manic laugh spouted from her lips. "Do? You can't do anything. You're so naïve. But I can't help but like you. Even after everything I've done, and yet you want to help me. If only you knew the truth."

"You mean about you having an affair with Joe? I'm not as naïve as you think." Margaret was shocked she'd said the words out loud. She lowered her voice, almost afraid of the answer. "Are you in love with Joe?"

"Love? No, Margie. An affair. Is that what you call it? No. It's sex, plain and simple." Anger rose in her voice. "It's a way to feel something. You'll see. They take you, and they use you, then they spit you out like something bad in their mouth. You become nothing more than a glorified housekeeper and mother to their children. That's when they start looking for something else. Something younger, more fun." She sucked in on her cigarette, wincing as it connected with the cut on her lip.

"But what about your husband? Don't you feel anything for him?" Margaret's question bore no judgment or rancor. If Pete beat her, maybe Mitzi felt she had no other choice.

"I was like you once. So enthralled with all of this." Mitzi waved her hand at her surroundings. "But you don't realize it's a trap. And once you're in it, you can't leave. Especially when you have sons. They want you to have more and more."

Margaret sat, stunned at what she was hearing. For a diamond ring and the home of her dreams, she'd willingly walked into a cage. She wondered how long it would be before she ended up like Mitzi. She had to escape.

She motioned to Mitzi's face. "Why?"

"I was careless." She shook her head. "Anyway, I'd been seeing

Joe for a while. Just a fling. Nothing serious."

"Does Pete know?"

"Of course, he does. But Joe's the big cheese. No one will go against Joe Senior. Joe Senior knows too many, um, let's call them 'protectors.' Now with Joey going to run for office, he needed a wife but not Italian. With you by his side, he can show that he's one of them. That's why he changed his last name from Martino to Martin. No more calling him Joey, only Joe or Joseph. They're going after the labor groups. His power will grow, and who knows where he'll end up. Maybe even governor."

"I can't believe Pete's okay with all this. Why doesn't he stand up to Joe?"

"He's not okay with it. But it's the way things work in the family. The higher-ups take what they want. If someone complains, well, let's just say you don't see them around anymore."

Margaret gulped. Mitzi couldn't mean what she thought. She wanted to ask, but the word—murder—wouldn't leave her lips. She clasped her hands tightly.

Mitzi continued, "But after you came, and I got to know you, I realized you were just a pawn. I didn't want to see you get hurt." She got up and walked over to the large secretary, opened a drawer, then pulled out a box. "I got this for you. It's a diaphragm. It's not even mine. But I left the bag on the counter, and Pete found it. He went nuts. He knows that the more children you have, the more it gives you an extra layer of protection. They won't come after your wife or kids. With lots of kids, they may beat you up but won't—anyway, I told him I hadn't used it, but he went crazy."

"Mitzi, I'm so sorry." Part of Margaret told her she shouldn't feel sorry for a woman who'd just admitted she'd been sleeping with her husband. Yet she did. She pitied Mitzi.

"You don't owe me anything. I'm the one who should be sorry. I stopped for a while, but Joe's like an alley cat, and he came slinking back around. I was lonely, desperate. You should hate me, and I wouldn't blame you."

"I don't hate you." Margaret realized the words were true. Mitzi had been as much a victim as she had in some respects.

"Listen, you can't let Joe win this commissioner race. If he wins, he'll never let you leave."

"What can we do?" Margaret had been aware that Joe had been starting to speak at events. She'd even attended a few, standing behind him as the doting wife.

"Not me. You."

"But you need to leave too."

Mitzi shook her head. "It's too late for me. What would I do? Where would I go? But you're still young. You have your looks, and I can tell you're smart. But I can do this. Let me think of something." She handed Margaret the box. "Try to avoid him as much as possible. I'm going to my sister's for a few days until the makeup can cover this." She waved at the bruises on her face. "Then we can think of a way forward."

She stood, and they hugged one another. "I've never had a genuine friend before you, Margie." Her eyes teared up. "I wish things would have been different, and we'd met at a different time or place."

"I'm still your friend."

Mitzi shook her head. "I don't deserve you as a friend after everything I've done. But I'll make it up to you. I'll figure out a way." She sniffed and pulled out a handkerchief from her pocket, wiping her nose. "Now go. Don't come back here. No one should see you here. I'll call you. No, that won't work. Too many ears. If Joe were to get wind of me contacting you now, I think it could be trouble. He's been starting to back off anyway in case anyone saw him come here without Pete being home. He can't take the chance of any scandal at this point."

Scandal. Margaret's mind whirled at what she'd just heard.

Mitzi tapped her fingers. "If I need to send you a message, I'll figure it out somehow." Um, borrowing sugar. That's it." Then she rushed Margaret out the door.

Margaret drove home, her mind on what she could do to stop Joe from being nominated to run. She had to get to the men.

An idea came to her. *Of course.* The best plan was often the simplest. If she wanted to affect the man, she would get to him through his wife.

CHAPTER THIRTY-SIX

Margaret set the table with her best china and a buffet of tomato aspic, a tray of various cucumber, egg, and pickle sandwiches, and crudites.

Weeks had gone by since she'd spoken to Mitzi. She'd seen her a few times at the grocer's, but Mitzi made it a point to put on a show of walking away whenever she saw Margaret. But Margaret hadn't spent her days waiting. She'd crafted a plan that would stop Joe from ever holding office.

The women were abuzz with the latest gossip as they gathered their food and found places to sit. Margaret made sure she sat down next to Sophia, who couldn't keep a secret if her life depended on it. The chief thing was to steer the conversation in the right direction.

"Sophia, that's a pretty dress you're wearing today."

"Thank you. I enjoy sewing my own day dresses. It keeps me busy. Hank likes me to stay occupied. He says it keeps me out of trouble." She giggled, but it fell flat.

"Well, I'm sure that we'll probably all be stretching our budgets and making our own day dresses soon."

Sophia cocked her head. "What do you mean?"

"Oh, nothing. I'm just wondering how long the factory is going to stay put is all."

"What are you talking about? That factory's been here forever."

"It's a nice piece of property. I bet developers could make a lot of money shutting down the factory and selling it."

"Selling the land?" Sophia balked. Margaret saw she had the other women's attention as well. "Not with the labor group in charge."

"Oh, I thought I heard differently." She took a bite of the aspic. "I enjoy this with the gelatin."

The women all exchanged looks before Sophia said, "I've heard Joe is running for commissioner and backing the party's platform. He's definitely on the side of labor."

"Is he? Maybe I'm mistaken. I thought he'd said..." She stopped and let the insinuation hang in the air. "I'm a terrible hostess. Will you excuse me?" She wiped her mouth with her napkin and went over to the other table, where the ladies were laughing and joking, knowing that the whispers behind her were just the beginning, or should she say, ending Joe's political aspirations.

After the woman left, Margaret peeked from the upstairs curtains as the women congregated in animated conversation out by their vehicles. It only took a little miscommunication to let the women fill in the blanks. Tonight, they would share it with their husbands, and word would spread that while Joe was telling them one thing, he planned to do another.

However, her risk made her presence there with Joe also more precarious. If it came back that she'd been the one to start the rumor, she might end up with a bruised face like Mitzi—or worse. That night, she hugged the girls tightly and wondered if she'd made a terrible error in judgment that would come back to haunt her.

~

Margaret lingered over her coffee and dry toast, the daily newspaper open in front of her. Her mind drifted as she recalled hearing the news that Pete had been mugged one evening and walked with a limp after. She suspected Mitzi had shown Joe her face before she left, and Joe had made sure Pete wouldn't touch her again. Or Mitzi's family had decided to teach Pete a lesson. Either way, Pete would think twice before laying a hand on Mitzi if he knew what was good for him.

Mrs. Bohannon interrupted Margaret as she reclined outside on a chaise, reading a new Agatha Christie novel, while the girls played with dolls nearby and Annabelle napped. "Mrs. Martin, you have a visitor. She wouldn't come inside but asked if you'd see her for a minute." Margaret knew immediately who was at her door by the tone of Mrs. Bohannon's voice.

"Okay." She rose and dusted off her tan slacks. "Can you watch the girls for a minute?"

She went over to where Mitzi waited by the back door in dark glasses, her hair covered in a wrap. "Come inside."

"No. I don't think anyone saw me, but it's important that we don't appear friendly. I'm going to give you this magazine, and when I leave, I want you to yell at me. Take it up to your room. Don't leave it lying around anywhere."

Margaret nodded.

Mitzi turned and spoke loudly, "I shouldn't even have returned it to you."

"Never come back or show your face here!" Margaret yelled after her. She closed the door and looked down at the magazine. But as she flipped through it, no note or envelope spilled out. She took it upstairs and put it on her bedside table before returning to the girls.

Later that evening, she opened the magazine, trying to figure out what Mitzi had wanted to tell her. Frustrated, she sat back and perused the pages of articles, ads, and photographs. Something caught her eye. A word had been underlined. Over on the next page, a little star was next to a picture. She went over to her dressing table and pulled out a pad and pencil. She wrote the letters as words and sentences formed.

Don't use the phone. Operator listening in on calls.

A picture of a dinner party. An advertisement for a bottle of aspirin.

Margaret stared at the information she'd compiled and the pictures that were marked in the book. Finally, she realized what Mitzi was communicating. They had been invited to a party, and Mitzi was advising her to stay home.

On the day of the dinner, Margaret told Joe that she was worried that Annabelle didn't seem well, and she didn't want to leave her for the evening in case her fever went higher. Joe okayed it, but she could tell he was distracted.

"Is everything okay, Joe?"

He rubbed his hands through his hair. "Nothing."

The rumor mill must be working. She decided not to keep questioning him. The last thing she needed right then was him angry with her. He might start wondering if she'd had any part of the gossip.

As she moved in front of him, he gazed at her. "You look like you're losing weight. Is everything okay?"

"Yes, just want to stay trim for you, darling." Margaret couldn't tell him she'd been buying less food at the grocer's and only eating broth when he wasn't at home. That had allowed her to stash away money. She refused to be without any way to care for herself and the girls in case something happened.

"You sure it's for me?"

"Why would you say such a thing? Of course, it's for you."

Joe slunk off to his study with Margaret glad the conversation had come to an end. She stayed up in June's room, playing with the girls until it was their bedtime. After kissing each on the head, she made her way downstairs, tired and ready for a reprieve. She was pouring herself a drink when the doorbell rang.

Who could that be this late? She went to the door and was surprised to find Pete standing there. His forehead and hand still bore the signs of a fight.

"Pete, what are you doing here?" She stood in the doorway.

"Is Joe here?"

"No. Was he expecting you?" She wondered why he wasn't at the party, but maybe he and Mitzi hadn't been invited.

"I got a message to meet him here at the house. He wanted to talk about the campaign tonight." He shrugged. "That's all I know."

"Oh, well. I guess you should come inside, then." Joe hadn't said he was meeting with Pete after the party, but it wasn't unusual for her not to know her husband's plans. She ushered him into the living room. "Would you like a drink while you wait?"

"Sure." He loosened his tie. "Mitzi tells me you two don't see each other much anymore."

The hairs on her neck stood up. "We've both been busy, I guess. But she was very helpful when I first moved here." Margaret realized she'd been living the façade of a perfect life. Handsome husband, beautiful home, children—but underneath was deceit and dirt and the death of everything good.

"Thanks." He took the drink she offered him.

"I guess Joe's not home a lot. Must get lonely." He sipped at the drink, and Margaret felt icy fear well up inside her.

"Not so much. In fact, I bet he'll be home any minute."

The phone rang. Thankful for the interruption, Margaret raced down the hall to the telephone stand. She picked up the receiver.

It was Mitzi.

That was strange. She remembered what Mitzi had said about people listening in on conversations. "Hello, Mitzi, can I help you?"

"I'm looking for Pete."

"He's right here." Margaret stopped. Something was wrong. "He's waiting to talk to Joe."

"Joe's not there? You're all alone?"

What is she doing? She stumbled to come up with a response, but saying the children were there only made it seem more sordid. Nothing was happening. But it sounded like it was. "Pete said Joe told him to come here to meet after the dinner. He just arrived."

"Joe's at the card game. He went there after dinner ended. You knew that, right?"

Margaret swallowed. "Oh, I must have forgotten. I'll tell Pete, and he can go over there right now. Unless you'd like to speak to him first." Her chest tightened.

"No. I'll talk to him when he gets home."

What game is Mitzi playing?

Margaret heard another click on the line. Someone had been listening in on the party line, or it had been the operator. Neither was good. Margaret had already drawn her curtains for the night and was alone with a man in her house. Anyone would question it with Joe gone.

She should have realized she was dealing with a cunning foe. She slammed the phone down on the receiver then flew back to the living room, where Pete sprawled against the couch. His glass looked full, so he must have gotten more while she was on the phone.

"Hey, baby. Why don't you come sit next to me?" He patted the couch.

"No. Leave. Now. Joe's at a card game. I think you may have been mistaken."

"Ah, come on. One more drink. You're very attractive, you know. Joe's a lucky man."

She went over to the door and opened it. "You need to leave. Now!"

"Fine." He threw back the whiskey and set the glass down on the side table. Walking out the door, he leaned in close to her ear, whispering, "Let's do this again sometime when I can stay longer."

He stumbled off the porch, righting himself before he made his way to the car. As she slammed the door shut, she pressed her back against it. Fear gripped her. Mitzi had played her, and she'd fallen right into her trap. She pushed up from the door, pacing as her mind sought answers that evaded her. In the end, she wondered if she had been beaten at her own game.

CHAPTER THIRTY-SEVEN

The phone's ringing pulled Margaret out of a deep, troubled sleep. It rang again, insistent.

She wrapped a robe around herself and made her way downstairs. Picking up the headset, she heard a familiar voice.

"Hello, Margaret?"

Margaret roused out of her stupor. "Katie? What's wrong? Is everything all right?"

"No. You've got to get out of the house. Now."

She clutched at her nightgown, suddenly alert. "What are you talking about?"

"I can't tell you much, but Tom was out with some other drivers tonight at a party. He overheard some of the guys talking. He recognized Joe's voice." She hesitated. "It's bad, Maggie. They're going to say you're having an affair. Joe is going to try and take Annabelle away from you."

"What are you saying? This is crazy talk."

"We don't have time. You have to trust me. Get the girls ready. Tom and I are on our way. Do it. Now!" The line went dead.

Margaret rushed into her bedroom and dug the suitcase out from the back of her wardrobe where she'd stashed it. She'd already packed it with clothes for her and the girls, but she'd never thought she would need to use it so soon.

Next, Margaret went into the bathroom and emptied the Kotex box where she'd stashed the money she'd been saving. But more importantly, a set of photographs she'd taken. Those would be the proof she needed to obtain a divorce from Joe. It was Mitzi who'd given her the idea when she'd spoken of scandals. It had never occurred to Joe or Mitzi that she would follow them and find them *in flagrante*. She pulled the damaging photographs from the box and set them inside her suitcase.

Margaret shed her gown and was reaching for one of her dresses when she stopped. She didn't—wouldn't—take anything from there. Dressing quickly, she heard a door open and steps on the stairs. She grabbed for a lamp as the door opened. It was Tom.

"I'll get the bigger girls, and you get the baby. Hurry." He saw the suitcase and grabbed it too. She looked around at the room that she'd dreamed of as a young girl, with its queen-size bed, satin coverlet, dressing table, and chaise. She had one more thing to do. Mitzi might have called her naïve, but she wasn't stupid. She found the bag she'd retrieved from the traitor's house.

After smoothing out the covers, she laid her peignoir set down on her side of the bed. She pulled her ring from her finger then placed it on top.

Margaret had finally realized what it was about Joe that bothered

300

her. It was the smell on him when he'd come home on certain nights. Mitzi's perfume. She wanted to send a message to him that she'd known all along. When she had visited Mitzi, she confirmed her suspicions. There it was. The same nightgown Mitzi had instructed Margaret to purchase. She dumped Mitzi's gown on his side of the bed.

Finally, she ran from the room to get Annabelle from her crib. The baby in her arms, she raced down the stairs, out of the house, then into the alleyway to where she could see Tom standing next to the car. Inside, the girls were on the backseat, Gennie and June crying at being woken and taken out of their warm beds.

"Mommy!" Gennie reached for her.

"Shh. It's okay, sweetie. Put your head in my lap."

Gennie laid her head down as Margaret stroked her hair, cooing softly. "It's okay, honey. Go back to sleep." June had snuggled up next to them while Katie held Annabelle in her arms in the front seat.

Tom closed the door behind her, and they headed off into the night.

"How did you find out all of this?" She slumped against the seat, the adrenaline coursing through her veins.

"You should know that house staff talk. Turns out, you're not the easy, compliant wife Joe wanted. Plus, when it got back about where people had heard he was going against labor, well, that was it. Someone sent Pete over there so they could get you both."

"I would never." She put a hand to her temple. "Mitzi was setting me up to take the fall. She'd get rid of me and Pete in one swoop.

Wait, Pete left hours ago. How—"

"Someone was going to wait outside to take pictures, but luckily, you got him to leave. From what I understand, they were on their way to confront you before you fled. The housekeeper overheard all this and told her husband. The next thing I know, I found out. That's when I had Katie call you."

Katie reached over and took Margaret's hand in her own. "What are you going to do, Margie?"

"I need to talk to Joe Senior. First thing tomorrow."

Katie shot her a worried look. "Are you sure that's wise?"

"I don't know, but it's the only thing that I think can give me back my freedom."

"We have little room, but you and the girls are welcome to stay as long as you like."

Margaret stretched. "I can't impose. I need to get this settled quickly. They're going to be looking for me."

"Where will you go?"

A name popped into her mind. "Leland. I've kept in touch with him about June. I think he'd come if I asked him, if only for June's sake. I can see if he'll let me stay with them for a while. He didn't remarry after all when she lost the baby, and he's living with his sister again. She hates me, but I do believe he'll do it for June.

"Plus, it will give me enough time to figure things out, and I don't think Joe would think to look for me there. I'll call him in a little bit. But I have a few loose ends I need to tie up first."

~

The following morning, Margaret felt more determined than ever. She watched as Katie cleaned up the breakfast dishes. "What first?"

"I need to go to the grocery store."

"I'm sure I have what you might need."

Margaret shook her head. "No. I need to buy a bag of sugar and some salt."

"I have that at home."

Margaret shook her head. "It's not just buying it. It's something I have to do—someplace I have to go."

"Okay, well, you let me know. We'll do whatever we can." She squeezed Margaret's hand. "It's so good seeing you again, though I hate the circumstances."

Margaret nodded. "I really don't know how I'll ever repay you and Tom for what you did last night."

After Katie took the children to the park, Margaret got to work. From her suitcase, she pulled out a black wig she'd bought at the thrift store. She put on a pair of sunglasses and made her way to the grocery store. Joe Senior was laughing with a customer, and she waited until the woman had left.

"Hello, miss. Can I help you?"

"That depends. I think we can help each other."

His eyes darkened. "Smart disguise. How's about we go in the back and talk?"

"No, thanks. I like it right here. More public."

"Okay, so talk."

She reached into her pocket and slid out a picture of Joe with

Mitzi. "You can thank your son for buying me a camera and for him and his whore not thinking I would use it on them." She pointed at it. "Pretty compromising for a possible political candidate. So much for his run."

Joe Senior pushed it back at her. "That's disgusting."

She stuck it back in her pocket. "Oh, I agree with you. It would be horrible if this disgusting picture got leaked to the press."

"Are you threatening me?"

"No. I just want my children. He never sees Annabelle again. That's all. If that happens, these pictures—"

"Pictures?"

"Oh, yes. This was mild compared to the others. We can have a quiet divorce, and you can do an annulment or whatever for the church. Otherwise, he'll never be able to marry in the church again."

His hands gripped the edge of the counter. If he could have, she knew he would've strangled her right then and there.

"Do we have a deal?"

He crossed his arms across his burly chest. "How do I know you'll keep your word?"

"How do I know you will?"

He threw back his head and laughed. "Okay. I'll talk to Joe. Where can we find you if we need to talk?"

"You don't." She reached into her bag. "One more thing. I need a bag of sugar and some salt." She handed him some coins.

He set the paper bags on the counter. "No charge. Consider it a parting gift."

Margaret took the bags and walked out of the store, feeling a strength that she'd never felt before.

Since she didn't want anyone to follow her back to Tom and Katie's, she took a series of buses. In some ways, it felt foolish, but it made her feel more secure. She had one more errand to run.

She walked up the drive to Mitzi's back entrance under the portico. She looked inside and saw a woman washing the dishes. She rang the bell.

"Hello, will you give this sugar to Mitzi, please? I borrowed it, but I wanted to return it to her."

"Would you like to come in? She's just out in the back. I can call her."

"No, I don't want to disturb her." Margaret walked off but not far. She hid behind a tree across from the house. A few minutes later, the door flew open, and Mitzi stood there, holding the bag of sugar filled with salt and the photograph of her and Joe which read, *Only a fool trusts a cheat.*

She waited until Mitzi had slammed the door shut before taking another bus back to the girls.

~

That night, she called Leland, who'd moved to Georgia with his sister. After Margaret explained that Joe was involved in some shady dealings, he'd agreed to pick them up. She thanked Tom and Katie for all their help and promised to keep in touch. She snoozed on the drive and only woke when they reached the house, its light blazing. A stern

Ida stood on the steps, her face pinched and angry. She moved out of the way as Leland led them up to the attic area.

Ida ushered them into the room tucked under the eaves of the attic. "This will be your room. I've made pallets for the girls on the floor over here, and we have a crib for Annabelle. It's not much, but beggars can't be choosers."

"It's wonderful. Thank you." That night, Margaret slept deeply for the first time in months, and for once, she wasn't left with nightmares.

The sun was already high in the sky when she made her way down to the kitchen. Ida turned from the stove. "Breakfast is over. I don't suppose you want some eggs?"

"That would be lovely. If you don't mind." Margaret went over and helped herself to some coffee while Ida banged the iron skillet onto the stove. "I can do it if you prefer."

"I won't have no other woman cooking in my kitchen while I'm still good and able."

Margaret shrugged. "Okay." She peeked into the living room. "Where are the girls?"

Ida tipped her head to an alcove, where Gennie sat next to Annabelle. "What are you two doing in here?"

"Auntie Ida said I'm to watch over Annabelle, but all she's doing is sleeping."

Margaret looked around the room. "Where's June?"

Gennie shrugged.

"Come and eat these here eggs while they're hot!" Ida called.

"Thank you. Where's June?"

"Leland took her out for a stroll. She *is* his daughter."

"I know. I just wondered."

At that moment, the kitchen door opened, and Leland entered with June perched on his shoulders. "Okay, that's enough for now."

She gurgled with laughter. "More, Daddy, more!"

"Later." He pulled out two lollipops from his pocket then offered them to her.

She hugged his neck before running off to find Gennie.

While Ida went outside to hang clothes on the line, Leland sat across from Margaret. "How'd you sleep?"

"Like the dead. I didn't even hear them leave the room this morning."

"Not surprising." He broke off a piece of her bacon and popped it into his mouth.

She studied his features. He was still the handsome man she remembered when they'd met. *Where did we go wrong?*

"I was sorry to hear about—um, Catherine, was it?"

"Some things aren't meant to be. She was never pregnant. Thankfully, I found out before we got married."

"Oh. That's horrible."

"Yes." He picked up a cup from the dish strainer and poured coffee into it. "What are your plans now?"

"Okay if I smoke?" She held up a packet of cigarettes.

"Ida won't have it in the house."

Margaret didn't want to cause any problems, so she put the

cigarettes back in her pocket. "I don't know, really. I guess I'll need to find a job, but that's going to be fun with three children."

"Well, you can't stay here. A few days at most. Then we'll need to figure some place for you to go."

"What about you? Are you here temporarily?"

He nodded. "I'll be traveling to start a new job soon if I don't get the promotion here."

"Well, thank you for coming and getting me. I need to tell Ida thanks for putting up with us for a few days too."

"You've lost a lot of weight. Have you been ill?"

"No. It's a long story, and right now, I'd rather not think about it."

"Okay. You better get thinking about where you want to go, because I'll need to take you this weekend." He left the room.

Ida returned and gathered the dishes to start washing up.

"I could do that." Margaret got up from the table.

"No need." She kept her back to Margaret.

She really needed a smoke, so she went out back to the far corner of the yard. In a few moments, Ida came outside with June, talking and laughing.

Margaret sat and watched them as she puffed on her cigarette, her only option growing stronger in her mind. She dreaded what she had to do, but she had no other choice.

She was going home.

CHAPTER THIRTY-EIGHT

After telephoning Mama about staying with them until she found a place, Margaret cried tears of joy to hear she would be welcome with the children. Instead of the normal dread that she had felt so often in the past when they pulled up in front of the house, relief flooded her. She was home, and whatever that meant, for good or for bad, it was a comforting embrace.

Her mother flew down the steps, the screen door banging behind her. Margaret raced into her arms and collapsed into tears.

"Oh, child, let me look at you. Haven't you been eating? No worry, we'll take care of that soon enough." Mama wiped Margaret's face with her gnarled hand.

A noise startled her, and she looked up to see Papa, James, and Bobby coming around the corner. James waved with a dirty red mechanic's rag. "Hey, Maggie!"

"Hi, James. You've gotten so tall. And you, too, Bobby."

James pointed to the car. "Should I help Leland with the girls?"

Margaret nodded. "Yes, thank you. They're all in the backseat." She faced her pa.

"Margaret Rose."

"Papa."

"You're home now where you're safe." He bent his head and passed by her to help with the luggage, though there wasn't much of it.

Safe. The word held so much weight. She prayed Joe Senior wouldn't go back on his word about coming after her. Mama took her inside, and the sameness of the home's interior felt like a comfortable blanket enveloping her in its embrace.

Deep in her soul, she wanted to be despondent and feel like a failure at starting again at the very place she had sought so hard to escape. But she couldn't. Instead, her heart soared at returning to what felt normal. It was the first time she'd ever felt content that she was home.

Leland declined to stay for lunch, as he wanted to get home before darkness fell. As they had the night before, he would pull off the highway and sleep for the night on a cot set up outside the Packard. Mama handed him a towel wrapped with a slab of ham, some brown bread, and a mason jar of buttermilk.

Mama stood on her tiptoes and kissed him on the cheek. "Thank you kindly for bringing our girls back to us." The woman patted his shoulder, and Margaret knew that they all wished things had worked out between them.

"You're welcome, Granny Locke."

Margaret joined him by the door to his vehicle, and the others left to give them some privacy. "I can't thank you enough, Leland. I don't know what I would have done—"

He held up his hand before removing his wallet and holding out some bills. "It's okay. I still care about what happens to you, and of course, Gennie and June. Listen, it's not much, but it will help for a bit."

"Leland, I—" She had the money she'd saved. Even though she wanted to take it, she didn't want him to think she was back where she was before. "Thank you, but I have my own money." She kissed him on the cheek and waved him off, thanking him for allowing her and the girls to stay and for driving them home.

Margaret stood looking at the road for a long time as a wave of fatigue enveloped her. Her girls were also bearing the weight of moving from one place to another. Gennie, especially, had grown clingy and cried as she fought monsters in her sleep.

As she faced the old house, the desire to collapse in a heap overwhelmed her, the comfort of being home replaced with the cruel reality of returning. She felt like she would never break free of the tentacles that wrapped her so tightly to this place. But even with Joe Senior's word and the hundreds of miles between them, she knew she would constantly be looking over her shoulder.

Over the next weeks, Margaret was able to find some low-income housing for her and the girls. It allowed her to be closer to town and more work opportunities, but she worried how long the money she'd saved would last. She and the girls slept on a mattress on the floor with Annabelle in a dresser drawer. Other than a table and chairs and a rocker, the apartment was bare.

So far removed from New York, Margaret worried about what her children thought of the constant upheaval in their lives. She did her best to make the apartment into an adventure, using sheets to make a tent over the bed. With a small lamp for light, they would cuddle together at night, reading of animals that talked and fun adventures.

It should have felt like a hardship, but the girls' laughter and the time spent with them made it that much sweeter. She'd gotten caught up in so many other things that she'd forgotten that she had three wonderful daughters. They didn't care if they lived in a palace or slept under a magic tent made up of linen sheets. They were happy. Margaret was too. Love had always been there. She'd just been looking in the wrong place for it.

After a few months had passed, Margaret began to relax. She no longer waited for the other shoe to drop. There was no sign of Joe other than a letter, which she would pick up from her parents' house that Sunday.

Arriving at the house, Margaret pulled a jump rope from her bag, and the girls played. Mama retrieved a large official-looking envelope that could only contain one thing—divorce papers. She read through the information as the front door opened.

"Hey, sis. Good to see you." Edsol came inside and kissed Mama before sitting down across from Margaret.

"Nice to see you, too, Edsol."

"How's the apartment working out?"

"We have a roof over our heads. I'm content with that."

"I think you're learning what's important in life."

"I guess. It's a nice day. Let's go outside."

They found the girls by the nearby tree with the swinging tire. Margaret settled Annabelle on the step to play pattycake. Edsol went over and gave Gennie a push before gathering June up on his shoulders. She squealed with delight as he pretended he was going to drop her. Gennie gave Margaret a wave as the tire soared through the air, and Margaret blew her a kiss. Her eldest had lost some of her baby fat and was growing taller and leaner each day. It wouldn't be long before she would be a young woman with dreams of her own.

The clock was ticking. She had to make up for the times she hadn't given her children the attention and love they deserved.

Yet with three girls to support, it would be even more important to find steady work. That had already proved more difficult with the war over. With the men returning home to their old jobs, many women who had taken over had been forced out, back into impoverished circumstances. Margaret tried to make more money, even taking in ironing while the girls were in school, but with her small apartment, there wasn't much she could do at home.

Doc Albert had taken on a male assistant who was also a doctor and would take over the practice when Doc retired, so that had been a closed door. Even with all her experience and the training she'd received as a nurse, many doors remained firmly shut for women with children. Once Annabelle was in school full-time, it would help, but transportation was also an issue. She'd finally gotten back on with the commissary, but the part-time hours wouldn't sustain her and the girls. Still, she was grateful for anything.

She watched Edsol swing June before setting her down.

"Hey, let's play hide-and-seek!" Gennie said. "Mommy, come with us."

The older girls squealed and designated Edsol as the first seeker. Margaret hid with June, who gave away their hiding spot when she giggled as Edsol passed. Margaret knew he'd heard the soft laughter but pretended to keep looking.

"Come on, June. Let's run for it." They sprinted toward the porch post while Edsol feigned a hurt leg.

"Home free!" June yelled, but she hugged Margaret.

They continued the game the rest of the afternoon, hiding as best they could as Mama laughed at their antics, Annabelle cradled against her. Finally, Margaret and Edsol collapsed on the porch while Gennie and June ran back over to the tire swing.

"Oh, to have their energy again." Margaret rested her head against a peeling white post.

They stayed for supper, and the banter at the table over the simple meal was heartening. Even Pa was in a good mood. Margaret wondered if her youthful emotions had made him seem mean and strict. She still didn't want to raise her girls the way she'd been raised, but it was nice to be around her true family.

After dinner, Nellie took Margaret aside. "There's a job opening where I work. A lady just left. I think you'd be a great fit. Plus, wouldn't it be fun to work together?"

"I'm open to pretty much anything. What is it you do?"

"It's a linen shop. From hankies to drapes. Pretty much anything you need for your home."

"That sounds nice."

"It is, and the job would be full-time."

"But isn't it in Pensacola?"

"Yes. It takes about an hour on the bus."

Margaret sighed. That meant for time away from the girls in the morning and evening, but she couldn't be picky. They needed the money.

"Should I tell Mr. Smithson you're interested?"

"Yes. That's wonderful. Thanks, Nellie."

"Don't thank me yet, and I go by Nell at the store." She hugged Maggie and the others before leaving for the evening with some girlfriends to go see a film.

That night, the moon loomed large and heavy in the sky. Margaret and Edsol sat on the front porch, taking in the sounds of crickets rubbing their legs together as the girls chased fireflies. Margaret sipped on her sweetened iced tea and relished the moment.

Edsol drove them back to the apartment, and as Margaret climbed the stairs with the girls, she felt a sense of peace within. She put the girls to bed, excited about the job opportunity as she worked on the ironing from that day. Since it was full-time, she would need to hire someone to care for the girls during the day. That would be much of her paycheck at first, but once school started, it would be like getting a pay raise. She hummed to herself as she sprinkled water on a man's blued shirt. Steam rose as she dragged the heavy iron across the sleeve, creasing it perfectly. Everything was going to be all right.

~

Though she had little in common with the unmarried shopgirls, Margaret enjoyed the pace of the shop. On Nellie's advice, she'd simply told the other ladies that she'd lost her husband in the war, which stopped more prying. The shame of two divorces clung to her even as she fought against it.

Except for a Saturday spent at Ma's, she kept pretty much to herself. She took the girls to see Franny, but they barely got to chat with so many children running around the large room and Franny tiring so easily. Margaret wished she could have Franny at her place so she could care for her, but it was just a dream. She'd even done some research on people who were struggling with her sister's ailments. There was a place in Colorado that specialized in lung treatments, but that was for the rich.

Margaret finished ironing the shirt and began working on handkerchiefs. Another sitter had quit. It seemed the young women would leave as soon as any fella took an interest. She could ask her neighbor to help out for a few days in exchange for doing the ironing, but that was a temporary solution. She had to find steady help.

Things finally came to a head when the latest sitter didn't show up. Margaret had no choice but to take the girls with her. Gennie was old enough to watch Annabelle for a bit until she could call Ma to come get them.

They'd barely made it to the store on time, but it was no conciliation. Her boss had already given her a talking-to the last time she'd been late, and Mr. Smithson fumed when she entered the shop with the girls in tow.

She settled the girls in the backroom with coloring books and crayons when her boss marched into the room.

"What's this?"

"My sitter didn't show up. I couldn't leave them by themselves all day."

"I'm not running a childcare here."

"Mr. Smithson, they're good girls. They'll sit quietly while I'm waiting on customers until my ma can come get them. Come September, they'll attend school. That's only a few months away. Please, Mr. Smithson. I need this job."

Mr. Smithson considered her a moment then stepped closer. "How *much* do you need this job?" He caressed her arm.

Shocked, she backed away, hoping the girls hadn't seen it. "You know I'm a good worker. I saved you money by telling you that your linen distributor was cutting a penny's worth of goods off each order." She wanted to take the girls and never come back, but she couldn't lose that job.

He sighed. "Fine. We'll try it, but I'm going to have to take five cents off your pay."

"Why?"

"I told you. I'm not a childminder, and you will be distracted. Take it or leave it. Plenty of other girls would jump at the chance to have this job."

She stifled her anger. "Yes sir, Mr. Smithson. I'm very lucky to have this job and for you to let me bring the girls until they start school." As soon as he was gone, she raced to the back to put in a call to Ma as shaking overtook her.

The following weeks, Margaret worked to avoid her boss as much as possible. She kept her nose to the grindstone, but she had to admit that having her children around wasn't working. Plus, with the withholding from her check, she was barely making ends meet. It was looking more and more like she would lose her job anyway. With Ma spending so much time helping Franny and caretaking for her children, she couldn't watch Margaret's too.

That night, Margaret sat down and wrote to Leland. June was his daughter. He should help pay for some of her living expenses. In the end, she poured out everything about her work situation and the struggle for childcare for the girls. She hated asking him for money again, but her next paycheck might be her last. She certainly wouldn't ask Joe for a cent. All the money she'd saved when she'd left was gone.

Mama agreed to let the girls stay with her until Margaret could find a sitter, which gave her a reprieve. At work, Margaret walked on eggshells, grateful at the end of each day that she hadn't been sacked.

Finally, she received a letter from Leland. Inside was a ten-dollar bill, but his words were full of vitriol about her inability to care for her children. He was worried about June growing up in poverty and without a mother at home.

Margaret wept. That night, she paced the apartment, smoking cigarette after cigarette, her anger and bitterness growing. *What does he know about it?* She had three young children that she was doing her utmost to provide for, and he had the gall to call her an unfit mother. She pulled out a bottle of whiskey from the boxes Edsol and James had brought over. She poured herself a glass then downed it straight. Fire coursed down her throat to her belly. She needed to calm down. To think about how to respond to such blatant accusations. Margaret poured herself another drink and took it over to the table, where she smoked another cigarette.

Her mother had raised a passel of kids on barely any money, but she'd had Pa to support the family. Neither of them could understand the constant demand of being a single mother. She had to work to put food on the table and stay up all night when her children were sick with a fever. She cooked, cleaned, and mended, then got up the next day to do it all over again.

Margaret threw back another shot of the whiskey, its bite giving her fortitude. She pulled a sheet of paper from the counter then sat down to respond to Leland. She thanked him for the money, reminding him it would go to help care for his child—his responsibility. Her pen almost tore through the paper as she refuted every accusation. Her anger boiled over as she ended the letter.

If you think you can do a better job, you should try it.

CHAPTER THIRTY-NINE

The following morning, Margaret's head ached as she boarded the bus to work. She'd never drunk that much liquor in her life. *Why do people drink that stuff?*

After a breakfast of cereal, she'd left the girls with the portly neighbor woman. She'd promised the woman a good payment but only if she stayed the entire day with the girls. Margaret hoped it had been enough incentive.

She put on the round sunglasses and silk scarf given to her by Bette as a wedding gift. The smells of ladies' perfume and men's aftershave mixed with the bus exhaust and made her hold a handkerchief to her nose. Coupled with the motion of the bus, nausea finally forced her off a few stops before the store.

Margaret checked her watch. She should be able to have a much-needed cup of coffee and still make it to the store in time. After the last fiasco at work, she'd started coming in early to prove her merit. Margaret walked down the sidewalk until she found a diner. She went inside and slid into a booth.

A woman came up to the table wearing a pink shift with a white frilly apron on it. She wore heavy white stockings and sturdy white shoes like a nurse. Her hair was pulled back with a fishnet, holding the bun in place, and she wore a matching frilly cap.

"Oh, honey. You don't look so good. Hard night?"

Margaret swallowed against the cotton in her mouth. "Coffee, please. Black."

"Right up." The woman moved away from the table, grabbing some plates on her way back to the coffee station.

Margaret pulled out a cigarette, but even that caused her stomach to roil. She stubbed it out in the glass ashtray. Behind her, she could hear two men talking. They were planning to shortchange the waitress the cost of a side of bacon. Margaret's anger returned in full force. The waitress was just trying to make a living, and they were trying to cheat her out of the money. If she came up short, it would be out of her pocket. Margaret had seen it happen too often to young women at the commissary too. They hadn't believed a customer would lie to them.

The waitress—Sally, by her nametag—returned to set down an off-white cup and saucer on Margaret's table, pouring the steaming black coffee from a carafe.

Margaret jotted down her name then slipped Sally the note she'd been working on. When Sally gazed at it in confusion, Margaret motioned for her to put it in her pocket.

"I'll be back to check on you in a bit, miss." Sally then walked to the kitchen before returning to the next table where the two men sat.

"Hey, babe. How's about a date?"

"No, thank you. Are you ready to pay your bill?"

"Yeah, sure. I had the eggs and steak, and he had the eggs and toast."

"And a side of bacon," Sally added.

"No, I don't think so," the shorter man replied.

Margaret wanted desperately to turn around and shout, but Sally kept her calm.

"You must have forgotten, sir. You also ordered and received a side of bacon." Sally's voice was deliberate.

"I don't think so." The man's voice had risen. "I think you're trying to add to our bill. Well, I don't know about you, Stan, but I think she's trying to cheat us. I don't think we should have to pay for any of our meal."

Sally cleared her throat. "No, sir. In fact—" She pulled out the paper from her uniform pocket. "I always write each table's order. Just to ensure that I get it right for the cook. See? Right here's what you ordered."

"Fine, but we're not paying any tip."

Margaret felt her hands grip the table when she noticed a burly man in a white cap and matching apron covering his paunch approach their table. The left arm of his T-shirt pocket held his Camels, while the other one had been rolled up to reveal a large tattoo with an anchor.

"Sally here is a good waitress. Now, I don't enjoy thinking that you may have been trying to take advantage of how nice she is. Here's what's gonna happen. I think you'll pay your bill and leave Sally here a fine tip, and we'll never see your ugly mugs in here again, or I may just make them uglier." He cracked his knuckles. "What's it going to be, gents?"

Margaret heard the men hurry for their coats and hats before throwing the money on the table and fleeing the diner. She could help it no longer and turned to see them go with a satisfied smile.

The waitress pointed to her. "Huck, this is the young lady who helped me."

"Hangover, huh?" He motioned to his eyes.

Margaret had forgotten about her sunglasses. There was no point in pretending, so she nodded, but that caused a moan to escape her lips.

"Coffee ain't going to do the trick. What you need is hair of the dog. I'll make it for you."

"I really need to get going—I have work." She bent and clutched at her stomach as another wave of nausea overtook her.

Sally patted her shoulder. "Honey, there's no way you're going to work like that. You look like something you scrape off the bottom of your shoe, and that's putting it mildly. Here." She slid a nickel over the table to Margaret. "Go use the payphone in back, and tell your boss you're not coming in, that you're sick. I'm going to bring you some dry toast and oatmeal."

"I can't eat anything." She swallowed the awful taste in her mouth.

"It's on the house. Plus, once you get a load of Huck's concoction, you'll want something to eat."

After calling into the store, she returned to find a tall glass that looked like it held tomato juice.

Sally came over. "The best way is to chug it down. Huck used this on plenty of sailors back in the day when they needed to be fit for duty."

Margaret picked up the drink and took a swallow. She gagged at its harsh taste with a strong hint of horseradish and tried to set it on the table, but Sally handed it back to her.

"Bottoms up. I'm not leaving until this is gone."

Margaret downed the horrible tonic then laid her head against the cool plastic of the booth.

"Got your call done?"

Margaret nodded. She wanted to lay her hands in her head and weep. With another day's pay gone, it would mean a lot more laundry to make up the difference. She'd been so stupid.

Sally tilted her head. "You saw the bathroom next to the payphone, correct?"

"Yes, why—" Margaret shot from the booth and over to the bathroom. After she had thrown up what felt like the last five years of her life, she turned on the tap, rinsing her mouth before spitting in the sink. She pulled a rough brown paper towel from a stack and blotted her face with it, drawing in deep, cleansing breaths. When she finally made her way back to her booth, on the table sat a bowl of oatmeal, two pieces of dry toast, a glass of freshly squeezed orange juice, and more coffee.

Ugh. She forced herself to take a bite of the toast and then another. She poured heavy cream over the oatmeal, and when she'd devoured that bowl, Sally brought her another, which Margaret ate as well. When she was satiated, Sally came over and slid into the seat across from her.

"Okay if I smoke? I rarely get off my feet, so when we have a break, I try to sit down."

Margaret hadn't noticed that the breakfast crowd had thinned out, and only a few couples sat at tables, being waited on by another waitress.

"I can't believe how much better I feel. That drink's gross but a miracle." She reached over to her purse. "I really need to pay for all this. I can't have it coming out of your salary."

Sally took a drag of the cigarette, blowing smoke in the air. "I told you. On the house. Huck owns the place, and he said you helped him take out the garbage. Who knows what they would try next? Good riddance." She leaned over the table. "Though I have to say, one day, I'd love to see Huck lose his temper and hammer someone. He was a boxer in the navy. I don't think anyone beat him. Oh, and the cook. He decided to open this place when he got discharged. He can't hear very well now."

Margaret nodded. That explained the cauliflower ears, the jagged scars that stood out white against his mottled skin, and the crooked nose.

Sally took a puff of the cigarette. "I need to quit these things. They can't be good for you. Anyway, Huck's ship was hit, and he only survived because he was in the freezer area. He says cooking really saved his life."

"My husband's ship was hit too." Margaret struggled, and when she looked up, Huck was standing by her side.

"I'm sorry you lost your man. We lost a lot of good men in that dammed—oh, pardon me, ma'am. Sometimes the sailor in me sneaks out."

"It's okay." She reached into her purse, but she'd forgotten to add a clean handkerchief. Instead, she used the napkin to wipe her eyes. "Please, you all have been so helpful. I think I could actually go to work. I have three girls, so I need to work when I can."

Huck wiped his hands with a white towel he slung over his shoulder. "It's nice to meet you…"

"Margaret. But I'm often called Maggie." She extended her hand, and he took it in his calloused one with hairy knuckles. Margaret winced at the strength of his grip, thankful when he released it.

"Maggie, you ever need a job, you come here. I can tell good people when I see them. You're one of the good ones."

"Thank you, Mr.—"

"Huck's fine. That's what everyone calls me."

She nodded, and he helped her up as she slid out of the booth. Sally walked her to the door, advising her to add lip color. As horrible as she felt, she couldn't lose a full day's salary. She would explain that it must have been a passing stomach bug. She hoped there wouldn't be any questions.

Sally hugged Margaret's neck. "Come back and see us, Maggie."

Margaret stepped out into the sunshine, feeling much better about herself and the future. She hurried the remaining blocks to the store.

Inside, Nellie was out on an errand, but the other girls stared at her as she walked in. She walked to the back, where she looked in the mirror and adjusted her loose hairpins. She'd just pulled her timecard when one of the salesclerks sidled up to her.

"I thought you were sick." The shopgirl glared at her and crossed her arms.

"Trust me, I was." Margaret patted her hair down.

"That's a strange sickness. Ill in the morning and then fine." Her eyes went to Margaret's abdomen.

The last thing she needed was another fight. "It must have been a stomach bug from eating something that had gone off. I feel much better now. And I *won't* be getting sick again." She wanted to make her point clear.

"No skin off my nose." She sashayed toward the door before turning back to Margaret. "Mr. Smithson wants to see you in his office."

Oh, no. She'd forgotten that Mr. Smithson's upstairs office had a window that overlooked the sales floor. It made her shiver to think of the times she'd felt someone watching her. She looked up just as the curtain fell back into place. She gathered up her courage and made her way up the back stairs to his office. Adjusting her jacket, she knocked on the wooden door.

"Come in." He sat at his desk, swiveling back and forth in his chair, his hands steepled in front of him. "I'm confused. I thought they said you called some hours ago saying you were ill and not coming in today."

"Yes, sir. I must have had a stomach bug, but I'm feeling much better now. I wanted to ensure you had enough staff for the shift, so I came on. I can work my remaining shift. I feel fine now."

"You know, Mrs. Martin, I've bent over backward to help you. I let you bring your daughters here when you couldn't find help. I've been patient when you've been late with your excuses that the sitter didn't show up on time. And now I have you calling in sick? I'm just not sure—"

"Mr. Smithson, it will never happen again. I really think it was something off with my food. I'm fine. I can even stay later today and work on the stock orders."

"I'm afraid that's not going to work." He clasped his hands on the desk. "I had to hire someone that I could depend on, you can understand. A woman with a child, much less children, is not a good fit for the work we do here."

"But Mr. Smithson, I need this job."

He rose from his desk. "Maybe we could come to some arrangement?" He moved toward her, but she stepped out of his reach. He frowned.

"Mr. Smithson, I don't bring my children anymore, yet you've not added the five cents back into my paycheck. I rarely take a break, and if I'm late, I work through lunch."

"Be that as it may, I'm afraid that we here at Smithson and Sons no longer have a place for you."

A cry escaped her throat. "Please—"

"Don't make this harder than it needs to be." He sat down at the desk and opened his checkbook. "Here are your wages until this point. I believe you can escort yourself out."

She clenched her fists, wanting to knock the smug look off his face as he wrote out her last measly paycheck. Margaret's fury spilled over. "You're a heartless perversion of a man!"

"You're fired! Never come in this store again." He pointed toward the door, his face beet red. He threw the check at her.

"No, I quit!" She snatched up the check before rushing toward the door. On the way, she spied a selection of handkerchiefs spread out on a table. She picked up three and waved them at him. "And I'm taking these for the money you stole from me."

She raced out of his office then slammed the door behind her. As she hurried down the stairs, she wondered if he would come after her, accusing her of theft. *Let him.* She grabbed her purse from the shelf and stalked down the aisle, her heels clicking loudly against the floor. As she reached the front of the store, a thought came to her—*in for a penny, in for a pound.* She pulled a lace tablecloth from a display and held it up to where she knew he would be watching. After folding it under her arm, she made her departure, leaving the shopgirls agape.

As she stepped onto the bus, she shook her head. She couldn't believe that she'd stood up to her boss like that or, even more, that she'd had the gumption to take items from the store. He could have the police come after her for theft. She groaned. *And what about poor Nellie?* She prayed her sister wouldn't lose her job over it.

Foolish, foolish woman. She thought about giving the items to Nellie to return. She certainly didn't have the money to pay for them.

She couldn't face the girls or the neighbor if she went back early to the apartment, but it was the consequence of choosing to say no to her repulsive boss. That was what her life had come to—a series of choices—and somehow, it seemed like she always chose wrong.

When she made her way up the stairs, the neighbor was not happy about losing the extra money. But Margaret stood her ground and only paid for the time she'd watched the girls. As the woman got up from the dining room table, Margaret looked to where she'd put the letter to Leland in an envelope. In the light of day, her rant of last night had taken on a different view. She planned to tear it up, but she didn't see it on the table or the counter.

"I had a letter on the table. Did you see it?" Margaret searched the floor under the table.

"You had a stamp over in the cubby, so I mailed it."

CHAPTER FORTY

Inside the apartment, Margaret shucked off her jacket, placing it on a hanger before putting it back on the peg on the wall. In the bedroom, she slipped out of her skirt then her slip before removing her shoes and carefully taking off her hose. A sigh escaped her lips as she shimmied out of her girdle, and she rubbed the red marks left by the stays. She flopped on her bed and stared at the ceiling as she thought back to the scene at the store.

I sure told him. What a louse. She felt sorry for his poor wife. Margaret flipped on her side, closing her eyes. She had expected tears or some emotional response, but she felt nothing. Maybe it was because of the hangover. All she knew was that she was more tired than she could ever remember. She pulled up the worn chenille bedspread with its simple medallion and scalloped hem with decorative fringe.

"Mama." The words came to her in the darkness as she struggled from sleep. "Mama." Louder.

Margaret blinked and saw Gennie standing next to her in the light of the lone bulb in their room.

"Why are you in bed, Mama?"

She sat up, still groggy. "I wasn't feeling well, sweetie. But don't worry, I'm feeling better now." She tousled Gennie's curls with her hand.

"I made peanut butter and jelly sandwiches." She held out a plate. "Do you want some supper?"

Margaret shook her head. "Sorry, sweetie. I'm still a bit tired. Can you watch June and Annabelle for a little bit longer? You can color at the table, okay? If you need anything, you wake me up, all right?"

"Okay, Mama." Gennie gave her a wet kiss on the cheek before scurrying off. Margaret lay back down on the bed and closed her eyes.

The sound of a warbler woke her the next morning. She shot up, clasping her hand over her mouth. She'd forgotten about the girls. Margaret threw back the covers before she looked over and saw Annabelle in her crib. She glanced over to see the girls asleep in the bed next to her. *Thank heavens for Gennie.*

She ran her hands through her hair and plodded over to the bathroom with its ugly cream tile floor. After yesterday's ordeal, she needed a bath. Running the water in the cracked pink porcelain tub, she said a silent prayer of thanks for indoor plumbing. She lowered herself into the hot water, added a scoop of bath salts, then stirred the water with her hand, sighing as the warm water lapped at her neck.

Her thoughts drifted to work. If she could make it for another month, the girls would start school. She had enough to pay her rent, but they would have to be careful with their food stores. The girls loved macaroni and cheese with cut-up weenies, so she could stretch that with more noodles and smaller bits of hotdogs. She had a bag of beans and rice that would work for a while if she added a few other items. If she could take in more ironing, that would help too. She sat up in the tub, water sloshing over the side. Once the girls were in school, she could look for a morning job, and in the evening, she could do the ironing.

She stood up in the tub, pulled a terrycloth towel from a hook, then wrapped it around her. After brushing her teeth and hair, she felt much better. She made a vow never to be so stupid again.

After Margaret dressed, she headed to the kitchen. On the metal pantry was a fresh loaf of bread and a jar of preserves. A note sat next to it.

Came to check in on you. Didn't want to wake you, so put the girls to bed. Love, Nell.

So Nellie had watched over the girls. It made sense why everything was so tidy. Margaret bit her nails. *Was Nellie sacked too?* She needed to find out if her outburst had caused any repercussions for her sister.

She scooped some coffee grounds into the percolator and sat down at the wooden table. One cigarette remained in its pack, and she set it back down. If money was going to be tight for a while, she would need to ration her smokes. Or even give them up completely. That twenty cents a pack would add up over the month.

The coffee finished, and she poured herself a cup and sat at the table. On a sheet of paper, she started a tally. All the money she had on hand plus her ironing income wouldn't be enough. She did the math in her head. If she could add on three to five more clients, she could break even.

She took a swig of the hot, bitter brew, her thoughts going back to the letter she'd written to Leland. *That's what I get for writing anything when I was angry.* It would be difficult to seek his forgiveness, but she would have to give up her pride, call him, and apologize.

Margaret heard the shuffling of feet. She looked up to see Gennie wiping the sleep from her eyes. "Do you feel better now, Mama?"

"Yes, I do." She opened her arms, and Gennie climbed up on her lap. "You're almost too big to sit on my lap anymore. Pretty soon, you'll be off and married."

"Oh, Mama." Gennie rolled her eyes, laughing.

"Gennie, do you know you're my bestest girl?"

"I am?" Her eyes went wide as saucers.

"Yes, you are. You help me with June and Annabelle. You're a trooper. I couldn't do it without you." She leaned over and kissed her on the head, breathing in her smell. "Now, let's get your sisters up because we have lots to do today." She tickled Gennie lightly, who laughed and scampered off, calling, "June, wake up!"

They spent the day over at Ma's, harvesting beans and potatoes from the garden, and she made a big pot of turnip greens with drippings, cornbread, and white beans for supper. The day passed lazily even with the chores they were doing, and Margaret spent some of the afternoon sitting on the porch swing with Annabelle in her lap while Gennie and June played hopscotch in the dirt.

Nellie arrived later in the day, and Margaret waved her over. "Nellie—"

"I prefer Nell. Remember?"

"Yes, sorry. Can't help it. I've known you as Nellie all my life. Thanks for coming over and checking on me yesterday."

"You're welcome." She joined Margaret on the swing as Annabelle slept.

"I'm really sorry about yesterday."

Nell laughed. "That was some scene you pulled in front of God and everybody. At least, so I've been told. I think some of the girls were applauding you."

"Really? Well, whatever it was, I don't know what came over me. But I wasn't going to let him walk all over me." Margaret wrung her hands. "When I realized what I'd done, I felt horrible. Not for chewing him out but if I'd caused any trouble for you."

As her little sister rocked beside her, it was the first time Margaret noticed that Nell had indeed become a young woman and quite pretty. Her baby face had slimmed, and her demeanor was much more refined.

"No trouble," Nell said. "I planned on quitting there soon, anyway."

"You did? Why? Do you have another position?"

"No. I'm getting married."

"What? When did this happen?"

"He came in one day with his mother, and well, as he says it, he fell for me hook, line, and sinker." She grinned at the memory.

"What about Papa? You know how he can be. Look at what happened with Franny."

"He'd already been going into the barbershop, first when he was enlisted and since then. His parents are the Calhouns."

Margaret raised her eyebrows. The Calhouns were one of the wealthiest families in the county. Surely they wouldn't want their son to marry Nell. What made that cruel reality worse was that Nell was evidently in love with him. Her chest contracted at the pain that Nell would experience when everything she dreamed of would dissolve under her feet.

Nell pointed her finger at Margaret. "I know exactly what you're thinking, Margaret Rose. But this time, you're wrong."

"Nellie—I mean, Nell—I don't know how to say this, but to be honest… they're not going to allow this marriage to go forward."

"That's where you're wrong. Just like I said. I've already met his family, and his mother commended me for raising myself up in my work, my deportment with no outside help, and well, she said she could tell that I loved Arnold. That was the best recommendation. She also confided to me she had been born on the wrong side of the tracks as well." Nell smiled and threw up her hands. "See? Just goes to show you. He's already asked Papa for my hand, and Papa said yes. We'll be married next summer."

Relief flooded Margaret. "I'm so happy for you." She leaned over and hugged her neck. "Where will you live?"

"We're looking at somewhere on North Hill, but we're not sure. We may even move down to Miami. There's a place there called Coral

Gables, and they're planning a new shopping area, Miracle Boulevard or something. Anyway, this would be an opportunity to have our own store. He and his father are already discussing the details."

"That's wonderful. I hate to see you move so far away though."

"Says the one that moved to New York!" Nell caught herself. "I'm sorry, Maggie. I shouldn't have brought that up."

"No, it's fine. I left to go to New York to follow a dream. But I didn't get my nursing certificate. I thought I'd finally gotten everything I wanted when I married Joe, but I didn't realize it came at a high price. I hadn't thought it through. But that's done now. I'm home, I've got my girls, and—"

"But what are you going to do since you don't have a job anymore?"

After Margaret laid out her plan to her sister, Nell insisted on giving her money.

"I won't have it," Margaret said. "We'll get by. I'm going to call Leland, apologize for the letter, and I'm sure he'll give me some more money to tide me over."

Nell took her hand. "Please let me help. I want to."

"No, and the subject's closed." She rose from the porch swing. "Are you staying for supper?"

"I can't. We're going out for dinner, but thanks for the offer." She pressed her cheek against Margaret's then descended the porch as a car drove up. A handsome man with a toothy grin met Nell before opening the car door for her.

"Bye!" She waved to Margaret.

"Bye!" As she watched Nell go, the happiness for her sister was tainted by the ball of envy underneath. *Is this the way Ma felt when I left home?*

Margaret waited a week to call Leland. She knew that he would be livid when he received her letter, and she needed him to calm down before they talked. Ida answered the phone, and Margaret could almost feel the vitriol through the receiver.

Finally, Leland came to the phone. A deep silence ensued before she rushed into her explanation about being angry and tired after a long day of work.

"Leland, I'm sorry for what I wrote. You have no idea what it's like, trying to raise three little girls on your own." She waited, but he didn't respond. She swallowed her pride and relayed the information about losing her job. If he could send a bit of money, it would sustain them until she gained some more ironing work and found a part-time job while the girls were in school.

"Wait, first you're telling me you were drunk when you wrote that letter, you ask for my forgiveness, and now you tell me you got fired and you need more money? What about the other money I gave you?"

"I'm grateful, but I've got three children, plus myself. With the electric and food plus bus fare, it's tight. I'm just asking for it until the girls start school. That's all."

"But what if you can't get another job? What if you get fired again?"

"I'm not going to let that happen. I've got it figured out."

There was silence on the other end.

"Leland? Leland, are you there?"

A quiet, steely voice came through the phone. "I'm here."

"I don't know what you want me to say. I said I was sorry. I'm at my wits' end here." She stopped before she went too far. "I just need this money for now. That's all."

He was quiet for a moment. "Let me think about this, and I'll get back to you." Then the line went dead.

She set the receiver back on the cradle. If he refused her, she would have to think of another way forward. She's started over before. She could do it again. But hopefully, it wouldn't come to that.

A day went by.

Then a week.

Then another.

No letter. No phone call from Leland. She couldn't wait much longer. She'd gained a few ironing clients, but she would need more to cover all her bills. Plus, the girls would need some new clothes and shoes for school along with pencils and red paper tablets.

That evening, she made grilled cheese and canned tomato soup for supper. Gennie had gone next door to listen to the radio with her friend, while Annabelle watched as June played with dolls in the bedroom. Margaret was washing the dishes when she heard a knock at the apartment door. She wiped her hands on the dishtowel and went to the door.

It was Leland.

CHAPTER FORTY-ONE

"Leland, what are you doing here?"

He took off his hat and held it in his hands. "Let's not do this out here. Let me come inside."

She chuckled. "Okay." As she opened the door for him, movement caught her eye. Someone dressed in dark clothing was standing in the shadow of the stairwell.

Inside, Leland stood with his back to her before facing her. "I've come for my daughter."

Margaret laughed. "What are you talking about?"

"I'm serious, Maggie. I'm here for June."

She stepped back, shock registering on her face. "You're scaring me, Leland. What do you mean?"

"I mean, I'm taking her with me. Don't make this harder than it has to be." He moved past her, but she grabbed his arm.

"You're not taking my daughter!"

"Lower your voice. You don't want to frighten the girls."

Margaret was shaking as Leland continued, "She's my daughter too. I've already shown a lawyer your letter where you said you couldn't handle all three, that you didn't have the money, and you've also admitted you have no job or means of support. I left out the part of you being drunk to protect your reputation, but I could easily include that as well. Now, don't make a scene in front of the girls and scare them."

Margaret fell to her knees, wrapping her arms around his legs. "Please, I'm begging you. Don't take my child."

He brushed away her hands. "This is best for her. Later, you'll see it was good for you too."

She rose, pummeling his chest with her fist. "No. No. You can't be this cruel."

He pushed her away and sat her down on the chair before walking into the next room. June had come to the door, her eyes wide and alert.

"Daddy?"

"Hiya, Junebug. Guess what? We're going on a trip. You're going to come stay with me for a while so Mommy can have—" He paused. "That'll be fun, right?"

The little girl's lip quivered. "Is Mommy coming too?"

"No, not this time." He took her small hand in his large one and guided her into the living room, where Margaret clutched at her knees, rocking back and forth.

"Give your Mommy a kiss goodbye."

Margaret flew up from the chair, reaching for June, but Leland's gaze stopped her from grabbing her in a desperate embrace. He waited by the front door then took June up in his arms.

Margaret followed them out to the hallway, where a man in

uniform stepped out from the shadows. The policeman's eyes went everywhere but to Margaret, his face despondent at taking a child from its mother. She rushed over to him, pleading for his help, but the policeman only shook his head and explained that he couldn't do anything. He handed Margaret a set of folded papers.

Clutching the packet, she followed them down the stairs, her gaze fixed on June. It had to be a bad dream. This couldn't be real. She forced herself not to grab June and run away.

Leland walked to his car, parked next to the police cruiser. In the back seat, Ida took June into her arms before shutting the door.

As Leland climbed into the driver's seat, Margaret rushed over to him. "Leland, please. Give me another chance. Please don't do this. I'll do anything. I'm begging you. Don't do this."

"I'm sorry, Maggie. But you left me no choice." His voice was as hard as nails. He slammed the door and started up the car.

As his car rolled forward, Margaret stood paralyzed in the parking lot. She struggled to breathe, gasping as if she were drowning. She grabbed her stomach as waves of sorrow folded her in on herself. *No, this can't be real.*

As Leland's car turned onto the road, Margaret screamed, "No. Stop. June!" The reality of losing her daughter finally brought the feeling back into her legs. She sprinted after them. But the car sped up. The distance between them grew with every second, but she ran until she collapsed on the road, scraping her knees and hands.

"June. Junnnnne." She rocked back and forth, calling over and over for her baby.

The following moments were blurry. Arms rushed to gather her up and help her to her feet. Whispers assaulted her ears as she was taken back up to her apartment, but she didn't care if they thought she was a spectacle. All that mattered were her girls. Rushing over to Annabelle, she gathered the toddler in her arms, weeping into her neck. Her hands and knees burned from where they'd been bloodied by the pavement, but she ignored them, holding on to Annabelle until the girl squirmed free.

Margaret flung herself on her bed and buried her head in her pillow, screaming into it until her voice was hoarse and her throat throbbed. Exhausted, she wept until she fell into a tortured sleep, clutching June's doll to her chest.

Sometime later, she awoke to see Gennie standing over her as she held Annabelle, who had her thumb stuck in her mouth.

Tears welled up in Margaret's eyes. "Come here, you two." She sat up and pulled them into an embrace. "It's going to be all right. You'll see." She repeated it as she rocked the girls, recognizing she was trying to convince herself.

Annabelle pointed at Margaret's hand. "Mommy, give me?"

Margaret lifted it to see she was still clutching June's doll, her grip tight on it. "No, sweetie. This is all I have to hold on to right now."

CHAPTER FORTY-TWO

Margaret spent the following days in a trance. She wouldn't even go to Ma's for lunch on Saturdays. She couldn't stand the thought of her Pa's eyes on her. She couldn't face any of them. Plus, every hour she wasn't taking care of Gennie and Annabelle, she was either ironing or trying to look for an additional job, but the only offer she'd gotten was from the diner, and that wouldn't work with the upcoming school schedule. Her only option was to hold out and keep looking. She got up each day, determined to overcome the coming challenges.

She made sure to give the girls more attention and love as they too mourned June's absence. Margaret told them that June's daddy had missed her, so she'd gone to stay with him for a while. Gennie had been told her daddy died in the war, but Margaret resisted telling Annabelle too much about Joseph, other than he lived far, far away and it was difficult to visit her because he worked so much. She urged both of them not to worry about June. She would be home soon.

Margaret picked at her cuticle. Her hands were rough and bore ugly red welts from times when the iron had slipped and caught her hand. Every night, she would apply Pond's Cold Cream to her hands and face, hoping that the burns wouldn't leave scars.

Days went by without any word from Leland. She would dial their number but was rebuffed by Ida or Leland, stating that there was no going back. While a black cloud surrounded her, it didn't negate the fact that she couldn't simply curl up into a ball and cry. In the meantime, Margaret spent all day and part of the night ironing. Gennie asked if she could learn how, so while Margaret sat nearby on the sofa, her daughter would iron all the handkerchiefs or pillowcases. It gave Margaret a chance to get off her feet for a bit along with time to study Gennie. The girl had gotten her height from Eugene, and her strawberry-blond hair was always a source of playful envy and compliments.

Gennie looked up and smiled at her. "Don't worry, Mama. I'll do a good job."

"I know you will, sweetie."

That afternoon, they loaded up the laundry into a pair of wagons that Margaret had found at the thrift store. It would make it easier to transport laundry and help do her rounds quicker.

Margaret pulled one wagon with Annabelle riding in it while, behind her, Gennie pulled the other. In an attempt to make it fun, they would play I spy as they made their way over to the beautiful homes Margaret had dreamed about as a young girl. It had taken her years to learn that a big, fancy house didn't mean happiness.

They walked to the back door for their deliveries, where uniformed maids took in the clean laundry and handed her the ironing in sacks or pillowcases. The walk seemed longer as they headed back to their apartment, going up and down the stairs until all the bags were unloaded.

When a letter finally arrived from Leland, Margaret tore into it with the hope that he had changed his mind, but he only stated that June was healthy and happy. He'd also enclosed a ten-dollar bill. She picked it up and tore the bill in half, but she knew she would tape it back together later. She needed the money—even if it came from the man who had betrayed her.

When a call came for her to come for lunch at Ma and Pa's, she wanted to refuse, but Edsol wouldn't take no for an answer. "You can't be a hermit forever, Maggie. The girls need to get out of that apartment. Now, you come Saturday 'cause I've got something to show you."

"I'll try."

"No, I'm holding you to it. Pick you up at eleven." The line went dead before she could reply. She placed the handset back on the cradle and made her way back to her apartment.

~

When Edsol pulled up in his truck, Margaret and the girls were waiting for him. After fighting over who got to sit next to their uncle, it was decided that Gennie would take the front seat and Annabelle would get a turn on the way home. The girls piled in, followed by Margaret. They drove in silence until they reached the house.

"What is—" Margaret squinted as they passed the hedge. "Did you build yourself a house?"

He smiled. "I've been building it all right. James and Bobby have been helping me, along with some of my work buddies." He stopped the truck then helped the girls out, who ran over to where Mama waited on the porch. He turned to Margaret. "I don't know if you heard, but it's been confirmed that Bud Simpson died in a camp in the South Pacific."

"No, I'm sorry." She was. Even though she hadn't wanted to marry him, he had been a friend growing up. So many of her classmates had not come home from the war. She thanked God every night that Edsol had been spared.

After lunch, when the girls were playing on the tire swing, Edsol led Margaret across the yard toward the new house. It looked tiny and was tucked back from her parents' house.

Edsol held out his hand for her to walk up the wooden porch. "Here, let me show you. Of course, it's not done yet, but we've made progress."

Margaret followed Edsol into the house. A small living room led through to a bedroom and back to a kitchen at the rear. She envisioned a rocking chair next to the woodstove and a rag rug close by where kids could sprawl out and read books.

"This is really nice, Edsol. Does this mean you're finally done sowing your wild oats and settling down with a family?"

He shook his head. "It's not for me, Maggie. It's for you."

"What?"

"Papa said you needed your own house. He didn't like you living so far away, and he's heard some bad people live at those places."

"Then I fit right in. I've definitely made some bad choices in my life." She tried to appear flippant, but it stung because it was true.

Edsol looked at her sadly and shook his head. "I think sometimes you let your heart convince your head that someone was good when they weren't. It's not a crime to be a bad judge of character."

"Maybe so. But it certainly has its consequences." She looked around the living room, unwilling to meet his eyes. It was the biggest of the three rooms. Her heart lightened. With just the three of them, it would work nicely. There would even be room for June.

Edsol beckoned to her. She followed him through the shotgun house into the bedroom, which held a double bed. They walked around the bed and into the kitchen, where a stove sat against one wall, with an older icebox in the corner. On the other side of the cozy room, a white sink with side drains had been attached to the wall. It would be easy to sew a skirt to cover up the shelving underneath it. On her left by the back door stood a metal cabinet for holding plates and canned goods. Drawers and a roll-down top covered part of it for keeping bread and other perishables.

"I don't know what to say, Edsol." Though the thought of being so close to home wasn't what she wanted, it would inevitably make things easier. Beggars couldn't be choosers, and she certainly felt that she had fallen and needed the help.

"You, Margaret Rose, speechless?" He laughed. "Wait, you haven't seen the best part." He led the way back through the bedroom and into a bathroom. A white bathtub dominated the room, along with a standing sink.

"Right now, you'll still have to use the privy outside, but look." He uncovered a porcelain toilet.

She went over and hugged his neck. One thing she had dreaded was going back to the lack of indoor plumbing. "Edsol, I don't know what to say. It's perfect."

"The plumbing still needs to be set up, but this will work for now. When you're ready, you can give notice at the apartment and move here."

Giddiness overtook her. No more rent would make a huge difference in her income. "This means the world to me. I know the materials weren't free."

"Thanks, Maggie. But it was all Pa. He paid for it. He didn't want his girls not having a proper home of their own. Plus, he thinks you need to be close to family."

"Yes. I've wanted to get away for so long, I hadn't realized that there is no perfect place or perfect family. But family matters so much."

Edsol moved back to the living room. "Obviously, we still have quite a bit of work until it's finished, but we made some real progress." They went outside, Margaret grinning widely.

"Oh, I forgot something." Edsol bounded over to his truck, parked under a neighboring oak heavy with lichen. Edsol pulled at a rope securing something on the truck's bed. He reached over and threw the tarp to the side. It was a porch swing. "Here, give me a hand, will you?"

Margaret helped him carry the white swing over to where he

attached the chain and hung it from hooks in the ceiling she hadn't noticed before.

"You can't have a porch without a good ol' porch swing. This way, you can sit here and watch the girls while they're playing outside. Also, a good place to shuck peas. Speaking of..." He took her hand, and they moved around to the side of the house. "We thought this would be a good place for a garden. Mama wanted to do something, too, so she planted this for you. Beans, squash, and who knows what else. Should make for a good fall crop for putting up for winter."

Margaret wiped her eyes. "It's too much. Thank you."

"Thank Pa." He patted her on the shoulder and moved away, leaving her standing in front of her house. "He loves you, Maggie."

"He sure has a strange way of showing it."

"Maggie, I've seen things that no man should ever see. Pa saw it and worse. Out of his company of hundreds, only he and a few others came home. We never know what another person is dealing with from their past. That's why we have to give grace to the people even when they seem to be the farthest from receiving it."

She elbowed him. "Okay, preacher man."

"That's another subject for another day." He turned toward the girls, who were calling him over to push them on the tire swing.

Margaret turned to take in the house. *Her* house. A place of her own.

She took a deep breath, ready to begin once again.

CHAPTER FORTY-THREE

The girls would be starting school in a few weeks, so Margaret wanted to get settled into the new place as soon as possible. She took her Singer sewing machine over to Ma's, and they spent the day making dresses for the girls, curtains for the house, and some day dresses for Margaret.

Along with setting up the house, she spent her days searching for work but had no luck. One day, she took Annabelle over to see Doc Albert for a check-up because her tonsils looked inflamed.

His office was busy, so she and Annabelle sat on the porch outdoors, waiting. In a while, a black girl in her teens came around the building, carrying a bundle.

Margaret studied her face. "Hello. Aren't you Ceril's daughter?"

The girl stopped, the bandanna covering her tight braids flapping with her nod. "Yes, ma'am, I am."

"I'm Margaret. I mean, Maggie. I used to work here. What was your name again?"

"Sure. I remember you." She adjusted her bundle to her hip. "I'm Cassia."

"That was it. Such a pretty name. From the cassia tree, right?"

Cassia smiled. "Yes. Few people know that."

Margaret swatted a fly away. "Well, I hope your papa's well."

The girl nodded. "Come spring, we may be moving to Alabama."

"Why?"

"To pick cotton."

Margaret groaned, having spent days with her hands sore and cut from pulling the cotton bulbs from the plant while her neck blistered. She'd never been happier than when they'd moved to Florida and away from that labor when Pa started his barbershop. "I hate picking cotton."

"Me too. But we all haves to do what we have to do."

"From the mouths of babes."

The girl cocked her head. "What?"

"Oh, nothing. I'm just talking to myself." Margaret looked back at Cassia, a question forming. "What about your schooling?"

"Pappy says there's no need for schooling, me being a girl and all."

Margaret bristled. "Of course there's a need for schooling. I bet you're a smart girl too."

"I tries, but it's so hard. I really want to learn enough and become a teacher so I can help other children."

In Margaret's lap, Annabelle swallowed then cried out. Cassia bent down, picking a daisy growing by Doc's steps. She handed it to Annabelle and told her that she often made daisy chains and wore them in her hair. Their conversation kept Annabelle occupied, and as

Margaret watched the pair, an idea sprang to her mind.

"Cassia, I could use some help at my house with my two girls. Do you think your pa would consider you staying here and helping me with Gennie and Annabelle? That way, he could go south and pick oranges instead of moving to Alabama. What do you think? I believe it's better pay for a shorter time away. You wouldn't have to move, and you wouldn't have to miss out on school."

Cassia smiled, but it faltered. "Could you talk to him, ma'am?"

"I will. Is he around? Let's get this figured out right now."

At first, Ceril was hesitant. "I dunno."

"Ceril, I'll be honest. I need some help. I'm trying to get a job, but most start early in the morning or go until after the girls are home. My mama can't be there all the time, as she's spending more and more time over at my sister's."

Margaret realized she was rambling, but the idea of this girl dropping out of school upset her. She wanted to share the importance of education, but Ceril believed his daughter wouldn't make it academically. When Margaret mentioned she would also tutor Cassia in math and reading so that she could possibly become a teacher, Ceril's eyes lit up. "A teacher. Well, that's a fine profession."

"It is. Respectable and no having to work in the fields anymore." She hoped he wouldn't take her words as an insult. "Also, everyone will see Cassia is helping me with my girls, she'll have a home while you're away and still be able to go to school, and the tutoring will be our secret. Right, Cassia?" Margaret knew that there were still some who bore terrible ideas of who should be granted an education.

He looked at her. "I always knew you were a good woman, Miss Margaret. I think it'll be fine for her to stay with you. I should be back around the end of March or April."

"Great. Part of her chores will be writing to you. Now, let's shake on it."

He stared at her for a while before he took her small hand in his strong one.

Thankfully, Annabelle's tonsils would heal naturally from her episode, though Doc's assistant said she may have to have them removed if they kept having problems. Margaret smiled. In addition to gaining Cassia's help, she didn't leave the office with a major expense to worry about.

~

With Cassia around, Margaret found a new fervor to find a good job. Even though she didn't need to worry about rent, as the girls grew, expenses would too. Plus, she didn't want to live hand-to-mouth forever. She wanted more for her daughters.

She also needed to find a bed for the girls. She created an alcove for Cassia with a twin bed. Edsol helped move a bed she'd found at a local thrift store, which they added to the front room. It was tight with the bed, a couch, and the table in chairs, but it was workable. Knowing that Cassia would be there when Gennie got home meant that she could cast a wider net for work, and she knew exactly where she was going first.

The next morning, she dressed in her best suit and caught the bus as she had done on so many other occasions. She'd taken Annabelle over to Mama's, who was once again heading to Franny's house, as she'd had a setback and had started coughing up blood.

As soon as Margaret stepped into the diner, Sally waved at her. She stood in the doorway for a moment then decided to take the initiative and headed to the kitchen. Huck was busy frying up eggs and bacon. Margaret chastised herself on her timing. The diner was packed. He wouldn't want to talk to her then.

But when Huck spied her, a big grin broke out over his face. "Maggie, good to see you, girl." He reached over and flipped some flapjacks.

Sally came in. "I'm rushed off my feet here today. Good for business, but these tootsies will be sore tonight!"

"Can I help in any way?" Margaret asked.

"Not that you'll want to do it, but we have a pile of dishes, and our dishwasher called in sick."

"I'll do it. Just give me an apron."

Sally blinked. "Really?"

"Yes, really. I do know how to wash dishes."

"Great! Hang your jacket over on that hook and you can put your purse in this cabinet." She thrust an apron at Margaret. "I've got to get back to the tables."

Margaret faced the sink full of dirty dishes and noted the garbage bin in the corner. She rolled up the sleeves of her blouse and filled up a large pot with hot, sudsy water. In no time, she'd scraped the plates then put them into the water to soak until she had cleared the sink. As more came in, she repeated the pattern. When the dishes were caught up, she wiped down the counters, filled up the salt and pepper shakers, and got cups and glasses ready for Sally. Finally, the lunch rush was over. Huck went to the door and flipped the sign to Closed.

"That was the busiest it's been in a while. I'm beat." Sally slumped into the nearest booth. Huck had gone to the kitchen, and he returned carrying three plates of the day's special of pot roast, cabbage, and carrots. Margaret dug into the meal with gusto.

When they finished, Huck reached up and pulled the cigarette from behind his ear and lit it. "You're hired."

She hadn't thought of being a dishwasher, but she would do anything. She glanced down at her hands, raw and red from the hot water and detergent.

He must have spied her looking at her hands because he added, "As a waitress. We still have the dishwasher. He had a spell today, but he'll be okay tomorrow."

Margaret did not know what Huck meant by "a spell," but she was thrilled to hear about the job. Next was the hard part. "I appreciate it, Huck. But I can only work the breakfast and lunch shifts. Then I have to be home with my girls."

"Done." He took a drag of the cigarette. "Sally will give you the details about pay, uniform, and tips. Show up at five tomorrow morning."

Five? She didn't know if the bus even ran that early. "I need to figure out the transportation."

"Okay, well, get here when you can. We open at six." He stamped out his cigarette into the last puddle of gravy before picking up the plates and heading for the kitchen.

"He's a man of few words, isn't he?" Margaret tilted her head.

"Yes, but his word is his bond. You have a job here as long as you want it. He always helps those in need."

"I'm not—" Margaret stopped when Sally's brow rose.

"Okay, yes, I'm in need. What about the dishwasher?"

She took a drink of water. "Shell shock. Huck lets him work, and then, if they get better, another one shows up. Plus, he feeds some stray dogs out the back with scraps. He may look tough, but he's as soft inside as a dough ball." She crumpled a napkin in her hand. "So, how do you plan on getting here?"

"I don't know. There's no way I can walk it, and if the bus doesn't run until later… I may not be able to take this job. I hadn't thought about that."

"Listen, if you can get to Miller's Point, I can pick you up there. What do you think?"

Margaret counted the miles in her head. "I think so."

"Okay, well, see you then. Four-thirty. Don't be late."

Margaret gathered her jacket and purse from the back. She turned as Huck reached out his hand. "Here's for today. I pay on Fridays, but you can keep your daily tips." He dropped six quarters in her palm. "Good work, kid."

On the bus home, Margaret calculated how much she would make per hour plus tips. If she got enough, she might not have to worry about finding a job for the evenings. She could still do ironing if needed. But she knew that she needed something she hadn't realized before—a vehicle. Even though she was exhausted, she got off the bus before her stop at home and headed for the commissary, where she could get a job from five to closing at eight. That would give her a full eight hours at the diner and time to get home to see Gennie and Annabelle before going to work at the commissary. She rested her head against the metal bar of the bus. She had to show Leland that she had money saved and plenty of income before he might consider bringing June back.

In her lap, she held a new pair of ugly-looking shoes and heavy hose, but Sally had sworn by them. She'd spent the money Huck had given her plus a bit more for those, along with a new wind-up alarm clock so she wouldn't oversleep.

At home, she found Cassia cooking a pot of soup on the stove, the smell of cornbread in the oven wafting in the air.

"That smells delicious."

"It's icebox soup."

Margaret grinned. "Icebox soup?"

"Yes. You find what's in the icebox, and in it goes to the pot." She picked up the ladle, holding it out for Margaret to try some.

"That's wonderful." Margaret looked around. "Where are the girls?"

"Your mama took them over to see their auntie. I 'spect that they'll be coming home soon. Now go change, and I'll ladle this up for you."

Margaret stripped out of her clothes, putting on a day dress. She left her feet bare even though the floor was chilly from the night air sweeping in through the cracks. As she dug into the simple meal, she fretted over Franny. She needed to go see her sister soon, especially if Mama was worried. She would go that weekend since she wasn't working then. She needed to keep her mind occupied until Mama came home with the girls.

"Now, where were we?" Margaret pointed to the book on the table.

Cassia picked it up and read about Tom meeting another boy named Huckleberry Finn.

CHAPTER FORTY-FOUR

Margaret rose each morning as the clock clanged, the bells on top ringing. The weeks passed quickly as she went from one job to the next, spending a few precious moments with the girls in the afternoons, playing a game or reading together.

She'd also kept her word to Ceril with tutoring Cassia, who had a talent for figures. While Cassia didn't have Margaret's memory, she was further ahead in her math skills. Margaret knew she wouldn't be able to provide the tutoring the girl needed to excel.

One night, after Cassia had solved a complex problem, Margaret sat back in her chair, gazing at the young woman. "You have a natural gift for mathematics. I think you could go beyond teaching children. You could teach in a university or put that math to use in some other way."

"You think so?" Cassia bowed her head.

"Cassia, look at me. It's not wrong to be proud of your abilities or acknowledge your talent."

All of a sudden, Margaret wished someone had told her those words as a young girl. She'd never admitted that her exceptional memory or skills were worth recognizing or that they could possibly help her get a better job. She pushed it to the back of her mind. Right then, she needed to focus on working hard, saving her money, and getting June back. While she hated to admit that she owed Pa a huge debt for having the house built, her life had become much easier because of him, and she would be able to get ahead for once in her life.

"Cassia, I'm going to speak with my math teacher and see what she says we should do."

That night, as she lay in bed, Margaret thought through the coming weeks. Ceril would be returning from the orange season. She would speak to him about considering higher courses for the girl. She had to think of the best way to approach him, as she'd often found men to be warier of women pursuing any higher education. If she focused on Cassia becoming a teacher, she might convince him. She fell asleep with a plan she felt would work.

Margaret stretched. She hoped she would get used to those early mornings soon. She rolled over and stared at June's doll, which she'd left propped up on the windowsill every night since June had left. The pain of missing her would come in waves, and sometimes, Margaret didn't know if she could bear it. She had no choice but to carry on. Even while she might cry herself to sleep after the girls had gone to bed, the next morning, she would start all over again. She would show Leland what a capable mother she was. Then maybe June could come home. It was that hope that drove her every day.

Arriving at the diner, Margaret pulled on her apron and set to putting the baskets of condiments on the tables. The familiarity of the morning and Huck, always ready with a strong cup of coffee, helped start the day in a comforting consistency. Then it would be his command to unlock the front door when he would yell from the back, "Order up!"

At that, she or Sally would head over to the door, where Huck's long-time patrons were almost always waiting to enter. Margaret would greet them and address many by name, and often, she didn't even have to ask for their orders.

She was in the back, picking up an order of chicken and dumplings with a side of turnip greens, when Sally came up to her. "The Sisters are here. Let's flip for them."

When Margaret had first seen the four women come in for lunch, she had been in awe of the way they carried themselves and their demeanors. They worked in the Defense Department and, more importantly, they tipped very well.

"Heads." Margaret picked the same choice every time.

"Bummer. Heads it is." Sally picked up a tray laden with salads and scooted off toward the dining area.

Margaret placed the Sisters' drink order on the tray, along with salads. She then spouted their favorite omelet orders to Huck with one daily special. She went out to the table and greeted the women. "Good morning, ladies. Here are your drinks."

"Thanks, Maggie. All well?" The leader of the group looked up at her through cat-eye glasses, her black hair tucked back in a chignon under a smart pillbox hat.

"Yes, very well. Thanks. I've got your orders on, and Katherine, the special today is fried fish, collards, coleslaw, and, of course, hushpuppies."

"What if we'd like something different?" Katherine asked.

"Would you?" Margaret smirked.

"No." The woman laughed. "I think you've got us pegged."

"It's not really you so much. It's people in general. We tend to do and like the same things. Sit in the same pew at church. Eat the same meals at the restaurants we choose. Follow the same habits, even down to things we do subconsciously."

The woman swiveled and looked at her with a furrowed brow. "So you're a student of habit, then?"

"I don't know about that. I've just always had a good memory."

The woman smiled. "I have to say, that's impressive if you can remember beyond the day-to-day things that go into regular memory."

Margaret shrugged. "I guess. I need to go wait on that couple that just walked in, but I'll be back to get your plates."

She went over to an elderly couple who had been coming into Huck's for years, and he always charged them the same thing no matter what they ordered. She and Sally also gave a big smile at the five-cent tip he would leave as they exited the diner, he on his cane and his wife tucked up next to him. Those two were survivors. He had been injured in World War I, and they had lost both sons in World War II. It was a wonder that Huck ever made money with all the discounts he gave out, but Margaret was happy to work hard for someone who cared so much for others who had been dealt bad hands in life.

She returned to the women, who had finished their salads.

"Carolyn wants to test your memory. Are you game?"

"As long as it doesn't take a long time. I have a break now, but I'll have to wait on others that come in."

The woman waved her manicured hand in the air. "This should be quick. How about telling us what we wore last week? Obviously, you know what we ordered." Carolyn laughed.

Margaret paused for a moment. "Carolyn wore a twin set in a pale blue, a pencil skirt, and black peep-toe pumps. Pearls in her ears, which matched the pearl trim on her hat... I'm sorry, I don't know your name, but you wore a smart brown tweed suit with a blouse with a tie at the collar. You had a beautiful gold brooch on your—" Margaret stopped and thought. "On your left side. I had to recall what side I'm looking from. You wore brown oxfords. And you'd cut your finger. Probably a paper cut. You had a Band-Aid on your index finger."

She turned to Katherine, sitting closest. "You wore a lovely pale-yellow dress with a coordinating belt and a white sweater. You also wore pearls, and I think you had gloves on that day as well. You also wore a pair of Mary Janes with an ankle strap. Finally—"

"Sylvia. Sylvia Mathers."

"Miss Mathers, you also wore a suit. Dark blue. You prefer that because it's a responsible color, and I gather that you are a manager or something of that nature. You had on a white blouse and wore white gloves. You wore navy slingbacks."

"That's amazing. I didn't remember any of that until you said it. That's exactly what I wore." Carolyn placed both hands on her chest. The other two women nodded.

"Anything else you'd want to convey?" Sylvia asked, and at that moment, Margaret felt their conversation had gone from a simple game to a test.

"You have a cat, and while you wear those glasses, I think you do it more because you think it makes you look serious. While your fingernails are painted clear, I'd guess that your toenails are a bright red."

Sylvia threw back her head and laughed. "You are a master at this!"

The chime on the door sounded, and Margaret looked up. "Another group's come in. I need to check on them, and then your orders should be up." Margaret left, wondering what had just transpired. She'd amazed herself too. She knew she had a strong memory, but it was the first time that she'd been called upon to test it for others.

When Margaret returned with the food, the women were deep in conversation. When the three other women moved toward the door, Sylvia stayed back. "Margaret, you have a gift that few people have. I know you're a good waitress, but I think your talents are wasted here. I bet that we could easily triple what you make here in salary." She handed Margaret a card. "Call me, and let's discuss this further."

She walked away, and Margaret stared at the business card. *A job? Doing what?* She tucked the card into her pocket and picked up the tip, which was even more generous than usual.

Later, she grabbed Sally and pulled her aside. "The Sisters were in a great mood today, so let's split the tips." She handed Sally her share.

"That's wonderful. But it was more than them being in a good mood, wasn't it? I saw her give you her card." She frowned. "I knew you wouldn't be here for long the first time I saw you deliver all the orders word-for-word to Huck without writing it down and how you add up the bill in your head." She took Margaret's hands. "This is so exciting!"

"I don't know. If she knew I had children, she may not have."

"Just call her! Don't waste this opportunity. It could change your life. And your daughters'." She moved around Margaret, grabbing plates of fish on the way.

That evening, Margaret kept flipping the card between her fingers. Finally, she set it on the windowsill and drifted off to sleep.

When she woke, rain pattered on the roof, and wind whipped the trees. She jolted from the bed, fearing she had overslept, but she fell back on her pillow and pulled Annabelle closer when she remembered it was Saturday. She was thankful that Huck had the weekends covered, as it gave her time with the girls and to catch up on that week's chores and errands. She rolled over and lay on her side, listening to the rain beating against the glass. It was growing stronger, and a burst of thunder had Gennie and Cassia rushing into her room while Annabelle stirred, crying.

She set Annabelle next to her and adjusted her pillows against the wall. "Come on, girls, jump in."

Margaret pulled the covers back, and Cassia and Gennie piled into the bed.

"I hate thunder, Mommy." Gennie cuddled up to her.

"I know. I'm not a fan either. But we'll be okay. Now go back to sleep."

Margaret reached over and clasped Cassia's hand, smiling. She visibly relaxed as Margaret hummed about mares and oats and ivy. Soon, the girls drifted back into slumber. Margaret listened as the wind outside howled on, trying to claw its way inside, whistling through unseen cracks in the wood.

CHAPTER FORTY-FIVE

Downed tree branches covered the ground, and puddles of muddy water dotted the landscape. *The spirits were really wrestling last night.* Margaret smiled at how Mama's superstitions had crept into her thoughts. She put on some overalls to go out and pull the branches around to the back. She could use them for kindling come winter.

The percolator finished just as the back door came open. It was Mama. "We have to go to Franny's today. Now."

"Mama—"

"Didn't you see outside? It's a sign." Mama lowered her voice. "Words need to be said."

Mama left, and Margaret almost dropped to her knees. She sat in the chair and rocked. Mama had to be wrong that time. Franny couldn't die. It wasn't fair.

Margaret forced herself up then went over to where the girls dozed. She tapped lightly on Cassia's shoulders, holding up a finger in front of her lips. "I'm going to Franny's. I should be home after lunch. On top of the icebox, there's a treat for you girls."

Cassia nodded then closed her eyes again.

Margaret grabbed a red bandanna and tied it around her hair, holding it back from her face. She pulled on her penny loafers and headed over to where Mama was already in Edsol's truck. He must have come over to pick up some of the tools he kept in the barn. No one spoke as they made their way over to Franny's.

When they arrived, Mama and Edsol stayed back to allow Margaret time with Franny since they'd seen her recently. Margaret made her way over to the frail woman, her hair so light you could almost see her scalp, giving her an angelic glow. Franny was propped up on pillows, a rag against her head and a compress on her chest. The room was hot, and the woodstove had a fire going in it, making the air stuffy and cloying.

Through parched lips, Franny whispered, "If I knew you were comin'—" She stopped as a coughing fit overtook her. When she pulled back the cloth, Margaret winced at the blood left behind.

Margaret tried to lighten the mood. "What kind of cake?"

"Whatever kind you want, sister." Her eyes teared up. "I love you."

"I love you too." Margaret pressed Franny's hand to her cheek. "You can fight this."

"No. God's calling me home. But before I go, I have to make my peace with you."

"What are you talking about?" Margaret released Franny's hand, who pointed to a drawer.

"There's a letter inside. Don't read it until you get home. I want you to know, Maggie. I'm so, so sorry. I hope that in time, you'll

369

forgive me."

"What are you talking about? There's nothing I need to forgive you for." Margaret took the cloth from Franny's head, dipped it in the basin, then wiped her face before she reapplied the rag to her head. Finally, she went over to the drawer and pulled out the letter.

"You know, I've always looked up to you."

"Me? Why?" Margaret sat back in her chair.

"You've pushed on. No matter what. No matter how many setbacks. You didn't take no for an answer. In fact, I think that your troubles have propelled you even further into becoming the woman you should be." After the next coughing fit was over, she sighed then took in a shallow breath. "I'm proud of you."

"Proud of me?" Tears fell from Margaret's eyes as she shook her head.

"Yes." Franny's eyelids fluttered. "I'm tired, Maggie. Can you get Mama? I want Mama."

"Of course." Margaret stuffed the letter into her overalls pocket, running outdoors to where her family was standing under a large oak tree. "Mama, Franny wants you."

Mama sat in the chair vacated by Margaret, holding Franny's hand as her breathing slowed and she moved between earth and heaven. The minutes ticked by like hours until Franny exhaled one last time.

Margaret fell into Mama's arms, weeping. Edsol, who had stood by stoically with Robbie, directed the grief-stricken man outside to where their children had gathered. The wails at the loss of their mother met Margaret's ears, but she was too wrapped up in her own sorrow to go to them. Her sister, her best friend in the world, was gone.

Later that night, after the Simpsons had come home with a wooden coffin, Margaret sat on their porch as Mama and Robbie's mother prepared Franny's body. In the front room, the coffin rested on ice blocks covered in black fabric. Franny would be buried on Sunday, as she'd been the pianist for the church choir and a big part of the church.

They drove home, the sorrow in the truck's cab palpable. Margaret kissed Edsol goodnight before she led Mama up the steps to the house. Inside, Mama nodded to Papa, who rose from his rocking chair and strode out the back, the screen door slapping behind him.

Why didn't he come to Franny? At that moment, she hated her father.

After settling Mama in her chair with a knitted throw over her legs, Margaret made her way out of the house, but instead of going across to her home, she walked down the road.

After the initial grief, Margaret felt numb, her mind and body adrift from one another even as tears slid down her cheeks. Franny, the kindest, most caring person on earth, was gone. She was young, too young to be taken.

"Why?" she screamed. But no answer returned from the dark void that surrounded her.

Her emotions raw and spent, she returned home to find that the girls were all in bed. In the kitchen, her coffee cup still sat on the table, stained with the dregs of that morning's brew. Margaret collapsed into the kitchen chair, her head in her hands. As she moved, the letter Franny had given her rustled in her pocket. But she couldn't face it then. It would have to wait until after the funeral.

She stripped out of her clothes and drew a hot bath. Sinking into its depths, she wondered how much more pain and heartache she could take.

~

At the funeral, the church piano had been draped in black in honor of Franny. Robbie sat in the pew at the front with his children, his shoulders stooped in grief. He had lost two wives then. *Will he marry again?* Margaret chastised herself for considering it.

The pastor spoke of Franny's service, her devotion to God and her fellow man, but Margaret wanted to scream. Her hands balled into fists in her lap. All Franny had ever done was give, give, give. And look what it had done to her. An early grave.

She didn't want to stay for the requisite meal, where people would chat and laugh as if it were any other day. But she faced the long ordeal of condolences, especially the "She's in a better place" or "She's with God now."

Margaret didn't care. She wanted Franny there—with them. Her anger mounted at the words even though she knew the women were trying to be kind. But the women who had lost sons in the war didn't spout such words. They understood it was okay to be angry, to question God for taking someone so young. Those women would simply hug her or share a story about Franny when she was a girl or some impact she'd made on their children.

The church's women had outdone themselves, as usual, with their potluck dishes and desserts. While the food looked delicious, Margaret had no appetite, so she went outside. She sat on some steps in the back, her arms crossed over her knees as all the children romped and played with each other. Their peals of laughter couldn't help but make her smile.

Life would go on. Even amidst horrific grief, the nagging pain would be replaced with fresh joy.

Margaret rose from her place and rushed over to the children. She swung Annabelle around, the toddler's squeals of laughter filling the air. "Faster, Mama, faster!"

After she'd worn herself out and was dizzy with the effort of swinging all the children, she sat on the stoop. Nell joined her, laying her head on Margaret's shoulder as she had done as a child.

"I still can't believe it, Maggie. It feels like it's not real."

"I know. I keep expecting her to come through that door and try to boss us around."

Nell gave a sad smile. "Yes, she wanted to be bossy, but she never could. She was too nice."

"That was Franny, all right. Too nice." She patted her little sister's hand. "I hear that you will be moving after the wedding."

Nell nodded. "You and the girls will need to come visit once we set up house."

"At least your wedding is coming up soon. That will be a bright spot of joy in all this sorrow."

Margaret and Nellie touched foreheads, neither speaking, each holding back tears that threatened yet again.

"I need to get inside." Nell stood and brushed off the back of her dress.

After endless condolences, goodbyes, and hugs from relatives and friends, the family made their way home. Margaret had the girls settle in with books and found herself fingering the letter Franny had written her. Finally, she ripped the letter open and unfolded the pages within. Inside, she found various bills. She laid out the money and gasped. It added up to two hundred dollars.

She began reading.

My dearest Maggie,

Oh, how I have longed to be free of this burden. Now I am to be free of every burden soon, and so I write this while I'm still able. I know the first thing you're thinking is, "I can't accept this money." I want you to have it. I know that you have struggled, and I know this will be a big help to you and the girls. I should have given it to you earlier. Maybe that would have saved June, but that is only one of my many regrets. Sadly, as I unburden those regrets to you, I will not be releasing them but merely transferring them to your shoulders. But I must do this. I have to.

I guess the easiest way to tell you is to come out with it. But know this, I'm a coward. I freely admit it. I couldn't go up against him. I was too afraid that he'd send me to the sanitarium as he'd threatened. Or send you there.

Margaret paused at the words of the last sentence. A shiver of fear went up her spine. Franny had worried about their father's horrible punishment. *But why?* Still confused, she kept reading.

I have to clear my conscience before I stand before my Maker.

Eugene is alive. Papa had the marriage annulled. He then told you that his ship had gone down and Eugene was killed. Later, when Papa found out that you were pregnant with Gennie, he had to change it to a divorce. He has power, but that time, it cost him. For us, that's when the radio went away, so he had money for the bribe.

Later, when Eugene returned home, you had already left, and Papa told Eugene that you never wanted to see him again. All those letters you wrote—they were never mailed. He also told Eugene that Gennie had died with croup. I'm sorry, Maggie. I wish I could have been braver. Had more courage. This disease is my punishment for living my life in fear and regret.

Please forgive me, Maggie. I love you.

Franny.

Margaret stared off into space. She read the letter two more times, the words penetrating her marrow. The reality of the betrayal started in her gut and rose until she wanted to scream at the top of her lungs. She raced over to her parent's house, where her father was sitting in his chair.

She shook the letter at him, her body trembling with anger. "Franny told me *everything*. How could you? You're evil. I hate you. I hate you!"

He spat tobacco into the can. "It's over and done."

Margaret let out a primal scream that sent her siblings scattering from the house. Her mother rushed toward her.

Margaret spun on her mother. "Don't touch me. You had to have known about this, too. And you said nothing. Nothing!" Margaret sobbed with such intensity that she couldn't catch her breath. She leaned over and put her hands on her thighs, trying to calm herself, but she couldn't stop panting, her body trembling with a mix of anger and sorrow.

"You're dead to me." She rushed from the room, his words echoing behind her.

"I did what I thought was best."

CHAPTER FORTY-SIX

Margaret paced the room until her anger had been spent. She clutched the letter from Franny, which was crumpled and torn. She had to find Eugene. But her body was ragged with mourning and anger at the betrayal. First thing in the morning, she would begin her search.

After breakfast of cereal and milk, Margaret took Cassia aside. "Don't take the girls over to Mama's anymore. Stay here, or they can play out in the back. I have to go into town."

With the girls occupied, she focused her energy on digging through her old boxes. She found the home address of Irene, an old friend who'd lived across from her while Margaret was married to Leland. She'd moved not long before Margaret had, and they'd written to each other for a while, though they'd lost touch other than the yearly Christmas card. She found the last card and sat down to write a letter. Maybe if she wrote to her, she could see if her husband still worked in the Records Department. It would take some time, but it was her only lead.

After a few weeks, Margaret received a letter from her friend's parents along with a phone number where she could be reached.

Margaret's hand shook as she dialed zero for the operator. Thankfully, it wasn't a long distance. Margaret waited until the operator connected them. After a quick catch-up on the kids, Margaret came to the real reason for the call.

"I need to talk to your husband. When will he be in? Can I come to your home and meet him this Saturday?"

After confirming their meeting time, she ended the call. Margaret dropped a nickel into the slot as the operator came on, instructing how much to deposit. She stepped out from the booth, folding the door closed behind her. As she pushed her bike down a back alley, she heard her name being called. She shaded her eyes to see a woman in a scarf and glasses discreetly waving at her.

Margaret squinted. *Bunny?* It'd been years. Looking both ways, Margaret jogged over with her bike.

Bunny eyed her. "Child, you don't look good. What's going on with you?"

Margaret broke down in tears.

"Oh, honey, come on. Let's get you where you can sit down." They walked back to Irma's, where Bunny led her into the familiar kitchen. Women were gathered around the table, and they jumped up to greet her.

"Aren't you a sight for sore eyes," Lucy said brightly.

"Maggie, what's wrong?" Bunny asked as she sat her in a chair vacated by a woman Margaret didn't recognize.

She was handed a coffee, along with a plate of cookies. She sipped the coffee before spilling her story of Franny and of her secret about Eugene. The women were shocked by her recounting, murmuring, "Oh, no." Some had left ladylike language behind and called her father everything under the sun.

"Leave it to a man to decide what he thinks is best for you." Margaret swiveled in her chair to see Irma, her hair in curlers, wearing a sleeveless white blouse and khaki capris. Irma took a drag of her cigarette before leaning against the counter. "I thought I told you not to come here. You're going to have people talking."

"I don't give a rat's ass what people say. I'm fed up with living by other people's rules and prejudices."

Bunny grinned. "Whoa. Something's lit a fire in your belly."

"I'm just tired, is all. I work hard. I've tried to do everything the right way. And every time I feel I'm getting ahead, something, or someone, comes along and knocks me back down. First my papa then my husbands. I have to take charge of my own life. I have to pursue what I think's best."

One of the other women vacated a chair so Irma could sit. "And you think that finding your first husband is what's best?" Irma gave her a hard look. "You've changed. He's changed."

"I don't know. But I have to find him. If nothing else, to close that chapter in my life."

Irma nodded. "Fair enough. What's your plan?"

"First, I'm going to see if they can tell me where Eugene is. I know someone who may be able to find out for me."

"Sounds good."

"Then I'll go there and see if I can find out where he lives. That's going to be harder. I don't know if I'll be able to take the bus, if I'll be able to ride my bike, or walk. I'm going to look for a used car. I need one anyway with me, working so far away. If I didn't have to ride my bike partway, it would save on time."

Irma gazed at Margaret. "Buying a car is expensive. You got money? You know, I'm getting a new car and am looking to sell my ol' girl."

"I doubt I could afford it." Margaret pursed her lips.

"How much you got?"

"Two hundred and fifty dollars." It was the money Franny had given her, along with what she'd saved thus far. She hated to use the money, but a car would make it easier to go see June too.

"Okay. Let me see what I can find out about a car for you. Now, I keep telling you not to come here, and you keep showing up like a bad penny. So scat. I'll have Bunny contact you when we find you a vehicle. I'm serious, Maggie. Don't come here again. You may not care, but you will. You don't want rumors to start around you that may affect your daughters."

"I guess you're right." Margaret clasped her hands around the coffee cup.

"I am. And don't worry. We'll figure this out. You do what you have to do." Irma stood.

"Thanks, Irma." She surprised the woman by hugging her before telling the others goodbye.

Saturday arrived, and Margaret took Gennie with her so she could reunite with Irene and Roy's daughter while Annabelle stayed with

Cassia. After the girls had been settled in the front yard with jump ropes, Margaret took a seat on the yellow mohair loveseat. "Thanks for seeing me, Roy. Has Irene told you what this is about?"

He sat in the chair opposite, leaning forward, his fingers tapping against each other nervously. "Yes. I don't know, Maggie. I'm not sure about this. I can't give information about personnel out to anyone."

She scooted forward. "Just imagine if it were you. Wouldn't you want to know the truth? Wouldn't you want to see your child?"

He rubbed his hands against his Ivy League haircut but remained silent.

Margaret went to the door and called to Gennie.

"Yes, Mama?"

"I just wanted to see how you're doing." She gestured to Roy, who stiffened in his seat. "This is Linda's daddy. Can you say hello?"

"Hello." She stuck out her hand for him, and his features softened. She really was a sweet, beautiful child. Margaret should have been ashamed of the ploy in using Gennie to get him to do what she'd requested, but she had no choice.

After they shook hands, Margaret said, "Run along now, sweetie."

"That was wrong on so many levels. But you made your point. I'll see if I can access his records and if there was any forwarding address or other information that can help. I can't promise you anything." He left the room.

Margaret closed her eyes and whispered a "thank you." Without help from Roy, she wouldn't know how to contact Eugene, assuming he was alive. And if not, at least she would have closure.

That night, Margaret arrived home to find a message from Bunny to stop by the next day. They'd found her a car for four hundred dollars. Irma agreed to cover the difference, and Margaret could pay her back as she got the money.

Margaret grinned as she took the wheel behind her 1942 Chevy Master and drove to the diner. There was such freedom in being able to go anywhere, anytime she wanted. No more dealing with busted bike tires or bus schedules. Even though she'd had access to a car in New York, it had been Joe's. This was entirely hers. She sang to herself, enjoying her new independence.

The following weekend after she got the Chevy, she surprised the girls with a day trip. They crossed the bridge toward Gulf Breeze on the Fairpoint Peninsula and on over to the beach. Margaret laid back on her beach towel as the girls filled then dumped their sand buckets. After returning home for a lunch of sandwiches on white bread, they'd lazed the rest of the day, reading or playing Chutes and Ladders.

She'd also rented a phone from the phone company, which would enable Roy to contact her directly as soon as he found anything out about Eugene. Finally, she got the call.

Eugene was alive and closer than she expected. His new address was in Gainesville. Before he hung up the line, Roy warned Margaret about not seeking Eugene out and to let the past remain in the past. But for Margaret, that was never an option.

The new a conundrum was that she didn't have anyone to watch the girls. With the picking season over, Cassia was back living with her father. She considered asking Ma and found that, in the weeks since the revelation and Franny's death, her anger had softened. Her mother had been no more able to tell her the truth than Franny because she, too, was under Pa's thumb.

Margaret waited until Pa had left for the barbershop before heading over to the house. Inside, Ma sat at the table, her shoulders hunched, a shell of her former self. Franny's death and Margaret's own cruel words had done considerable damage. She should have been there for Ma in her grief, but instead, she'd stormed off like a child and made it that much worse.

Margaret rushed over to her. "Mama, I'm sorry. Please forgive me." She sat on the floor, burying her head in her mother's lap.

Her mother stroked her head. "I felt like I had lost both my daughters that day. But now—" She cupped her hand under Margaret's chin and raised it to look at her, "Now I have one back."

Margaret hugged her then took her by the shoulders. "I found Eugene, Mama."

"I feared as much." Mama sighed deeply. "What do you plan on doing, child?"

"I have to go see him. I have to tell him I didn't reject him, and that Gennie is alive. I can't leave this in the past until it's done."

"Yes, I know. You've always been like a dog with a bone when you set your mind to it."

"If you can watch Annabelle, Gennie and I can go next week. I figure if the speed limit's been raised to forty-five, I can probably make it there in a day. If it's still at thirty-five in parts, it may take a bit longer."

"You don't need to be taking Gennie with you this time. I'm not in favor of you traveling all by yourself either. You need to take one of your brothers."

Margaret didn't see how taking her brother would help, but she conceded it would be nice to have someone to help change a tire if needed. "Fine, I'll see if James will want to come. He's always up for an adventure. Plus, we can stay at a motel with a pool, and that'll seal the deal."

After taking a few days off from the diner, promising to work a weekend shift to make it up, Margaret and James hit the road toward Gainesville. About midday, they pulled off the road and had a picnic lunch from items Mama had packed for them. They arrived at the Stardust Motel just as the sun was dipping low in the sky. Margaret handed over the eight dollars to the manager, who looked down his nose at her. "Are you alone?"

Margaret realized the implied question. "No," she said cheerfully. "My brother is with me. We're on our way to see family in Gainesville. Mama's sister is sick, so I'm going to help with the children."

Her fake story seemed to satisfy the manager's concerns about allowing a woman of ill repute to check into his establishment. She retrieved the keys and drove over to park in front of room number ten. Inside, the walls were paneled, and two double beds were separated by a wood table with a tall orange ceramic lamp on it, along with a

Gideon Bible. They dropped their bags on the double beds before going back to ask the manager for directions to the closest diner, where they ate chicken and dumplings with pecan pie for dessert.

Margaret tossed and turned all night. The air was hot, and even with the windows open and running the box fan, the room remained stuffy. She took a hot bath and dressed before leaving James to enjoy sleeping in and pool time. She'd purchased a map at Texaco, which she laid out on the hood of her car, searching for the street name. After folding it up, she put on her sunglasses then covered her hair in a scarf. Though she was excited to see Eugene after all that time, she wanted to keep her distance at first.

After a lot of false starts and missed turns, she found the subdivision she'd been looking for. She parked the car and walked over to a large tree, where she would have a safe vantage point of the house. It was white with blue shutters. Cheerful window boxes held red geraniums, and the green grass was clipped and neat next to the gravel driveway. Margaret checked her watch. She probably had hours before Eugene would be home from work, so she could come back later.

At the motel, Margaret unloaded the drive-in hamburgers and shakes she'd picked up on the way back. James devoured his, and after a dip in the motel's pool, Margaret reclined on a plastic lounger, a rickety, old striped umbrella providing a bit of shade against the soothing warmth.

She awoke to children's laughter as they splashed in the shallow end of the pool. Margaret smiled at the display of affection between the mother and father as they admonished their children to stay close by and not run around. Maybe she and Eugene could be a happy family like them. She picked up the worn white towel she'd taken from the motel room and slipped her feet into her sandals.

After taking her time dressing, she gave James money for dinner then headed back to Eugene's. Her heart thumped as she climbed from her car and positioned herself behind the tree.

A black Oldsmobile drove down the road then turned slowly into the driveway. A tall man in a gray suit exited the car, taking his hat and a briefcase with him.

Gene!

Margaret dug her fingers into the tree bark. She'd decided to move from her spot when the front door flew open, and two children, a girl and a boy, ran out to him. They wrapped their arms around his legs as the girl called, "Daddy!"

Tousling the boy's hair, Gene handed him the briefcase and his hat. Then he lifted the girl into his arms, pressing a kiss on her cheek as she threw her arms around his neck.

A woman's voice called out over the laughing children. "Let Daddy get inside!" She appeared at the screen door and held it open for Gene and the kids. Margaret spied her pregnancy top, which did nothing to hide the blossoming belly underneath.

Eugene flipped the girl to his back then carried her piggyback to the front steps. There, he kissed the woman before they all went inside.

The door closed.

Margaret felt sick to her stomach. She sank against the tree, its rough bark catching on her shoulders. *What did I expect?*

She had moved on. He would have too. Married with two children and one, or maybe twins, on the way.

If she confronted him with the truth then, who knew what would happen? Would he leave his family for her? Would she even want him to? Her mind spun as her heart ached.

She looked up to see a boy studying her strangely. He tossed a ball into his baseball glove, up and down, up and down. "Are you okay, lady?"

She nodded, too upset to speak. Margaret made it over to her car. Inside, she stared at the house as minutes ticked past. Darkness crept over her as lights in the house came on.

Finally, she put the key in the ignition then drove away.

CHAPTER FORTY-SEVEN

Back home, she avoided conversation by simply stating that once she'd arrived, she'd changed her mind about talking to Eugene. But Edsol finally convinced her to open up about it.

"Maggie, you did the right thing. I know it hurts, but people move on. For all he knew, he thought you hated him, and that Gennie had died."

"Did you know too, Edsol?"

He shook his head. "No. I was already off serving. But I do feel guilty sometimes."

"Why would you say that?"

"Well, you never would have met him if it weren't for me. Your life could have been different."

She sighed. "You know, I've finally figured out that no matter how you think your life is going to turn out, it ends up different. I've been blessed though. Even though I haven't been lucky in marriage, I have been lucky in love. I have three daughters. I've made wonderful friends that I'm still in contact with, in New York and in California."

His forehead wrinkled. "Will you ever tell Gennie the truth?"

"I've been thinking about that. Maybe later, when she's older. By then, Eugene's kids will be older too. But for now, I think it's best to let the past remain in the past."

He put his hand on her shoulder. "I think that's a smart idea."

~

Margaret hadn't forgotten Sylvia's offer. Once the dust settled after her trip to Gainesville, she called her up, and the women met on Saturday at a restaurant. She didn't want to take any chances that Huck or Sally would overhear their conversation.

Margaret picked at her flapjacks. "So, tell me again what an administrative assistant does." She took a bite of the warm, fluffy pancakes, butter melting on top and sweetened with maple syrup.

"You'll be taking dictation, typing up letters—" Sylvia held up her hand. "Don't worry if you don't know how to type or take shorthand. With your memory, you probably won't need it, but you'll learn both in the training."

"But I still don't have experience."

"That's true. But you have two things that are needed in this position."

Margaret took a sip of her coffee. "What's that?"

"You're a hard worker. I watched you over the weeks and how you were constantly looking for something to do. You were never idle. The next thing, and this is the most important, is your way with people and your memory. When I explained how you could remember things from weeks in the past, that's a skill that will be extremely beneficial to the ambassador."

Margaret fought to pinch herself when she'd learned the job was in the administrative offices of the French ambassador.

Sylvia continued, "He meets so many people. You can be there to tell him the person's name or remind him of other information about them."

"I still can't believe that you want me for this job." Margaret sat back against the plastic booth seat.

"Well, believe it. I'll be his executive assistant, but the fact is that I don't have the amazing recall you do. I want you to be part of my staff."

"I appreciate it, Sylvia. But I have children. I'm not a single woman. I can't—no, I won't go overseas and leave them. I've left them before, and I won't do it again, not even for all the tea in China."

Sylvia responded, "Neither would the other women you've met. Carolyn has a child. No husband, as he died in the war. Anne's married. No children yet. I'm the only old maid here. It doesn't matter, Maggie. It's your brain that's important. And your work ethic. Plus, there's an American school there for the children, and they can learn French too. It will be an amazing adventure for them. What do you say?"

"I really need to think about it."

"Okay, but don't take too long. Let me know soon so we can get everything arranged. In a month, we'll be going over to get everything settled. Plus, with your skills, I wouldn't be surprised to see if it doesn't lead to a promotion." She waved the waitress over to get the bill.

The older woman appeared, fatigue evident in her demeanor. Margaret felt like she was looking at a future version of herself.

Sylvia rose and held out her hand to Margaret. "If I were you, I'd jump at the chance to go to Paris."

Paris. It couldn't have been more unreal than if Sylvia had said Mars.

~

Margaret pulled her kid gloves on before grasping the Samsonite cosmetic case in her hands as Edsol pulled the rest of the new matching luggage set from the trunk of the car. She'd already said her goodbyes to the rest of the family before driving to the airport. In her pocketbook, she had placed the most recent letter from Cassia. The young woman's future appeared bright—she'd been accepted to Howard University and would focus on gaining a teaching degree. Margaret's heart swelled as she thought of the girl's humble beginnings and how, like Margaret, she was setting off on an adventure of her own.

Mama had advised Margaret to let her daughters join her later since they had begun school. Besides, it would be a busy first few weeks in her new role. Nell had even promised that she would escort the girls herself and spend the summer with them in Paris. But in the end, Margaret brought them along. She smiled as they gathered their things in the backseat, knowing that she could no longer separate her role as a mother from the life she would live. She wanted her daughters to know that she'd always be there for them.

With her daughters beside her, Margaret stood on the edge of a brand new life as an assistant and aide to the French ambassador. Because of her great knack with memory, she'd quickly picked up some basic French vocabulary, which she hoped to expand once she arrived in Paris. Being able to speak the language well would make her even more valuable.

As Sylvia had promised, the salary was much higher than what she was making at the diner. Once she'd received her first paycheck, she bought three smart suits. She'd gone to visit June, and while she still wanted to take her child back, it was best that June not be uprooted again. Plus, Leland wouldn't even consider Margaret taking June overseas. Still, she was thankful Leland had allowed her and the girls to spend time with June. She left the girl with a teddy bear wearing a French beret she'd made for it. After she'd hugged and kissed June that last time before the trip, she said, "Know that I am always thinking of you and love you."

Edsol came from around the back of the trunk, carrying the bags. "Sis, you look swell. I can't believe you're that gangly kid that used to follow me around when we were younger, begging me to take you along."

"Oh, stop it." She jostled him.

"No, I mean it. You've grown into a beautiful woman. But more than that, you've become a strong, independent woman." He yelled, "Watch out, world, here comes Maggie!"

She laughed as she tried to shush him, but he simply gathered her up and swung her around.

"Put me down. What are people going to think?"

"Do you care?"

"No." She yelled, "Watch out, world, here I come!"

"There's my old Maggie." He shut the trunk then gathered up the suitcases. "Ready?"

"Just about. Come on, girls." She ushered Gennie and Annabelle from the backseat of the car, both adorned in pretty new dresses, white socks with lace, and polished Buster Browns. Gennie held onto Annabelle's hand as they walked behind Margaret and Edsol inside the airport.

At the check-in desk, the ticket agent handed her the tickets and her passport. Margaret took Gennie's hand, and the four of them walked to the waiting area.

After the girls had run over to the large glass windows to watch the planes, Edsol turned to her. "I want to say something to you."

She turned and faced him. "Okay."

"You did the right thing. In fact, you did the selfless thing by not confronting Eugene."

"I don't know about selfless. It just wouldn't have helped him and may have caused more harm. Plus, who's to say that we wouldn't have hated each other?" She laughed.

"You also need to forgive Pa."

She shook her head. "No. I can't do that."

"Maybe not now. But you need to do it. Forgiveness isn't for the other person. It's for you. Unforgiveness will eat you alive."

She smirked. "Since when have you gotten all philosophical?"

"Actually, I'm going into the seminary. I'm going to become a pastor. Forgiveness is a big thing there, or so I've heard." He winked. "But seriously, I've felt this calling for most of my life. Like you, I tried to run away from where I needed to be. I believe you have a calling, too, Maggie. I bought you something." He reached into his coat pocket and pulled out a small box.

She opened it and found a picture of Ma and Pa and her daughters standing in front of her little house. In the corner, almost out of the frame, was the gardenia bush she'd planted.

"To remind you of home."

Margaret put the photograph in her purse, clicking the bag shut. "Thanks, Edsol. You write to me, you hear?"

"I will, and I'll be praying for you too."

"Thanks." She kissed him on the cheek and wiped off the smudge of lipstick. "Well, this is goodbye."

"Not goodbye, just until later."

"Yes." She wiped at her eyes. "It's funny, but I'm scared."

"I know. But maybe you'll find your heart's desires there."

"Maybe I will."

Margaret picked up her bag and took the first step toward her future.

AUTHOR'S NOTE

I never really knew my mother.

I don't think any of us can say that we really know our mothers other than as a woman whose very existence seems to revolve around us. Some of you never met your birth mothers, but even for those of us who have, there's a chasm that we seldom recognize. We struggle to wrap our minds around the person we call Mother having a life apart from us. This became very clear to me the year I turned fifteen and was told that a sister I'd never known existed was coming to visit.

At that point, I already had two older sisters, one younger sister, and one brother. As the eldest of my sisters lived in a neighboring town, I imagined that this mysterious half-sister must've lived far away, maybe in another state. But that wasn't the case.

I recall asking my mother why she'd never told me about her, and she replied, "It was none of your business."

The differences in the relationships between parent and child have always been a puzzle. At that moment, I was to see my first glimpse of a puzzle piece of my mother's life that had been hidden up to that point. It was also my first glimpse of the chasm that is the parent–child relationship. But in many cases, parents have secrets that they don't want to share with their children for whatever reason. Over the decades, parents have become more open with their children, and things like divorce are sadly a part of everyday life and conversation now. But during the time my mother grew up, there was a chasm between parents and their children, and what, if anything, should be revealed. The things that seem so strange to us now were a matter of form for previous generations. You didn't talk about things. You stuffed them down, hid them until they were forced out into the light.

After I found out my mother had a child who was secret from me, my sister who lived in the adjoining town stopped by for a visit. As we walked outside, I shared how it was strange to think I had another sister. I'd assumed that my mother had only been married once—to my father. Why would I have thought anything different?

Then my sister turned to me and dropped the next admission— we were only half-sisters. Her father had been killed in World War II, and my other older sister also had another father. My father was my mother's fourth husband. Now, in the 1970s, you expected such news to be associated with some Hollywood star like Elizabeth Taylor, not your own mother, who wore her hair in rollers every Saturday and covered it with a scarf if she went out grocery shopping as if that made it look any better.

How had this average woman had four husbands?

Now, you might think that's where the story begins, but when you're in your teen years, you're—at least I was—pretty self-absorbed. My sister did come to visit, but I don't recall any conversation with her. She was older, had a young son, and we were in very different stages of life. It occurred to me then that I had met this older half-sister once, but the entire incident had left my mind. We never talked about her, and it was as if she had never existed. I don't know why she visited then—maybe it was closure for her and my mother—but I never saw my sister again.

Decades passed, and life went on. I became a writer, but my mother's story kept calling to me, so here we are today.

While the plot is loosely based on true events that occurred in my mother's life, all the characters are of my imagination. Even the main character, which would have been my mother, is from my imagination, as I never knew the woman between these pages. I only knew of a middle-aged housewife who'd been married to my father. Thus, the characters, their stories, personalities, and foibles are all fiction. Much of the setting is fictional except for the occasional reference to a city or town or store or a particular item in keeping with that timeline.

That said, I know you're wondering—what are the facts?

First, my mother eloped with an older man, and her father was dead set against the marriage. As depicted in the story, my grandfather held some power in the community or sway over officials, so it was easy for him to obtain an annulment while telling my mother that her husband's ship had gone down from a torpedo.

As a young woman of that era, my mother wouldn't have even questioned that what her father told her. Parents were the absolute authority. While my grandfather altered the course of her life by using the tragedy of so many killed in the war, we'll never truly know his motive. As with the story, when it was found that my mother was pregnant with my eldest sister, my grandfather had the annulment changed to a divorce. I've often wondered how a barber living at the poverty line had held so much power to have these things done. It's another question I'll never have answered. For decades, my mother never knew that my grandfather had lied to her or that he had sent her husband away, denying her a husband and my sister her father.

While Margaret finds out her father's betrayal as a young woman, in actual accounts, my mother didn't discover that her first husband was alive until much later, when my sister, Annabelle in the story, started doing ancestor research.

I can still vividly see my mother's face as she stared into the void, in shock at what her father had done. All those years, she had thought her first husband dead.

Even more devastating was to discover that my aunt knew about it when my mother's first husband had been turned away, saying she wasn't there. All while his child slept in the room just beyond the front porch.

After learning that he hadn't died in the war, my mother and sisters began a search for him. They were able to discover that he had lived in the same town in Texas, mere miles from his firstborn child.

But sadly, he'd died just two months before they discovered the truth. He and his daughter never got to meet because of my grandfather's deceit.

I only recall visiting my grandfather once, though I know we went there on many vacations over the years. I thought he was dying, as I'd never seen anyone spit tobacco juice into a can. Decades later, after learning what he had done to my mother and sister, I was angry and hated him. How could he do that to them?

It was only later, when I was sharing the oft-repeated story, that a lady I was having lunch with replied, "Maybe he did what he thought was best."

It was the first time that someone hadn't been shocked or dismayed by my grandfather's actions, and it made me step back and think about his reasoning.

Maybe he'd seen something of himself in the man—a mean drunk or a man fighting against hidden demons, most likely unaddressed posttraumatic stress disorder from the First World War. Or was it simply that he was older than my mother? Or something else entirely?

We'll never know why my grandfather chose to interfere in my mother's life, my sister's, and consequently, my own. The fact is that I wouldn't be here if it weren't for his horrible deed. I have to acknowledge that, but my heart still breaks for what was lost.

The next biggest tragedy in my mother's life was losing her second child. As you can imagine, it's tough enough on a single mother today, but back in the 1940s, there was no childcare. While many places bounced back after the war, it was still hard on more rural communities.

Imagine trying to work to support yourself and your three children as a single mother. At the time, she didn't have family nearby to help out with her children.

Sadly, though I doubt she had been drinking at the time, my mother did write that damning line, "If you think you can do better, then try it." My half-sister, June in the story, was taken from my mother, and they never spoke of her again. I can't imagine the pain that caused, but as I wrote that scene, I glimpsed the horrible pain my mother must have felt over the betrayal of what she'd written being used against her to take her daughter. While Margaret does get to reconnect with June, sadly, my mother never saw her June again until her daughter was old enough to seek her out on her own.

It may have been why my mother had been so curt to me when I'd questioned her on why she'd never spoken of my sister before. The pain must have been tucked away to never be opened up again.

My "Gennie" also recalled asking my mother for a toy and my mother replying with the line, "No, it's all I have to hold on to."

I don't know when that occurred, but I added it into the story. We can all relate to feeling that we need something, anything to hold on to when tragedy strikes. My mother had a life taken from her, she lost a daughter, then she went through two divorces in a time where such things were unheard of. Is it any wonder that she felt she had nothing firm to grasp in her life?

In the story as in my mother's life, she thought her first husband had died in the war, which was very common for those serving in the US Merchant Marine Academy. From what I'd gathered, he was too old to be in the navy. Unlike the navy, the merchant mariners received no pension. Because most men were supposed to be single, it's unknown whether his marriage to my mother was ever announced to anyone.

Margaret marries Leland out of necessity, but it's unknown if this was the case with my mother. There was animosity between her and his sister, and from looking at records, it appears that "June" grew up living with her aunt after the divorce. That's another piece of history that will remain hidden behind a closed door.

My older sister, Annabelle in the story, often visited her father, my mother's third husband, in New York when she was older, but I never got to meet him either. Many years after my mother passed away, I was shown a picture of my mother with her third husband. I stared long and hard at the picture. There was no way this glamourous woman with a fur stole was my mother. She looked like a forties movie star, and her husband, with his slicked-back hair and suit, was dashing. Whether he or his father were involved with the mafia is pure speculation and fiction that I created for the story.

My mother had always wanted a house with a white picket fence, and she was well off financially while married to her third husband. Sadly, wealth didn't provide happiness for her. That life came to a halt when she was forced to flee in the middle of the night, just like Margaret does with her children. For whatever reason, he planned to set it up to look like she was committing adultery in order to take his daughter and obtain a divorce. In real life, my mother's second husband also came to her rescue, which makes me think that they must have stayed in touch during that time. It may have been that he also still loved her. Whether he did it for his child or to help my mother, he got them out. This is why his actions later of taking his daughter from my mother seemed so cruel. It makes me wonder if so many women in that era stayed in bad marriages simply because they lacked any way to support their children.

These are the primary areas that form the basis for this story, but other small details about my mother, like her tearing our gum in half, made their way into the narrative. Growing up, I could never figure out why we couldn't have a whole stick of gum. But the remnants of an impoverished early life stuck with my mother.

One day, while we were sitting drinking coffee at my mom's house, she casually remarked, "I lived in the same apartment building as Bette Davis in New York." I can't recall why it was even part of the conversation, but years after my mother had passed away, I told my older sister about it as I was thinking through the plot of this book.

"Oh, no. That's not right. But we did go to her house. I remember I got in trouble as I sat on her lap and said she was fat." Davis had been pregnant at the time. That was another strange moment. My mother had not only known Bette Davis but had been invited to her home. I doubt that she had any interactions like Margaret does in the story, but it just confirmed how little I knew of the woman who was my mother.

I also included a line that my mother said about "helping that poor woman" who was giving birth. I was that breech kiddo, and childbirth was much different than it is today. Though my birth came later in my mother's life, I added in how differently childbirth was handled in those days.

In many ways, this is a girl's coming-of-age story during a time when women were told to use mouthwash for feminine hygiene as well as other uses. Today, some of the things Margaret experiences wouldn't be tolerated, but it was a different time and place in history. While some desire to erase the mistakes of the past, it's good to see what transpired before and choose to do things differently now.

In the story, Franny knows the truth of her father's lies about Eugene. She ends up being forced into marriage because her father threatens her with being confined to a sanitorium. Sadly, many people who were considered trouble had barbaric procedures performed on them such as lobotomies. It's been said that my grandfather did threaten my mom's sister with being sent to a sanitarium, but his reason is unknown. It's scary to realize how much power was wielded against anyone who dared to buck the conventions of the day.

When I was around ten or so, I can recall visiting a wrinkled woman who lived in what I would now call a shack or a one-room house. I'd asked to go to the bathroom, and they'd pointed to a door, but when I opened it, the door led outside. When I told them it was the wrong door, they'd laughed. I'd never been in a house that didn't have indoor plumbing.

When I was doing research for this book, I discovered that my mother's sister had died in her late forties, so the woman who had looked old to me then was most likely her sister. I used her as the basis for Franny in the story, a woman who was never in control of her own destiny.

As for the song lyrics Franny shares with Margaret at her deathbed, these were the words my own dear sister said to me shortly before she passed from this life. It's like one of those songs that get stuck in your head and won't let up. I know if my sister were here, she'd be tickled to know that I have included some of her words in this book. Like Franny, my sister was also in her forties when she died from lung cancer.

While the main premise of the story is based on true events, many are simply from my imagination. My mother did study to become a nurse, but Margaret's special memory and mathematical ability were all made up. I doubt my mother ever knew any prostitutes, but Irma showed up, and that character just took off. My grandfather was long gone by the time my mother found out the truth about her first husband, but I wanted to give Margaret time to confront him in the book.

And while my mother's story didn't end happily in real life, in the story, she takes charge of her life and embraces the talent and skills she's had all along. She's able to be open to the possibilities and opportunities ahead of her.

My mother did go to Paris, but it was with me and my sister as we flew over to be with my father, who was in the Air Force. There's much more that happens after that, but I may save that for my memoir.

When I began delving into this story, I wanted to reach out to my estranged half-sister. We found where she had grown up, living primarily with her father's aunt. But sadly, she, too, had passed away. Another casualty of the past. Of not taking the chance when it was there and grasping it firmly with both hands.

As I began thinking of this story, I had a different title in mind.

But one day, this title came to me. My mother loved gardenias, and I recall her pouring pickle juice around them because they wouldn't bloom without the acid. In some ways, I relate that to Margaret and what my mother endured during the first part of her life. There were constant struggles, but they only ended up causing her to bloom later.

When I was approximately the same age as my mother had been when she had me, she was diagnosed with colon and pancreatic cancer. It's interesting to note that issues with the pancreas are often indicated emotionally as "the sweetness has gone out of life." She was given three months but lived for another decade.

I may have never really known the woman whose story I imagined within these pages, but I did know my mother. She was a fighter and a survivor and one of the strongest women I've ever been blessed to meet. She made me into the woman I am today. For that, I'm grateful. We each go through tragedy in this lifetime. For some, it may be limited, while for others, tragedies are major parts of their story. In every instance, it doesn't matter how big or serious the tragedy is, as it does not negate the pain of going through a tragedy of any size.

As of writing this, my eldest sister, who experienced so much in her young life as my mother fought to find a way forward, and I are the only remaining members of our family. My father, mother, sisters, and brother are gone.

Secrets that were uncovered will soon settle into the dust again, where they will remain buried forever. But for a brief moment, they will live on the pages of this book.

And in them, I hope my mother would be proud.

ACKNOWLEDGMENTS

It's difficult to know where to begin with all the help that I received in bringing this book to fruition. Having told my mother's story to so many individuals, it would be a long list to include, so many of them will need to remain nameless, though I'm forever grateful for their insights. They goaded me on to write my mother's story.

Yet it's those who provided constructive criticism and professional expertise that enables you to hold the book you read.

I'd like to begin with Lisa Poisso, book coach and editor, who freed me from the facts to write a fictional account that opened the door to so many characters and events. She encouraged me to dig deep into the main character's emotions and motivations, thus creating a much better storyline.

Once I'd written that last word on that last draft of the manuscript, the hard work began. This is where I worked with content editor Angie Lovell, who gave me insights on the big picture, along with Marirose Smith, line editor, who made the editing process fairly painless and manageable, while proofreader Kim Husband dotted all the i's and crossed all the t's. I'm thankful for Lynn and her excellent team at

Red Adept Editing. Any mistakes that you find are all mine.

In addition, I'd like to express my gratitude to Bryan Cohen and his team at Best Page Forward for their experience and expertise for the writing of the book's description and other assistance.

There are a few individuals I would like to acknowledge. First, those who helped me with their insights during the initial stages and onward. In no particular order: James Cudney, Jean Dukes, Kris Burgoyne, and Laverne Stanley, who agreed to answer my questions and give critical input. Sometimes you need a firsthand account of what occurred, thus I appreciate Marilyn Mahoney supplying with me with her knowledge and insights of the era.

I also want to express my appreciation for Ali and Erik Spear, who allowed me to stay in their cozy home while I wrote and did a bit of research around the Pensacola area. While a hurricane approaching kept me hunkered down over the computer keyboard, I had two wonderful furry companions named Frank and Walter at my side. Yet I was still able to find that my grandfather's house and my aunt's house (where Margaret ends up living in the book) are still standing.

I'm also thankful for my family and friends who supported me through this endeavor. Your encouragement, love, and support are the best gifts of all.

Whenever you're writing historical events, you have to dig into the time period. I did lots of research and found out so much about it. I was able to visit the Admiral Nimitz Museum (also known as the National Museum of the Pacific War) in Fredericksburg, Texas. There, I was able to see the uniform worn by the Merchant Marines and learned about that time in history.

I don't specify a particular tragic event that occurred when Sarge writes back about the devastation she's encountering, but when I was writing, my thoughts were on Slapton Sands, located in South Devon. I only found out about the tragic disaster while staying at a bed-and-breakfast in Kingswear. I listened, enthralled, to an older gentlemen tell me about his life, fleeing London on the train as a child and watching a submarine rise in front of his eyes in the River Dart. Sadly, I didn't get their names, but I never would have known of that history myself, and so I would love to thank them for their kindness. It was also the first time I'd ever been called a "Yank."

While I've tried as much as possible to accurately portray the culture, events, manners, and nuances of the time, I am human. If you find something that doesn't line up with the timeline or is off historically, I hope you'll give me grace.

~

Sign up at www.lorrainehaas.com to receive book club discussion questions, get news on similar books from other authors, and stay tuned for news of any upcoming projects.

Made in the USA
Middletown, DE
03 June 2022

66612647R00246